FROM THE ASHES:

Paradise One

Jack Bandemer

And

Marat M. Bandemer III

FROM THE ASHES:
Paradise One

Published by

PHOENIX PRESS

Janesville, Wisconsin

(in association with lulu.com)

© 2007 by Jack Bandemer and Marat M. Bandemer III

ISBN 978-0-6151-8313-8

For our children,
because they've grown up with "the book".

May they never have to live it.

PROLOG

The Big Win

"The world is a dangerous place to live, not because of the people who are evil, but because of the people who don't do anything about it."

Albert Einstein

AUGUST 2011

Jesse Walker was in a bad mood. He hadn't had a cigarette in days, his refrigerator was nearly empty, and he had forty-nine cents in pocket change to his name.

Now, all of this was not unusual; however, what made it particularly frustrating was the fact that he had wanted to go to the beach with some friends and was secretly embarrassed that he could not afford to fuel up his beat-up, oil-burning '99 Chevy. So, rather than beg a loan from Jon or Patti, he had made an excuse for not going.

Jesse looked out the window of his tiny two-room apartment. A warm, fragrant breeze blew the tattered gauze curtains into the room, and Jesse fumed. *I'm stuck here on such a perfect day,* he thought, *and nowhere else to go.* He turned away from the open window and paced nervously across the room. He opened the refrigerator and looked forlornly at the meager contents: an inch of flat Pepsi at the bottom of its two liter jug; two apples, their green and red skins wrinkled and unappealing; and a plastic container that held a leftover casserole of his own devising—a meal that was old a week earlier, and was probably even now sprouting furry mold.

With a sigh, he grabbed one of the apples, slammed the refrigerator door, and absently began polishing the puckered fruit on the leg of his Levi's. He went to the ancient stereo that sat on shelves made of bricks and boards and began to finger through his collection of rare LP's. He owned over three hundred of the old vinyl discs, but none of them was any newer than 1990.

5

He had never gotten around to purchasing a compact disc player, and since the record companies had largely stopped producing 'records' in the late Eighties and nineties, his stock of music was growing more out-of-date with each passing year.

Jesse gave up his search for something to listen to and punched the 'on' button of the tuner. The old speakers crackled with static as the radio came on; he fiddled with the tuning knob until he found an FM music station.

I wanna be your baby, I wanna be your squeeze,
Oh, baby, don't you tell me no – I'm begging, baby, please!
I'll get down on my knees for you, I'll lick your –

In disgust, Jesse switched the radio off. The song, which he recognized as a 'ballad' by the Sex Eaters, was just one of a trend of new songs that began as semi-romantic tunes and quickly degenerated into pornographic filth. That they were allowed to be recorded, let alone played over the public airwaves, was a sad commentary on the state of affairs in the country.

Jesse flopped down on the threadbare sofa and bit into the apple. The skin felt like leather, and the meat of the fruit, while soft almost to the point of being mushy, was tart and bitter. Regardless, he chewed on the piece in his mouth, managing to take several more bites before he tossed the core into the trash.

This is all Ben's fault, Jesse decided. *If I hadn't let him sucker me into giving him my last couple of dollars, at least I'd have cigarettes.*

"Damn!" Jesse looked a final time out the window of the apartment at the blazing noon sun deep in its vault of blue sky, and threw his feet onto the couch. Still fuming, he closed his eyes and dozed.

The front door rattled on its hinges and Jesse struggled reluctantly up from a dream of warm, white sand beaches and blue, sunlit waves. "Just a goddam minute," he muttered as he wiped his eyes and ran his tongue over his teeth. The taste of the apple was still in his mouth, and he quickly poured a glass of tepid water to rinse it out. He spat in the sink, set the glass on the drainer, and walked to the door.

He ran a hand through his long brown hair to straighten it and opened the door.

On the stoop stood his brother, Ben. He smiled at Jesse through his bushy beard and pushed past him and into the apartment.

"What the hell do *you* want," Jesse snapped. "Where's my money?"

Ben ignored him and walked to the small table in the kitchenette. He set down the grocery bag he was carrying and reached inside it. He pulled out an oblong carton, tossing it to his brother. "Here, you crabby son of a bitch."

Jesse snatched the thrown carton from mid-air; he had recognized it as soon as Ben took it from the bag, and now he tore into it. He opened one of the packs of premium cigarettes, dug into his jeans for a lighter, and took a long, slow drag.

"Thanks, Ben," Jesse said in an apologetic tone. "Sorry that I was so grumpy, but I just woke up."

Ben cocked an eyebrow at his younger brother. "At three o'clock on a Saturday afternoon? Don't you think that's a bit unusual?"

Jesse smiled crookedly. "I was awake earlier, but I was bored to death. I must have dozed off." He turned his attention to the cloth mesh grocery bag. "What's in the bag? Anything to eat?" The memory of the apple and the thought of the biology experiment growing in his 'fridge nearly gagged him, and his lean and empty belly grumbled in protest.

Ben grinned and returned to the table. "Let's see. I think that I remember getting something—here it is." He tossed a paper wrapped sandwich to Jesse, and pulled a package of corn chips from the bag. "And to wash it all down," he continued, "how about a Heineken?"

Jesse's mouth watered as he swallowed a large bite of the ham and Swiss sandwich. He almost forgot his hunger in his haste to open the green glass bottle that Ben handed him. "Have a seat," he said around a mouthful of beer, "and tell me how you can afford all of this, but can't pay back the money you owe me." Though sarcastic, Jesse was still curious.

Ben sat in the armchair across from Jesse and opened his beer. Both men sat in companionable silence punctuated only by the gurgling of beer, the sounds of chewing, and traffic noises from without. Finally, as Jesse finished his sandwich and washed it down with a mouthful of brew, Ben reached back and pulled out his worn biker's wallet. He removed a slip of paper, carefully unfolded it, and held it out to Jesse.

"What's this? Why'd you write a check?" Jesse held the paper up without glancing at it. "If you could afford to buy beer, not to mention black market Marlboros, you should have had the cash to pay me back. What good is a check to me when the banks are all closed?" Jesse's earlier fury was returning; sometimes he wished his brother used the genius that God had bestowed upon him.

Ben shook his head and drained his remaining beer in two swallows. In an exasperated tone, he said, "Just look at the damned thing!" He reached for another beer, his face creasing into a smile that quickly became quiet laughter.

Jesse could not see what the joke was, but he was afraid that Ben was pulling a fast one. He took a final drag from his second cigarette, stamped it out in the ashtray, and turned to examine the check.

As he read the front of the draft, his jaw dropped open. His breathing came hard and fast, and his eyes widened in stunned disbelief. Suddenly, to Ben's dismay, all the color drained from Jesse's face and he slumped forward.

Ben rushed over to catch him, carefully stretching his unconscious brother out on the couch. He picked up the draft from where Jesse had dropped it, and set it on the coffee table with a smile. "Jesse, you never could handle stress, could you?" he mumbled.

The draft was on multi-hued paper imprinted with flowery, engraved script. In the upper corner was written **Banque du Montreal.** Below that, in large block letters, it read **GOLD CERTIFICATE.**

What had most likely been the cause of Jesse's reaction, however, was the line following. In tiny letters it said, Pay to the Order of **Jesse Adam Walker** the Sum of Ten Million Dollars ($10,000,000.00) in Gold or the Equivalent Currency of the Government of Canada.

Ben grinned so hard that his face hurt, and he sat down to finish his beer. He was on his fourth when Jesse finally regained consciousness.

It has to be a dream, Jesse thought as he swam back to the land of the living. *Ten million dollars would be like having my wildest dreams come true!* Slowly, savoring the glow of his thoughts, he opened his eyes. He blinked against the stream of brilliant sunlight that was warming him through the window, and propped himself up on one arm. He saw Ben sitting across from him beer in hand, and his eyes flew to the table.

There was a check! Quickly—so much so that he almost passed out again—Jesse sat upright and grabbed the paper. He saw the words *Ten Million Dollars* and felt himself swoon.

"Now, Jess, don't you go and faint on me again," Ben slurred. "Open a beer, relax, and we'll talk." Jesse complied, and lit another cigarette. "Is—is this real, Ben?" Jesse put his beer to his lips and realized that his hands were shaking. As he set it down in a puddle of condensation on the coffee table, he found that his entire body was trembling.

Ben finished his beer and asked Jesse for a cigarette. Jesse handed him one, tossed him the lighter, and nervously waited for him to speak.

"Jesse," Ben began in a hushed voice, "that check is as real as I am." He let that sink in before continuing. "That check should more than cover the couple of dollars you lent me last week—with interest!

"You are now the co-winner of the New Canadian Lottery, which your 'investment' helped me to win!"

Jesse had heard of the Lottery, of course; everyone had. It was less than a year old, and had already paid out more than a billion dollars in prizes around the world.

As Canada had fallen further and further into debt, it had become desperate for revenue; their finance minister had finally come up with a plan to have a world-wide lottery, one that did not pay over a span of years, but rather paid a lump sum equal to roughly half of the money taken in bi-weekly. The scheme had been a hit from the onset. So far, the smallest prize that had been awarded was a little over five million dollars, and that had been the first week. Bi-weekly prizes now averaged between twenty and thirty million dollars. It was open to people of all nations, and tens of millions played the game each week.

"Are you serious? How did my money help to win the Lottery?" Jesse was still overwhelmed by the impact of going from destitute to wealthy in the same day.

"As you know, Jess, the Lottery is based upon a series of seven numbers ranging from one to nine hundred and ninety-nine. For the past eleven months, since the Lottery began, I've been working on a program to deduce the winning numbers, based upon past winners, random number theory, and the element of chance.

"It was the chance bit that had me stumped until I added that very element into the system. It was like having the computer figure random numbers on a double-random basis, with the past winning sequences for a guide." Ben smoked his cigarette in silence for a moment, then took a deep breath.

"Each time they announced the winners, I'd enter the winning numbers into the system and have the computer print out a list of seven number sequences. Over time, I noticed that my numbers were getting closer and closer to the winning numbers—one week I'd get three numbers right, another time five.

"Two weeks ago, my numbers matched the winner's exactly—some guy in Zambia won thirty-two million dollars—so I figured that it was time to put my system to the test. I had to have a ticket!"

Ben's hands shook as he put out his cigarette and took a swig of his beer. "Unfortunately, I didn't have the five dollars for the ticket, and the deadline was fast approaching. That's why I hit you up for the loan."

Jesse was still in a state of shock, but managed to stammer out a question. "You won the Lottery?" He knew that it was a stupid question the minute it left his mouth; the evidence was right in front of him. "How much?"

"Twenty-five million, four hundred and seventy-four dollars," Ben replied slowly. "I figure since your investment of two dollars came to forty percent, that you should get forty percent of the return. I rounded it off to ten million dollars, and kept the extra four hundred and seventy-four as my fee for the computer time. It works out to about fifty dollars an hour; not bad for a hacker." Ben sat back in his chair with a sigh, and for the first time Jesse noticed how exhausted he looked.

"Are you all right, Ben?"

"Yeah, I'm fine, Jess," Ben answered wearily. "How could anything be wrong?" He smiled, and some of the vitality seeped back into his drawn and pale countenance. "You just don't know what it's been like having to sit on a secret like this...I wanted to tell you when I called Wednesday, but decided that I should have the check in hand before I said anything." Ben did not know it then, but it would not be the last time that he would keep a secret from his brother.

"It took me two days of haggling with a brokerage firm and several banks in Canada before I could arrange the transfer to you of the ten million.

It would have been nice of you to tell me that you were a Canadian citizen!" Ben glared at Jesse for a moment, and the younger man colored.

"That's a long story, Ben. I'm sorry if it caused you any trouble."

"Well, not a lot. You're going to have to fill in some papers to arrange for taxes and the like; as a non-Canadian, I don't have to pay taxes on my share." Ben smiled.

"I wanted to surprise you, Jess; I guess it worked, didn't it?" He laughed quietly, and said to himself more than to Jesse, "I'm going to have one hell of a phone bill."

Jesse thought about his own phone; it still hung from the wall, but had been disconnected earlier that week. A list of other debts came to mind, and he mentally totaled them up and subtracted them from the amount of his new riches. A bright, happy smile spread across his face, and he rubbed his beard vigorously.

No more working two jobs to make ends meet; no more struggling to make his paycheck stretch for two weeks, and ending up with nothing to show for it but a roof over his head. Jesse looked at his brother with admiration, affection, and respect. Ben would finally be able to realize his dreams, too.

Jesse began to feel the full impact of what that wealth meant, and he looked at his twenty-nine year old brother with wide eyes. "Ben, do you know what this means?"

Ben smile slightly, the fatigue visible in his face but not in the bright glowing of his eyes as he looked at Jesse, five years his junior.

"Paradise," Ben said.

PART ONE: MARCH 2022

Beginnings and Loose Ends

Riding into the sunset, Frank looked over his shoulder at his companions. He gunned the cycle's engine, and with a sad and silent smile, disappeared over the crest of the hill.

He knew not where he was bound, but he was sure that the journey was his to make.

From **Riders** – Jesse Walker, 2007

CHAPTER ONE

A thin, ragged whirlpool of mist was beginning to rise around the base of the tower in the faint gray light of dawn. The cool air of the surrounding forest was silent except for the occasional chirp of an early-risen bird.

Jesse Walker sat high in the tower; his bottom was nestled on a straight-backed chair that was tilted back just far enough for him to place his booted feet on the wooden railing in front of him. A large, shaggy brown dog of indeterminate breed lay curled on the rough plank floor next to Jesse, its slow, regular breaths puffing out in clouds of steam. Jesse, too, appeared to be dozing, and his chair seemed constantly on the verge of capsizing as each breath caused it to rock back and forth.

He wore a heavy overcoat, and his hands were pushed deep into the pockets to protect them from the early morning chill. He wore no hat, but his bushy mane of shoulder length brown hair served just as well to shield his ears from the elements. His full mustache and curly beard were lightly frosted and joined together by tiny icicles that had formed below his nostrils. An M16 assault rifle lay balanced precariously across his lap; however, the shoulder strap was looped around one of Jesse's arms.

Suddenly, Jesse rocked forward and heaved a great sigh. His piercing, dark brown eyes were wide open. He took his hands from his pockets and brushed the ice from his beard with one as he roughly tousled the ears of the inquisitive dog with the other. "It's okay, Ralph," he muttered through numb lips. "I've just got to stretch."

He stood slowly, hands on hips, and curled his spine backward to pop out the kinks that had settled in during the last half hour of sitting. He set the rifle gingerly against the railing and rubbed his hands together to restore some warmth and circulation. Reaching into his breast pocket, he removed a worn leather pouch that he unzipped with a grimace. He pulled out a hand-rolled cigarette and a wooden match, allowing the pouch to drop carelessly to the chair. He turned away from the breeze that was wafting through the tower, struck the match, and lit the smoke.

Jesse carefully blew out the match and dropped it into the sand-filled ash can near his feet. He took several drags on the cigarette before he moved again, but his eyes were constantly scanning his surroundings.

He glanced at his watch: 4:57 A.M. "Time to call in," he said, and Ralph's ears perked up. Jesse slowly walked along the perimeter of the tower, peering through his sensitive eyes at the shadowy woods and the misty clearing around the base of the tower.

He saw nothing out of the ordinary, but...maybe it was the peculiar quality of the gray dawn, or perhaps the smell of the damp air. He could not decide what, exactly, was causing the hairs on the back of his neck to stand on end, but something sure as hell was!

Jesse unconsciously rubbed his left shoulder, feeling the knotty scar even through the thick folds of the coat. It was not until he noticed what he was doing that the feeling came clear—it was on a morning like this, late last October, that the attack had come.

Jesse remembered little of that attack. Most of what he knew he had picked up second-hand from others who had been less involved than he. Doc Riley said that was just his subconscious mind's way of dealing with the trauma of the attack and injuries. What Jesse did know was that a band of nomadic ruffians, the Rovers, had made a concerted effort to attack Paradise. The tower they had hit first was the one in which Jesse was doing morning sentry duty.

Jesse had been shot in the shoulder and nearly killed in a grenade blast that had leveled the watchtower. The Rovers themselves, however, had sustained the brunt of the blast effect.

Jesse kneaded his shoulder ruefully, and then shook his head to dispel the half-formed memories. He took a last drag from his cigarette, crushed it out in the can, and turned to where a forty-channel radio hung suspended from a tarnished brass hook.

He gave the power meter a cursory glance to check the battery charge, and double-checked the channel display. The LED shone brightly to his night- adjusted eyes and he read: 17. He pressed the SEND switch with his thumb.

"Walker." He released the switch and waited for the central dispatcher to reply. The radio hissed quietly, and Jesse was reminded of a time, so long ago, when a citizen's band radio had to be squelched to reduce interference.

"Seventeen, this is Central. How's it hangin', Jess ?"

Jesse recognized his brother's voice with a smile. He brought the mike up to his face and spoke. "It's hanging like the icicles on my face, Ben—it's cold out here!" His smile broadened. He knew that Ben would have an answer for that.

"Well, Bro', if your face is so cold, you can always stick it between your legs. Better yet," and Ben chuckled, *"set it on fire with one of your butts."* The laughter was still emanating from the speaker when Ben cut off.

"Very funny, Ben. At least you're inside, and more than likely, you're snuggled up with a nice warm bottle of Isaac's rotgut, too." This last was a joke between the two brothers. Everyone was well aware that Ben drank his share, and then some; however, Jesse knew that Ben seldom indulged in this vice when on duty. "When can I come in? I thought that my shift was over at five o'clock."

"Five minutes, Jess. I'm sending Frank out with one of the four-wheelers, so you can be inside building a fire in ten. Is that all right with your Royal Coldness?" Ben's tone belied the sarcasm of his words.

"That meets with Our approval, knave," Jesse quipped. "Is Frank taking the day shift then?" Jesse envisioned Frank sitting in the tower for the next five hours, and could not help but laugh. Frank Post was, in all likelihood, the most restless person in Paradise; the picture of him pacing the ten by ten foot floor of the tower for hours was amusing.

Ben came back on the radio. *"Yeah, Frank has the shift. He was supposed to be here at four-thirty, but he says that the kids had him up late and he overslept."* Ben paused, and Jesse could hear muffled voices in the background. *"I'm going to have him to foot patrols of that sector every hour. Wouldn't want him to doze off now, would we?"* Jesse overheard Ben and Frank's conversation again, but could not make out the words.

"Jesse? Frank says that we're both supposed to take a flying leap—or words to that effect." Ben laughed heartily. *"He's leaving the compound now; I heard the four-wheeler start."*

"What time is school today?" Typically, Ben changed the subject without warning—but rarely without reason.

Jesse studied his watch in silence for a moment, and yawned. "Eleven, I guess. I'd like to get some shut-eye before class, and I'm sure that the kids would appreciate it, too." Jesse quickly ran through the day's lesson plan in his head. "We'll run until about two or two-thirty; then, if you have the time, I'd like to discuss an idea I've been toying with." Jesse grinned, knowing that Ben could never resist a brainstorming session.

"*That sounds good, Jess. Could we make it closer to three, though? I've got some things to do before that, and I don't think I'll be free until then.*"

"Okay, Ben," Jesse replied, though he wondered at the furtive tone in his brother's voice. "I have some errands to take care of myself." He heard the muffled roar of the four-wheeled cycle approaching, and bent down to quiet Ralph.

"Ben? I'm going to sign off and let you get back to that bottle. Frank is almost here, and Ralph is going to make a nasty puddle on the floor if we don't leave now. Seventeen out." He thumbed the radio to standby and put it into one of the cavernous pockets of his overcoat.

Jesse turned to the chair and picked up his tobacco pouch. Grabbing the M16 with his other hand, he checked the safety. He took a few steps to the center of the tower and bent over to grasp the heavy ring that served as the handle for the trap door set into the floor of the tower. "Let's go, Ralph. Come!"

The dog ran to Jesse and jumped into his already heavily laden arms. With a minimum of fuss, Jesse maneuvered Ralph into a one-armed carry, kicked open the door, and slid down the polished brass pole that ran next to the ladder to the ground below.

Ralph jumped from Jesse's arms as soon as they hit the ground, and began cavorting around the idling motorbike as it pulled up.

Frank hopped off of the four-wheeler and walked over to Jesse, pointedly ignoring the dog. "Easy night, eh?"

Jesse snorted. "Not bad, if you don't mind freezing your balls off. Looks like it's going to warm up for you, though." He yawned and called to Ralph. "I don't want to seem rude, Frank, but I've got school in a couple of hours, and I'm bushed."

Frank nodded, and a faint smile cracked his normally sober face. "Can I get a couple of smokes from you? I left in such a hurry this morning that I forgot to grab some."

Jesse tossed his pouch to Frank. "Hang onto that. I've got some more at home."

Frank smiled again, his left eye twitching slightly, and thanked Jesse. Then the turned and began his ascent to the tower.

Jesse stretched, yawned, and mounted the idling four-wheeler. Ralph jumped into the small cargo bed in back and curled into a ball.

Jesse looked at the eastern horizon, and smiled to himself at the sight of the rose and golden sunrise. He turned his attention to the vehicle, and gave the throttle a twist. Bending low over the handlebars, he deliberately exceeded the fifteen mile per hour speed limit and drove toward home.

Jesse entered the small, one room schoolhouse and inhaled deeply of the air redolent with the scent of aged pine and chalk dust. A smile crossed his bearded face, and a familiar shiver ran through him—the same excitement and awe that he felt each time that he allowed himself to accept the reality of his tremendous responsibility as Teacher.

For the better part of ten years, this classroom had been Jesse's domain: the slate chalkboards; bookshelves filled with the much-loved and battered books; the rough-hewn tables and chairs with their histories etched in graffiti all seemed to him to be the very essence of what a place of learning should be. Perhaps it was the warmth that the room seemed to exude even through the chill of the air; or maybe it was that this was the place where so many young minds had shared with one another—each reaching, in its own way, for some small part of what was theirs to learn.

Yes, Jesse thought, *this is where I belong.* The tiny building had been more of a home to Jesse than was his own cabin, and it was here that he did his utmost to bring out the best in his students by giving them his best. The young, the old, the merely curious, and those with a deep, aching hunger for knowledge—these were his pupils, and he was their teacher.

As he walked to the front of the room, Jesse glanced at the slates still lying on the tables from the previous day. Several of them had not been wiped clean, and one in particular caught his eye.

Mike Johnson, a clever but somber thirteen year old, had drawn a scene of wonderful intricacy. A sphere, obviously intended to be the Earth, hung suspended in the black void of the slate. Through a chalk haze, hordes of tiny people were scattered across the face of the planet. In a corner of the slate, far from the Earth, a lonely little sphere circled its primary. Beneath the drawing, Mike's neat hand had written the word *Dad.*

Jesse allowed a sad smile to cross his lips as he recalled that Mike's father had been one of a team of astronaut/engineers who had been stranded aboard the NASASAT orbital platform after the destruction of the Cape. The terrorist attack occurred only hours before all Hell broke loose on Labor Day,

2012, and no one was able to render assistance or aid to the fourteen men and women who were doomed to circle the Earth until the platform's orbit began decaying—in the year 2027. They had been equipped with enough supplies of food, water, and air to last them through the end of September 2012. No one knew what their eventual fate had been.

Jesse had to dig deeply to dredge up this memory. The information had been gathered second- and third-hand over the span of several months, and to Jesse it had been a horrible piece of news to be filed and, hopefully, forgotten.

It seemed that Mike would never forget.

Jesse sighed and set the slate down almost reverently. He made a mental note to talk to Mike about his father when the time seemed right. He walked to his desk, double-checked his lesson plans, and jotted down a few notes in the margin of a precious legal pad.

Jesse chided himself with having wasted so much time. He turned and walked to the woodpile next to the Franklin stove and pulled out several pieces of dry tinder. He opened the front of the stove and poked among the ashes hoping to find a live coal. Luck was with him, and he placed the dry wood over the dimly glowing ember, pumping the bellows gently with his foot. Within minutes he had a healthy blaze going, and he closed the door.

His knees cracked as he stood, and he shook his legs to get the blood flowing freely again. His circulation regained, he walked to the heavy wooden door, opened it, and grasped the dangling length of rope hanging just outside the portal.

As the school bell clanged, he heard the approaching laughter of the children, and smiled.

Times may change, he thought, *but some things never do.*

CHAPTER TWO

As Ben awaited Jesse's arrival for their meeting he paced angrily back and forth across his small, well-furnished office. *Why, after all this time,* he pondered, *have the damn Cencoms decided to annex Paradise?* Until today they had attempted to negotiate a peaceful takeover rather than try to take the community by force; however, Ben harbored few doubts about their ability to do so.

The Central Command, a self-appointed peer group that consisted of a core of ex-military and political leaders, had remained in control of the major cities of the Midwest; over the years, they had organized them into a loose-knit confederation that wielded considerable force in certain areas. They had a loyal, albeit fanatical following, basing their leadership on a mixture of political propaganda and evangelistic fervor. The leaders of Cencom claimed publicly that they were the Chosen survivors of the Collapse. As expected, if you tell a largely uneducated, desperate public that they are God's favorites (backing it up with enough food to keep their bellies from grumbling), they will believe whatever they are told. Thus it was only natural that the leaders of Cencom were successful in nearly all their attempts to consolidate their power.   Only a select few of the better-organized communities in the Midwest, such as Paradise, had managed to hold out against their manipulations for this long.

Of course, the Cencoms rarely attacked openly, preferring to exhaust the diplomatic methods before resorting to force. Old habits die hard, and the leaders of Cencom still clung tenaciously to the old American way of doing things whenever possible. Only when the avenues of diplomacy failed had they been known to enlist the aid of any one of several renegade raider bands that survived on the edges of what little remained of society. Ben was firmly convinced that last year's attack by the Rovers had been orchestrated by the Central Command, not only as a softening up measure, but also as a way to test the strength of Paradise's defenses.

Well, Ben mused with a touch of arrogant pride, *if they want to soften me up, they've picked the wrong target.*

He stomped over to the concealed cabinet (which was hidden from no one who knew him well) and withdrew a pint bottle of his favorite booze, the now rare and priceless *Seagram's Crown Royal*. It was one of few luxuries that

Ben allowed himself to indulge in openly, feeling that he had to maintain certain Spartan standards for the community. Though he was a heavy drinker, he had proven on more than one occasion that he could think more clearly and act with more control after a few stiff drinks than most men could manage stone-cold sober.

Ben caught sight of his reflection in the mirror above the sink on the far wall and raised the bottle in mock salute. He chuckled softly, his deep voice resonant in the enclosed space, and tilted the pint up to his mouth. The liquid set his throat and abdomen burning, and he began to relax. He walked over to his desk and settled into the large leather chair behind it.

Ben took several deep, cleansing breaths, another swig of whiskey, and let his mind drift. The Cencom situation, however, kept cropping up. . .

Dwight C. Cochran, the titular leader of the Central Command, was a man with both the appearance and the nature of a weasel. He had been the majority leader during his several terms as a United States Senator, having forced his way into the position through a number of shrewd political moves. His outspoken nature, scathing wit, and cunning, coupled with his Missouri upbringing, had caused his detractors to dub him *Mark Twain from Hell*--but only when his back was turned.

Cochran was a man who believed in living life to its fullest, even if that meant that someone else had to live it a little bit less fully than he did. On the eve of the Collapse he had been on the verge of being indicted for various infringements of tax, trade, and sodomy laws, and a Senate investigating committee had been convened to decide whether he was fit to remain in office. Only the fact that the central government had fallen saved him from being ousted from office as well as being prosecuted for his nefarious activities. Cochran's involvement in the events leading up to the Collapse was merely a coincidence.

Still in a position of power and prominence at the time of the Collapse, Cochran had seen a void in the power structure appear after things settled down to a semblance of order—and he had grasped the opportunity with both hands. As a world saver he left much to be desired; he was, however, a capable administrator, and he had a knack for getting men to follow him.

Cochran sat in his office in a nondescript brownstone building in St.

Louis and stared out of the single large window. On the desk before him were a series of reports dealing with a tiny community in north-central Wisconsin.

"Paradise," he muttered. "I'll give them Paradise!" He rummaged through the papers on his desk; finally, he located the one for which he was looking. **Recommendations Regarding the Disposition of the Paradise Community** it read. Cochran scanned through the concise report, and nodded.

He affixed his signature to the bottom of the report and placed it in his out box. He smiled, secure in the knowledge that the fate of Paradise had been sealed. His crooked yellow teeth protruded from between tobacco-stained lips as he sat back in his chair.

He stared out the window and promptly forgot about Paradise.

Ben gazed out of the window in his office atop the central administration building and allowed a wave of pride to wash over him.

For over eight years, Ben and his community of Paradise had been left mostly unscathed by the aftermath of the Collapse, due in large part to the foresight shown by Ben and others. As a result, Paradise was thriving while most other areas of the country — and possibly the world — were not.

A lot of blood, sweat, and tears had gone into the construction, organization, and protection of Paradise over the years of its existence. Ben thought of the hardships they had endured to make Paradise what it had become; however, his sense of pride was shattered abruptly as he recalled the friends and neighbors who had given their lives. In the warmth of the sun, he shivered.

Since the Collapse, Paradise had lost forty-two people: in the beginning, to the mobs driven to desperation by their plight; then, in 2017, fifteen of the remaining one hundred and thirty-eight had died of the Plague. Ben silently remembered those whom the Plague had killed so horribly — nine of them young children — and once again he swore an oath of vengeance against those who had loosed the genetically altered bacteria upon the world. He had no way of knowing how many had died elsewhere; however, if local conditions were any indication, Ben guessed the death toll to have been in the tens of millions.

Ben shook his head and rose from the desk. He stepped to the window and leaned close to the glass. As he squinted against the afternoon sun that beat down upon the small town spread below him, he sighed.

Paradise had grown considerably from its earlier, humble beginnings. When he, Jesse, and nine others had taken residence, Paradise had consisted of roughly one square mile of wooded land, a pole barn, a farmhouse, and three small cabins. Now, as Ben looked out upon his town, he could see the small, thriving community center, trade district, distillery, and the nearly completed research center. Of almost sixty cabins, there was no indication; tall trees, mostly pine and red oak, obscured the view with their freshly budded boughs.

Ben watched the dozen or so people at work on the research center. His pet project was going along smoothly. The packed earth, bermed structure, built with salvaged steel beams and glass, was truly an impressive accomplishment. It contrasted sharply against the more primitive buildings and idyllic scenery that surrounded it, being of a more modern design. Ben, and Paradise as a whole, was rightfully proud of the center.

The interior work was completed and the finishing touches were being put on the exterior walls. Several groups of volunteers had begun stocking the library portion of the center with materials salvaged from neighboring areas, as well as with books, tapes, and discs gathered from Ben's personal collection. The library now boasted a complete edition of the 2012 Encyclopedia Britannica, as well as editions of the published works of both Walker brothers.

All but one of the original eleven founders was still living. Raiders had ambushed Mike Barton, a childhood friend of Ben's, on a foraging trip north of Wausau in the spring of 2016. Ben missed him still.

Each of the remaining founders kept busy with the day-to-day details of running the community; most of them, however, found time to work on projects that interested them or made use of their special talents.

Jesse's project was on-going and open-ended. He had always been interested in teaching, and he had a way with children that most men could not hope to match. From the day that the first child had entered Paradise, Jesse had been in charge of academic education. He felt that it was his duty to make sure that Paradise did not sink into the general barbarism and ignorance to which the rest of the world was succumbing; to this end, he saw to it that everyone, young or old, had at the very least a good sound knowledge of the three R's. From there, it was up to them to decide what, if any, further education they had a need or desire for.

Even such abstract and seemingly useless subjects as Sociology and Calculus were not deleted from the curriculum. "If we're going to learn from our past mistakes," Jesse was fond of saying, "then we'd damn well better know what they were and how we can do things better this time around. The past makes the present."

Jesse was an intelligent and daring teacher, but he was not an expert in all subjects. He had many assistants, mostly laymen, who guest lectured for his classes as needed. The average Paradisan was far better educated than the old norms, due in large part to the fact that the inhabitants of Paradise were those with the intelligence and foresight to prepare for the worst before it happened.

In many ways, Jesse's self-imposed duties made his project the roughest. He had been forced to operate a functioning school from day one; the projects of others were allowed the time to go through lengthy planning stages, if necessary, before they were put into use. Jesse had been constrained, out of necessity, to build the school as he went along.

Resources were limited, so the most ingenious thinking was rewarded. Unfortunately, the library/research center had eaten away at their reserves of building materials and manpower, and Ben suspected that was one of the reasons that Jesse had requested a meeting. The school was badly in need of upgrading and expansion now that they had decided to accept students from nearby areas. Ben regretted that it did not seem likely that the necessary changes had any chance of happening in the near future.

As the leader of Paradise, Ben exercised almost total control over the distribution of resources; however, many of the residents had resources of their own. Items brought into the community at the onset and not deemed as necessities for the survival of the community were allowed to stay in the hands of the original owners.

Paradise was Ben's resource; it had been his dreams and ingenuity that had enabled Paradise to become a reality. Without him, none of the people who made Paradise their home would be there now. As long as he continued to make the right decisions and administer necessities fairly, chances were good that he would live to see another day. Such were his convictions that he felt that an assassination would be necessary for him to accept taking a back seat in the governing council. Ben could never allow Paradise to be taken from him!

Ben returned to his desk and rummaged through one of the drawers until he found a crumpled, hand-rolled cigarette. He rarely smoked these days, having given up the habit back in '01, long before the days of having to rely on home-grown tobacco and stockpiled paper. Now he smoked only when under extreme stress—and then, almost without conscious volition.

Ben inhaled deeply as he lit the stale cigarette, and barked out a dry cloud of smoke as his lungs protested the intrusion. He took a long pull on the bottle of whiskey to clear his throat, replaced the cap, and put the half-empty pint back into its hidden niche. He took another drag of the cigarette and absently sent smoke rings wafting across the still air of the office. He glanced at the clock; at the same moment, the door to his office reverberated with a loud knock and swung open.

Jesse entered the room, his arms swinging freely at his sides. He turned and pushed the door shut, removed his overcoat, and carelessly tossed it on the floor beneath the coat rack inside the door. As he crossed the floor he swept his wind-blown mane of hair out of his face.

"Hey, Little Brother," Ben greeted him. His dark mood lifted as it so often did in the presence of his sibling. "How did school go today?"

Jesse scowled, his brow furrowing slightly. He dropped into the chair, threw his feet up on the edge of the desk, and pulled a cigarette from the breast pocket of his faded flannel shirt. He dug in a pocket of his tattered Levi's and pulled out a brass lighter, making a show of lighting the cigarette. "As well as can be expected—under the circumstances," he snapped. He smiled suddenly, his countenance brightening, and blew out a dense cloud of smoke. "How are you doing?"

Ben refused to be baited by Jesse's veiled reference to conditions at the school, and decided to run the conversation in the direction of what was troubling him. "Not so good, Jess."

Jesse nodded as he leaned his supple torso forward to tap ash into the tray on the desk. He slumped back into the chair in his customary slouch, and sniffed the air like a wild animal tracking his prey. "I knew something was up the minute I came in." Jesse pointed at the ashtray.

"You've been smoking, which is always a bad sign—but drinking? At this hour? What's got you so uptight?"

Ben glanced with a guilty expression at the burning cigarette in his right hand and the cloud of bluish smoke circling above him. He angrily crushed the butt out in the ashtray, and then turned to face his brother.

24

"Well, Jess—" Ben paused, and took a deep breath. "We're in a heap of shit. That's all I'll say until we've gone over what's on your mind, okay?"

Jesse began to protest, but after a long, searching look at Ben's hardened features, nodded his acceptance.

"To make a long story short," Jesse began, "I'm running out of room at the school."

"I know that—" Ben started to say, but Jesse cut him off.

"Let me finish. Recently, several families have approached me here in Paradise as well as some from the outlying areas. These folks are mostly farmers, and need their kids to help make what little living they can get from the land. They also remember that a good education used to mean something—sometimes the difference between making it and not making it— and they want their kids to have the benefit of as much education as they can get. Of course," and he winked, "our new agriculture class might have something to do with it.

"Anyway—the kids can't make their way to school during the day because they have to work the farms; even if they did, where in hell would I put them? I've got at least ten too many students in there as it is, and Moira and I spend more time entertaining them than teaching!" Jesse finished his cigarette and stamped it out in a gesture reminiscent of Ben's just a few minutes earlier. The younger man sat back in the chair, took a deep breath to calm himself, and looked Ben right in the eyes.

"I've been thinking about that fancy new research center that's going up," Jesse continued, choosing his words with great care. "It's really going to augment the amount of research space we have available. I figure that some of the advanced students ought to be able to transfer their work over there where they'll be able to take advantage of the facilities."

"That sounds reasonable," Ben mused. "But you want more, don't you?"

Jesse sat forward abruptly, his eyes blazing. "You're damned right I want more! I've been struggling along for years with the bare minimum, and now that we have a place tailor-made for teaching, I have to come begging to use it. Where would you find another teacher willing to put in the hours I do? Yeah, I want more—I want the council hall!"

Ben was taken aback by Jesse's vehemence, but his request was not totally unexpected. "So, you want to have the hall for night classes? Next, I suppose you'll be wanting a steady paycheck." Ben smiled and rubbed a hand through his salt and pepper beard. "The hall you'll get; the pay is still under advisement."

"Yeah, like it's been since 2014," Jesse quipped with a hint of a smile.

Ben nodded. "When the hall is completed—note the emphasis on *'when '*—you can have it three or four nights a week. I'll rearrange the meeting schedule around your classes.

"I have to tell you, though, that it may be some time before it's finished. Effective tomorrow, I am going to be transferring the bulk of our manpower to the distillery. We may need a great deal of fuel in the near future."

Jesse had been set to wrangle with Ben over the use of the hall, so his brother's enigmatic statement startled him. Slowly, an expression of concern crossed his tanned and bearded face. "The Cencoms?"

"I'm afraid so. Cochran sent another message—actually more of an ultimatum—by courier. We've been given sixty days to clear out before he sends his goons in to take over." Ben's hands clenched in fists of rage, though his voice remained dispassionate.

"What the hell are we going to do?" Jesse exclaimed. "We can't fight the combined strength of the Cencoms! The odds must be ten thousand to one against us."

"I know the odds, Jess; however, we have certain factors in our favor. We have greater mobility that the Cencom troops and we're more familiar with the territory. We have an efficient fuel source for our vehicles and limited air power with the ultra lights. That alone can give us an extra edge in both reconnaissance and attack capability." Ben grimaced. "Hell, Bro', we could nibble at their flanks in guerilla fashion and they wouldn't know what hit them."

"Are they in that bad of shape, or are you just doing some wishful thinking?" Jesse lit another cigarette and began puffing furiously on it.

"I've received enough reports from various sources to make me confident of one fact: the Cencom army, as it stands, is little more than a mob. As near as I can tell, roughly ninety-five percent of their troops are foot soldiers—literally." Ben ran his fingers through his thatch of black hair, and a crooked grin crossed his face.

"They have a bigger problem than that, though; if they were to attack us, they'd have every group in the area ganging up on them in self-defense. Of course, that will be of little consolation to us, since they'll have already wiped us out. With a little planning ahead, however we may be able to consolidate our position. Even Cencom can't win against us if we show a united front." Ben paused, and his brow furrowed.

"Well, they *could* win, but they probably wouldn't even try. They can hardly afford to feed a large armed force for any length of time, especially if they're cut off from their main base by our hit and run tactics. They can't waste precious fuel moving people and goods several hundred miles—nor can they risk losing any supplies to raiders.

"Something else we have in our favor—we're spread mighty thin up here. Oh, I don't mean Paradise; but our nearest neighbors are nearly ten miles from us, and their neighbors aren't any closer to them."

"But what if they decided to go for the easy target first? Paradise is the biggest concentration of people and technology for hundreds of miles." Jesse's eyes were worried. "How do we defend against an army of ten thousand, no matter how poorly equipped they are? Dammit, Ben, we have less than seventy-five people here who could actually be classified as combatants, and most of them barely know how to use a gun, let alone kill anyone."

Without responding, Ben got out of his seat and walked to the door. He opened it, peered down the hallway, then closed and bolted the door. He sat on a corner of his desk and faced his bemused brother.

"Pour yourself a drink, Jess. I've got a surprise."

CHAPTER THREE

"Get yourself a drink," Ben repeated. "You're probably going to need it."

As Jesse went to the 'concealed' liquor cabinet, Ben paced nervously around the desk. He watched impatiently as Jesse took a small sip from the pint, and waited for Jesse to sit down again before he continued.

"Jess, when we designed Paradise, we designed for practicality, not defense; however, it was always in the back of my mind.

"When you decided to take a break in June of 2012--which you'll remember I urged you to take—I decided the time was right to implement some of my plans. You don't know how pleased I was that you decided to stay away for six weeks instead of a month."

Jesse nodded, remembering the six idyllic weeks that he had spent that summer traveling, partying, and generally living the life of Riley. He also remembered the plans of his own that had reached fruition that summer. He handed the pint to Ben, who took advantage of the pause to take a large swallow.

"I made some calls and had some experts come here to give me advice. One of them, an old service buddy of mine, was of invaluable assistance. Between us, we made some changes in the original plans."

Ben passed the bottle back to Jesse and walked over to the large, multi-monitor display that dominated the small office. The six-foot diameter cylinder boasted some twenty small view screens; their panoramic views slowly changed as the cameras to which they were linked scanned a three hundred and sixty degree field of view.

Jesse focused on the screen that showed the view from the camera mounted on the roof of the tower that topped the central administration building. The hustle and bustle of late afternoon Paradise was just beginning: plows--both horse-drawn and powered--were returning from the fields; children were running in the grassy plazas; and a small crowd was lining up outside of Isaac's, waiting for the inn to open. He gave a cursory glance to several of the other screens, making note that the view of Duesouth Road was being obscured by early growth on the trees. Jesse knew the importance that Ben place on his security system, an enthusiasm and reliance that Jesse did not share since the failure of the system to give forewarning of the Rover's attack last fall. He began to wonder, now, at Ben's preoccupation.

As if reading his mind, Ben said, "I know you've scoffed at my attack headquarters in the past, Jess. What you don't know is that I never intended this to be anything but the most minimal of security measures." As if reading his brother's mind, he added, "That was proven by its failure to alert us last year."

Ben pointed at the bottle. "Take another slug of that, and come over here."

Jesse complied, and with the warmth of the alcohol in his belly, joined Ben at the monitor column.

"Observe carefully," Ben ordered as he turned to the displays. "If anything should ever happen to me, you'll be in a position to preserve Paradise.

"It's high time that I let you in on my secret."

"What secret?" Jesse asked in a bewildered tone.

In answer to Jesse's question, Ben slid his fingers under the right corner of the central display. There was an audible click, and the entire unit swung out on hinges. Jesse peered into the exposed cavity, and his eyes grew wide as he saw a tiny alphanumeric keypad and LCD screen set into the base of the cabinet.

He stood transfixed as he watched Ben deliberately type in a phrase:

PARADISE IS NOT YET LOST

There was a quiet electric hum from inside the column; without warning, the entire column split down the middle and the two halves swung apart. A dark, gaping hole was revealed in the floor—something that Jesse had never suspected, though he had seen the column thousands of times.

"Follow me," Ben said enigmatically as he stepped into the column and disappeared down the hole. Jesse leaned forward and looked down.

It was not as dark as he had originally thought, though the lighting within was quite dim. He saw a ladder set into the center of a narrow shaft, dropping out of sight into the nether regions of whatever it was that Ben had so carefully hidden. Jesse fought down his feelings of claustrophobia and stepped into the interior of the column. There was a whine of electric motors as the two sections snapped shut behind him.

He took a deep breath and willed his rising panic away. He bent down, stepped onto the ladder, and began the descent into the dimly lit shaft.

Hours—or seconds—later, Jesse reached the bottom of the ladder. Ben was waiting for him and held out a hand to steady his brother as he teetered, week-kneed, at the base of the shaft.

"Well, what do you think?" Ben had a huge grin on his face as he awaited Jesse's reaction.

The younger man blinked his eyes in the fluorescent lighting and stared at the chamber around him. A full thirty feet in diameter, most of the space was taken up by computer mainframes, terminals, video displays, and printers. Across the room from the shaft were two airlock-style hatches. Above each was a lighted sign that read EXIT.

"Wh-what is this?"

"This," Ben remarked proudly, "is our defense headquarters. Think of it as the Pentagon War Room on a microcosmic scale." He gestured to the view screens.

"The radar is limited to a one hundred mile radius, but can be correlated with satellite data, though I'm only getting one satellite feed right now. Most of them have gone off-line in the past year or so.

"The radar, satellite data, and visual remotes are used to direct drone tanks, land-to-land missiles, and two airborne recon drones."

Ben's grin faded. "I blew a helluva wad on this, just on the off chance that things would go to hell and some petty little tyrant would declare himself God." He shrugged self-consciously. "I never actually expected to make use of all of this—I just don't like to get caught with my pants down. You've heard the saying, 'The man who dies with the most toys wins'?"

Jesse nodded, momentarily too stunned to speak. He bent closer to one of the terminals and read **DRONE CONTROL**. He turned back to Ben, and stared at him intently for a moment.

"How effective will this be is Cencom attacks?" he managed to say.

Ben's smile returned, and he gestured to a small sign on the wall above the central terminal.

Jesse followed Ben's pointing finger, and he read the simple words emblazoned in royal blue on a platinum plaque. He shook his head, amazed at the confident arrogance that his brother continually displayed.

Jesse glanced once more at the plaque.

WE WIN it read.

CHAPTER FOUR

Excerpted from the Memoirs of Benjamin Walker:

...childhood was nondescript, as was my early adulthood. In fact, it was not until I decided to attend college at twenty-six that things began to work out for me.

I had survived a bad marriage—six long years—and was recovering; I found my life empty, and vowed to do what I must to begin living my life again. College seemed like the logical place to start finding out what I wanted to do with the rest of my life, so I enrolled in a junior college some thirty miles from where I was living at the time. I took courses in almost every major discipline, but found politics and sociology to be my favorites.

The real turning point in my life came six months after I began school. I obtained an obsolete Pentium PC at a swap meet, and after toying with it for several weeks, stumbled upon a word-processing program cached on the hard drive that piqued my interest in writing. I determined to try my hand at writing a novel, something that I had attempted before but had always failed to do.

My schoolwork suffered to the point where I was forced to drop out of my classes; however, the writing flourished, and I completed my first novel late in 2003. I wrote a sequel to that in the ensuing four months, and submitted the pair to various publishers with lukewarm success.

In 2007, my brother Jesse approached me with a completed manuscript, as well as an idea for a new novel. A moderately successful collaboration followed, and from 2007 through 2011, Jesse and I managed to publish a total of seven novels, mostly through a university press.

During those three years, we talked and dreamed of starting our own community. We envisioned a self-sufficient, self-governed establishment, with a maximum of two hundred to five hundred people. Unfortunately, it remained a dream until the day that one of my experiments panned out. . .

The Journal of Jesse Walker: November 12, 2011

Ben and I finalized the deal on our property today. Paradise is on its way to becoming a reality!

After searching through hundreds of real estate databases and going on countless unsuccessful and disappointing trips to look at land, we finally located a nearly perfect parcel. Situated as it is in the sparsely populated farm lands of north-central Wisconsin, it has many of the features that we were looking for: relative isolation; a large amount of readily available timber; rich farm land; and most important of all, two sources of water--a deep artesian well, and the Spirit River Flowage.

We have a square mile (approximately six hundred and forty acres) that is roughly half old growth timber and half empty farmland, bordered on the north by a county road and the river. The closest town is a little place called Spirit, seven or eight miles north of us. Tomahawk, twenty miles away, is the only town of appreciable size within striking distance.

Both Ben and I are excited about beginning. I think that he must be more anxious than I am, however; this has been a dream of his since he was a kid, whereas I came around to his way of thinking later in life.

To make things easier (almost as if it was meant to be), there *are some existing buildings on the land--an old farmhouse, a barn, several outbuildings, and three small tourist cabins, all in good repair...*

The Journal of Ben Walker: December 19, 2011

TODAY, I CONTACTED SEVERAL MORE PEOPLE ABOUT JOINING US IN PARADISE. IT SEEMS LIKE IT'S BEEN A DREAM OF MINE FOR MOST OF MY LIFE, AND NOW—COURTESY OF THE CANADIAN GOVERNMENT—THE DREAM IS CLOSE TO BECOMING A REALITY.

I SPENT THE LAST WEEKS OF NOVEMBER (AFTER CLOSING THE $300,000 DEAL ON THE LAND) LOCATING THE CONTRACTORS WHO WILL BE DOING THE WORK AND PROVIDING SUPPLIES FOR PARADISE. I SPENT THE MOST TIME PETITIONING FOR THE RIGHT TO INSTALL A STANDARD SEPTIC SYSTEM, RATHER THAN THE MORE EFFICIENT MOUND SYSTEM. IT'S AMAZING WHAT A LITTLE SQUEEZE WILL DO WHEN DEALING WITH HUNGRY RURAL OFFICIALS.

MY PLANS FOR THE IMMEDIATE LAYOUT ARE TO CONSTRUCT A CENTRAL ADMINISTRATION BUILDING, UTILIZING THE SHELL OF THE EXISTING FARMHOUSE; ALL THE OTHER MAIN BUILDINGS WILL BE ERECTED AROUND IT TO FORM A CENTRAL PLAZA. AS I MULL OVER MY PLANS, I AM DAUNTED BY WHAT AN UNDERTAKING I HAVE BEFORE ME...

MY RECRUITING SESSIONS WENT FAIRLY WELL. I RE-APPROACHED SEVERAL PEOPLE TO WHOM I HAD SPOKEN OF MY IDEAS BEFORE THE DREAM BECAME A REALITY. IT'S ODD—THE PEOPLE WHO WERE EXCITED ABOUT THE IDEA WHEN I COULDN'T PULL IT OFF ARE UNENTHUSIASTIC NOW, WHILE THOSE WHO SHOWED LITTLE OR NO INTEREST ARE VERY EXCITED.

I HOPE TO ENLIST AT LEAST FIFTEEN ADULTS FOR THE INITIAL POPULATION. LATER ON I'LL WORRY ABOUT VITAL OCCUPATIONS; FOR NOW, I NEED ABLE-BODIED LABORERS WHO WILL BE PERSONALLY LOYAL TO ME.

I AM PLANNING AHEAD TO A WORST-CASE SCENARIO—THE DECLINE AND FALL OF THE WORLD AS WE KNOW IT. TO THIS END, I HAVE WRITTEN A CONTRACT, OR CHARTER, THAT INSTITUTES A SERIES OF CHECKS AND BALANCES

WHICH, WHILE GIVING ME ABSOLUTE AUTHORITY OVER DECISIONS IN THE ECONOMIC, POLITICAL, AND SOCIAL ARENA, NECESSARILY LIMITS MY POWER OVER INDIVIDUALS. I THINK THIS IS THE ONE POINT THAT IS DETERRING MANY FROM JUMPING INTO THIS PROJECT: THAT I PLAN FOR MYSELF TO BE THE FINAL PUBLIC AUTHORITY—THOUGH THERE WILL BE A COUNCIL TO DECIDE THE LESS WEIGHTY ISSUES. I REALIZE THAT IN THE PAST I HAVE BEEN A PAIN IN THE ASS TO SOME, BUT MY DESIRE TO SEE THIS DREAM FULFILLED HAS, TO SOME EXTENT, OVERRIDDEN THAT TRAIT—I HOPE. IN THAT MANNER, I WILL BE MEDIATOR OF DISPUTES. I'LL ATTEMPT TO SETTLE DISPUTES OF ALL NATURES, AND MY WORD WILL BE BINDING IF ACCEPTED BY BOTH PARTIES; IF NOT, THE MATTER WILL CARRY OVER TO PUBLIC VOTE, OF WHICH I AM MERELY ONE BALLOT.

I HAVE NOT SET THIS UP TO BE A DEMOCRACY—IT IS AN EXTREMELY CONSERVATIVE ORDER, BASED UPON MY RECOGNITION OF INDIVIDUAL RIGHTS. I WILL NEVER ALLOW IT TO DETERIORATE INTO A VOTING SITUATION ON ANY MATTER OF SURVIVAL. AFTER ALL, THIS WAS ORIGINALLY MY DREAM, AND I HAVE SPENT TOO MUCH TIME PLANNING AND PREPARING TO SEE IT LOST THROUGH PARLIAMENTARY PROCEDURE.

JESSE AND I HAVE DECIDED THAT THERE WILL BE ONLY ONE GENERAL RULE IN PARADISE: DO NOT HURT ANOTHER PERSON WITHOUT JUST CAUSE. IT WILL BE UP TO THE COUNCIL AND MYSELF TO DETERMINE `JUST CAUSE´.

IT IS MY FERVENT HOPE THAT IN PARADISE WE CAN FOSTER A SOCIETY FREE FROM POLLUTION, HATE, BIGOTRY, AND RESTRICTIONS. I WISH TO FOMENT CREATIVITY, BOTH IN ADULTS AND THE CHILDREN WHO WILL INHERIT WHAT WE BUILD HERE.

SOME HAVE ACCUSED ME OF DESIGNING A COMMUNE—A WELFARE STATE IN MINIATURE. NOTHING COULD BE FARTHER FROM THE TRUTH! EVERYONE WHO IS IN THE COMMUNITY WILL RECEIVE THEIR BASIC SUBSISTENCE FOR TWENTY HOURS OF COMMUNITY SERVICE PER WEEK—TO BE DETERMINED BY MUTUAL CONSENT AND NEED (THIS, OF COURSE, EXCLUDES CHILDREN UNDER TEN YEARS OF AGE). THIS DOES NOT CONSTITUTE WELFARE. BEYOND THAT MINIMUM, PEOPLE WILL BE FREE TO START A BUSINESS, PROVIDE A SERVICE, OR LOAF. LUXURIES—ANYTHING BEYOND THE BASIC NEEDS—WILL BE EARNED BY

PRODUCTIVITY. MY OWN LOT WILL BE TO FUNCTION AS LEADER, BY RIGHT AS FOUNDER; I WILL DO MY BEST TO PROVIDE DIRECTION AND GUIDANCE FOR INDIVIDUALS, ALWAYS WITH THE BEST INTERESTS OF PARADISE AS A WHOLE IN MIND. AND THIS WILL BE OVER AND ABOVE THE TWENTY HOURS OF SERVICE THAT I, TOO, WILL BE REQUIRED TO PROVIDE THE COMMUNITY.

...HAS ME STUMPED IS EMERGENCY TRANSPORTATION. SUPPOSE THE WORST HAPPENS, AND THERE IS A NUCLEAR WAR: THERE IS NO WAY OF STOCKPILING SUFFICIENT FUEL AND VEHICLES TO TRAVEL CROSS-COUNTRY TO A NEW LOCATION, SHOULD THE NEED ARISE...

...I HAVE PURCHASED EIGHT TWO-PASSENGER ULTRA LIGHTS, ABLE TO CRUISE AT A MAXIMUM OF SIXTY-FIVE MILES PER HOUR AT TEN THOUSAND FEET, OR GLIDE AT TREE TOP LEVEL. FIVE OF THESE ARE BEING MODIFIED TO CARRY AN ADDITIONAL PAYLOAD OF TWO HUNDRED POUNDS EACH, EITHER IN FUEL, SUPPLIES, OR WEAPONS. THE OTHER THREE ARE REMAINING STANDARD WITH OPTIONAL PONTOON/SKIS FOR THE WINTER MONTHS.

...JESSE HAS LEFT TO FIND A CONTRACTOR WHO CAN PAVE OUR INTERNAL ROADS, INSTALL PERIMETER FENCING (FOUR MILES WORTH!), AND CONSTRUCT WATCH TOWERS. WITH NEARLY FOUR MILES OF FENCING ENCLOSING OUR BORDERS, WE PLAN TO HAVE EIGHT SIXTY-FOOT TOWERS, AND EIGHT ADDITIONAL THIRTY-FOOT AUXILIARY TOWERS MIDWAY BETWEEN THE MAIN TOWERS AND THE CENTRAL PLAZA. THE PLAZA ITSELF WILL CONTAIN ALL OF THE NECESSARY FUNCTIONS FOR THE COMMUNITY TO SURVIVE: WAREHOUSING FOR FOOD AND EQUIPMENT STORAGE; A DISTILLERY FOR FUEL AND CONSUMABLE ALCOHOL; GRAIN ELEVATORS, ETC.

I AM GOING OUT THIS AFTERNOON TO PRICE SOME HOVERCRAFTS...

CHAPTER FIVE

"You're pretty sure of yourself, aren't you?" Jesse asked his brother as he stared at the polished sign. "Out-numbered ten thousand to one, and you think that *this*," as he indicated the 'war room' with a gesture of contempt, "will win the war?"

Jesse snorted, and shook his head. "Don't you think that it would be better to avoid a conflict in the first place?" He pulled out a chair and dropped into it, his frustration and outrage making him unable to speak coherently. He fumbled with shaking hands in his shirt pocket for a cigarette, then gave up the attempt.

Ben smiled at Jesse, a mirthless expression that would have made the blood run cold in most people, but which only served to enhance Jesse's anger. The younger man opened his mouth to speak, but Ben cut him off.

"You don't fully realize what we're up against here, Jesse," Ben said in a quiet voice. He sat down and faced his brother. "Our friend and neighbor, Mr. Cochran, contacted me on channel forty late last night, using one of our own security codes to get through. He added some interesting points to his ultimatum."

As he paused to let this sink in, Jesse frowned. "Forty, our private emergency channel? I guess that it was only a matter of time before someone broke the codes, and it figures that it would be someone from Cencom. Who else would want to?" Jesse looked at Ben, most of his anger dissipated in light of this new development. "What did Dwight have to say? He already gave us our walking papers — now what?"

"For starters, he reiterated his formal position as outlined in the message that was delivered by his courier," Ben stated with outward calm. "The newest wrinkle is his offer of jobs with the Central Command."

Jesse's eyes grew wide in disbelief, but Ben forestalled any questions with a glance.

"Dwight said that it would make the transition easier for Cencom, as well as us, if the nominal leadership of Paradise appeared relatively unchanged during the initial stages of the take-over. He offered high-ranking positions to us and anyone else who would willingly assist him in developing Paradise for his purposes." Ben spat the last of these words, and his face flushed in anger.

"He outlined special plans for the school, too."

"What plans?" Jesse hissed. "That snake wouldn't know a curriculum if it bit him on the ass!" Jesse clenched his fists and imagined what it would feel like to squeeze the life out of Dwight Cochran.

"He may not know how to run a school, Jess, but he is a master of the art of propaganda. He intends to use the school as a training ground for young recruits." Ben watched helplessly as Jesse's anger intensified, and braced himself for the inevitable explosion.

"*My* school!" Jesse screamed. "I won't see him take it from me—us— without a fight! I've put too much into it, trying to teach kids how to live peaceful, intelligent lives, to see it perverted by that son of a bitch!" Jesse concentrated intently for a moment, managed to get a cigarette from his pocket, and began to light up. Ben held up his hand for attention, and Jesse paused.

"Let's go back up to the office if you really need that," Ben said. "The smoke isn't very good for some of the components down here, and I don't have the ventilators on." Ben gestured toward the ladder, and Jesse got up and walked toward it, pocketing the unlit cigarette.

Ben was secretly delighted at his brother's reaction; the threat to the school had served to make Ben's point like no other argument could have. As he came up behind Jesse, Ben pointed to a small monitor screen at the ladder's base. "That's the office monitor. It allows whoever is down here to check whether the office is unoccupied before going back up. There are monitors by each of the lower exits as well." He pressed a button below the screen, and a view of the office appeared in clear, minute detail. As they watched, the view panned across the entire office. Satisfied that the room was vacant, Ben switched off the screen.

"Let's go," Ben said. Jesse began the ascent in the dimly lit shaft, but paused, panting, halfway up the ladder.

"Do you mind telling me how to open the door when I get to the top? I really don't want to stay in here any longer than I have to." Jesse's voice quivered, and he laughed nervously. "Since you've finally decided to let me in on your little secret, I might as well get all the details."

"There's an infrared detector at the top of the ladder that's keyed into the switch for the hatch," Ben explained. "It only has a range of about five feet, directed away from the office to avoid accidental triggering. It'll open the hatch automatically when you get to the top of the ladder, and won't close again until I've passed through after you."

Ben smiled in the dark and tapped Jesse's boot with one hand. "It works the same way, in reverse, when you go down the ladder. You probably noticed that the hatch closed behind you when you got into the shaft. The switch was keyed by your body heat to stay open until you were far enough inside for safety. For emergencies, there's a manual latch on the inside of the hatch; however, with solar power and battery back-ups, chances are you'll never need to use it."

Ben saw a sliver of light appear above him as the hatch opened, and Jesse gave an appreciative grunt. If nothing else, Jesse appreciated good machinery, and he watched with a smile on his face as the hatch closed silently seconds after he and Ben were safely inside the office. He took several deep breaths to dispel his claustrophobia, and walked over to the desk.

"That's quite a gizmo, Ben. What I don't understand is why you never told me about this before—didn't you think I could be trusted? Or is there something else you haven't told me?" Jesse resumed his former position on the chair, and swung his feet onto the desk. He lit his cigarette thoughtfully, an expression of confused dejection on his face. He unconsciously took a swig from the open bottle on the desk, draining the last of the amber liquid within. He gave a little cough to clear his throat and looked at Ben.

"You've taken me this far, Ben—don't leave me hanging."

Ben sat behind the desk, pushing idly at some papers with the point of a pencil. Absently, he held his hand out for the bottle. Jesse tapped the empty pint with his fingernails, making the glass sing.

Ben sighed and looked at his brother. Silence hung in the air between them. This was not the silence of two brothers who knew each other's moods inside and out; rather, it was a pause between two businessmen who are trying to negotiate a deal. Jesse nervously tapped the ash from his cigarette and waited for Ben to speak.

Ben took a deep breath. "I hope you don't think that it's been easy for me to keep this a secret from you, Jess. Every day I considered telling you, and every day I seemed to find a reason to put it off. I guess that part of it was my reluctance to see your reaction.

"I know," Ben said with a smile, "that you aren't nearly as 'war-like' as your big brother. You'd rather walk away from a fight, if possible, or talk it out with the other party—and your method works well, in most cases. You know, however, that if someone gets out of hand I prefer to knock him on his ass first, and ask questions later.

"The 'war room' is my way of being prepared to do just that—kick someone's ass if they won't listen to reason." Ben paused and stroked his beard with one hand.

"I wasn't sure how you'd react to my idea of defense. While I don't need your approval, I want very much to have it. Besides, I suppose I knew that you wouldn't approve; however, there it is—the only way we can respond to Cencom.

"They're the new bully on the block, and they've gotten out of hand. They leave me no choice but to kick their ass before they kick ours!"

Jesse slowly smoked his cigarette, finally stamping out the butt in the ashtray with a contemplative expression. "Can you tell me anything more about our situation, Ben? I really need to know as much as possible before I can make a decision."

Worry lines deepened on Ben's face, and he reached for the whiskey, remembering at the last second that the bottle was drained. "Yes, there's more. I think that we have a spy among us."

Jesse sat up abruptly, his feet sliding from the desk with a thump. His eyes, normally soft and glowing, turned hard, and his voice was harsh when he spoke. "Do you know who it is?"

Ben slowly shook his head. "I have my suspicions, but no hard evidence. We can go over my notes later; maybe you can see something new. In the meantime, keep your eyes and ears open." He glanced at the empty bottle, and opened a drawer on the desk. He pulled out a small flask and took a sip from it before handing it across the desk to Jesse.

"Dammit! I thought that we were all in this together, and now I don't know who to trust." Ben's shoulders slumped; in his eyes Jesse could see how this revelation had shattered his brother's dream of what Paradise should be.

Jesse frowned, then a faint smile of decision touched his lips. "Ben, no matter how I feel about your 'war room', I have to admit that you've shown a helluva lot more forethought than I have." Ben managed to smile, accepting the compliment.

"Show me how everything works, and I'll do my best to run things if you aren't available." Jesse lit another cigarette, and gestured toward the central hub. "Just turn on the ventilators, okay?" Ben grinned and walked to the hub. He opened the control console and entered the password. Glancing over his shoulder to be sure that Jesse was watching, he typed in an additional phrase. The screen read:

PARADISE IS NOT YET LOST
AND THE AIR IS STILL AS SWEET

Jesse chuckled softly as he felt a slight throbbing in the soles of his feet. As the hatch opened, a gentle breeze stirred wisps of hair about his face, and cigarette smoke was carried away from him to a hidden vent in the shaft. "Nice," he whispered.

Ben entered the shaft and began to climb down, Jesse following close behind. He paused long just long enough to watch the hatch close above him. As they made their descent, Ben began his instruction.

"This should be right up your alley, Jess. You were always good with video games, and to a certain extent, that's why I designed the layout as I did. The remotes are all handled with joysticks and remote cameras, with special instructions entered through a keyboard menu."

Ben reached the bottom and helped Jesse with the last step. "Let's see what we can do."

The Journal of Jesse Walker: April 3, 2013--

I have been feeling rather melancholy lately; things are going almost too well. Yet, I find myself indulging in that vice of old men: nostalgia.

It's funny--no matter how bad the old days were, they tend to look better to us as we grow older and farther away from who and what we were back then. Maybe it's because I'm into my thirties now; or maybe not.   Regardless, I've found myself remembering things, and wishing for things, that I know I may never have again.

Sometimes I miss the old world, like it was before the Collapse.   There was so much good in that world; unfortunately, it was overshadowed by so much evil.

Later:

I have compiled a list of **Things that I miss**:

Driving seventy miles per hour down the interstate, the music blaring and the cruise control on.

Pepsi.

Channel flipping through a hundred different programs on cable TV.

Filtered cigarettes.

Decent FM radio (and the daily news!).

Central heating. Air conditioning.

Microwave ovens.

Soft, gentle toilet paper.

Noxzema.

Vacuum cleaners.

Running down to the liquor store for a Cold six pack.

The list could go on and on; however, in re-reading it, I realize that many of these things carried negative vibes with them, and that I don't truly miss them at all (with the notable exception of the toilet paper!). It's just that I was raised in an age of technological wonders—it's a shame that so much was wasted and abused.

My life now carries with it so many little joys, so many bright moments, that I wouldn't have the time or the incentive for many of the things I thought I missed. Or maybe I have too much time. I have replaced those things with others that are so much more important to me than they ever were. To that end, I now compose another list:

Things that I have:

The smiles of my students when they learn something new.

Walks in the woods.

Hard, sweaty work that lets me know I'm alive.

The friendship that comes from being an integral part of a community.

I have no master—my life is my own.

Empty pockets (and no need of full ones).

My own home.

Ralph (the best darn mutt anyone ever had!).

My health.

My brother.

I guess that everyone has to go through a selfish streak every once in a while to truly understand what really matters.

I see now that I am probably one of the richest men on the face of the Earth. I just needed to rub my nose in it to see it. What's that old saying? "You can't see the forest for the trees."

You can. You just have to look at the trees from the right perspective.

As Jesse left Ben's office several hours later, his thoughts were troubled by visions of tanks, missiles, and drones, all causing mass destruction.

The simulations that he and Ben had gone through in the 'war room' were very much like video games; however, Jesse knew that in this 'game' real lives were at stake, not just phantasms made up of pixels on a screen.

Jesse looked back over his shoulder, and saw that the lights were still burning in Ben's office. *He wanted the worry seat,* Jesse thought. *Fine – let him have it.*

Jesse felt in his heart that there had to be another way of dealing with Cencom. A trade agreement, a truce--anything in order to avoid the bloodshed that would result from an armed confrontation.

Jesse stopped to light a cigarette, and then resumed walking toward the garage. He felt with a measure of distaste the weight of the 9mm Ruger automatic slapping his thigh. Ben had insisted that he begin wearing it at all times, but that did not mean he had to like it. He did feel more secure with it on, and with the possibility of a spy in Paradise, it was probably a wise move.

He still found it hard to accept that there was a traitor in their midst; however, Ben's evidence was convincing. There were the broken codes to think about, as well as Cochran's obvious familiarity with the set-up in Paradise. They still didn't know who the spy was, but they would find out sooner or later. And then. . .

Jesse grimaced and patted the pistol on his hip. He neared the garage, and in the dim twilight could barely make out the face of the sentry. He pulled out his pass, a small, slightly fluorescent rectangle of blue LISA plastic, and flashed it at the sentry. He moved to enter the garage, but the guard stopped him.

"Gotta look at it," he said in a low-pitched, slurred voice. He held out his hand, and Jesse passed over the card. The sentry scrutinized it carefully, then handed it back to Jesse. At that moment the automatic night-lights came on, and Jesse recognized the face of Paul Anton.

"Hello, Paul," Jesse said. He watched with tolerant amusement as the man saw who he was, and smiled in answer to the sheepish grin that planted itself on Paul's chubby features.

"Gotta look, no matter what, Mr. Walker," Paul stammered. "The, uh, other Mr. Walker—he says so, and I do just like he says." Paul looked down at his feet, obviously torn between his embarrassment and his sense of duty.

"You did fine, Paul," Jesse assured him. "I follow Ben's orders, too." Paul beamed happily. "Why don't you call me 'Jesse', like everyone else does? You aren't in school anymore. Hell, you have an important job—maybe I should call you 'Mr. Anton'?"

Paul swelled with pride at the suggestion, but was quick to add, "Oh, no, Mr. Walk—I mean, Jesse." He smiled, his large teeth gleaming in the light. "You just call me plain ol' Paul, like you always do. What you takin' tonight?"

"I'd like to take one of the hovercrafts, if any are ready to go. This one all right?" Jesse indicated the nearest one, a sleek black craft.

Paul's head bobbed up and down, and Jesse thanked him. He seated himself in the cockpit, pulled on a helmet, and cinched the noise baffles down over his ears. Driving one of these contraptions was akin to being tied inside a tornado, and Jesse took no chances with going deaf just to drive one. He checked the fuel gauge, logged in on the clipboard, and inserted the plastic card into the magnetic reader that served as an ignition.

With a roar and a cloud of dust, the hovercraft slowly rose from the ground. Jesse gently applied throttle to the thrusters, and maneuvered the craft out of the garage. He waved to Paul, and headed down the road.

When Jesse reached the corner of Duenorth, he turned and headed for the dam. As he wrestled with the ungainly machine, he remembered all the trouble he had gone through to get Paul his job at the garage.

"He can't be trusted," people had said. "He's a feeb," others had shouted, Ben among them. But Jesse had taught Paul all that he was capable of learning—a surprising amount—and in the course of that teaching, had discovered that Paul had an amazing and intuitive aptitude for machinery. If it did not work, Paul could fix it; if he could not fix it, he could use the parts to make something else both unique and useful.

Jesse had learned a lot about human nature from his work with Paul. He learned that it was okay to show affection, and all right to be happy.

Jesse had finally convinced Ben to allow Paul to apprentice at the garage under the present caretaker, Jack Barker. It was not long before reports began to come in—favorable reports.

"I don't understand how he does it," Jack said, shaking his head. "That boy can start with a piece of junk that I'd scrap, and make it purr like a kitten. I've never seen him look at a manual for either the hovercrafts or the ultra lights—can he read?--but he tunes them up in half the time I can. Maybe I should resign."

Jack was persuaded to remain in charge of the garage; while Paul may have turned out to be the better mechanic, he was lost when it came to organizing a work schedule or doing an inventory.

All in all, Paul's position had worked out to everyone's benefit, a fact that even Ben had grudgingly admitted. It was one of Jesse's greatest success stories, and he was justifiably proud.

Jesse's thoughts turned to Cencom once again as he was compelled to stop and show his ID at both the inner and outer watchtowers, something he rarely had to do. He continued driving after the last checkpoint, and went through the gate that marked the boundary of Paradise. As he crossed the old county road, he was forced to swerve to avoid a large tree limb that was lying across his path. He frowned as he went around it; there were no trees within thirty feet, and it was altogether odd that a branch had landed at that particular spot. He made a mental note to move the limb on his way back.

For the moment, he forgot about Cencom, and focused his attention on driving up the winding road that led to the dam, and the home of his friend, Harry.

CHAPTER SIX

When Jesse arrived at the dam, he slowed the hovercraft and circled around the gravel clearing. He located a spot close to the main building, and with a hissing sound, allowed the craft to settle to a stop. Fumbling for his card in the full darkness, he cursed softly under his breath as it dropped to the floor near his feet.

As he bent over to retrieve the card-key, Jesse heard the distinctive sound of a shotgun barrel being snapped into place. Keeping his head low, he peered over the dashboard into the murky night.

"Who's there?" a deep voice shouted. "I've got my gun aimed right at you, so you've got about two seconds to answer me before I put a few holes in that pretty little runabout of yours." The speaker gave an evil chuckle, and Jesse could imagine the barrels of the shotgun swinging up to take aim.

"Hold your fire, Harry!" Jesse cried out. "It's Jesse Walker. I've just come out for a visit. I thought that you might want to shoot the shit for a while." Jesse took a deep breath and waited for Harry to recognize him.

Harry Miller was fanatical about his privacy, resenting any unwarranted intrusions. The dam was the only place in Paradise, besides the watch towers, that required 'round the clock attention; unlike the watch towers, however, the dam and its accompanying hydroelectric station required manning by someone with expertise in electrical engineering to ensure its smooth, efficient operation. Harry had the knowledge, and his crusty, hermit-like personality made it a convenient set-up for everyone. Jesse was one of the few people that Harry would allow on the grounds without being invited first—and he rarely issued invitations. Even Ben was not welcome; though if he chose to stop by, there was little Harry could do other than bitch about it. Jesse had always wondered why Harry and Ben did not get along, but since his coming to Paradise had been at Jesse's bidding, Ben had allowed Jesse to deal with both Harry and the maintenance responsibilities of the dam.

"Is that really you, Jesse?" Harry squinted, trying to see past the end of his unusually protuberant nose. "C'mon up to the house where I can see you better." As Jesse crawled over the side of the hovercraft, the beam of a high-power spotlight hit him. "Yep, you're you, all right," Harry laughed. "Gimme a smoke, boy, and let's go up to the house and set a spell."

Harry shifted the shotgun to his other arm as Jesse handed him a cigarette. They walked up the small, neatly manicured lawn to the building that Harry called 'home'.

Once inside, Harry gestured toward an old, overstuffed chair near the fireplace. Jesse ambled over, sat down, and stirred up the embers of the dying fire with a poker. "You know, Harry, I think that this is the most comfortable chair in Paradise." Jesse slouched back into the cushions with a sigh, and pulled out another cigarette.

Harry looked at Jesse with his flinty gray eyes and smiled faintly. "You say that every time you come out, Jesse," he reminded the younger man. "I guess that I'll just have to leave it to you in my will." Both men laughed as Harry walked over to Jesse and handed him a tumbler.

Jesse took the glass, and as he put it to his lips, noticed a strange yet familiar odor. Gingerly, he took a small sip, and the icy fire that poured down his throat was at once revolting and appealing. He stared at Harry in astonishment.

"Is this what I think it is? Where the hell did you get it?" Jesse took another drink as Harry smiled and followed suit.

Harry sat down across from Jesse and set his glass down on the table between them. He lit his cigarette with a burning twig from the fire, and settled back into his chair. "Well, it's a long story. I guess you probably know that I do a little trading with some of the local river people, Indians mostly." He shrugged. "Once in a while, I ask them to get me something personal in addition to what I get for Paradise. I think it's what your brother calls 'skimming the top'."

Harry paused to take another drink, and he carefully eyed Jesse for any hint of disapproval. "This schnapps came from somewhere near St. Paul, near as I can figure. The Indians said that they found a whole warehouse of the stuff, and they just wanted to share some with me as a gesture of good will. So they gave me a nice little stock of it, as well as some other things." Harry got out of his chair and walked to a door at the back of his cabin. He stopped short of opening the door, and turned to Jesse. "Mind you, none of this stuff was traded for with Paradise goods." Jesse followed Harry to the door, and the old man ushered him into the storage room within.

The back room, which Jesse knew Harry used not only as storage for parts for the dam, but also as a warehouse for trade goods, was nearly half full of cardboard cases of liquor. Jesse saw several more cases of the schnapps, as well as cases of Korbel brandy, Southern Comfort, and Jack Daniel's. Over in a far corner was another stack of cartons, but these were not liquor. Jesse gaped in amazement as he made out the labels on the tattered cartons.

"Nestlé's Quik?" he whispered almost reverently. "Hershey's Syrup?" Jesse backed slowly out of the room, and went back to his chair in a daze.

As Harry carefully locked the door to the storage room, Jesse spoke. "Those aren't normal trade goods you've got there, Harry. In fact, you've got things there that I haven't even seen in over five years." Jesse looked with suspicion and an unspoken accusation at the older man, whose eyes dropped from Jesse's under the obvious scrutiny.

"Hell, Jesse, who knows where the Indians get their stuff? I just take delivery; I don't ask too many questions — unlike some people." Harry stared at Jesse, his eyes cold and hard. "Nobody likes to be asked too many questions these days. 'Sides, I don't remember you bitching too much when I traded for those M1 carbines a couple of years ago. And you didn't complain when I got you that carton of filtered cigarettes last month." Harry's tone began to sound self-righteous, and Jesse hastened to soothe him.

"Hey — calm down! I didn't mean to sound like I was interrogating. I don't have the right, especially since I don't have any reason. I was just curious — naturally, I think. It is kind of strange that none of this makes it into Paradise."

Harry merely shrugged as he calmed down, while Jesse mulled over what he had just seen. It was probably true that Harry had not been trading away any goods from Paradise; inventory control was too tight to allow for any major discrepancies — and the goods in the back room would have cost Paradise dearly in normal trading. *What then,* Jesse wondered, *had Harry traded for them? What could he offer, besides his 'good will', that would be worth these kinds of riches?* A nagging suspicion began to nibble at the back of his mind, but Jesse rejected it for the time being. What he needed was answers, not conjecture. He removed a couple of cigarettes from his pouch and laid them on the table. He forced a grin for Harry's benefit, slammed down the remaining schnapps in his glass, and stood.

"I have to be getting back, Harry. I only signed out the hovercraft for a couple of hours, and I have some other rounds to make. Do you mind if I take a look at the works as long as I'm out here? Ben asked me to check on things if I was out this way, and to find out if you need any parts for the power plant."

Harry roused from his sullen reverie and looked doubtfully at the younger man. Smiling when he saw nothing more than amiable curiosity in Jesse's manner, he said, "Sure, we can take a gander at the plant. 'Sides, I have something else that I suppose I should show you." Harry led the way out of the cabin, locking the heavy door behind them.

Jesse followed Harry through the darkness to the waterfront, where above the sound of rushing water he could hear the creaking of the waterwheel and the quiet hum of the electrical generators. A dim night-light shone on the area, enabling Harry to see it at all times in case of trouble.

"What's new out here?" Jesse looked around as his eyes grew accustomed to the gloom, but he saw nothing out of the ordinary.

"Just a minute," Harry replied. His voice sounded strained as he fumbled around on one of the wheel braces. "Here goes!" he shouted finally, his voice echoing flatly from across the water.

Suddenly, the area for about a hundred yards around the dam became as bright as day. Jesse blinked furiously until his eyes adjusted to the abrupt change. Shading his eyes with his hand, he peered around for the source of the illumination.

From the roof of Harry's cabin, Jesse saw a ten-foot pole thrusting skyward. Atop the tower, gleaming with harsh brilliance, were four spotlights. Each of the lights faced in a different direction, effectively lighting the entire area.

Jesse heard a muffled click, and the lights were extinguished. As his eyes struggled to readjust to the dark, Harry chuckled.

"What d'ya think? I just finished installing them this afternoon, and this is the first time that I've tried them out in full dark. I don't know where your brother got the parts, but I'm sure glad he did."

Jesse was suitably impressed; the lights would serve to make the dam area more secure, since it would now be visible to the guard in the north-central tower. He could not restrain a stab of jealousy at the fact that Harry had seen another of his goals realized, while he still had to make do with the antiquated resources of his school. He shrugged and began walking across the gravel turnaround to his hovercraft.

"Helluva display, Harry," Jesse said, feigning more enthusiasm than he felt. "I'm sure that Ben will appreciate the work you've put into this."

Jesse reached the craft and climbed into the front seat. He pulled out his card/key, and slid it into the ignition. "Thanks for the drink, Harry. I'll drop by again next week, okay?" He pulled on his helmet, adjusted the baffles, and pressed the starter. The hovercraft arose in a cloud of dust.

Harry jumped back to avoid the maelstrom. "Wait a minute!" he shouted over the din, adding a wave of his arms to gain Jesse's attention. He ran back to the cabin, returning shortly with a bottle in his hand.

"Take this with you," he yelled as he handed it to Jesse. "It'll keep you warm." He smiled and gave Jesse a conspiratorial wink. "Just forget where you got it." Harry backed away and waved to Jesse.

Jesse waved back, set the bottle on the seat, and turned on the bank of halogen lights that lined the roll bar above his head. With a light touch on the controls, he turned the craft around and headed slowly toward the north-central gate. It was not until he came upon it that he remembered the limb lying in the road. He slowed the craft and hopped out of it as soon as it settled to a full stop.

Jesse hurried around to the thick end of the limb, and bent over to grasp it. As his hands ran over the bark, he noted in the glare of the headlights that the end of the branch was not cracked, but rather cut cleanly.

That's odd, Jesse thought as he resumed tugging the heavy branch to the side of the road. *It's almost as if it was put there intentionally. But by whom? And why?*

He wiped his hands on his pants legs, and with a shrug, got back into the hovercraft. He drove to the gate of Paradise and silently showed his ID to the guard, still puzzling over the unusual event.

Jesse pulled into the garage a few minutes later, shut down the craft, and signed in. Since he had not seen Isaac for several days, and he was hungry, he decided to stop at the inn for a bite to eat. Also, he felt like he could use a stiff drink to help him sort out the unusual events of the day. Wrapping his jacket around him, he began the short hike to the inn.

It had been a busy day.

The first thing that Jesse noticed as he entered the tavern was the size of the crowd. He glanced across the heads of several patrons at Isaac, who caught his eye and grinned.

"C'mon over, Jesse," Isaac boomed cheerfully. "Good crowd tonight, don't you think?" Isaac handed Jesse a mug of beer, spilling a large head of foam on the bar in the process. He wiped up the spill with a clean rag, winked at his friend, and hustled down to the far end of the bar in response to a cry for more beer. Jesse smiled as he set his beer on the bar, and shrugged off his jacket. He settled onto his stool, sipped his beer, and surveyed the crowd.

So many familiar faces, he mused. He knew everyone at the inn, not only by name but on a personal level. Some of them had children in his school, others were involved with projects of their own. But Jesse was familiar with each and every person, through his position as teacher as well as his place on the council. He made friends easily; many of the people waved to him as he sat down, and he returned their greetings with a smile.

The door opened, and Jesse saw Doc Riley enter into the smoke-filled room. "Over here, Doc," Jesse called. The older gentleman saw Jesse and hurried over.

"Buy you a drink, Doc?" Jesse noticed how tired Doc looked, and he expressed his concern. "Have you been working overtime again? You should really let Marty do a little more of your running around, you know."

The doctor sat down next to Jesse, and looked at him sternly. "You young spalpeens just don't know what work is anymore," he snapped, his rough Irish brogue accompanied by a twinkle in his eyes. "All you want to do is eat, drink, and be merry, when there are more important things to be doing." He paused just long enough to get Isaac's attention. "Besides, 'twasn't work that wore me out." The older man winked, and a smile creased his weather-beaten features.

Jesse threw back his head and laughed, the first time that he had felt good all day. "Dammit, Doc—what are you doing here talking to me when you could be in a nice warm bed? Do you believe this guy, Ike?"

The tall black innkeeper set a jigger and bottle of whiskey down in front of the doctor. "What's that? Is this old coot giving you his 'I'm so tired 'cause she wore me out' spiel?" Isaac laughed heartily, reached over the bar, and gave the doctor a good-natured thump on the shoulder. "The day this old goat stops working long enough to grab some tail is the day that I stop spilling beer on the bar." To illustrate his point, Isaac swiped at the bar before him. All three men laughed, since Isaac was notorious for getting as much beer on the bar and his customers as he did in the mugs. "Seriously, Doc, you've been working too hard. Hell, you haven't been in here for nearly a week. I was beginning to wonder what to do with all my surplus whiskey." Isaac smiled, his perfect white teeth gleaming against his ebony skin.

Jesse looked shocked. "A week? What have you been doing that's kept you out of circulation for that long?" Jesse turned all his attention to the doctor, and Isaac stood silently, wiping the bar absently with his rag.

Doc Riley downed a shot of whiskey, and looked at Isaac disapprovingly. "Last week's batch, Isaac?" Isaac nodded soberly. "Not bad," Doc grudgingly admitted, "but I don't think it will ever be a national brand."

Isaac pretended to be insulted and stalked off. He shot a look of amused affection over his shoulder at his two friends, and turned to other customers.

"One hell of a man, our Isaac," Doc said. He turned to Jesse and grinned. "Now, what was on your mind?"

Jesse swallowed another mouthful of the warm, bitter beer, and set his mug down on the spotless bar. "I was wondering what has you so busy that you can't even find the time to have a drink with your friends." Jesse's brow furrowed as a horrible thought entered his mind, and he lowered his voice. "You didn't find a plague victim, did you?" He pitched his voice so that only the doctor could hear; there was no use starting a rumor that would end in panic.

Doc Riley had an almost fanatical obsession with the plague, though it was only natural for a man to become obsessed with tracking down and eliminating the killer of his beloved wife. It had been the skill and compassion of Riley that had enabled Paradise to survive the plague—he had been the first one to spot and identify it, and it had been his techniques of diagnosis, quarantine, and treatment that had kept it from spreading into the general populace. Everyone in Paradise owed their lives to the doctor, and it was obvious that all knew it by the deferential, loving treatment that he received from each and every person.

Doc shook his head slowly. "And what would make you think that, boyo? No, 'tis something nearly as bad I'm checking on." Doc picked up his empty glass and looked at it mournfully for a moment before speaking again. "I've found some peculiar things in some of my water samples lately. I've not talked to your brother about it yet, but I think that our ground water is being contaminated."

The words hung in the air, and the hustle and bustle of the inn seemed to intensify. Jesse mulled over the significance of the doctor's disclosure, and was seriously frightened by some of the implications.

"What kind of contamination, Doc?" Jesse asked in a near whisper. "In it's own way, a loss of potable ground water could prove as serious as another plague. Is it natural, or is it some form of pollution?"

"I'm not sure, Jesse," Doc answered carefully. "I've talked to a few people—Isaac, for example—and I'm thinking that the contaminants are artificial. But that doesn't mean that they are being deliberately introduced into the water, if that's what you're thinking," he hastened to add at the look of anger on Jesse's face. "I cannot be sure without further tests."

"You'd best talk to Ben about this as soon as possible," Jesse decided. "It's something he needs to know about, and he may be able to get you some help for your investigation."

Jesse drank down the rest of his beer and decided to take his leave. He could get himself something to eat at home. Standing, he noticed Doc looking askance at the pistol hanging from his belt. "Things are not always what they appear to be," Jesse said cryptically. "Take it easy, Doc, and keep us posted." He waved at Isaac and left the inn.

He began the short walk to his cabin, but had not gotten as far as the central plaza when he heard hurried footsteps approaching from behind. He turned and saw Moira Doyle running after him.

"I saw you leaving the inn," she gasped as she tried to regain her composure, "and I thought that I'd never catch up. What's your hurry?" She flipped a stray wisp of auburn hair from her forehead with a flip of her head, and smiled at Jesse.

"No hurry, Mo'," Jesse replied. "Just a bit chilly, I guess." He slipped his arm around her waist and resumed walking. "Want to come over to my place for a late supper? I was going to eat at Isaac's, but it was too crowded for my liking."

Moira gazed up at him through emerald green eyes. "Sure, Jess. I wanted to talk to you about school tomorrow, anyway. I want to take the day off, and my lesson plans may take a little deciphering." They both chuckled.

"Yeah, I suppose we could do that," Jesse laughed, giving her a squeeze. "Do you mind if I stop at Ben's office first? I have to drop something off and leave him a note." He felt the weight of the bottle inside his jacket, and felt a similar weight press down upon his soul.

When they reached the office, Jesse saw that his brother was no longer there. He reached into his pocket for a pen and paper, and left a note:

Ben,

Have to talk to you about new info. Something strange going on at the dam, but I can't put my finger on it. This bottle might have something to do with it.

Jesse

Jesse dropped the note and bottle in Ben's mail chute, and he and Moira left the administration building.

They began walking in the direction of Jesse's place, and Moira kept silent. She was dying to ask him about the bottle, as well as the gun hanging at his side, but the look of intense concentration on Jesse's face kept her from doing so. She knew that expression far too well, and knew better than to interrupt his thought processes. Tonight, however, she saw a new expression that she had never seen before: the lines etched in his tanned face and the haunted look in his eyes spelled *worry*. She hugged him tightly with one arm, pressing her slender frame against his lean body. She wanted so much to please him, to make him happy, but she knew better than to press him into divulging something that he was not yet ready to volunteer.

Moira had been working closely with Jesse at the school since her arrival in Paradise in the summer of '16. She had maintained the school and filled in as teacher during the weeks that Jesse spent recovering from wounds received in the Rovers' attack.

The two of them had hit it off immediately. She appreciated his gentle good humor, his winning way with the children, and his love of knowledge. It had not been long before the two became lovers, and that had only served to strengthen and enhance their relationship. For Moira, however, it was a relationship that was often sad and lonely. Jesse did not seem disposed to making a commitment, though his attentions and affections seemed centered on her. Still, she felt sometimes that she was placed after Jesse's relationship with his brother, his work, and his many projects.

Moira gazed through loving eyes at Jesse as they walked to his home.

It doesn't matter to me if I come second in his life, Moira told herself firmly, *as long as I'm part of it.*

They finished the walk in silence; neither of them mentioned Moira's lesson plans again that night.

CHAPTER SEVEN

The Journal of Ben Walker: May 4, 2012--

IT'S HARD TO RESIST THE URGE TO PLAY GOD WITH PARADISE AND MY FRIENDS AND NEIGHBORS. I'VE LIVED SO LONG FOR THIS TIME THAT I CANNOT BEAR TO SEE ANYTHING FAIL TO WORK AS I'VE ENVISIONED IT. I HAVEN'T SPOKEN TO ANYONE ABOUT THIS, LEAST OF ALL JESSE; MY FEARS AND DOUBTS ARE TOO PRIVATE, TOO WEAK. I MUST BEAR THIS PARTICULAR CROSS BY MYSELF...

...CONSTRUCTION HAS BEGUN ON MANY OF THE PRIVATE HOMES. WE WERE VERY FORTUNATE TO HAVE LOCATED A TRACT OF LAND WITH BOTH A READY SOURCE OF WATER AND TIMBER—MANY OF OUR HOMES AND OTHER STRUCTURES ARE BEING CONSTRUCTED OF PINE LOGS. MY HOME, A SIMPLE A-FRAME, HAS A DUAL LOFT; ON ONE END IS MY STUDY, ON THE OTHER IS MY BEDROOM. A NARROW CATWALK THAT TRAVERSES THE EMPTY SPACE SOME TWELVE FEET ABOVE THE GROUND FLOOR CONNECTS THE TWO. THE HOUSE IS SMALL, BUT WELL-DESIGNED AND COMFORTABLE FOR ONE PERSON. I HAVE TAKEN ADVANTAGE OF THE WEALTH THAT WE'VE ACQUIRED TO COVER THE SOUTHERN SLOPE OF THE HOUSE WITH SOME OF THE NEWER HIGH-YIELD SOLAR CELLS. ON A SUNNY DAY I CAN PULL IN NEARLY SIXTY KILOWATTS AT TWELVE VOLTS, MORE THAN AMPLE FOR MY NEEDS.

THE FIRST OF THE ULTRA LIGHTS ARRIVED TODAY—WHAT A THRILL! I HAVE ALWAYS WANTED TO FLY, BUT NEVER HAD THE TIME OR OPPORTUNITY TO LEARN THE REGULAR WAY. NOW I'LL BE ABLE TO GET ALOFT WHENEVER THE URGE HITS ME. IT'S GREAT, BEING UP IN THE SKY WITH THE FRESH AIR AND SUNLIGHT. I WAS TOO CAUTIOUS ON MY FIRST FLIGHT TO TAKE IT OVER A FEW HUNDRED FEET UP, EVEN THOUGH I KNOW THAT IT'S ACTUALLY SAFER AT A GREATER ALTITUDE—MORE TIME TO CORRECT MISTAKES. HOWEVER, SOMETHING ABOUT SITTING SO EXPOSED TO ALL THAT EMPTY SPACE KEEPS ME ON EDGE. I SUPPOSE THAT IT'S ONLY A MATTER OF TIME AND EXPERIENCE BEFORE I WILL BE TRULY AT EASE IN THE SKY...

THE FENCING CONTRACTOR FINISHED THE JOB TODAY—PARADISE IS NOW COMPLETELY ENCLOSED BY A PERIMETER OF EIGHT-FOOT CYCLONE FENCE.

I HAD GIVEN THOUGHT TO HAVING ANGLED, ELECTRIFIED BARBED WIRE ON THE FENCE TOPS; HOWEVER, THE ADDITIONAL EXPENSE AND POWER REQUIREMENTS CHANGED MY MIND FOR ME. ALSO, AS JESSE POINTED OUT, IT WOULD MAKE PARADISE LOOK LIKE A POW CAMP.

...AS I'VE BEEN URGING HIM TO DO, JESSE IS GOING ON A VACATION FOR ABOUT THE NEXT MONTH. HE SAYS THAT HE MAY JUST FLY TO IRELAND; HE'S ALWAYS WANTED TO SEE THAT, AND A WALK THROUGH A REAL CASTLE WOULD MAKE HIM A HAPPY MAN.

I AM ASKING EVERYONE TO TAKE THE NEXT MONTH OFF TO VISIT FRIENDS AND FAMILY, TRAVEL, OR WHATEVER—ALL EXPENSES PAID BY PARADISE, OF COURSE. I HAVE A PROJECT PLANNED THAT WILL REQUIRE ABSOLUTE SECRECY TO IMPLEMENT. JESSE WOULD HATE ME IF HE KNEW, NOT ONLY FOR THE WASTE OF MONEY, BUT FOR THE INTENT BEHIND MY PROJECT. REGARDLESS, I FEEL THAT THE ULTIMATE SAFETY AND SECURITY OF PARADISE, GIVEN THE PRESENT STATE OF AFFAIRS IN THE WORLD, MUST BE MY PRIMARY CONCERN.

...OLD FARMHOUSE MODIFIED TO MY SPECIFICATIONS, AND WILL SERVE AS A CENTRAL ADMINISTRATION BUILDING—AND MORE. JESSE WON'T FIND OUT ABOUT THE CHANGES UNTIL IT IS ABSOLUTELY NECESSARY. I LOVE MY BROTHER, BUT HE IS SOMETIMES TOO PACIFIC FOR DEALING WITH THE HARSHER REALITIES. I, ON THE OTHER HAND, WILL DO ANYTHING TO DEFEND MY PRINCIPLES.

I HAVE BEEN IN COMMUNICATION WITH A RETIRED SYSTEMS ENGINEER WHO WORKED ON REMOTE SURVEILLANCE FOR THE ARMY. FOR FIVE MILLION DOLLARS, HE IS DESIGNING A SYSTEM THAT WILL INCORPORATE DRONE TANKS, AIRBORNE DRONES, AND RADAR INTO A COMPLETE DEFENSIVE ARRAY. WE WILL HAVE COMPLETE RADAR COVERAGE FOR A ONE HUNDRED MILE RADIUS, AS WELL AS LIMITED SATELLITE COVERAGE. THE TANKS WILL BE CONSTRUCTED OF LAMINATED PLYWOOD AND FIBERGLASS, WITH A SHEET METAL OUTER SHELL. THE AIR DRONES WILL BE NOTHING MORE THAN TINY POWERED GLIDERS DESIGNED TO CARRY A CAMERA AND TRANSCEIVER.

MY CONSULTANT ASSURES ME THAT THE SYSTEM WILL SERVE TO HALT ALL BUT THE MOST CONCERTED ATTACKS. HE LOOKED AT ME LIKE I WAS MAD

WHEN I FIRST ASKED HIM TO BUILD THE SYSTEM FOR ME, BUT HE CAN READ THE PAPERS, TOO. HE IS NOW CONSIDERING JOINING US IN PARADISE BEFORE THE YEAR IS OUT.

HOPEFULLY, THINGS WON'T GET AS BAD AS I FEAR, AND THIS SYSTEM WILL BE ALLOWED TO RUST. JUST IN CASE, THOUGH, I WANT TO HEDGE MY BETS. IN ADDITION TO THE CONTROLLERS FOR THE DRONES, I HAVE HAD A COMPUTER NETWORK INSTALLED IN A SECRET LOCATION. I TIED IN THE CONTROLS FOR THE DRONES, AND WROTE A PROGRAM THAT WILL ENABLE MANY OF THE FUNCTIONS—ESPECIALLY SURVEILLANCE—TO BE AUTOMATED. WITH LUCK— IF IT COMES TO SOME SORT OF POST-HOLOCAUST SITUATION—THE WORST WE WILL HAVE TO FEAR IS A POORLY ARMED AND EQUIPPED MOB. IF, HOWEVER, WE DO RUN UP AGAINST SOMETHING MORE ORGANIZED, MY PLAN IS TO BREAK THEIR FRONT LINE SO COMPLETELY THAT THE REMAINDER WILL BE TOO DEMORALIZED TO ATTEMPT ANOTHER SFOUR-WHEELER. ANY ERSTWHILE AGGRESSOR WILL THEN THINK TWICE BEFORE ATTEMPTING TO SFOUR-WHEELER AGAIN...

TOMORROW MORNING, JESSE AND I ARE FLYING INTO ST. PAUL ON AN ULTRA LIGHT. WE ARE GOING SHOPPING FOR HOVERCRAFTS—WE NEED A VEHICLE WITH DECENT SPEED AND CARGO CAPACITY TO TAKE THE PLACE OF BOTH BOATS AND LIGHT TRUCKS. A FIRM IN MINNESOTA MAKES A TWO PASSENGER CRAFT THAT WILL TRAVEL AT SPEEDS UP TO FIFTY MILES PER HOUR ON LEVEL LAND, AND TWENTY-FIVE ON WATER OR MARSHLANDS. WE DECIDED AGAINST THE LARGER CAPACITY, FOUR-PASSENGER MODEL BECAUSE IT WAS NOT FUEL-EFFICIENT.

...SUBJECT OF FUEL: THE FIRST OF FOUR STILLS IS UP AND RUNNING. BY THE END OF THE WEEK, WE WILL HAVE ENOUGH ALCOHOL FUEL TO RUN OUR TEN, FIVE THOUSAND WATT GENERATORS. THE STILL SHOULD PRODUCE ABOUT THREE HUNDRED GALLONS PER MONTH, OR ENOUGH TO POWER THE GENERATORS FOR SEVEN DAYS NON-STOP. HOWEVER, MUCH OF THE FUEL WILL EVENTUALLY BE RESERVED FOR TRANSPORTATION NEEDS; THEREFORE, I HAVE MADE PLANS TO ALTER THE GENERATORS TO RUN OFF OF A WATERWHEEL, AS WELL AS CHANGING THE FUEL SYSTEMS ON THE VEHICLES TO A METHANOL/ETHANOL SYSTEM WHERE POSSIBLE.

Jesse suggested that we leave several of the generators running at twelve volt, and the rest at one-twenty. I decided to split it half and half for now: five generators running at twelve volt for lighting and related applications; five generators running at one-twenty for appliances, computers, etc. The furnaces will also need the higher output of the generators, because if we have to rely on wood-burners all winter, we'll freeze. All the buildings are insulated, some to the point of super-insulated (the perishables warehouse, for instance); however, our survival as intrepid 'pioneers' still depends to a large extent on the effectiveness of my planning.

Paradise now has almost twenty-two permanent inhabitants. I say 'almost' because Karen Mitchell is expecting her first baby in two months. I am planning a large celebration, as the baby will be the first born in Paradise.

Greg Mitchell, Karen's husband, is an old high school buddy of mine. I ran into him at a lumberyard in Marshfield where he was working as a foreman. We went out for a few beers, and I outlined my schemes for him; days later, he was working for me, and a short time after that, I had convinced Greg and Karen to join Paradise.

...And with our growing population, several tasks have become easier. I have mounted a night guard in the watchtowers, more to keep out curiosity seekers than from any real need. We began with an eight-hour watch schedule, but with the addition of Greg, Jack Barker, and Roger Dooley, we can drop the rotation to one four-hour watch per person.

Frank just called in; he's on his way back to the house (administration building), and Jesse should be here any minute.

Business as usual.

CHAPTER EIGHT

Ben awoke, earlier than usual, with a start. He took a quick, bracing shower, made a sandwich of rough corn bread and smoked venison, and headed to the site of the new library and research center. This was Ben's own pet project; ruefully, he recalled the difficulty he had experienced trying to convince the council of the necessity. They had been stubborn almost to the point of selfishness, but with the control that he and Jesse wielded in the council, it had been a foregone conclusion who would prevail.

Some of the newer members of the council—who had never been in charge of anything—had objected on the grounds that the effort would be better spent in improving their own standard of living. Ben and Jesse scoffed at the notion; Paradise had been set up to allow for a minimal amount of luxuries. Together, the Walkers had expressed the opinion that if the council members wanted to improve their own personal living standard, they would be best served by working to that end themselves.

Ben and Jesse had defeated the council—which was becoming increasingly more hostile and conservative—only by a show of force. They had told the others quite simply that if they did not like the way things were being run, they were free to leave Paradise at any time. Jesse had indelicately reminded the councilors, resting his eyes on a select few, that Ben had subsidized their entrance into Paradise, and they owed their very existence to him. The final vote had been unanimously, if grudgingly, in favor of the project.

Ben smiled as he recalled the debate. He approached the construction site and surveyed the work. He was gratified to see that the building was coming along swiftly; already the roof and outside walls were up. The southern wall, which was constructed of a many-faceted wall of glass, still needed work, since behind the glass were to be put the special banks of photovoltaic cells that would provide light and heat for the entire complex.

Labor teams were just beginning to arrive at the site. Ben had recruited locals from the Tomahawk area for this venture. They needed many things that Paradise had in abundance, such as medicines, clothing, and tools. Ben had made them a fair offer that the townsfolk, in their need, had readily accepted.

The foremen had arrived, and work was commencing. Ben stood to one side and watched as the crews rapidly fitted together the pre-assembled sections. Soon they were beginning to work on the nearly completed interior assemblies, even as the outer walls were being finished.

The complex consisted of three closely spaced buildings. The library was a twenty-two by forty-eight foot rectangle, with huge, many-paned windows on the southern face to take advantage of both light and heat. The glass had been scavenged from abandoned homes and buildings in the surrounding area, and pieced together into large frameworks. The result was almost artistic, resembling a large mosaic, since most of the glass was of differing sizes, shapes, and colors. It was here that the solar cells were to be installed. The central building in the complex was going to contain a series of small laboratories, designed for experiments in physics, chemistry, biology, and other disciplines. The largest of the three buildings was the auditorium, suitable for everything from showing films to holding town meetings. It would, upon completion, seat nearly three hundred people in bleachers. Ben's dream for the complex was that it would someday become a Mecca of science and culture for the fragmented upper Midwest.

Ben was suddenly aware of a presence at his side. Turning slightly, he glanced over.

"Good morning," he greeted Anna Graycloud, Paradise's security chief. Raven-haired, half-Chippewa, Anna was a lovely sight on such a fine morning. Ben watched her appraisingly, and saw a tall, slender woman with coppery skin, lean figure, and deep black eyes. She looked at Ben briefly, and both averted their eyes in uncomfortable embarrassment.

Anna had joined Paradise eight years earlier, a disaffected product of both the white man's world and the Chippewa tradition. Her interests, because of an early exposure to a dedicated Protestant missionary, had been to enter the ministry—a rather strange calling for a young Amerindian girl. Therefore, at seventeen, she had entered a Lutheran college; her intentions were to become the first female Chippewa pastor. It only took a short time for her to become disenchanted with the new changes within the church, however; she soon left the college and pursued her second interest—police science.

At eighteen, she entered the police academy; one year later, she graduated at the top of her class. The Green Bay Area Federal Police immediately hired her, where she served with distinction from early 2011 until the Collapse of late 2012. She remained in Green Bay doing her best to keep order, until the whole population fled from the starving, dying, and disease-ridden city.

Anna, due more to her own ingenuity than her heritage, had managed to survive through the winter months of 2012-13 alone, until Ben had chanced upon her camp nearly thirty miles northwest of Paradise. Ben remembered that day as if it was only yesterday...

It was an extremely cold January day in 2013. Ben was out testing one of the newly winterized hovercrafts, something he had hoped Jesse wanted to be in on; however, because of the weather, Jesse had decided to hold class instead.

Ben was some thirty miles from home, just outside a small town named Phillips. He was hovering in neutral, deciding whether to turn back or go on, when he noticed a trail leading off to the right. The trail, beaten by foot through the fresh snow, led deep into the forest. His curiosity piqued, he guided the craft to the side of the road, shut it down, and pulled the camouflage tarp over it. He removed an M16 from its case, checked the clip, and entered the woods.

He crept quietly down the trail, hating the scrunch of frozen snow beneath his boots but unable to avoid it. His view was obscured by the densely packed pine and fir trees, and the day was overcast, making the gloom nearly night-dark within the woods.

He followed the trail for several hundred yards, finally coming to a clearing. He paused just within the tree-line and scanned the area. He saw a small, ramshackle cabin at one side of the clearing, but would not have given it a second glance had it not been for the tiny streamer of smoke rising from the stovepipe in the roof.

Ben had learned caution in the months since the Collapse — without conscious thought, he had the M16 cocked and ready as he made a stealthy approach to the cabin. He circled around the back of the dilapidated structure, not leaving the relative safety of the forest until he was at his closest approach. Silently, he made his way around to the front of the cabin, and stood listening for several minutes before he moved again.

He reached out with the butt of the M16 and rapped loudly on the door. There was no response, so he struck the door harder, causing it to open several inches. He jumped back from the opening as he heard someone cry out softly.

"Is anyone there?" Ben called out. Again, he heard the soft voice, sounding feeble and ill. Throwing caution to the wind, Ben pushed the door open and entered the cabin.

A pile of furs lay to one side of the tiny room, and a wood stove was throwing off some heat, but there was no one in sight. The hackles on Ben's neck rose, and he readied the gun for action. "Where are you?" he asked.

The pile of furs in the corner moved slightly, and he heard a moan. He went quickly to the corner and removed the top layer of covers. In the dim light, all he could see was a dirty face topped with ragged black hair — a face that could have belonged to anyone. He helped the weak, bedraggled figure to its feet, and moved closer to the stove. He stoked the fire and removed the Thermos from his pack. He poured a steaming cup of chicory coffee into the cup and held it up to the huddled figure's mouth.

The cabin's inhabitant drank the coffee greedily, and muttered a quiet word of thanks in a shivering voice. Ben handed the Thermos to — her, he decided, and looked around the room.

He saw an old card table against one wall with a folding chair in front of it. On the table, pushed behind a plate and some silverware, was a stack of dog-eared paperback books. Bending closer, he saw *The Boy Scout Handbook*, *A Camper's Guide*, and several novels. He smiled at the titles of several of the books; science fiction was good entertainment for someone living alone, and the others were among the best survival books ever written.

Ben roamed around the rest of the room. What he was looking for was weapons, and finally he saw them. On the wall above the piled furs, a holstered .38 Special was hanging. There were only about a dozen bullets in the belt. Next to the pistol, a twelve-gauge riot gun was hung from another hook. Ben turned to look at the girl sitting by the fire, and a dawning respect for her passed through him. Here was a person who had made it through the worst of the Collapse on her own; however, it was obvious to Ben that she now needed help.

Ben walked back to the stove and the girl backed away, fear and defiance in her black eyes. Ben hastily explained where he was from and why he was here. She began by casting doubtful looks at him, but eventually seemed to believe his story.

"I have a hovercraft back on the main road if you want to come back with me," Ben offered. "We can be back in Paradise in just an hour or so, where you can get something to eat, get cleaned up, and get warm." At the last suggestion, the girl's eyes lit up; her decision was made.

"Can you make it that far?" Ben asked. He really did not want to have to carry the filthy woman any farther than he had to. Being in the enclosed hovercraft for an hour would be bad enough.

She nodded, and Ben helped her to gather her things in a blanket: the guns, the books, and a tiny bundle of clothes were her only belongings.

Ben half-carried her to the waiting vehicle. He stowed the tarp, secured his passenger, and with a silent prayer, pressed the starter button. To his grateful amazement, the vehicle started right up, and he allowed it to warm. With the heaters on full, he spun the craft around and began the return trip to Paradise.

The girl, no more than twenty by Ben's estimate, promptly fell asleep. *Malnourished, by the looks of it,* Ben thought. He decided that it could wait until she was fed and clothed to determine who and what she was.

They arrived back at Ben's late; he carried the sleeping woman into his place and laid her on the couch. After calling Jack at the garage to let him know that the hovercraft was at his place, Ben proceeded to unwrap the woman from the smelly blankets and furs. He winced when he saw just how emaciated she was — but she was definitely female.

She awoke while Ben was unwrapping her, and some of her earlier fright returned. Ben assured her that he was just going to dispose of the filthy blankets, and asked her if she wanted some soup. She nodded vigorously, and wolfed down the bowl of stew Ben brought her without waiting for it to cool.

When she had finished, Ben asked if she wanted to take a hot shower. She looked surprised, then nodded slowly.

"I suppose that introductions are in order," Ben told his guest. "I'm Ben Walker, and I run this place we call Paradise. Who might you be?"

The girl cleared her throat. "Anna. Anna Graycloud."

"Well, Anna, take a shower while I try to rustle up some clothes for you. You can get some rest, and we'll talk in the morning."

Ben showed her where everything was, and soon he heard the water running. He pondered the problem of clothing for Anna; she could wear any of his shirts, but while he wore pants with a thirty-four inch waist, she looked like she could get by with a twenty-four. Oh well, he decided, she'll just have to tie off the waist.

He laid out the clothes on the bed outside the bathroom, and sat down with a cup of coffee in the small kitchen downstairs. He thought that his guest would want to go right to sleep, so was surprised when she came out of the bedroom.

Ben suppressed a smile at her appearance. She looked both fragile and comical in his clothes; she was, also, quite lovely — though she needed to regain a few pounds.

Ben gave her a cup of coffee and another bowl of soup, and in between bites, she gave him her story. When Ben discovered that she had been a fedcop, he toyed with the idea of making her security chief — a job which he had been filling, but was more than willing to give up.

Over the next several days he had outfitted her, and at the next council meeting, presented her for membership in Paradise. She had been readily accepted, and a month later, took over the position of security chief.

She had been the fifty-eighth member of Paradise.

"Your project seems to be coming along nicely," Anna said, breaking Ben from his reverie. She had shown an interest in all aspects of Paradise from the beginning. "How long until it's ready for use?"

Ben smiled. "Hopefully, in about a month. Why? Have you got some research project in mind?"

"Not really, Ben. I was just thinking how nice it would be to have a forensics lab in Paradise — not that we need it. We could, however, expand out police protection to the surrounding communities now that things are settling down locally." She glanced significantly at the Outsiders on the construction site.

"Do you really think we could make a go of it?" Ben asked. "It would be helpful to have eyes and ears outside of our borders; however, with the Cencoms breathing down our necks, I wouldn't want to jeopardize the safety of any of our people, either."

Anna grinned and said with a trace of sarcasm, "You still can't accept that a mere woman can do anything better than you, can you? Ben Walker, if I didn't like you so much, I could learn to hate you!"

Ben laughed. "We're kindred spirits, you and I; that's why we never really fight. I look upon us as competitors, but on terms of mutual respect. That respect is why you're security chief here, and not one of the men who are nearly as qualified."

Ben paused, and his tone became serious. "You're right, though. I don't believe that the average woman is as capable as the average man. But you, my dear, are the obvious exception. You're highly skilled in your area of expertise, and don't run from danger. Why is that?"

Anna stood silently gazing at the upturned dirt of the construction site. When she spoke, her voice sounded sad and distant. "We all have dreams, Ben. Unlike you and your dream of 'Paradise', I may never realize mine. Even all the gold you have could not buy me my dream. Maybe that's why I try so hard." She stopped talking, and for the first time since they had met, she looked frail and innocent to Ben.

"I wish that I could help, Anna," Ben said softly, "but I can't—at least, not until you choose to share your dream with me. I want to help you; you've been a good friend, and an indispensable ally. But there's always this—thing—between us."

Anna turned away, but not before Ben had seen the glistening tear on her cheek. "I can't, Ben. Not now—maybe never. Please don't push me."

They stood together, facing the early morning sun, their bodies lightly touching. Anna's hand slowly, deliberately crept upward and found Ben's. They held hands, sharing her silent hurt, well into the morning.

CHAPTER NINE

Ben sat in his office, wishing for perhaps the millionth time that he had installed air conditioning. It was an exceptionally warm day for March, and just thinking of everything that needed doing made Ben thirsty. He pushed aside the papers on his desk, and sighed. Isaac's seemed like a great place to while away a couple of hours before getting back into the mass of work that had piled up over the past few days. Ben grabbed his jacket, locked the door, and walked out of the building into the sunny March afternoon.

Isaac's was the social center of Paradise, being at once a tavern, inn, social club, and recreation area. Isaac Peters had made an easy transition from big city college professor to small town bartender, distiller, and part-time chemist. The Peters family had been readily accepted into the community of Paradise, which had warmed Ben's heart. He had hoped that in the wake of a dead nation, old prejudices would also be wiped out.

Perhaps it was simply the man himself; Isaac was six and a half feet tall, two hundred and seventy pounds of muscle, and had an easy, disarming grin that instantly made anyone near him feel as if they were old friends. He was gentle with women and children, gruffly affectionate toward his male friends, and easy around strangers.

His over-sized Teddy bear exterior, however, hid the fact that he had a keen mind. He was a leading organic chemist, and had been working as a professor and researcher at the University of Wisconsin campus in Madison when the Collapse occurred.

Ben opened the door of the inn and walked in with the expectation of finding the place deserted; instead, it seemed that half the community was there. The crowd was talking, laughing, eating, and drinking, and no one took notice of Ben's arrival—except for the ever- watchful Isaac. Ben thought that there was way too much drinking going on, so he determined to buy a round for the house.

"Hi, Isaac," he called. The big man waved a greeting, and set up a glass for Ben as he reached the bar. "Buy everyone a round on me, okay?"

Isaac grinned, his teeth flashing in the dim light, and nodded his approval. He passed the order to his wife, who assisted him in managing the inn and serving the customers. She was also one of the finest cooks in Paradise, able to make venison stew taste like an Epicurean delight. An

69

attractive woman of forty-two with skin the color of mahogany and beautiful, almond-shaped eyes, Josslyn Peters ambled over to where Ben was sitting.

"Hi, Ben. Do you want another?" Ben nodded, and she pulled a bottle from beneath the bar. "Whiskey, straight up?" Without waiting for an answer, she poured a jigger of the whiskey; in the past eight years, she had never poured anything but that for Ben.

Their fifteen-year-old daughter Marissa, who waited tables and generally brightened up the place, assisted the Peters'. Ben wondered where Nathan was until he saw his lanky, eleven year old frame dodging in and out of the kitchen bearing trays of dishes.

"Thanks, gorgeous," Ben quipped. "What's the occasion? Is someone having a party that I wasn't invited to?"

"It's the heat," Josslyn explained. "Most of the kids are splashing around in the pond, but the adults are in here drinking Isaac's latest." She nodded at the glass before Ben. "He thinks that he's duplicated the formula for Seagram's Seven; if he had only a couple of ounces of the real thing, he'd be able to tell for sure—but I guess that's just a dream, right?" She sighed and looked wistful, remembering things past.

"Maybe Jesse and I can locate some on our next scavenging trip, all right?" Ben smiled at the woman, admiring her support of her husband's work. She returned his smile, patted his hand gently, and then moved down the bar to serve another customer.

Ben took the bottle and his glass and circulated around the room, nodding hello and stopping occasionally for a few words with his neighbors. Finally, he located a relatively quiet table and pulled up a chair. He poured another shot, and sat in the corner drinking his whiskey.

"Uncle Ben?" The timid young girl's voice caused him to start. Opening his eyes, he peered at Isaac's daughter Marissa, who was standing nervously before him. By her side was a young man of sixteen with tousled, blond hair and brilliant, blue eyes. Ben recognized the face, but could not immediately name him; then, with a smile, he remembered—Jeff Barker, son of Jack Barker. Jesse had spoken highly of him because of his attentiveness to his studies; it also seemed that he was destined to follow in his father's footsteps, for he was a fine mechanic in his own right.

"Hi, 'Rissa, Jeff. Why don't you have a seat, and tell me what's on your minds." Ben smiled brightly to put the youngster at ease.

"Oh, no," Marissa stammered, "we couldn't—I mean, we don't want to bother you. It's just that we were wondering—that is..." She trailed off into embarrassed silence.

"What she's trying to say, sir, is that we want," and Jeff took a deep breath, "we want to get married!"

Marissa blushed, her skin turning a purplish hue, but her dark eyes glittered. "That's right," she said, nodding vigorously.

Ben was momentarily stunned. Married? These two kids? He took a slow sip of his drink, and motioned for the two to sit down across from him. This time they did not argue, perhaps more confident since Ben had not immediately berated them for their request.

"Have you talked to your folks yet? Jeff, what does your dad think?" The boy lowered his head. "I didn't think you'd approached him yet. Marissa, I know that you haven't talked to your parents yet."

Ben leaned forward and managed to catch both of their eyes. His next question he asked in a quiet, gentle tone. "Marissa, are you pregnant?"

Jeff looked startled, then embarrassed. Marissa, however, looked indignant. "Of course not! We know that if we fooled around, we could get in serious trouble; besides, we're not ready to raise a family. We're going to wait for—that—until we're married."

Ben nodded his approval. Here was a young woman with some sense! "Very sensible of you. Now, why are you telling me when you haven't told your parents yet?"

Marissa looked ready to say something, then stopped. She glanced at Jeff, who nodded slowly. Marissa smiled shyly, and then began again.

"We were hoping that you could talk to our parents for us, Uncle Ben. You and my father are friends, and you've known Mr. Barker, well, just about forever.

"If I were to tell my dad," she continued, "he'd throw a fit. First, he'd assume that I was pregnant; then he would want to go out and kill Jeff. After that, he'd probably come home and kill me, too."

Ben struggled to restrain a burst of laughter; somehow, he could not see Isaac getting that mad. It was a remote possibility, however, and Marissa was taking this very seriously, so he decided to treat her with the respect she deserved. "I don't think that it would come to that, 'Rissa." He turned to Jeff.

"Is this what you really want? Do you want to spend the rest of your life with this young lady?" Jeff nodded vehemently.

"And you, Marissa? Do you want to marry this young man, and spend the rest of your life with him?" She looked at her beau and nodded gravely.

"Yes."

"Then, by the authority vested in my by the Paradise charter, I now pronounce you engaged. I'll talk to your parents later; however, this is something that *you'll* have to discuss with them, too."

Marissa came around the table, and wrapped her arms around her 'uncle'. "Thank you," she whispered in his ear.

Jeff stood and extended his hand. Ben grasped it, surprised at the firm grip of the boy. "Thank you, sir. I'll speak to my father tonight. I'm sure that once he knows that you approve, he'll rest easier."

Ben watched as the young couple moved away through the thinning crowd. They look so happy, he thought, and so young. The weight of his years was suddenly heavy upon him. We need kids like that to ensure the future of Paradise.

He reflected for a moment on the memory of the skinny little tomboy that Marissa had been just—what was it? --eight years ago. He remembered her big, wide eyes and bright smile. Now, she was a beautiful young woman preparing for marriage. He sighed and sipped the last of his drink. I'm getting old, he thought bitterly.

Sensing Ben's mood, most of the inn's customers steered clear of his table. Everyone knew that Ben could get to brooding, and was better off left alone. Even Isaac and Josslyn stayed away, but kept an eye on him to make sure that he had something to eat. Shortly after three, Josslyn put a plate of fried potatoes, onions, and rabbit stew in front of him; half an hour later, she removed the plate, untouched, from his table.   After the day had cooled down enough for the crowd to return to their labors, Isaac walked over and towered over Ben, shaking his head. Ben finally noticed him, and managed to smile faintly.

"Sit down, Ike. I'll pour you a drink."

"Ben, you know that I never touch that stuff. Remember, I'm the guy that made it. You think that old Oscar Mayer ate his own hot dogs?" The two friends laughed gently, and Ben seemed to cheer up.

"So, Ben," Isaac began, "where the hell have you been lately? You don't seem to come in here much anymore."

Ben looked at the mock pain in Isaac's eyes, and could not help but smile. "You know how it is, big man — the responsibilities of leadership and all that happy horseshit."

Isaac's laughter boomed off of the walls. "Yeah, I guess so. Is it true that Cencom is after our asses? Jesse mentioned that you had been in contact with Cochran, and he still hasn't backed off."

"True enough, Ike, though I don't want it to get around — yet. I expect them to hit us any time after the end of the month," Ben said, lowering his voice, "since I'm sure that they'll wait for the weather to settle down before making their move. Amateur troops tend to stray in bad weather, and I'm betting that Cochran's army is just that — amateurs."

Isaac rubbed his hands together, and his face was deadly serious. "What can I do to help, Ben? I was in the Marines for a six year hitch — special combat tactics."

"I know, Isaac, and I'm counting on your support in this; however, I'd rather have you stay here and take care of your family for the time being. We have a little time before the shooting starts." *I hope*, Ben added silently.

"You might think of a way to up the alcohol fuel reserves, Ike. I have a feeling that we'll need all we can get." Isaac nodded, and the two sat in silence for a moment.

"Oh yeah," Ben said, remembering his earlier conversation with the young couple. "You know Jeff Barker, Jack's son?" Isaac nodded absently.

"It seems that he and 'Rissa are an item, and they want to get married."

Isaac's jaw dropped, and Ben could almost see the steam beginning to pour from his ears. "She is not pregnant, if that's what you're thinking. They've decided to hold off on, shall we say, conjugal relations until they're married — which I think is damned responsible of them. Were you able to keep it in your pants when you were sixteen?"

Ben poured an ounce of whiskey in his glass, and sipped it as he looked at his stunned friend. "I don't think that you've taken a good look at your daughter lately. Marissa is pretty enough to turn heads at a beauty pageant, and in this community, it was only a matter of time before some young stud began chasing after her.

"You should consider yourself lucky that she chose to be caught by Jeff. He's good looking, intelligent, good with his hands, and highly thought of by both his peers and the adults with whom he's had any dealings."

Isaac slowly closed his mouth, and the flush drained from his face. "But Ben—this is my baby we're talking about!"

"Ike, she's not a baby any more. She's nearly sixteen, which is plenty old enough in Paradise for her to make her own decisions. Why don't you go talk to Jack, and work something out. Just remember, this is what you daughter wants—and I think that Jeff can make her happy."

"So—you approve of this?" Isaac looked sharply at Ben as he nodded. The play of emotions on Isaac's face was almost painful for Ben to watch.

Suddenly, Isaac's face was split by a tentative grin. "I guess that I'm gonna be a father-in-law, then! Thanks for telling me about this, Ben—and thanks for making me see reason, when all I was thinking about was where my shotgun was!" Isaac stood, grasped Ben's hand in his huge paw, and gave it a squeeze. "You're all right, for a white boy."

Both men laughed at the joke from another era, and Isaac walked away singing softly under his breath.

That man has a gentle soul, thought Ben with affection, *but I wouldn't want to cross him.*

He stood up, walked to the empty bar, and set the bottle and glass down. He leered at Josslyn down at the far end of the bar, winked, and staggered his way to the door.

CHAPTER TEN

The Journal of Jesse Walker: March 3, 2013

Today was the first decent day of the year. The weather was nearly perfect--unseasonably warm breezes, clear blue skies, and snow remaining in only the most shadowed and remote areas.

I got up early this morning. Breakfast: Two eggs, potatoes, and goat's milk. Packed a lunch, travel gear, and weapons--20 gauge, 9mm, and knife. Called Ben and told him I was ready.

Met Ben, Anna [Graycloud], and Mike [Barton] at the garage. Our little scavenging party was complete. Mike and I were assigned to the cargo hovercraft; Ben and Anna would be aloft in ultralights to cover us.

Our plan was to head overland for the Merrill area to check on a rumored supply of gasoline; however, the best laid plans of mice and men...

Jesse and Mike had been driving the noisy hovercraft for nearly twenty miles when they decided it was time to take a break. They pulled the craft off to one side of the rutted road they were traveling down, and Mike reached back to grab a couple of sandwiches from the cooler. Ben and Anna, meanwhile, were circling overhead in the matching ultralights.

Jesse had just taken a bite from his snack when the radio squawked. *"Ground One, this is Air Two."* Anna always was one for protocol. *"I have sighted smoke sign roughly two miles due north of your position."*

Jesse hastened to swallow his mouthful of bread and venison, and picked up the microphone. "Roger, Air Two. Air One, did you copy?" *Two can play that game*, Jesse thought with a grin.

"*Got you, Ground One. Smoke sign confirmed two miles north of your position. Let's take a look, folks!* "

The two small aircraft banked and headed north. Jesse started the hovercraft, and with a glance at the compass set into the dashboard, moved to follow. Mike grinned ruefully at Jesse as he put away the sandwiches.

"So much for a nice quiet lunch, Jesse," he bellowed over the cyclonic roar of the hovercraft. He held onto the side of the craft with white knuckles as Jesse dodged in and out of the trees.

They dipped and swayed along for about ten minutes when they came out of the forest and onto a pitted asphalt road. Jesse called in their position, and one of the ultralights circled over them.

"*Ground One,*" Ben radioed, "*it looks like the smoke is just up the road from you about four hundred yards. I suggest you park that moving wind tunnel, get out your guns, and approach with caution.*"

Mike was laughing so hard that tears were streaming down his cheeks. "What's so funny, Mike?" Jesse asked.

"How are we supposed to 'approach with caution' in something that sounds like a goddam tornado?" He rolled back in his seat, and Jesse gave him a light punch on the shoulder as he, too, laughed. When the two sobered up, Jesse proceeded to pull the craft to one side of the road.

He parked the hovercraft in a small clearing, skirting around the crumbling and rotted remains of a picnic table. They loaded and cocked their weapons, tossed their packs in the cargo bay, and moved out.

They chose to walk along the washed out gravel shoulder of the road rather that in the woods. Their visibility would be better, they decided, and it was quieter on the soft shoulder than in the dense dry underbrush of the forest. They were exposed to any would-be aggressors, but the cover of the ditch and forest were only a few feet away.

Mike was nervous; Jesse could tell by the way his shoulders and arms twitched as he walked down the road. Jesse could hardly fault him for his apprehension, however; sweat was running down his back in rivulets. They had gone several hundred yards up the road when they smelled the pungent odor of wood smoke.

"Ground One to Air Two," Mike whispered into the radio. "Have you landed yet?" The radio hissed for a moment, then Anna replied.

"*Air Two to Ground One,*" she said, and Mike scrambled to reduce the volume on the radio. "*I have just landed, and Ben is coming around on his approach now. We're about three hundred yards south of the smoke sign—what is your position? *"

Mike informed Anna that they were almost on top of the position, and Ben came on the radio.

"*I'm down now, guys; wait where you are for us to reach you. We have no idea what we're up against.*"

Mike and Jesse waited, and took advantage of the wait to relieve themselves in the trees. As Jesse returned to where Mike was stationed, the older man pointed up the road.

Jesse followed his gesture and saw a little black boy, three years old or so; the child was hanging onto the end of a tether, and rounding the bend at the other end of the rope was another child, a girl of seven.

The children were singing Old MacDonald in high, off key voices, and seemed totally oblivious to the presence of the Paradisans. With a look at Mike, he and Jesse faded into the cover of the ditch.

Jesse held out his hand for the radio, but as Mike pressed it into his hands he was stopped short by the snapping of a branch behind them. He made a half-hearted attempt to grab his pistol, but a deep voice from the rear, coupled with the distinctive cocking of a rifle, stopped him in mid-reach.

"Don't either of you make a move, or I'll blow a hole in you that you could drive a truck through." The voice was deep and melodious, but Jesse detected a hint of nervousness in it. "I want you to slowly toss your weapons over to the left, put your hands in your pockets, and roll onto your backs—now!"

They did as instructed, and Jesse threw the radio with the guns—making sure that the circuit was locked open as a warning to Ben and Anna. When they rolled over, Jesse was surprised at what he saw.

Their captor was a black man, an imposing six and a half feet tall or better. He was wearing tattered but clean Levi's, a blue cotton work shirt, and a pair of the biggest Colorado Hikers that Jesse had ever seen. His arms were as big around as Jesse's thighs, and he looked like he could have given a professional 'wrestler' a run for his money.

He had close-cropped, kinky black hair with just a trace of salt and pepper to it. His eyes were a deep brown, and they shifted back and forth uneasily between the two men. His rifle was pointed at Mike, more than likely because he assumed that the older and more rugged of the two men was the leader.

"What do you want here?" the man asked, directing his question at Mike. "We don't want any trouble, but if you're here to give us any, we'll give it right back to you." He looked over our prone bodies for a moment, and Jesse heard the scuffle of footsteps coming from across the road. "C'mon out, baby," he called, "but keep your eyes and ears open for others."

Jesse watched the big man as he spoke gently, yet with a tone of firm command, to his accomplice. He saw through the frightened, desperate exterior to the reasonable and civilized man inside.

"May I speak?" Jesse asked. When the man nodded, his eyes full of frank curiosity, Jesse continued.

"We aren't here to hurt you, sir. My partner and I were out scouting supplies for Paradise when we saw your smoke." Jesse saw his eyebrows go up at the mention of Paradise; that was a good sign. If he had heard of the community, then perhaps he knew of their reputation.

"We decided to detour, just in case there was a forest fire starting, or if it was an isolated settlement. We're always on the lookout for new people, and we're always willing to lend a hand if necessary. However," and Jesse gave him his most winning smile, "I see that you have the situation well in hand."

At that point, Jesse thought that he heard something from down the road, and hastened to keep their captor's attention. "My name is Jesse Walker, and this is Mike Barton. Down the road," he added in a louder voice, having come to the conclusion that the man was of no danger to them, "is my brother Ben and our security chief, Anna Graycloud."

As he said this, Ben and Anna strolled around the bend, Ben whistling aimlessly, and Anna smiling brightly after an initial glare in Jesse's direction. Their guns were holstered and slung over their shoulders, and they looked relatively harmless.

The big man who was holding them captive looked down the road, too startled to react. Jesse took this opportunity to kick his feet out from under him, and as he fell, Mike grabbed the rifle from him and threw it on the pile with their own weapons.

"It's okay," Jesse shouted as he saw the woman across the road raise her gun in their direction. "Tell her it's okay!" he yelled at the big man as he sat on the ground rubbing his side.

He looked from Jesse to where his rifle lay, and spoke quietly to the woman. "Go ahead, Josslyn; put your gun down." She hesitated for a moment, and then lowered the barrel of the .22; however, she did not put the gun down.

Jesse noticed that the man was moving to stand up, and offered him a hand. "Just leave the children be, that's all I ask," the defeated man whispered. Jesse saw a tear roll down his cheek, and hurried to reassure him.

"We're not here to hurt anyone," Jesse explained. "We're just what I said we are—a group from Paradise out looking for supplies. We saw your smoke, and felt obligated to check it out. Tell him, Ben; he doesn't believe me." Jesse turned away from him, and lit a cigarette. Ben was the leader—let him handle this.

Ben walked up and offered his hand. "Ben Walker. Who are you," he gestured, "and the woman?"

"I'm Isaac Peters, and that is my wife, Josslyn." His voice cracked with emotion, and he wiped sweat and tears from his face.

Ben smiled and stroked his beard. "I'm the head of a little community near Tomahawk called Paradise; perhaps you've heard of it?" Isaac nodded. "You live here? I thought that this was a state park. The map calls this 'Council Grounds'."

"We live here—now," Isaac stated. "We've been staying in the old ranger station since last September." He smiled faintly. "Of course, it's nothing like our place in Madison, but it's a roof over our heads."

Ben gestured at his party, and we retrieved our weapons and the radio. At a signal from Ben, Mike gave the rifle back to Isaac, ignoring the scowl shot in his direction by Anna. He got them all heading down the road toward the station. As they neared it, Jesse heard the muffled whispering of the children, and Isaac cast a wary glance at the newcomers.

"Don't worry," Jesse assured him, moving closer and matching the larger man's stride. "We're not cannibals." Isaac tentatively returned Jesse's smile, and tension flowed away from him in nearly visible waves.

When they arrived at the station, Isaac called out to the children. They ran out and huddled behind their mother, peeking shyly around her now and then.

Dr. Isaac Peters, his wife Josslyn, and their children — Marissa, seven, and Nathan, three — had originally arrived at Council Grounds State Park for the Labor Day holiday weekend in 2012 (he told his uninvited guests). Isaac had taken a leave of absence from his job at the university after he had received notification that his petition for a research grant had been denied. He decided that he needed some time away from campus, so had packed up his family and gone camping.

Unfortunately, Labor Day was also the first day of the Collapse. In the ensuing confusion — made even stranger by the fact that they did not know what was going on — their car and nearly all of their camping equipment had been stolen, stranding the Peters' in the park. They had found weapons, blankets, emergency rations, and clothing in the ranger station; they had made the best of a bad situation, but between the rationing of food, the bitter cold winter, and the marauding bands that occasionally passed through, it had been a harrowing and horrifying season for the city folks. Isaac had been out trying to scare up some game when he heard the approach of the hovercraft.

"I couldn't help but notice the noise, and when I saw the two little planes fly over, I got ready for the worst," Isaac told them.

The Paradisans were the first people that they had seen in over two months, and because of their previous experiences in the park, they were understandably cautious. As the day progressed, they relaxed, and little Nathan even took a turn sitting on Jesse's lap.

Isaac, as it turned out, had a doctorate in organic chemistry. He and Ben talked at length about the best ways to produce fuel alcohol, and shortly the rest of the group became bored with their conversation.

"Just ask them, Ben," Jesse finally snapped, his patience at an end. Ben tended to ramble on once he had picked a subject. Jesse recalled many a night that he and his brother had sat up all night bouncing from topic to topic without getting anywhere; he wanted to forestall such an occurrence on this night.

Ben frowned at Jesse, obviously puzzled. "'Ask them'? Oh." He turned to Isaac and his wife. "Isaac, Josslyn — how would you like to join us in Paradise?" Ben went on — in great detail — to explain the set-up in the community. When he was finished, Isaac and Josslyn exchanged glances.

"We'd love to come with you — if you'll have us," Isaac said as he extended his hand to Ben.

They filled the hovercraft with what few belongings the Peters' had, and then put the children together in the cargo bay. Isaac was thrilled at the opportunity to ride in an ultra light with Anna, but Josslyn was extremely apprehensive. Ben finally convinced her that it would not take long, so she strapped in, gritted her teeth, and closed her eyes for the duration of the flight. Jesse and Mike waved as the two fully-laden planes took flight.

Mike and Jesse turned to their own craft, and prepared for their somewhat more leisurely trip home.

The Journal of Jesse Walker: March 3, 2013 (later)--

..finally arrived in Paradise about six-thirty tonight. With their ability to fly somewhat faster than we could traverse the landscape, the others had been back in Paradise for nearly an hour. We had, of course, kept in touch by radio, and twice someone from Paradise did a fly-over to check on our progress.

Anna, Ben, Isaac, Josslyn, and I got together at my place; Mike begged off, pleading a prior commitment, with a pledge from me to fill him in on anything interesting. We spent the evening getting better acquainted, but everyone was exhausted by ten o'clock. Ben took our new members to the inn, and helped them get settled.

We never did get to Merrill, but it has certainly been an eventful day.

We found something of greater value than we could ever have expected; today, we made some new friends.

..about one in the morning. I cant sleep, even though my body cries out for it.

Ben and Isaac are going to be laying the groundwork for improvements to the distillery tomorrow; it never ceases to amaze me how Ben can instill such enthusiasm in others for his ideas.

I wish I could do the same with my students. I try.

CHAPTER ELEVEN

The sun was sitting on the horizon as Ben left Isaac's place; it glowed like a tremendous ember, spreading crimson and god radiance through the late afternoon haze. *Nice day for a flight,* Ben thought as he gazed at the setting sun. He turned on his heels, veering away from his office and toward the hangar situated at the southwest corner of the community center.

When Ben arrived at the hangar, Paul Anton was just coming on shift. Ben flashed his blue pass, knowing that Paul took his duties seriously. He shook his head as he entered the Quonset building. *Just another of Jesse's pets,* thought Ben uncharitably.

Paul had apparently been abandoned by his parents during the early weeks of the Collapse—a mildly developmentally disabled youth with little chance of independent survival. Jesse had happened upon him wandering half-starved and terrified through the streets of the little town of Woodboro. He had brought the boy back to Paradise, to the consternation of Ben and many others. No matter how progressive and open-minded the inhabitants of Paradise thought themselves to be; no matter how free of racial prejudice they might appear; when it came to someone who was so—different, it made them uncomfortable at the least, and many were out and out repelled by the Down's Syndrome lad. The more outspoken of those who opposed Paul's entrance into the community said that he would be a drain on the already limited resources of Paradise without giving any fair return. Jesse, with characteristic caring and stubbornness, had set out to prove Paradise wrong.

Paul had moved in with Jesse, and by putting in long hours during the day and well into the night, Jesse had taught Paul to read, write, and almost by a process of osmosis, to handle machinery. Paul sat enchanted as Jesse worked on the various pieces of broken down machinery and appliances that came into his workshop—soon, Paul was assisting Jesse with the repairs. It had only been a matter of time before Jesse convinced—forced, really—the council and Paradise's chief mechanic to allow Paul to enter into an apprenticeship in the community's garage and hangar. His growing expertise with machinery, sunny disposition, and willingness to serve had soon gained him a permanent place in even the most begrudging hearts and minds of the Paradisans. In June of 2013, Paul had been formally adopted into the ranks of Paradise.

"Hey, Paul, how's my ultra light doing? Is the new engine in yet?"

Ben had given orders to have his plane, the *Screamin' Eagle,* modified. He had not yet had the opportunity to test it since giving the order.

Paul ran over, his grease-stained coveralls flapping around his skinny legs. "You bet, Mr. Walker," he replied with shining eyes. "I just finished checkin' on it today."

Ben walked over to the *Eagle* and ran an affectionate hand down her fuselage. "I'm going to take her up for a while, Paul; has she been fueled?"

Paul nodded affirmatively, and Ben strode to a set of lockers on the far wall. He opened the first one and took out his flight suit—a pair of insulated coveralls. He pulled the suit over his clothes, donned a pair of leather gloves, and placed amber goggles over his eyes. He walked back to the waiting plane and leaned over the port wing surface.

"Give me a hand, would you Paul?" Paul bent over the starboard wing strut, and together the two men wheeled the light craft out of the hangar and onto the smooth blacktop of the landing strip. Ben smiled at Paul.

"Thanks. I may be gone a couple of hours, so if you're going home before I get back, tell the watchman, okay?"

"Oh, I'll stay here until you get back, Mr. Walker," Paul said. "I have a lot of stuff to do before I go home. Besides," he added with a shy grin, "you might want me to do more things to your plane."

Ben flashed a smile at the youth, crawled into the reclined seat of the plane, and inserted his pass card into the starter. The throaty roar of the engine surprised him until he remembered that the stock ninety horsepower engine had been upgraded to a one hundred and fifty horsepower, super-charged engine. Ben pulled the pen off the log book, and paused. He toyed with several destinations before he wrote: MERRILL FLY-BY; TEST FLIGHT. He returned the pen, and with a wave to Paul, applied the throttle.

As he taxied down the strip, he applied more power to the pusher prop. He was nearly halfway down the strip when he pulled back on the stick and began a steep, swift ascent to eight thousand feet. The frigid air whipped his cheeks into numb ruddiness, and he could feel it biting even through the heavily insulated flight suit. He alternately applied the throttle and wiggled the stick, and the craft jumped at his command, as responsive with its new modifications as a thoroughbred racing horse.

Immediately after reaching his chosen altitude, he nosed the craft into a steep dive. As the air speed indicator topped one hundred he pulled back gradually into a climb, then at vertical, slapped the stick over to the right.

The little plane spun rapidly as it continued to climb. Suddenly, Ben heard the sound of a stall developing, and hastened to orient his craft into a more stable flight pattern. He stole a glance at the altimeter, which read ninety-five hundred feet.

Hunched down behind the small fairing to get out of the wind, Ben pushed the throttle full and engaged the supercharger. The engine took on a whining, whistling quality as the rush of air into the twin carburetors echoed past his ears. The air speed indicator read one-twenty and continued to climb slowly.

Better than I thought, Ben mused happily. This baby should be able to handle one-fifty in a dive and sustain a four-gee turn. He smiled in pleasure; the Screamin' Eagle was now aptly named.

Ben backed off the throttle to about sixty percent and heard the whine of the supercharger automatically cut off as his air speed dipped below eighty. He looked down and could already see the outskirts of the old county seat, Merrill, on the horizon. Checking his watch, he saw that he had been airborne for only thirty-three minutes, most of which he had spent in aerobatics. The forty-mile trip to Merrill had taken virtually no time at all!

Happily, Ben spun the plane about and headed through the twilight toward home.

Jesse stood at the hangar door watching the telltale red of his brother's plane as it approached the landing strip. He smiled in appreciation as he watched the plane make a perfect three-point landing and taxi up to the hangar.

"Hi, Jess," Ben exclaimed breathlessly as he unfastened the harness and jumped from the open cockpit. "You should try out this little darlin'! One thirty at ten thousand feet, and I pulled a vertical spin at eight thousand. She's a powerful wench now!" Ben grinned foolishly, a kid with a new toy.

Jesse smiled at his brother's excitement, and then his features took on a serious cast. "Where the hell have you been for the past hour? I tried to reach you by radio, but you didn't answer!"

"Maybe that's because I didn't have the radio on, Jess," Ben retorted. "Can't a guy have any privacy?"

"Not where the Central Command is concerned, he can't!" Jesse waited for the inevitable reaction from his brother, and it was not long in coming.

"The Cencoms? Now what?"

"We received another message from them about forty-five minutes ago — again, on one of our *secured* channels. It would appear that Cochran has gone over the edge; he's declared himself God's Chosen, and calls his followers 'Angels'. Dammit, but I hate to deal with that crazy son of a bitch!"

Ben nodded in commiseration. "What did he have to say? Has he altered his stand in any way?"

"Well, Ben, he wouldn't speak to me directly — I gathered that he would not sully himself by talking to a sinner such as myself — but I did speak to one of his flunkies, a guy named Donner.

"The gist of it was that Cochran has been patient with us far too long, and has been instructed to show us the error of our ways. If the heathen sinners," Jesse quoted, reading from a note pad, "of the community that calls itself Paradise do not repent their ghastly, ungodly ways, and make a gift of their worldly possessions and homes to the Crusaders of the Lord, then God's will instructs us to cleanse the den of iniquity and use it for God's purposes." Jesse handed the transcript to Ben, wiping his hands on his pants legs as is he could somehow wipe away the feeling he got when he thought about the perversion the Central Command had become. "I think we're in big trouble, Ben."

Ben handed the notebook back to Jesse. "You're right, Jess, but they can't do anything until the ground dries up. They can't move an army through the woods when they're this swampy, and even Cochran knows that we can pick them off at our leisure if they attempt to come by road."

Ben began walking toward the plaza, and motioned for Jesse to follow. "Let's go to my office and discuss this. Paul," he yelled in the direction of the hangar, "can you put the plane away? Thanks." He heard Paul's muffled answer from the depths of the hangar, and put the matter out of his mind.

As they walked, Ben unzipped the front of his flight suit and ran his hands nervously through his graying crew cut and neatly trimmed beard. He had hoped to avoid a confrontation with Cencom all along; now that Dwight Cochran seemed to have gone 'round the bend, that confrontation seemed inevitable.

Like his brother, Jesse ran his hands nervously through his long dark hair. (It was a habit both had developed when under stress; the only difference was that Jesse's shaggy, unkempt beard gave him more to tug on than Ben's well-trimmed growth). Jesse, too, had misgivings about the new development. His concern stemmed from the fact that he did not have the confidence in the war room that Ben did; rather, he was sure that if it came to a battle, Paradise and its citizens would surely be lost.

When they arrived at the three-story house that served Paradise as a central administration building, they walked through the reception area, up two flights of stairs, and down the narrow hallway that led to Ben's office. Ben unlocked the door, and the two men entered.

"Pull up a chair," Ben suggested as he shrugged out of his flight suit. He cast it carelessly to one side and went directly to his liquor cabinet. He took out a bottle of Isaac's whiskey and two glasses, walked to his desk, and sat down. He poured himself a drink, but as he went to pour one for his brother, Jesse shook his head no. Ben replaced the stopper in the neck of the bottle and set it next to the empty glass, an open invitation. Sipping slowly, he gazed out of the window for a moment before speaking.

"Now do you see why I thought we'd need the war room?"

Jesse sat forward abruptly and shouted, "Dammit! Your defense strategy is just fine—but will it be enough? How many of us are going to get killed to keep Paradise from falling into the hands of that fucking madman?"

Ben thought for a moment, utterly oblivious to his brother's agitation. "We have two weeks," he thought aloud, "three at the outside, to prepare. We'll have to close our borders to Outsiders within the first two weeks, and begin some intensive weapons training. I want every able-bodied person over the age of twelve issued either a handgun or rifle, and we'll need to set up some training—Frank Post can handle that end. Arrange for everyone in training to be issued fifty rounds of practice ammo. We'll set up a range in the Great Meadow; just make sure that all of the targets are all on the eastern side so that we don't have anyone shooting up somebody's cabin."

Ben paused to take a drink, and Jesse lit a cigarette before he resumed writing notes on his pad.

"We'll have to move everything that is easily damaged to a safe place," Ben continued. "Have the men build a wall of dirt around the distillery—I guess we'll have to take the pay loader out of storage. If a stray bullet hits one of the storage tanks, Cochran won't have to worry about taking Paradise, because it won't exist anymore."

Jesse looked up from taking notes, his brow furrowed with concern. "We can store some of the smaller, more portable valuables in the tunnel system, can't we? Also, if we fill the fuel tanks of all the vehicles, as well as all the reserve tanks, we could probably drain the bulk of the distillery's tanks before Cencom attacks."

"Make a note of that, Jess; it's a great idea. Now you know why I keep you around," Ben quipped, his tone momentarily lightening the somber mood in the room. "It'll definitely minimize the risk, and save a lot of time later." Ben raised his glass in salute to Jesse.

"Ben, how many drone tanks does your system operate? And how are they armed? I need to know before I begin these preparations that we have a fighting chance, not just a hopeless, last-ditch effort."

"We have twenty drone tanks," Ben explained, "each armed with an auto-loading rocket launcher and a .50 caliber machine gun. The rocket launcher has forty rounds with a range of fifteen hundred yards. The machine guns have five thousand rounds each, with an effective range of about three hundred yards.

"At each radar site there is a remote grenade launcher with twenty grenades. The airborne drones are equipped with cameras for surveillance, and there is one high altitude surveillance dirigible for complete area coverage."

Ben paused to let this sink in. "On the perimeter, we can outfit each of the watchtowers with two auto-fire machine guns. Once they're set, they'll fire on anything in their path that moves until their five hundred round magazines are spent.

"You're familiar with the regular arsenal; two hundred plus various firearms, ranging from .22 pistols to .44 magnum rifles. In addition to the more mundane firearms, I have five LAW's and three flamethrowers stashed."

Jesse gasped. "My God, Ben, do you want to kill everything in the area?" He was appalled at the potential for destruction that his brother had just outlined.

Ben shook his head. "Jesse, it's too late to back out now. Our asses are in a sling, and if we want to survive, we have to win—by any means at our disposal. By my definition, the winner is the side with men standing when the smoke clears."

"Do you know how may people we're going to have to kill to save our skins?" Jesse asked in horror. "If Cochran throws fifty thousand of his fanatics at us, and ten thousand of them make it here, we'll have to wipe out at least half of them to demoralize them enough to leave.

"That's five thousand people!" Jesse shouted, his voice shrill. "Real people just like you and me."

"Not like me," Ben said quietly. "I don't have any desire to take what isn't mine and pervert it to my own uses. All I want to do is protect our homes. If I can do that without killing, so be it. If I have to kill, I will. It's that simple."

Jesse forced himself to get a grip on his raging emotions. When Ben refilled his drink, Jesse allowed him to fill his glass, too. He downed the whiskey in a single gulp and stared at Ben through watery eyes. "Are you really capable of killing that many people, Ben? Can you look at them as you take their lives?"

A stony silence stretched between the brothers for what seemed an eternity. Ben sipped his drink thoughtfully, and then set the empty glass on the desk.

"I don't know, Jess," he said in a whisper. "I really don't know."

CHAPTER TWELVE

Ben was in his office when Jesse went looking for him; the Cencom problem had holed him up there for the past two days working out the details of Paradise's defense against the forthcoming attack.

It was a foregone conclusion that the Central Command was going to attack; the deadline had come and gone, and it was now just a matter of time. Ben had determined that any transportation of large numbers of troops would have to come straight up old Highway Fifty-one, and then spread out north of Merrill. The need, then, was to do one of two things: stop them before they dispersed into the heavily wooded Council Grounds area, or pick them off in small groups from the cover of the forest. The only problem with both plans was Ben's lack of personnel. He could hardly pull fifty or sixty combatants from Paradise to attack the Cencom forces; that would leave the community itself nearly defenseless. Angrily, Ben crumpled yet another battle plan and threw it onto the floor with ten or fifteen others that he had scrapped.

It was beginning to look as if Ben and the other Paradisans were going to be forced into a siege situation, huddled behind their defenses and trying to pick off the Cencom troops one by one. Ben's only consolation was the fact that they had the automated defense system to assist; if they had to rely on numbers alone, they were doomed.

Ben knew that even at this late juncture Jesse would still rather have negotiated a peaceful solution than go to battle; however, Ben was certain that such a move was a lost cause. Cochran and his Cencom associates would no more bend to verbalization and rhetoric than a cobra would be swayed from striking by the promise of retirement benefits.

Ben looked across the room, eventually focusing on the large, library-style table against one wall. The heavy table held a relief map of the entire area, showing in three-dimensions roughly twenty-five hundred square miles of terrain. On the map were blue, red, and yellow markers representing drone tanks, radar emplacements, and air drone hangars, respectively. The blue markers roughly outnumbered the others two to one.

Ben rose from his chair slowly, his knees stiff and crackling from long hours spent nearly motionless. *Damn*, he thought, *I must be getting old. I can't even sit for a long time without some part of me objecting.*

He walked over to the map, rubbing his numb rear end with one hand as he grasped a half-pint of whiskey in the other. He stared through red-rimmed eyes at the map as he absently sipped from the bottle.

Something just doesn't seem right, he pondered, frowning. *Where have I — what have I missed?* He studied the layout of the automated defenses and grimaced as he saw the flaw. *There!* He saw a hole in their defensive line where the Wisconsin River crossed the Spirit River Flowage. He moved two of the red markers to cover the open area, make similar adjustments to the tank emplacements, and made note of the map grid numbers on a slip of paper. He put the note in his breast pocket and walked over to the central console.

He took a deep drink of the whiskey, looked at the nearly empty bottle, and with a shrug, drained it. He set the empty on an end table and turned to the video display. He pulled out the monitor behind which was hidden the secret keypad, and concentrated on the task at hand.

Punching in the code sequence, he waited for the hiss of air as the hatchway opened; as an afterthought, he turned on the ventilators. *I may be down there quite a while,* he thought as he lowered himself into the dimly illuminated shaft.

The sixty-foot drop went quickly as Ben grasped the side rails of the ladder and began to slide downward. He checked his speed by squeezing his legs against the outside of the ladder, increasing the friction as he neared the bottom. He came to a halt mere inches from the floor, and stepped down into the war room. *Not bad for a guy pushing forty,* he commended himself.

He removed the scrap of paper from his pocket and turned to the banks of computer equipment on the opposite wall. Just as he was about to sit down, he heard the telltale chirp of the alarm that informed him someone was operating the entrance code. He moved quickly to the upstairs monitor, hand on his pistol, and breathed a sigh of relief when he saw Jesse's image on the screen.

Jesse chose a more sedate descent than his older brother, taking the ladder two rungs at a time; nonetheless, he arrived at the bottom of the shaft quickly. His face bore the look of someone who has been on the go for far too long.

"Hi, Jess," Ben greeted his brother with a grip on his upper arm. "You look like hell, boy. What have you been up to?"

Jesse looked at Ben's unkempt hair, bloodshot eyes, and rumpled clothes, and could not keep from smiling. "You don't look too hot yourself, big brother. When did you last eat or sleep?"

Ben shrugged. "What time is it?" He had no clocks in his office or the war room; he said that the constant reminder of time pressures drove him to drink. For the same reason, Jesse said that he should have the clocks—at least he'd have something to blame for his habit.

Jesse looked at his watch. "One a.m."

"One?" Ben asked, looking momentarily confused. "What day is it?"

Jesse looked at him strangely. "Tuesday. Why?"

"If it's Tuesday, then I've been going for," and Ben closed his eyes for a second, "about fifty hours. No wonder I look like shit!"

Jesse frowned pensively for a moment, then his face cleared as though a great decision had been made.

"Ben, I think I know who our traitor is. . ."

Ben turned abruptly to face Jesse. His face flushed red, then deepened to a shade of purple, such was his rage. Jesse wondered if this had been the best time to tell him.

"WHO!" Ben roared.

"Well," Jesse began slowly, "I can't be positive—I just have a suspicion. I think it's Harry out at the dam."   Ben nodded as some of his own suspicions were verified.

"He has a warehouse out there," Jesse continued, "that looks better stocked than some of the supermarkets I remember from ten years ago. He has things out there I haven't even seen in ten years—like the schnapps I dropped here the other night."

Ben suddenly recalled the bottle; he had wondered where it came from, but with the other worries on his mind, he had not given it more than a passing thought. Now, though, his rage returned in full force. "If Harry is a spy for Cencom, I'll kill the son of a bitch!"

Jesse sensed that Ben was too tired and drunk to listen to reason, but he tried anyway. "Ben, I said that I'm not positive! Harry says that the Chippewa have been to St. Paul and elsewhere--raiding warehouses. I think that we ought to give him the benefit of the doubt before we sentence him to death."

Ben, who was just drunk enough to lose his temper, still maintained enough control to realize that he was in no condition to judge a man on the basis of hearsay evidence. "You're right, Jess; let's go out to the dam and you can show me what you've found."

"Do you think that's such a good idea, Ben? You know how Harry feels about intruders, and regardless of whose dam it is, he's awfully quick with that shotgun of his."

Ben smiled faintly. "I know. That's why we'll have to come up inside his perimeter. I know what he's been doing with the spotlights, and I also know that he has a system of trip wires set up all over the area to protect his privacy. Tonight we won't bother with his half-assed security — we'll be in and out without his ever knowing."

Jesse was puzzled. "How are we going to do that? There are only two ways to get to the dam — overland by taking Duenorth Road, or approaching by water. Both ways are pretty obvious when the area is lit as bright as day."

"Jess, there are always options which are not readily apparent. Grab a couple of flashlights from that cabinet and follow me."

Jesse took the two squeeze generator lamps and turned to face Ben. Where Ben had been, one of the two doors marked EXIT stood open, revealing a dark and narrow tunnel extending far beyond the reach of the light.

"Ben!" Jesse cried out.

"Follow me," was Ben's muffled reply.

Jesse suppressed a shudder at crawling into the dark and confined space; nevertheless, his fear of enclosed spaces was not debilitating, so after a few deep breaths and a silent prayer, he turned on his light and entered the tunnel.

He scrambled along for what seemed an eternity until he caught up with Ben, who was sitting casually at an intersection.

"How do you like the emergency tunnel, Jess?"

"Dammit, Ben! You know that I hate tunnels — especially long, dark ones! Let me have a smoke, would you? My nerves are shot." Jesse moved into the intersection, a space about ten feet in diameter, and sat cross-legged facing his brother. He placed his lamp between them, handed Ben his own flashlight, and lit a cigarette. "Whatever gave you the idea for this monstrosity?"

Ben grinned. "Just imagine how you'd feel if you were ever in the war room if it was bombed and caved in. You'd have no chance. This," and he indicated the tunnels with a nod of his head, "is a chance, both for whomever is in the war room, and for Paradise as a whole, if need be."

He pointed at the left fork. "This branch goes west, outside the perimeter, and exits into the cellar of an abandoned farmhouse. The right branch comes up within the perimeter, but outside of the central plaza.

"The branch we'll be taking," he said, indicating the tunnel straight ahead of him, "heads north toward the base of the dam, where there is a hidden — and watertight — door."

Jesse considered this, mentally trying to envision the network of tunnels. "How do we get from the base of the dam to Harry's warehouse? It's got to be twenty-five or thirty yards of open ground."

"That's the easy part," Ben explained. "There's a utility shed less than twenty feet from the tunnel exit. We'll scoot across to that and get inside — I have the key. Once we're in there, all we have to do is pull up a floor plate.

"You see, Jess, the entire area out there is connected with crawlspaces; I had that done to allow for free circulation of heat, as well as to allow an access for wiring and plumbing. If we can make it to that shed, we're home free." Ben grimaced. "More tunnels, I'm afraid."

"I can handle it, Ben. I was just giving you a hard time." Jesse sighed, and stubbed out his cigarette. "If we're going to do it, 'twere best done quickly."

Jesse took the lead this time, while Ben directed him from behind.

For nearly half a mile they crawled through the four foot diameter concrete tunnel. They might possibly have made better time by squatting and running, but with five hours of dark left, they were in no hurry. Ben cursed as he banged his knee and thought, *I should have put a couple of skateboards in here; we'd really fly on wheels.* He called out to Jesse, some twenty-five feet ahead.

"Jess! Do you think you could rig up some skateboards or some such for the tunnels? They wouldn't have to be anything fancy, just good enough to roll. The culvert sections are joined smoothly to prevent leakage, so a skateboard would be both fun and efficient. Maybe you could even put a small seat on it?"

Ben's knees were not the only ones getting scraped and bruised. Plans were already going through Jesse's mind, though he envisioned something just a little more elaborate than skateboards. "Sure, Ben, I can figure something out," he said with a grimace.

The two were silent for the next forty minutes, except for a grunted expletive now and then when one or the other would scrape an elbow or bump his head. They passed one siding in their journey, and Jesse was certain that he smelled quicklime. He disregarded it, filed the information for later, and continued forward. Finally, they came upon the door at a dead-end. Ben squeezed by Jesse, pushed a small button to the right of the hatch-like portal, and a green light came on.

"I just activated a small infrared detector on the outside," Ben whispered. "When the light is green, it's safe to leave."

He pushed on the release bar and the door swung silently upward, revealing a dark and cloudy circle of sky. Ben exited first, and then turned to help Jesse out. The door swung shut behind them, revealing no trace of its existence save a patch of packed dirt like the rest of the area around it.

"Come on," Ben hissed. He scrambled up the bank of the earthen dam, Jesse close behind.

The dam had been Jesse's idea, but Ben had made it into a more highly technological project than Jesse's original plan. Earthen on the low side and concrete on the high-water side, it rose about thirty-five feet above the southern side of the Creek; on the northern side it had created a shallow lake where the banks of the Spirit River Flowage had been. Dikes had been erected along the new shoreline for several hundred feet in each direction to prevent more than irrigation water from entering and flooding the valuable croplands. Through trial and error, the Creek had been altered from a tiny trickle to a relatively fast-flowing, clear water stream.

They reached the top of the dam with a minimum of falling dirt, and lay motionless just below the dam's crest. After a moment Ben peeked over the edge, then motioned to Jesse.

The two brothers jumped over the low retaining wall, feeling horribly exposed in the brilliant light of the new spotlights. They ran crouched over and keeping to the shadows, and reached the back wall of the utility shed without incident. Cautiously, they rounded the building, and hunched down in front of the door. Ben removed a key from his pocket and slowly turned it in the lock, wincing at each tiny squeak and squeal as the old brass protested the intrusion. At last the door creaked open on its hinges, and the pair hurried inside. Ben shut the door behind them, and turned the bolt.

In the ambient light from outside, Ben pointed out a small grate set into the center of the floor. "There's our way in," he whispered.

Jesse fumbled in his pocket for a moment, then pulled out a battered Swiss Army knife. He popped open the screwdriver blade, and with practiced ease removed the four screws that held the grate to the floor. He tugged on the wire mesh, and pulled it free from the floor. Jesse handed the steel grating to Ben, and considered the dark aperture revealed. Ben set the mesh on the floor near the hole and proceeded to snake his way into the opening, barely able to pass through the narrow gap. Jesse, some thirty pounds lighter, knew that he would have no trouble getting into the ventilation duct. The very thought of entering that tiny, black hole made perspiration sprout on his forehead and underarms.

"Here goes," he whispered nervously as he followed Ben into the duct.

Ben led the way, his flashlight reflecting dully off of the interior of the shaft. Cobwebs fluttered gently in the wake of their passage, and once or twice they saw the shadows of fleeting rodents; however, other than that, the crawlspace was silent and deserted but for the sliding, scraping sounds of their own progress.

The intricacy of the ventilation network, which Ben seemed to know like the back of his hand, failed to surprise Jesse. Ben had shocked him too often of late for this new development to stir more than a grudging admiration for the devious manner in which his brother's mind worked.

At length they came to an intersecting duct; this one, Jesse guessed, was the one that would lead them under Harry's storeroom. As if to confirm his guess, Ben stopped abruptly, pointed upward, and signaled for silence. He twisted around and removed a flat case from his back pocket.

Jesse had to stifle a burst of laughter as Ben opened the case, put the earpiece in his ears, and applied the end of the stethoscope to the top of the duct. Jesse watched, amused, as Ben moved silently from one area to another, listening for something; suddenly he jerked the earpieces out, and Jesse knew why—he had heard the sharp thump of footsteps as well.

The tread of many feet came and went, punctuated by heavy thuds as cases were scraped and moved around on the floor above them. Finally, the movement stopped, and muffled voices reached them. Ben replaced earpieces with a look of triumph at Jesse, and listened:

"There's your stuff for this trip, Harry," a man's voice said. "I hope you appreciate what we're going through to get it for you."

"*Yeah, but the trade is going both ways,*" Harry drawled. "*If I get caught, I'd be in a real bind. You're not risking any more than I am.*"

"*Maybe not, Miller,*" a woman snapped, "*but if we get caught, it would mean our lives — not to mention the lives of all the people who use what we get from you. These goods are the lifeblood of the entire —* "

"*Shut up,*" the man hissed. "*You talk too much, woman!*"

Harry chuckled. "*I know what you need, and why you need it. I may be old, but I'm not nearly as stupid or ignorant as the Paradisans think — especially my little buddy.*"

"*We know about your friendship with Jesse Walker,*" an old man's voice rasped. "*Don't you think that it's dangerous to continue such a relationship?* "

"*No,*" Harry replied. "*He's a trusting sort; he prefers to think the best of people rather than harbor doubts and suspicions. He actually believes that you — or rather, the Chippewa — are doing this for me out of the kindness of your hearts. 'Sides, what I give you, they'll never miss.*"

"*Does no one keep an inventory of your supplies?* " The voice of the younger man sounded incredulous. "*We have taken a large amount of medical supplies. Will they not be missed?*"

"*We have more than we need,*" Harry said. "*Ben — now there's a sharp one — planned for supporting a maximum of one thousand people, so what I'm giving you is just part of the surplus. He's never going to check that; he trusts his people, and he's arrogant enough to believe that his judgment could never be wrong.*"

"Bullshit," Ben whispered. Ben did trust his people, but he kept an accurate inventory of all necessary items; that is how he had come to suspect that there was a spy among them in the first place. As for making mistakes ... "Bullshit!" Jesse looked at Ben, and wondered briefly what had him so riled. Then he resumed listening to the clandestine conversation.

"*It's long past time that we left,*" the old man ordered. "*Have you got our goods?* "

There was a rustling of paper, the clink of glass objects, and Ben heard a wordless exclamation from the woman. He swore silently; he knew that Jesse would be convinced that Harry had some altruistic motive, but Ben knew that the son of a bitch was deliberately shafting Paradise for his own

97

personal gain. Ben wondered who his patrons were, and how they had managed to contact Harry.

The voices above faded beyond Ben's ability to hear, and he pocketed the stethoscope. Ignoring Jesse's whispered questions, he led his brother through the vents for several minutes until he was certain that they were out of earshot.

"Let's get the hell out of here," Ben commanded quietly. He disappeared down the crawlspace, his progress visible by the light of the lamp. Jesse followed, propelling himself forward with his elbows in an attempt to match Ben's anger-driven haste.

They reached the opening that led up into the utility shed, and Ben turned off his light. He eased himself out of the hole carefully, followed shortly by Jesse, who slid the grate back into place and scooped up the screws. Ben kept watch at the single grimy window while Jesse hastened to replace the screws. When he was done, he nodded at Ben. Slowly, Ben opened the bolt, then motioned for Jesse to go out. Ben followed Jesse, shut the door, and scurried around to the shadowed side of the building.

The two men stood gasping for air for a moment, then with a quick glance around the area, sprinted for the base of the dam.

Ben and Jesse leaped over the wall in unison, and slid down the embankment to the base. Ben crept to the hidden door and lifted a large rock to expose the latch. He pulled on the lever and the door lifted free of its snug resting place. Ben scrambled into the opening, leaving Jesse to dive in before the automatic cycle closed the hatch.

Although Jesse still had his light on and Ben did not, he found it impossible to maintain the pace that the older, larger, and presumably less limber Ben was setting. When Jesse arrived at the intersection he called out to Ben, but received no response. Frustrated, angry, and increasingly oppressed by the prolonged exposure to enclosed spaces, Jesse plunged headlong into the last three hundred yards of tunnel. He shot breathlessly through the hatch and into the war room in a matter of minutes.

"Ben, you son of a. . ."   he began when he saw his brother sitting casually before one of the desks. Ben motioned him into silence and pointed at the view screen in front of him.

Jesse squelched his anger for the time being, and watched the monitor over Ben's shoulder. In it he saw three shadowy figures in white robes moving stealthily through the trees. He began to speak when Ben silenced him again.

"Angels!" Ben spat the word. "I guess Cochran's power doesn't relieve him of the need for good old-fashioned reconnaissance—or medicine, for that matter." Ben explained briefly what he had overheard, and corroborated it with a computer printout of the medicine inventory for the last six months.

Jesse watched in silence as the figures moved around the buildings on the screen. "Where are they?"

"The camera is in an old farmhouse about five miles east of here," Ben replied. "The camera is motion activated, and transmits its broadcast as soon as the motion is no longer detected. The film was taken about the same time we left for the dam—" A thought suddenly occurred to Ben.

"Dammit! If we'd held off leaving for another ten minutes, we could have gone to the dam openly and confronted Harry and his friends. Shit!" Ben slammed his fist down on the desk.

They watched the screen as the figures roamed around the grounds of the farmhouse, then disappeared from view. The screen went blank. "That's all we have," Ben said dejectedly.

Jesse sighed. "Those bastards are really serious, aren't they? I wonder if they might be planning to make their move sooner than you thought."

"Jesse, get Anna on the phone," Ben ordered. "I have to talk to her."

Jesse looked at his watch before moving to the phone on the desk. "Ben, it's four a.m. Do you want me to wake her?" Anna and Jesse had a shaky relationship at best, and he had no desire to rock its foundations by getting her up before dawn.

Ben rubbed his bleary eyes. "No, I suppose not; I'll talk to her later in the morning. We'll need to beef up local security, and Anna has proposed the creation of a larger police force with jurisdiction outside of Paradise. This may be just the impetus we need to run it through the council." He turned to Jesse.

"Why don't you go get some sleep, Jess. We can do what has to be done once the sun is up."

Jesse nodded. "What about Harry? Will you wait to deal with him until we can both confront him?"

Ben's face clouded, and for an instant he looked as if he was going to explode. "Yeah," he said slowly, "I'll leave him alone. However, when the time comes, I'll take him out myself."

"Get some sleep yourself, Ben," Jesse said with a bleak smile as he made his way to the ladder. Ben watched him in silence as he disappeared up the shaft.

Once he was sure that his brother was gone, Ben rubbed his tired eyes and turned to the computer keyboard. He entered the command for his battle plan menu, and the screen queried him for his password.

"**RAGNAROK**," he typed. He had a feeling that as far as Paradise was concerned, the upcoming battle might just as well be the Apocalypse.

The screen cleared, and a neatly centered menu entitled **Battle Options** was displayed. Ben chose the fourth selection, **Deployment**. Again, the screen cleared and another menu displayed itself. Ben pushed 4 for the drone tanks, and went down the list of tanks, selecting automatic or manual control. When he was finished, the tanks nearest the anticipated angle of the Cencom attack were switched so that a gunner could operate them with joystick control.

Satisfied, he exited the program and placed the computer on standby.

A very weary Ben Walker climbed the infinitely long way to the top of the ladder, entered his office, and slumped on the couch, falling into a fitful and nightmarish sleep before he hit the cushions.

PART TWO: APRIL 2022

Alterations

"Will we have evolved far enough in a million years to allow us to eliminate war?" the student asked.

My boy," the professor said with a shake of his head, "that is a moot point. In a million years, it will no longer be a problem for Man; I believe that Man will have long since gone the way of the Dodo and the Passenger Pigeon."

From *The Not-So-Mad Professor*, Benjamin Walker (2006)

CHAPTER THIRTEEN

He was in a large cage, redolent with the scent of shit and urine. On all sides were large, hairy chimpanzees with round, egg-shaped rocks grasped awkwardly in their hands. They took turns pelting him with the stones, and as each one struck, he felt intense pain; he was bleeding freely from several lumpish bruises on his head, and he had numerous other injuries all over his body. His sole means of defense, other than folding his arms over his head, was a Thompson machine gun placed thoughtfully beyond his reach outside the bars.

He strained, between missiles, to grasp the weapon, but every time he exposed himself to put his arms through the bars, the chimps would let loose with a fresh volley of rocks aimed at his head...

Ben awoke to the sun streaming in upon his sweat-oiled face. His head ached unmercifully, and he put a hand to his temple, half expecting it to come away bloody. *I hope this isn't going to be one of those days,* he thought as he got unsteadily to his feet. He stretched, yawned, and headed for the door.

HOME! his mind screamed at him. **GO HOME!**

Ben's cabin, which he seldom used these days, was located outside the normal housing area just south of the landing strip. He had insisted upon a setting of relative solitude, isolated enough to be somewhat difficult for visitors to reach; therefore, when he did receive visitors, he was assured that they were on an errand of some importance.

Ben trekked along Duesouth Road until he reached the first watchtower, his head throbbing and sweat streaming from every pore. The day was already warm, and he loosened the collar of his stained cotton shirt. He waved half-heartedly to the guard on duty in the tower, then turned off of the packed and tarred pea gravel road and into the dense, cool forest.

There was no trail; Ben had purposely kept it that way by taking a slightly different route to his cabin each time he went there. He climbed over a shelf of limestone, remnant of an ancient cliff face, and jumped the six-foot gap over a leaf-filled gully. He entered a small hollow in the wood, and inhaled the musty perfume of damp mushrooms and moss. He continued heading west, tramping through the undergrowth for several hundred feet until he spied the silhouette of his highly camouflaged home in the shade of an aged fir tree.

He entered the small, screened porch, slipped his shoes off, and padded softly into his cozy abode. He began to strip off his sweat-stained, smelly clothes as he walked across the living room toward the bathroom. He planned on taking a quick, cool shower and catching another couple hours of sleep before dealing with the pressing matters of the day.

As he walked under the lip of the bedroom loft, he froze. An unfamiliar sound, barely more than a whisper, came from above his head. He wrapped his shirt into a tight rope and quietly ascended the spiral staircase to the loft.

What he had expected to find he did not know; the last thing that he would have guessed, however, was the sight of Anna Graycloud lying asleep in his bed.

Damn! What is she doing here? Ben frowned. *Could it be that my long-lived lust for her had finally been realized?* He shook his head, putting thoughts of Anna aside for the moment as a stray draft carried the odor of his body to his sensitive nostrils. He dropped the shirt on the floor and turned to go back down the stairs.

He entered the bath and finished undressing. He turned the shower to a pleasantly bracing lukewarm temperature and stepped under the luxurious, needle-fine spray. His was one of the few homes so equipped, a luxury that he had incorporated into the original plans. Most of the other Paradisans shared a communal solar shower out back of the inn.

After scrubbing thoroughly, which he sorely needed after having spent over two days in his office as well as several hours crawling through tunnels, he slipped on a pair of cotton boxer shorts — his pajamas — and made his way up to the loft.

He hesitated as he reached the bed, unsure whether he should get into it or not. *What the hell,* he thought with a smile. *It's my bed!* He pulled the quilt back gently and eased himself onto the thick, soft mattress. As he covered himself and nestled onto his pillow, Anna moved closer to him and wrapped her arms around his waist and shoulders.

Her fragrance was simple yet provocative, the scent of clean woman and musk. He felt the warm tips of her nipples pressing into his back, realizing with a stir in his loins that she was nude beneath the blankets.

"Hello, Ben," she whispered.

Ben was nearly too stunned to speak. "Why are you here?" he finally asked, though he suspected the answer was obvious enough. He turned over and looked into her dark, red-rimmed eyes. "You've been crying."

Anna did not bother to deny it; instead, she drew herself even closer to Ben. "I've decided that we have shared but two things, and it's time — after more than eight years — that we shared them as well." She sighed deeply, and relaxed against Ben as her eyes slowly closed.

"I have a story to tell you," she began, "of a young girl — a girl who was of two worlds, but accepted by neither.

"My father was a white man, a teacher on the reservation where my mother lived. He was a good, kind, and gentle man, and highly respected by the elders of our tribe. My mother was the second daughter of her family, so was worth little in inter-tribal marriage. She was, therefore, spurned by the men of the tribe, even though she was as beautiful a woman as had ever been. My father was sympathetic to her plight, and befriended her.

"Although there were many differences between the two of them, they soon became attracted to one another. It was only a matter of time before they planned to marry." Anna gripped Ben tightly, and he silently returned her embrace.

"They were married in a Christian ceremony, further alienating my mother from the traditionalists among her people. My father saw her torment, and took her off of the reservation and into the city.

"One year later, I was born. My parents had high hopes for me; they couldn't believe that I would have any problems.

"They were wrong," she said bitterly. "I was teased, tormented, and taunted by the neighborhood children — it was an all-white area — and it only got worse when I entered school! It reached such a level that my parents finally took me out of school, and my father tutored me at home. I was lonely, but it was better than the alternative."

Anna sniffed back a tear, and absently wiped at her eyes with the back of her hand. "When I was thirteen, my father died of cancer. He had left little more than a teacher's life insurance settlement, and so with little means of support, we were forced to rely upon my mother's family for help. We moved back to the reservation.

"That was worse than the city. The taunting was replaced with outright violence; other children often beat me, and twice my mother had to meet me at the hospital emergency room. It was a time of hatred; I hated myself for being a half-breed, and I hated my parents for having given birth to me in the first place.

"Most of all, I hated my mother for bringing me back to that terrible place. I was neither Chippewa nor white, and like my mother before me, was banned from both worlds.

"I took to hiding in our cottage; I left only when necessary — to get food or water."

Anna's body shook with sobbing, and Ben wrapped his arms around her slender body and held her tightly.

"The teasing was bad enough," she continued, "but the boys took to taunting me in other ways. They said that I was no better than an animal, and that no member of the tribe would live if he took me for his woman. I began to feel as dirty as they said I was.

"That summer, a virgin was sacrificed," Anna whispered. "Don't look shocked, Ben — it was her virginity that was sacrificed. A bunch of men were out drinking at a local tavern, and one of the bar maids was in the wrong place at the wrong time. Some of the older boys saw the gang rape, and went out to relieve their excitement.

"I was on my way home from the market when they found me. One, sometimes two at a time, they had me. They forced themselves on me, and made me do things to them. . ."

Anna's voice broke, and she began to cry in great, heaving sobs. Her tears fell unheeded onto Ben's chest as he held her, allowing her pain to seep into and through him. *Anna,* he thought, *let it go. I'll take your pain for you. Let it go!*

After a time, she subsided into a fitful doze. Ben looked at her for a long while, amazed at the depth of his feelings for her and gratified that she had finally shared her pain with him. To know that the outwardly strong, sometimes cold, Anna Graycloud harbored such deep sorrow and hurt only served to enhance his feelings for her. Soon enough, he fell asleep, too.

Ben awoke to a most pleasant sensation. Anna was kissing him, her warm, full lips pressing gently against his. When she saw that he was awake, she lifted her head and smiled at him with sparkling eyes.

"That was one of the things that I wanted to share with you, Ben," she said as she pressed her nakedness against him. "This is the other."

Ben took her into his arms, and they kissed; at first, gently and tentatively, then with passion and hunger that made each want to devour the other. They began to touch one another, softly and tenderly, each learning the other's body by touch before they finally joined and moved as one toward a new brand of paradise.

Jesse called Ben's place a little after three that afternoon. "Are you planning to take the whole day off, you lazy bastard?" His tone was one of mock irritation. "We have to meet with Anna and discuss the expansion of the police force."

"I remember, Jess. I've already discussed it with her, and we'll meet you in an hour to let you know what we've come up with."

Jesse hesitated, and Ben could almost hear his brother frowning. "Is Anna there?"

Ben covered the mouthpiece with his hand and mouthed to Anna, Are you here? Anna's smile faltered for a moment, then she nodded.

"Yeah, Jess. She's here."

"I—I didn't interrupt anything, did I?"

"No," Ben laughed. "We'll meet you at Isaac's around four; save us a table, okay?"

"Okay, Ben. See you in an hour—maybe longer, eh?" Jesse hung up the phone laughing.

Ben turned to Anna. "So, you want us to be out in the open about this? You don't care if anyone knows?"

Anna was very quiet for a moment, and then she turned to Ben with her eyes flashing. "Dammit, Ben, everyone in Paradise is convinced that I'm a frigid bitch, so it will help enhance my standing as a human being. Even your brother gives me the cold shoulder and treats me as if I were incapable of emotions. It's just been so long since I felt comfortable trusting anyone—but not anymore!

"I don't know if you want anything long-term, Ben. I want you to know that I understand, either way; I'll take what I can get, and be glad of it. But if you're willing to take a chance on me, I'm ready for the long haul. I'd be proud to be your woman, Ben Walker!"

Ben frowned, unsure of his feelings and not ready to make a long-term commitment based upon one day's lovemaking. There was the grim specter of his failed marriage still hovering in the background to consider, too. "Let's see how it goes, Anna. You may find that, while we've been friends for years, living with me might not be all you'd expect. Besides, we still have Cencom to deal with."

"Okay," Anna replied simply. She got out of bed, allowing the covers to drop slowly and provocatively from her body. Ben smiled as he admired the view. "You keep one thing in mind, Ben Walker; what you see is yours — anytime." She turned around to head for the stairway, and Ben felt his ardor rising as he watched her taut buttocks twitch back and forth with each step.

While Anna showered, Ben considered all that had happened and what Anna had shared with him. It had been a long time ago, and a painful memory, since his one and only lengthy commitment; was he ready again? Ben lit a cigarette and sat back against the headboard.

If he committed himself to an intimate relationship with Anna, it would necessitate a sharing of more than just physical pleasures; he would have to share a part of his soul, allow another inside his emotional defenses. *Can I give myself to that degree?* That was the real crux of the matter, of course. He loved Anna — that much he would admit. He had loved her for years, but had distanced himself because, after his ill-fated marriage of long ago, he had vowed to never again become serious about another woman. To be sure, he had engaged in several liaisons over the years, but whenever he began to feel more than a passing attraction for the woman, he had abruptly ended the relationship.

Ben dredged up the memory of his earlier marriage. He had been twenty years old, full of energy, and hornier than hell. Her name was Vicki, and she had been beautiful: A perfect body, golden waist-length hair, sapphire blue eyes, and a spunky, fun-loving nature. They had married four months after meeting, and things went fine — for a while.

Ben soon became aware that Vicki did not share the same interests as he; where his pursuits were intellectual in nature, she was interested only in having a good time. Though he loved her totally and had poured his heart and soul into their relationship, he had soon found a wall growing up between them. In his pain, he had withdrawn into his own little world, further alienating Vicki and leaving her to her own devices much of the time.

It had devastated, but not truly surprised him when he came home from work one day to find her in his bed with another man.

Vicki had not even apologized; she had called him a fool, a hopeless dreamer—then she said that she hated him and never wanted to see him again.

Their divorce was quick and relatively painless; the ensuing months of empty loneliness had been another story.

He was crushed, and for several months had gone on a drinking binge of epic proportions. He had survived only by forcing himself to forget his feelings and get on with his life.

To salve his wounded heart, he swore to never fall in love again, and for fifteen years, he had held true to his promise.

It was at this point that he had decided to go into the service—and was appointed to the Federal Police (but *that* is another story).

Now, Anna had pledged herself to him, and he did not want to refuse. His hesitation was borne of fear; he would not be hurt again!

Ben's reverie was broken as he heard Anna climbing the stairs. He grinned at her dripping form, and she walked over to the bed and shook her black hair over him. "Where do you keep the towels, Ben?" she laughed as more water cascaded down upon her lover. "Or..." she eased into the bed, her warm, wet body squirming playfully against his, " ... do you want to..." She grabbed under the blanket. "Is this a tent pole?"

"Hey," Ben cried. "As much as I'd like to, we have a meeting in half an hour."

"But that leaves us fifteen minutes," she teased. "Oh, go ahead. Get up and take a long, cold shower, 'cause that's what you're going to need in about ten seconds." She rubbed her naked body against his and felt him starting to pay attention. Somewhat to Ben's dismay, she hopped out of bed and began to dress.

"Come on, Ben; get up!" She laughed merrily, knowing that no matter how adept a man may be in bed, there are certain states during which he prefers not to be exposed.

CHAPTER FOURTEEN

Jesse reached for the phone on his desk. When the operator — a shy, retiring woman named Sara Larson answered — he gave her the three-digit number and she connected him with Isaac's place. He waited patiently as the line hummed and clicked in his ear, and then heard the tell-tale sound of a receiver being picked up.

"Isaac here," a deep voice said. "What can I do for you? "

"Ike, this is Jesse. Ben and Anna are on their way over, and it's important that I see them at my place. I was supposed to meet them at the inn, but I can't make it."

"Why don't you just call them on the radio? " Isaac asked. *"It would save them the trouble of coming all the way over here."*

"You know that Ben will use any excuse to get a drink of your latest concoction," Jesse chuckled. "Besides, this isn't anything that I can discuss over an open channel. Operation Three-Dee, Ike."

The other end of the line was silent for a moment as Isaac pondered the enigmatic reference. *"Oh. In that case, I'll send them packing after one drink. Good luck."*

"Thanks, Ike; I appreciate it." Jesse hung up the phone and looked at the drawings on the desk blotter. He frowned in concentration as he flipped through the sheaf of papers, then bent over them, pencil in hand, to make additions to the sketches.

It seemed like only moments later when Jesse's watch alarm began to chirp. He looked at his wrist and was amazed to see that it was already three forty-five. He turned back to his drawings, pleased at what he had accomplished in such a short time.

Ben and Anna should be arriving soon, he thought. I guess that I'd better get ready for this meeting. He smiled with a gleam of anticipation in his eyes. This will be a real surprise for Ben.

Jesse pushed back from the desk and glanced around the room. His private study, perhaps the tidiest room he had ever inhabited, enveloped him in an aura of nineteenth century opulence. Though relatively small, he had managed to line two walls of the ten by fifteen foot room with floor to ceiling bookcases as well as squeezing in a solid cherry executive desk. The desk took up nearly a third of the available floor space, and was accompanied by an imposing leather wing-back chair. While Jesse found the chair uncomfortable for long hours at the desk, it fit in so well with the rest of the decor that he could not bear to part with it. When he became really uncomfortable, he had a small studio couch against one wall upon which to recline in meditation — or sleep.

He stood and pushed the chair under the desk. Looking at the mild disarray on the desktop, he briefly considered replacing his work in the drawers, then thought better of it. *Why do today what I can put off until tomorrow?* he reflected with a grin.

Jesse walked purposefully from the study, closing and locking the door behind him with an antique brass skeleton key that he had carried for over twenty years. He had become so fond of its warmth and antique charm that he had contracted to have all the locks in his home fashioned to make use of it.

He paused on his way out the door to pick up a piece of kindling from the small woodpile next to the hearth, and walked out to the front porch. He looked down the path to the graveled road, but saw no one approaching. He pursed his lips and let out a peculiar trilling whistle, and slumped onto the worn sofa on the porch. He felt the familiar protest of the worn springs and the tired wooden framework beneath his buttocks, and settled into the threadbare cushions.

Jesse whistled again and was answered faintly by excited barking from the direction of the Pond. His dog Ralph came into view briefly through the underbrush, only to vanish again. Jesse slowly got to his feet and walked off the porch, his boots crunching in the loose gravel of the path.

"Ralph!" he shouted in a good-natured but exasperated tone. "Get your lazy carcass over here!" Jesse heard Ralph bark again, and the dog ran up to him from behind the cabin, bowling him over onto his back. Jesse grabbed Ralph by the jowls and started shaking him in mock fury.

Ralph growled furiously and attempted to dislodge Jesse's grip by whipping his head back and forth. The dog's clear and smiling blue eyes stared directly into Jesse's brown ones, and it was the man, not the dog, who broke eye contact first.

"Damned dog," Jesse muttered as he released the dog. "Never could stare you down." He ruffled the dog's ears, and Ralph licked his face before running around the back of the cabin once again.

As Jesse wiped dog drool from his face with the cuff of one shirtsleeve, he heard voices and familiar laughter coming from behind him. He pivoted on the balls of his feet and saw Ben and Anna standing at the end of the path. Ben was trying, with little success, to ignore the fact that Ralph was gnawing intently on his boot. Anna, on the other hand, was alternating her laughter between Ben's predicament and Jesse's wide-eyed expression of consternation.

"Jesse, call off your mutt, will you?" Ben asked in a plaintive voice. "I just cleaned these boots, and they don't need a spit shine." All three of them chuckled, and Ralph's ears pricked up as he continued to show Ben's boots no mercy.

"Ralph—come!" Jesse commanded in a firm tone. With a final look of longing at Ben's feet, Ralph trotted over to sit next to Jesse. Jesse reached down to scratch the ears of the malamute-collie mix, and Ralph's bushy tail briskly brushed the gravel path.

Jesse gestured to Ben and Anna. "Let's hit the tank, all right? I appreciate the fact that you could meet me here," he added as an afterthought.

Ben nodded with a smile, and he and Anna followed Jesse to the remodeled mobile home that he used as a workshop and think tank. Ralph bounded up the stairs, pushed the light door open with his snout, and ran inside where he made himself comfortable under the large bay window.

Jesse held the door open for his brother and Anna as they entered the workshop. This gave him a moment in which to compose himself, as well as time to revaluate his estimation of Anna Graycloud.

He and Anna had experienced a rocky relationship from the day that she was sworn in as a citizen of Paradise. To a great extent this was Jesse's fault. He resented her attitudes toward many things; most of all, he was intolerant of the cold, dispassionate way she performed her duties as Paradise's chief security officer. Jesse's own pacifist tendencies and concern for others seemed to be constantly at odds with Anna's blunt, direct approach, and he had made no secret of the fact that he disagreed with her on many matters of policy and procedure. They had engaged in harsh arguments time and time again in closed council sessions over matters such as these.

It was understandable, therefore, that Jesse was bemused by this woman who accompanied Ben. To his recollection, Jesse could not recall having ever heard Anna laugh aloud. To be certain, she had chuckled now and then, and her derisive "HAH!" had been heard by all; however, what Jesse was seeing and hearing in his dooryard was uproarious, teary-eyed, no holds barred laughter.

Jesse took a deep breath and closed the door to the workshop. He indicated the sectional sofa to his two visitors, and they sat next to one another, their knees barely touching. Ben appeared at ease but curious, and Anna looked about her surroundings with a faint expression of unease. Jesse leaned lazily against one of the ceiling supports and grinned at his guests.

"Welcome to my 'think tank', Anna," he said cheerfully as his eyes slid from Anna to Ben, then back again. Ben smiled faintly, and Anna seemed to lose some of her tension. "Would either of you care for something to drink?"

Ben glanced longingly at Jesse's small wet bar, but shook his head. "No thanks, Jess. I think that we should keep our heads clear this evening. We have some plans to make." Ben stood up, and Jesse could tell from long experience that his brother was getting into an oratory mood. As he lit a cigarette, Jesse hastened to forestall him.

"Hold on a minute, Ben," Jesse said as he offered cigarettes to the others. Anna smiled as she accepted one, and Jesse continued.

"I have something to show you, Ben. I was going to show you sooner, but as you recently pointed out, it's often easier to keep a secret than to tell one." Jesse turned to leave the front room, and waved the others to follow.

Anna hesitated as Ben rose, feeling out of place in the domain of her erstwhile nemesis. Jesse noticed her discomfiture, walked over to her, and placed a companionable hand on her shoulder.

"Any friend of Ben's," he whispered, "*can* be a friend of mine." Jesse met Ben's eyes and winked.

"Come on," Jesse ordered as he turned from Anna, and Ben's eyebrows lifted at the unaccustomed tone of command in his easygoing brother's voice. "What I am about to show you may be important in the upcoming conflict.

"As you both know, I do most of my tinkering and repair work here. I don't think you've ever been here, have you Anna?" Having decided to give her a chance, Jesse made an attempt to draw her into the conversation.

"No, I've never been here," the woman replied. "I suppose that I've avoided coming here, if only for the fact that we've been such bitter opponents in council." She smiled tentatively, unsure how her honesty would sit with Jesse. She need not have worried; once his mind had been made up, Jesse was willing to go the extra yard to make amends with this possible new friend.

"Well, I've been busy doing some work," Jesse said, gesturing at what had once been the home's kitchen, "in what I refer to as the lab. Isaac and I have been working on a project for the past couple of months." Jesse gazed at the maze of glassware for a moment, then continued.

"Down this hall are my workshops for small appliances and motors. This is where I do most of the repair work and tinkering that I find time for." He paused to allow Anna a glance inside the two tiny, cluttered rooms.

"At this end," Jesse said as the trio entered the final area, "is where I handle the business end of the repairs, as well as trading some of the widgets and doodads that I've managed to put together over the years."

"My brother is too modest, Anna," Ben said flatly. "Those 'doodads' include some very innovative inventions; if fact, Jesse has managed to adapt, alter, or invent things that we never thought we'd need until we found out we needed them."

"This is very impressive, Jesse," Anna said in admiration. "This is a part of Paradise that I never knew existed."

"Yeah, yeah—we're all impressed by what you've managed to accomplish, Jess," Ben said sarcastically. "But I don't see what bearing this has on our present situation."

Jesse's eyes flared in anger, but his excitement superseded his ire. He walked to the back door and ran the latch home on the simple lock. He came back over to the others with a tight smile on his face.

"What you don't know, Ben," he snapped, "is where I do my real work." Anna looked uncomfortably from one brother to the other, but Ben's face was expressionless. "I have my secrets, too," Jesse concluded.

Leaving Ben and Anna to wonder what he was talking about, Jesse walked to the workbench against the back wall and tightened a small vise at one end. He grasped it firmly with both hands and pulled the bench toward him.

With a slight grating sound and a rush of cool air, the workbench and a section of the paneled wall swung away from the end of the room; in the revealed cavity, a small light bulb glowed dimly.

"A crawl space," Anna gasped. Jesse shook his head and turned to Ben.

Ben smiled crookedly, his eyes gleaming. "A hidden passage, perhaps? I thought that those were reserved for castles and haunted houses."

"Yeah," Jesse began, "that and..." He trailed off at a shake of the head from Ben.

Anna glanced at the two men and laughed. "Secrets, secrets. Go on, Jesse." She leaned over to look into the dimly lit passage.

"Let's get on with this show," Ben said in a steely voice that barely concealed his curiosity.

Jesse allowed Ben and Anna to enter the passage before him, and whistled for Ralph. The dog padded quickly down the hallway and sat panting on the floor in front of Jesse.

"Guard," he commanded as he pulled the panel shut.

With a soft click the wall closed, and Ralph settled down near the workbench. His eyes closed halfway as he dozed, but his ears were upright and alert as his master began a guided tour.

CHAPTER FIFTEEN

"Watch your heads!" Jesse called out as he led Ben and Anna down a short ladder and into a brightly lit tunnel. He waited at the foot of the ladder as first Ben, then Anna clambered down. "You'll notice, Ben, that this is some of that seamless culvert that you employed—elsewhere." Crouching down, Jesse walked through the first fifteen feet of the tunnel, smiling as he looked at the paintings bolted to the curving walls.

"Nice decor," Anna remarked with a grin. "Is there some reason why you have these paintings hidden down here?"

Ben glanced over his shoulder and chuckled, his voice echoing from the concrete. "My brother has a mild case of claustrophobia, Anna. I'm sure that the lights and artwork make it seem a little less confining down here." He glanced at Jesse for corroboration.

Jesse nodded, more to himself than to the others. "That just about covers it, I guess. Besides, I like the paintings. Turn here," he directed, indicating a side passage.

The three of them paused at the end of the ten-foot siding while Jesse entered a code on a numerical keypad. With a click and a rush of air, a four-foot diameter hatch swung open on well-oiled hinges.

Jesse stepped into the inner chamber and soft lighting came up almost instantly. He moved to one side and with a sweeping gesture beckoned the others to enter. Anna let out a gasp, and even the usually stolid Ben showed signs of amazement.

"My special projects room," Jesse stated.

Three sides of the room were covered with tools and apparatus suspended neatly from hooks set in pegboard. Metal work tables were set in front of each section of wall, and upon each were laid out intricate and enigmatic bits and pieces of both mechanical and electronic devices. A *CRAY 2M* portable computer, the first of its kind to employ the so-called 'room temperature' superconductors, sat upon one of the tables, a spaghetti tangle of wires and cables leading out of the back of the device to other areas of the room.

The fourth wall, however, was the obvious center of attention. Set directly opposite the entrance, it did not appear to be a wall at all; rather, it looked very much like a view from atop the central administration building.

As they watched in silence, the view slowly panned across the plaza. Ben slowly walked toward where the fourth wall should be, and saw the view change for his altered perspective. In fact, as he reached the apparent edge of the floor, he looked down into the floor, which appeared to be suspended from a dizzying height above the plaza. He stepped back rapidly as vertigo threatened to overcome him.

"What is this?" Ben could not tear his eyes away from the all too real panorama before him.

Jesse walked up to stand next to Ben with Anna trailing close behind him. Together, the three of them gazed upon Paradise.

"Look, Ben—there's Isaac!" Anna cried out. "He's heading for the distillery."

Ben frowned thoughtfully for a moment, then turned to cast an appraising eye at his brother. Jesse turned at the same time, and Ben's pensive scowl met Jesse's ear-to-ear grin.

"Jess, I asked Isaac to walk over and check on the stills around four o'clock. Isaac, as usual, is right on time." Ben peered into the depths of the vision, and muttered, "Live action holography, right?"

"Good guess, Ben," Jesse exclaimed with all the excitement of a child as he clapped his brother on the back. "Get a little closer and you can actually walk into the picture. It's kind of like floating fifty feet in the air." As no one made a move to comply, Jesse moved forward himself. Ben and Anna both let out an involuntary gasp as they saw Jesse walk through the open air to a spot apparently ten feet away and fifty feet above ground.

Jesse flapped his arms as if they were wings and did a little spin. Laughing, he hopped back to the floor of the room and dashed over to the laptop. With a clatter of keys, he began to type furiously.

"Care to take a walk through the woods, anyone?" Jesse punched a key on the computer, and the scene shimmered and swirled, finally coalescing into a scene of the deep woods. In the near distance, a camouflaged house was barely visible. "Want to go home, Ben?"

Ben slowly approached the 'forest', and when he unknowingly crossed the threshold, his steps faltered for an instant. He looked back over his shoulder and saw Anna standing in the woods behind him, and Jesse further back apparently leaning against a shrub.

"I didn't hear you follow me in here," Ben said. "You know, Jesse, I swear that I could reach down and grab this undergrowth." He bent over to make the attempt, but his hand closed on empty air. To his astonishment, however, the branch appeared to be in his hand.

"All the beauty, none of the substance," Jesse remarked. "You probably don't realize it, Ben, but neither Anna nor I have moved since you entered the hologram; it's simply that the three-dimensional qualities have encompassed you, and we're merely inserted by the program since we're within the perimeter of the pickups."

Anna approached Jesse and touched him lightly on the arm. "May I?" At Jesse's nod, she walked over the threshold and into the forest near Ben's home. The two of them stood transfixed as Jesse busied himself at the computer keyboard (which, Ben noticed, was altered by the holographic program to look like a flat, moss-covered rock.).

"Close your eyes," Jesse called as he poised his index finger over the ENTER key. He watched as his two astounded guests whirled around, their eyes squeezed tightly shut.

With a whirlpool of colors, the scene shifted around the two figures. "Okay, you can open your eyes now," Jesse said from behind Ben.

Ben shook his head, blinked, and found himself, accompanied by Anna and Jesse, apparently in the bowels of the main distillery. Twenty feet away stood Isaac Peters, a huge smile splitting his face.

"Howdy, Ben, Anna. Jesse, I see your sneaky mug back there someplace." Isaac laughed and turned to Ben. "I suppose that Jesse didn't bother to explain to you that his 3-D gizmo is rigged for two-way communications, did he? Well, don't just stand there gawking! Get that crazy brother of yours to explain what he's done. I have work to do back at the inn."

The big innkeeper walked forward and passed right through Ben, much to the amusement of Jesse as both Ben and Anna let out a yelp. Isaac turned around and flashed a toothy grin.

"By the way, Ben, the still is in fine shape; we'll be able to produce just about any amount you need, within reason." He walked away from the images of the trio, his huge shoulders shaking with laughter.

Ben whipped around to face Jesse, his eyes flashing with anger. "Why the hell didn't you tell me about this before?" He stalked over to Jesse, and only Anna's grip on his arm kept him from striking the smile from his brother's lips.

"Have a seat and calm down," Jesse said evenly as he walked over to the computer, "and I'll tell you all about it."   He pressed the power button on the computer and the scene of the distillery vanished, replaced with the barren, recessed space that extended five feet past the edge of the main room walls. He went to the nearest worktable, pulled out two chairs, and pushed them across the floor to Ben and Anna.

Anna sat immediately, her expression both curious and just a little frightened; Ben sat down more slowly, allowing his anger to dissipate as he made himself comfortable. Jesse leaned against the table behind him, took a deep breath, and pulled out a cigarette. He lit it methodically and threw the spent match on the floor.

"Where should I begin?"

Isaac chuckled softly to himself as he left the main building of the distillery. It had certainly been a fine surprise that he and Jesse had cooked up for Ben; however, Isaac had been nearly as surprised to see Anna accompanying the two brothers. He was well aware of the uneasy truce that existed between Anna and Jesse, having been caught in the middle of several debates that had raged between the two in the council chamber. He frowned, wondering what had occurred to bring the security chief into Jesse's circle of intimates.

Isaac shrugged, deciding that it was probably none of his business. With long strides he walked down the street, passing the storage warehouses, and found himself heading for Doc Riley's place. He saw a few of the younger children playing in the grassy field behind the infirmary, their happy cries coming to him clearly through the quiet air of the warm evening. One of the children caught his eye and he flashed a smile and waved.

As Isaac walked up the overgrown path to Doc's tiny house, his brow furrowed with concern. *I wonder if the old man has found out what's gotten into the water,* he thought. He stomped up the front porch stairs and was about to knock when the door flew open.

Doc Riley stood framed in the doorway, his wispy gray hair flying about his seamed face in disarray. He was smiling broadly; his faded blue eyes sparkled with delight as he shook some papers in Isaac's face. "Good to see you, my boy," he exclaimed as he ushered Isaac into his cluttered front room. "I've found the cause of the water contamination!" He pushed the sheaf of papers into the innkeeper's hands and sat down, only to pop up from his seat seconds later, such was his excitement.

Isaac flipped through the documents that Doc had thrust upon him, and noticed that many of them were surveys from before the Collapse. Among them, he saw one that dealt specifically with the local water tables. He read intently for several minutes with only an occasional grunt to show his reaction. Finally, he straightened the papers and placed them neatly on the table in front of him.

"Well, Doc, this certainly sheds a new light on things, doesn't it? It seems that we were worried for nothing." Isaac grinned at the doctor and wiped his forehead with the back of his hand. "The levels of sulfur in the water are within safe limits, and seem to be within the parameters in the old reports, and the other mineral levels seem to be okay, too. Have you told Ben yet?"

Doc shook his head. "No, I have not yet sent him my report; however, if you run into the lad, you might want to pass on the good news. Lord knows, he could use a ray of sunshine about now." He heaved a sigh, and relaxed wearily into his chair. "I'll take the report over to his office right now, I suppose."

Isaac held up a hand and smiled. "Ben isn't in his office now, Doc; he and his brother are busy on a project over at Jesse's. Why don't you just drop it in his mail chute over at the admin building?" Isaac suppressed a grin when he saw the older man roll his eyes, and gathered up the papers himself. "Or I could drop them off on my way back to the inn."

Doc smiled gratefully, and his energy seemed to return as soon as he knew that he would not have to make the walk to Ben's office. "That would be right kind of you, Isaac," he said. "It's me poor tired feet that'll be thankin' you, and I do have other things on the burner — my supper, for one."

Both men laughed heartily, and Isaac took his leave.

After dropping the report at Ben's office, Isaac resumed his leisurely walk home. As he approached the inn, he heard the soft whinnying of horses back by the stable, and decided that he had best check on the horses before going inside.

He was just rounding the corner when one of the horses trod out of the stable led by Moira Doyle. The horse was loaded with packs and supplies for several days' journey, and Moira was dressed in stout travel clothes, with small pack on her shoulders. Her back was turned to Isaac, and he had to clear his throat to get her attention.

She whirled around, and for a moment Isaac was sure that he had mistaken someone else for Moira. Her green eyes were hard and suspicious for just that second, then in a quick transformation the familiar Moira was there. It was almost as if someone had put on a mask that looked like Moira, but was not her. Isaac shook off the thought, feeling silly. I must be getting paranoid, he thought, with all this talk of battles and such going 'round.

"Hi, Moira," he said cheerfully, flashing her his trademark grin. "Looks like you're going on a trip."

"Oh—Isaac," she replied in a startled tone. "I'm going to Tomahawk to, um, get some things for the school."   She did not meet Isaac's eyes, and he got the impression that something was wrong.

"Is everything okay?" he asked with genuine concern. "You aren't ill or anything, are you?"

Moira shook her head. "No, Isaac; I'm fine. I'm just a little nervous about traveling alone in times like these."   She began to fiddle with the bridle, and her feet shuffled back and forth in the packed dirt of the yard.

"Why are you traveling alone, then? I'm sure that someone would be willing to accompany you. It really isn't safe to be leaving now—especially for a woman."   Another thought occurred to him. "Does Jesse know that you're going?"

The woman's eyes flashed in anger, and she snapped out her reply. "No, Jesse doesn't know that I'm going, and I don't have to report my movements to him, either! Dammit, I just work with the guy; I'm not his property!" She swung up onto the horse's back, and with a kick of her heels sent the beast galloping out of the stable area, leaving a stunned and bewildered Isaac in a cloud of dust.

Shaking his head, Isaac walked toward the rear entrance of the tavern, wiping dust from his pants and spitting grit from his mouth. He wondered what had set Moira on edge; more than likely, she and Jesse had been fighting—and that, too, was none of his business.

He could hear the muted din of the early evening crowd in the tavern, and his thoughts turned to the more mundane chores that awaited him inside. He entered and waved at Josslyn, who shot him a brief, angry glance from the kitchen before she blew him a kiss. She motioned him to get busy, and Isaac hastened over to the bar and smiled out at his customers.

"What'll it be?" he boomed

"I began to tinker around with holography after I had several near panic attacks down here," Jesse explained. "For some reason, this room always seems confining to me, but I've come to relish the complete privacy I have while I'm down here.

"In the early days, I still had a lot of bugs to work out, especially with the electrical system. I didn't want the power drain to show up on the community system, so I had to improvise." Jesse smiled grimly and caught Ben's eye. "I'm sure you can imagine how I felt the first time the lights went out while I was down here."

"I'm sure that wasn't much fun," Ben agreed. "I don't know that I'd want to be down here when that happened; however, I still don't see where all this is leading." He sat back in his seat and stared expectantly at his younger brother.

"Well, on one of our forays into St. Paul a couple of years ago," Jesse continued, "I was off by myself in one of the warehouse districts. I happened upon a scientific supply warehouse—I can't remember the name of the company—and broke in. I rummaged around until I found what I wanted: the lasers. I picked up everything from microchip lasers to a megawatt ruby pulse laser that'll punch a pinhole through a quarter inch steel plate, as well as some basic holography equipment and mirrors. I loaded everything into the hovercraft, and as soon as we returned to Paradise, lugged all of it down here."

Jesse took a breath and paused to light another cigarette. "It took me a long time to get things to the level that they're at now, believe me. I spent as much personal time as I could studying theory, until about six months later I felt that I was ready to begin some experimentation.

"My first trials were simple: still holography in monochromatic laser light. After I was successful with that, I began some more ambitious experiments with combinations of pure laser light and color filtering.

Finally, I created my first full-color holographic images, using a variety of techniques. It was about this time that I stumbled upon the technique for full-color, full-motion holograms." Jesse smiled sheepishly, almost embarrassed to admit that the discovery, while it had been his, had also not been an intended outcome of his research.

"I have to admit that it was an accident that led me to the process. I was doing some unrelated work with digital video, and using the microchip lasers as scanners; a glitch appeared in my control program, and in attempting to rectify my error, I inadvertently accessed my holography control program.

"To make a long story short ("Thank God," Ben muttered), the result was a brief, full-color, 3-D view of my hands moving in front of the scanners.

"I sat stunned for quite a while before I realized the significance of what had happened.

"It didn't take me long to rig up an experimental holography 'tank', and over the next several days I not only viewed several moving objects, but managed to digitally record the images on disk.

"What you've seen here is the result of two years of work which all began because I couldn't stand to be in a room without a window." Jesse smiled, and his chest swelled in pride.

"In addition to all this, I think that I may have invented the world's first fool-proof camouflage."

Ben and Anna sat in silence for a few moments, each lost in their own thoughts. Ben absently rubbed his mustache as he contemplated what Jesse had thus revealed, but it was Anna who spoke first.

"It's really impressive, Jesse, but I can't see how this can be used for camouflage; the equipment is much too bulky to be of any practical use in the field." She shrugged and looked apologetically at Jesse.

"I mentioned that I had recorded the images digitally, right? I suppose that I should have been more explicit.

"The set-up that I have here is for two-way viewing, not merely for projection; that's why it's so unwieldy. Besides, I just finished this array a couple of days ago, and I haven't had time to package it nice and neat. The means that I've devised for camouflage is much different."

Jesse turned to the table behind him and picked up what looked like a compact portable CD player. He attached it to his belt and reached down to a switch on the side of the case. "Observe," he said.

He flipped the switch, and with a swirl of color, he vanished. In his place was the crystal clear image of a birch sapling, its branches swaying in a breeze that was not there.

Ben stood mystified and walked across the room. He peered at the tree from all angles, and walked around it. His eyes squinted as he tried to look through the image. Finally, he thrust a hand into the center of the foliage, and was rewarded by a shout of protest.

"Get your goddam finger out of my eye, Ben," Jesse shouted.

A moment later, Jesse added, "It can also be switched for night use." Abruptly, the image faded, and the area around it became hazy with a twilight sort of darkness. "Unfortunately, the batteries are only good for about half an hour or so, but they can be constantly recharged with small solar cells during daylight use."

Ben remained standing in front of the tree for a moment, his features set in a poker face. Suddenly, his face split into a huge grin.

"Jesse, you're a genius! Is it possible to make more of these with different images?"

Jesse turned off the image projector and the birch tree disappeared. He walked across the room to a storage cabinet near the entrance, thumbed a hidden switch, and the door opened. Inside the cupboard, in neat rows, were roughly thirty devices similar to the one on Jesse's belt. They were labeled with names like BOULDER, PINE, BIRCH, and two were labeled with an enigmatic ZERO.

Jesse asked with a smile, "Will these do the trick?"

CHAPTER SIXTEEN

Ben began his inspection of Paradise early; he also planned to make himself highly visible over the next few days in order to consolidate his position. Isaac joined him at the recovery plant just as he was preparing to leave.

"Hey, boss man," Isaac called as he sauntered around one of the seven copper stills.

"'Hey', yourself," Ben responded. "How's business coming along?"

"Not too bad, Ben. Once we get the new stills up and running, we should be able to produce enough fuel alcohol to meet all our needs, and the three new methane recovery plants will supplement that for household needs."

"Sounds great, Ike. If you need additional help to get the job done soon, pull workers off of the library crew; they're almost finished there, but this has to take top priority."

"Ben..." Isaac trailed off hesitantly.

"Yeah?"

"Are you really expecting trouble so soon? I know that Cencom has been a thorn in our side for quite a while, but are they so much of a threat that we need to go into wartime production?"

"I can't say for certain," Ben temporized. "I only know that with a religious fanatic and crooked politician like Dwight Cochran in charge, the best thing to expect is the unexpected.

"Which brings me to another subject, Ike. Jesse and I are expecting a showdown in the next council session; it may even come down to a vote of confidence. Some of the younger members of council believe that we can go along with Cochran and keep Paradise running pretty much the same as ever. I think — and Jesse agrees — that if we give in to his demands, we'll lose everything, including our freedom and security.

"What I need to know is...can Jesse and I count on your vote if it comes down to the wire?"

Isaac stood quietly for a moment, and leaned his two hundred-seventy pound frame against one of the copper tanks. "Ben, it's like this: I've been here with my family for nearly ten years now, and in that time, you've had to make some tough decisions. Some I've agreed with, others I may not have agreed with, but wouldn't have wanted to make. It doesn't matter, though; what counts with me is that you aren't afraid to make the decisions that need to be made." Isaac smiled at his friend. "You have my vote and any others that I can get for you."

Ben took Isaac's huge hand in his and gripped it firmly. "Thanks, Ike. It feels good to hear someone tell me that I'm doing a decent job instead of bitching about things that I don't get done. I'll talk to you later, okay?" Ben walked off, his shoulders squared and renewed confidence evident in his stance.

Isaac watched silently as Ben receded into the distance, and considered the strange coincidences that had brought him and the Walker brothers together in this time and place.

Truth is *stranger than fiction*, he thought.

Ben strolled calmly toward his office, displaying none of the turmoil that raged beneath his outward composure. *One more vote*, he thought, *won't win the contest, but it will help.*

Damn it all, he growled to himself. *Here we are on the brink of what may be the last year of Paradise's existence, and I have to devote crucial time to this damn politicking! I should have made this a dictatorship instead of allowing the community to remove me if the majority rules.*

As he walked in the direction of the administration building, he pondered the changes that had occurred in his life over the past few days. First, there was Harry, the black marketer, with whom he still had to deal. Then there was the fantastic bombshell that Jesse had dropped in his lap — the holography equipment. Last, but certainly uppermost in his mind, was Anna.

Just when life gets good, some scrawny buzzard flies overhead and dumps a load of shit on you.

He entered the building, and waving off the secretarial staff, hurried up the stairs to his sanctum sanctorum. Pouring off a shot of the ever-present whiskey, Ben settled into his high back chair to draw a chart. On the left, he listed the votes he knew that he could count on; to the right went those against him, and in the middle he placed the uncertain votes — the waverers.

He occasionally broke off to make a quick phone call, more often than not ending the conversation with a despondent, "Thanks, anyway."

Eventually, Ben had a final tally. If the vote were held today, he'd be in deep trouble.

Pro	Neutral	Con
MYSELF	EDDIE GORDON	CAROL BARTON
ISAAC	LINDA TYLLIER	GENE VOLKMANN
ANNA	GREG MITCHELL	CHAD DAVIDSON
JESSE	DOUG ZIMMERMAN	LEN TYLLIER
	JACK BARKER	SARA McDOUGAL
	SUSAN WILDMAN	
	FRANK POST	
4	7	5

By Paradise law, Ben had to get sixty percent of a vote of confidence to remain leader. That meant that he would have to pick up six of the seven neutral votes; to lose, he only had to drop two of the neutrals.

It was going to be a fight, but Ben welcomed the challenge; after all, they couldn't kick him out of Paradise. The worst that could happen is that he would lose his seat on the council, Paradise would become a Cencom satellite, and Cochran would execute Ben. Not a very pleasant prospect, but the only realistic one at this point. If nothing else, the upcoming struggle with the council would be good practice for the battle with Cencom, and the thought made Ben's heart race. Not in a long while had he felt more alive!

He dialed Jesse's number and waited through several rings before he hung up.

Jesse and I have to discuss our contingency plans, just in case Paradise decides that they can do without us, Ben mused. Jesse might prefer to stay even without his seat on the council, even in the face of a Cencom takeover, but Ben was more pragmatic; he wanted to survive to reorganize and fight a winning battle.

Well, Ben thought, *tomorrow will come whether I want it to or not, so I might just as well greet it with a hangover and be in the right mood for a fight.* He opened a new bottle of whiskey, settled back in his chair, and inserted into his stereo a compact disk of Prokofiev's Sonata in D Major for Flute, one of his favorite pieces. He filled a medium snifter, sipped slowly, and closed his eyes.

In his workshop, Jesse was entertaining himself, too. He worked steadily, fine tuning the holography transceiver while listening to the somewhat more pronounced beat of *Time*, by a late twentieth century group called *Pink Floyd*. Jesse preferred classic music to classical, and this particular piece dated back more than forty years.

Jesse showed none of the concern that his brother exhibited, because he was not worried. He knew that the council meeting would take every bit of support that Ben and he could muster, but he also recognized that without the Walker brothers, Paradise was indeed lost. This was not conceit on Jesse's part; rather, it was just the situation as he saw it. Jesse and Ben had already discussed the alternatives if a vote of confidence was called. They had decided that if Ben lost, the secret of the war room and of Jesse's holography set-up would leave Paradise with them. They would not be alone in their exodus, if it came to that; Anna had announced her intention to follow Ben wherever he went. With characteristic disdain for the more mundane of life's little problems, Jesse had scarcely given a thought to whether Moira would follow him or not.

The workshop throbbed with the subsonics of *Pink Floyd* blasting through the subwoofers of Jesse's sound system. He made a final adjustment to the belt device he was working on, and snapped it onto the waistband of his jeans. He turned the knob to its first setting, and turned the device on. Suddenly, where he stood was—nothing. Jesse seemed to have vanished.

He walked over to the workbench and propped a mirror up against the wall. He looked into the silvered glass, and chuckled with satisfaction. While he cast no reflection in the mirror, he could still see himself if he looked down. His image was invisible to those outside the projector's field, not to the person wearing it.

The only problem he had yet to solve was that of shadows; he still cast a shadow in the shape of his silhouette, and he would have to exercise caution when using the Zero setting to align himself properly in well-lit situations.

Jesse reached down to his projector and clicked the toggle to the second setting. In the mirror he saw a small shrub appear, leafless enough that a potential aggressor would not even consider using it for cover. He turned the switch over to the last setting, and the air shimmered for a moment.

Jesse looked into the mirror, and saw his brother's face looking back out at him. *That ought to impress the hell out of the council,* he thought with a certain irreverent glee, *when they all end up looking like Ben.*

Anna climbed the stairs to Ben's office with a slight feeling of intrusion, although Ben had made it clear that she was welcome there. She stopped to adjust her skirt—she knew that Ben loved to see her in feminine garb—and mounted the final few steps to the narrow hallway.

Her feet, clad in knee-high moccasins, made soft padding sounds that were scarcely audible more than a few feet away. The rustle of her dress as it brushed the sides of the narrow hall made more noise than her feet, and she was slightly irritated by that fact.

She reached the door to Ben's office, and gently turned the knob. The latch clicked, and with a squeak, she opened the door on a sad sight.

Lying with his arms sprawled across the oak desktop was Ben, an almost empty fifth of whiskey by his elbow. His hand still held the extinguished stub of a cigarette, and the desktop was littered with ashes and cigarette butts from the overflowing ashtray.

Shaking her head in disgust, Anna moved gently to Ben's side, grabbed him under the arms, and hauled him to his feet. He mumbled incoherently as she put one of his arms around her shoulder and half walked, half carried him to the couch; as she laid him down and straightened his legs, the mumbling ceased and Ben regained the state of mind that he had so fervently sought: unconsciousness.

Anna went to the icebox and removed a small jar of apple cider, which she took over to a chair near the couch. She drank the chilled juice in slow sips, her eyes scanning the mess that Ben had made of both himself and the office. Finally, she dozed, the jar falling from her hand to the soft carpet.

The warbling shriek of the emergency alarms awakened Anna immediately, and her first thought was that she ought to rouse Ben. She glanced at the couch, but Ben was no longer there. She turned to the desk, ready to activate the communications console, only to see Ben already there. He smiled at her faintly, his eyes red and bleary, but alert.

Ben punched up the button that deactivated the alarm and contacted the north-central station guard, Brian McFarland.

"What's the situation, Brian?"

The answer came over the speaker. "An intruder tripped the perimeter alarm just west of my position; he was attempting to gain access by going under the fence where the Creek passes under it. I contacted Chad at north-central two, and we over-powered him. He appears to have been working alone, and we have him detained in the jail."

"Good work, Brian; I'll be there in five minutes. Send Chad out to man your station, and meet me at the jail with your report. Walker, out." Ben turned off the radio, and visibly slumped. "You're the foxiest cop I've ever seen," he said as he noticed Anna's attire. "Seems a shame that we have to work."

"Now you say that? Where were you three hours ago when I wanted you? Sleeping off a liter of booze!" Anna shook her head, but could not help laughing at the contrite look on Ben's haggard face.

"Let's get going, Ben — we can play later." She took off at a run, skirt flying, leaving Ben and his pounding head struggling to keep pace.

Just outside of the administration building was Anna's patrol ATV; although it was primarily a one-person vehicle, it could seat two in a pinch — if they didn't mind getting cozy. Anna clambered aboard, indicating the tiny rear seat for Ben. "You can't drive, Ben. Wait until your eyes stop bleeding."

The jail was located at the far end of the central plaza, and it took less than a minute to reach it. Anna drove the ATV with reckless abandon, only the narrow headlight illuminating their path in the deepening twilight. Ben hung on, eyes tightly closed, his trust in Anna's driving better than his trust in his queasy stomach.

Anna brought them to a halt, spraying dirt and gravel for thirty feet.

She literally jumped off of the cycle and ran into the jail, followed unsteadily by Ben, who was now totally awake—and wishing he was not.

Jesse had been asleep only minutes when the alarm reached him. He listened in on Ben's radioed communication, pulled on a pair of jeans and a T-shirt, and ran down the road to the jail. He nodded to Brian as he entered, and walked over to the cell to look in on the prisoner.

He gasped as he recognized the man's attire, and slowly backed away from the cell.

"Do you think ..."

"Yep. I think so, Jesse," Brian replied to Jesse's unasked question.

Jesse sat down at the desk, impatiently awaiting the arrival of his brother.

Ben allowed Anna to rush ahead of him into the jail, knowing that she would do her job well. He paused to talk to Jesse, who walked outside when Anna told him where Ben was waiting.

Jesse lit a cigarette and leaned against the wall of the jail, looking with amused contempt at his brother. "What have you been doing, Ben? Drinking the stills dry? You look like shit!"

Ben fumbled in his shirt pocket for a cigarette, then remembered that he had left them on his desk. Jesse, anticipating Ben's need, already had one out and lit as Ben looked up.

"Thanks," Ben muttered. "Do you know what's going on?"

Jesse shook his head. "I know that we have a prisoner, but that's all I'll say until we get Anna's report." He dropped his cigarette to the ground and stamped it out with a boot heel. The two men stood in silence for nearly half and hour, awaiting Anna's report.

The door to the jail finally opened and Anna walked out. "Jesse, Ben, I'm afraid that I have bad news. Cencom is not our only concern anymore." She frowned before continuing, letting her pronouncement sink in.

"The man we are holding, if his identification is to be believed, is a Major in the United States Air Force, stationed in Ohio. He claims that the area of 'reclaimed' states includes all those east of the Mississippi except Wisconsin and Missouri."

"That makes sense," Jesse agreed, "since Wisconsin is split into several areas, and Missouri is under Cencom control."

"What the hell does he want," Ben asked irritably. "What does he think gives him the right to break into Paradise?"

"What he wants is simple, Ben," Anna replied evenly. "He's here to negotiate the return of Wisconsin to the United States."

Jesse, who was taking this all in with a calm demeanor, asked, "What form of government does the U.S. have, according to the Major?"

Anna glanced at Jesse, surprised at the direction of his interest. "The same system of democracy as before the Collapse, apparently. Why?"

Jesse looked at Ben before responding. Ben nodded, and Jesse explained.

"Anna, if the U.S. has the same government as before, it stands to reason that they would make the same mistakes as before. People can learn; governments can't. Why should we consider rejoining, only to return to the same system that allowed the Collapse to occur in the first place?"

"I agree," Ben announced. "We have to keep this secret from the general populace for a while, until we can further investigate this man's claim.

"Anna, can you keep our guest under wraps for a few days? What do the guards know?"

"I think so," Anna considered. "Brian and Chad don't know anything, other than the fact that he's wearing U.S. insignia; however, we can't keep them from speculating. Where do you want him kept?"

Jesse suggested that Anna, Brian, and Chad escort him from Paradise that night; then, the next night, Ben and Jesse would arrange to guard adjoining stretches of the perimeter, allowing Anna to return with the Major. "Send Chad and Brian on a wild goose chase—have them do a sweep of the area for a ten mile radius to check for any other intruders. Then, Anna, you can tell them that you are heading for home. If we don't have any other prisoners, we can then return him to the jail," Jesse said. "It's only guarded when someone is in 'residence', so it would be as safe a place as any to keep him under wraps."

"I'll want to have a long talk with the Major after all this subterfuge is over," Ben stated. "I want to know how hard the U.S. will fight to reclaim its lost territory."

Ben instructed Anna in detail how to handle the Major; Jesse waited politely out of earshot.

As Anna left to see to the prisoner, Jesse suggested to Ben that they go back to his place. Since it was closer than going to his cabin, Ben merely nodded with an inquisitive expression on his face.

Jesse shook his head to forestall any further questions from his brother.

"Wait," he said.

Jesse's home was unique to his style of inventiveness. Some may have called it 'cluttered' or 'busy'. To Jesse, however, it was merely *HOME*.

Ben plopped into the chair nearest the kitchen; Jesse poured coffee, then joined him, slouching into the deep-seated chair that he had designed specifically for his dimensions.

"Well, Jess?" Ben's curiosity showed in his eyes as he sipped steaming coffee from his mug.

"Ben, here's the picture as I see it. We have a great danger of being attacked by Cencom, which may or may not have enough manpower to kick our asses. Along comes Mr. U.S. Major, offering to accept us back into the warm bosom of the same old United States. We have a choice of two evils; who do we fight first?

"If we manage to weaken Cencom, the U.S. government will step in and finish the job, then turn to confront us. If we attack the U.S., Cencom will do the same. Either way, we lose."

"I'm finally starting to get worried," Jesse said as he drained the last of his coffee and set the empty mug on the end table.

"It's about goddam time," Ben growled. He had worried constantly since he had received the first message from Cencom. "The way I see it, we have no simple solution.

"One. We can join the U.S., and by surviving, lose all the freedom and independence that we've fought for.

"Two. We can join Cochran and his merry band of loonies; the result would be the same — we lose.

"Three and four, you've outlined. What you haven't considered is a fifth possibility."

"What is that," Jesse asked. "I can't see any other possibilities."

"Scenario five," Ben explained. "We get Cencom to attack the U.S., which weakens them both, then go in for the takeover."

Jesse jumped from his chair, his face flushed with anger. "You've gone fucking nuts! Do you want to die that badly?"

"Hear me out, Bro'," Ben said. "We won't really take over anything; all we'll demand is a treaty which guarantees that we'll be left alone, as an independent principality or some such nonsense. No taxes, no obligations on our part — just a promise of non-aggression where the U.S. is concerned.

"It's beautiful. We get a couple more states for the U.S., and we lose two enemies at the same time. Cochran can't stand up to the entire eastern third of the continent!"

Jesse shakily lit a cigarette and thoughtfully inhaled each breath as if he was going to speak after each one. Finally, with just a smoldering butt in his hand, he said in disgust, "Dammit, Ben. It sounds too much like politics, but it's just crazy enough to work. All we have to do is keep the Major under lock and key until after the council declares its vote. Then we can release him with a message — fake, of course — about how Cochran wants to destroy the 'godless heathens' of the United States. Also, at the same time, we send a false message to Cochran, telling him that the Antichrist of the United States is going to attack him unless he attacks first." Jesse frowned as another thought occurred to him. "Unless Cochran and the U.S. are already talking, in which case we can kiss our asses goodbye!"

"Yeah," Ben agreed. "Or unless Cencom decides to attack us before we can get this plan in motion." Ben sat back, and drank the cooling dregs of his coffee.

"Still, it's our best shot, Jess."

Anna walked back into the jail, her mind racing with the plans that Ben and Jesse had outlined. She asked Brian to wait outside for a few moments while she interrogated the prisoner; the young man left immediately, glad to be shut of anything having to do with this new and disturbing development.

Anna closed and locked the door behind Brian and walked over to the cell that held Major Michael Mantey, USAF. She looked through the bars at the small, well-furnished room. The Major was sitting on the edge of the bed, his pose the classic one of Rodin's *Thinker*. Anna pulled up a chair, positioned it well away from the bars, and cleared her throat.

The Major looked up, his brow furrowed with an unspoken query. "I imagine that you're wondering what's to be done with you," Anna guessed.

"That was uppermost in my mind, ma'am," Mantey replied in a polite, urbane voice. "I realize that I've trespassed where I do not belong; however, I hope that you realize that I was simply following orders."

Anna frowned and shook her head. "That's no excuse, Major, for violating the privacy and borders of an independent municipality. I imagine that the guards at Auschwitz used much the same excuse to pardon their behavior as they put thousands of people to death! 'I was just following orders' is the excuse of every war criminal since time began." Mantey flushed, nostrils flaring, at the comparison, but he held his tongue.

"You are hereby formally charged with criminal trespass and espionage, Major. These are serious charges and, to be honest, ones that we've never had to deal with up until now. Our ruling council will have to meet and review the particulars of you case, as well as delve into the charter of Paradise, in order to best deal with you in a fair and just way. You see, Major," Anna said with a smile, "we are not barbarians—nor are we ignorant peasants to be trifled with."

Major Mantey chose his next words carefully. "I understand the gravity of the charges leveled against me, ma'am. I would, however, like to have some idea of what the penalties may be for my alleged crimes. Am I to be detained in your jail indefinitely? Or will I be put to death?"

Anna laughed merrily. "Oh, Major! I hardly think that the death penalty is warranted in this case—and I hold considerable sway in council where the matters of crime and punishment are concerned. However," and her tone became serious, "there is the possibility of a lengthy jail sentence. I would suggest to you that cooperation is your best course of action. Meanwhile, relax and enjoy your stay; the cook makes a great venison stew." Anna pushed back her chair and turned to leave, but the Major's next words halted her.

"I should tell you that I was given very specific instructions regarding my mission here, ma'am. The most important part of those orders was the time limit placed on the completion of my mission." The Major was standing at the bars now, his earnest expression radiating honesty.

"What was the time limit imposed upon you, Major?" Anna felt their plans beginning to crumble around her.

"Three days, ma'am. After that, I will be considered missing in action, and a patrol will be sent to complete my mission — and they will be considering my loss a hostile act."

"Thank you, Major." *Three days,* Anna thought bitterly. *A lot can happen in three days.*

CHAPTER SEVENTEEN

It was chilly and damp, and the horse's breath puffed out in great gouts of steam. The night was without a moon, and in the shadow of the hangar, both horse and rider were but deeper shadows, black on black. A breeze blew out of the north and the rider huddled against the beast as if to draw some warmth from the sweaty flanks. Night birds sang softly in the distance, and the dark shape of an occasional bat flitted through the midnight sky.

The horse had been ridden hard through a night, a day, and another night to bring it to this point, and it stood with head down lazily cropping on a clump of tough grass near its feet. The rider, too, was weary, and waited impatiently for the forthcoming rendezvous that was scheduled for midnight.

Suddenly the horse pricked up its ears and raised its head from the grass. It whinnied softly, and the rider strained to hear what the animal had already sensed.

There it was—the soft, whistling thrum of the helicopter's rotors. The noise gained in intensity until it became like that of a giant's heartbeat. The breeze grew until it was of near-gale strength, and the rider saw a shiny black shape separate itself from the encompassing darkness of the night sky.

Even before the chopper had landed, the rider had grabbed a saddlebag from the horse's back and was running through the tall grass of the abandoned airfield to the waiting craft.

A door opened in the side of the helicopter and the rider threw in the bag, then clambered in after it. Sitting in the copilot's seat, the passenger strapped in and looked forward with steely eyes as the pilot raised the craft from the ground. Once airborne, the pilot turned to his passenger and grinned wickedly through gapped and grimy teeth.

"Good to see you again, Miss," he said to the young woman beside him. She stared at the pilot with contempt, hugged the saddlebag close to her breast, and closed her eyes.

The sound of the helicopter beat its way across the night sky as it veered to the south.

"As of today," Jesse said with a smile, "classes will be cancelled—temporarily, I hope." He stared out at the room full of bright young faces, and his inner despair grew.

"As I'm sure most of you know from the gossip going around, we're about to reach a crisis point—that is, we can expect to be attacked at any time by a group called the Central Command.

"I'm sure that most of you remember the attack by the Rovers last fall? Well, the attack that is coming may be much worse than that, and we'll have to fight to keep what we have all worked so hard to build. There's the possibility that some of us (*A lot of us,* Jesse thought bitterly) may get hurt—and some of us may even die."

"Is that why you're wearing that gun, Teacher?" Suzie Post asked. Suzie was eight years old, and often too perceptive for her age.

"That's right, Suzie," Jesse answered with a sigh, deciding that honesty was called for here. "As a matter of fact, all children twelve years old and older will be staying after class today to be trained to use guns like this."

A loud murmur rose and fell across the group of youngsters, and Jesse noted that several of the older children seemed very excited by the prospect, although more than a few of them looked frightened and nervous as well.

"For those of you over twelve who will be issued weapons, I want you to realize that this is not a game. We'll be fighting with real weapons, against people who want to kill us and take away everything we have. The existence of—the whole community of Paradise—may rely upon what you do when we are attacked.

"I want you all to do your best, and help out by following orders that are given to you as quickly as possible." Jesse saw traces of puzzlement on many faces, and smiled. *Better that they should misunderstand than be terrified,* he thought.

"Frank Post and Greg Mitchell will be instructing you in the proper use of the weapons issued to you this afternoon in the Great Meadow. All of you who qualify are expected to be there by one o'clock sharp."

Several hands raised, and Jesse pointed to sixteen year old Jeff Barker.

"Does this mean that we'll get to fight?" His anxious tone belied the excitement in his eyes.

"Hopefully it won't come to that, Jeff. We'll save you younger troops to guard the home front. With any luck, we can even avoid that." Jesse looked out over the faces, usually so bright and cheerful; now, however, he saw mostly looks of fear and dismay.

"Are there any more questions?" The hands that had been in the air before now stayed down. "If not, then class is dismissed!" Jesse began to clear his desk as the children walked quietly from the schoolhouse, their subdued voices strange at the time of day when they were usually so wild and happy. *Why couldn't Moira have been here to help me explain this? Come to think of it,* Jesse thought with a start as he realized that he had not seen her for several days, *where is she?* Jesse frowned, but could not remember Moira saying that she was going anywhere.

When he looked up from the desk, Jesse saw a pair of blue eyes peering at him over the desk's edge. He leaned forward and recognized little Mary Barton, the six-year-old daughter of Mike and Carol Barton.

"What can I do for you, little lady?"

Mary looked around the room to see if anyone was listening, then stared up at Jesse with an expression both shy and puzzled.

"What's a 'crisis'?" the little girl asked.

Ben sat in his office and for the fifth time that day, he reviewed the list of able-bodied, trained troops that Jesse, Anna, and he had compiled. It was, to be honest, very disheartening.

Out of a population of over two hundred, only thirty-seven could be considered as trained troops—and of that number, eleven were in vital occupations that required almost constant vigilance.

Ben shook his head. The 'home guard' that Frank and Greg were training was laughably inadequate; it was made up of thirty kids—children!--ranging in ages from twelve to seventeen. *How the hell are we supposed to hold off an armed attack by, at best guess, thousands of determined adults with fifty or sixty people?* Ben slammed his fist down on the desk in frustration.

The war room defense would be of great help, especially coupled with Jesse's technique of holographic camouflage; however, Ben was beginning to think that even his well-laid plans might not be enough. It was time for him to relinquish his pride and admit that he was not omniscient.

Ben got up from his seat, walked over to the main console, and pulled the cover from the one thing that he had avoided using in the past ten years — the emergency council call. He hesitated, hand over the switch, silently praying for a last minute brainstorm. Nothing.

Ben heaved a sigh and pushed the button that would, in all likelihood, force him to abdicate his seat of power.

From the roof of the administration building rose a steel shaft upon which was poised a brilliant red pennant. From hidden loud speakers a shrill, warbling siren blared forth.

Throughout Paradise, people stopped dead in their tracks. Those who did not know what the siren signified stared nervously at their neighbors, and many ran for their homes. The members of the council, upon hearing the siren, turned sharp eyes toward the center of the community.

Jesse ran out of the schoolhouse, directed his gaze to the plaza, and swore softly to himself as he saw the red flag.

"It's begun," he whispered to himself in fear and anticipation.

The brownstone office building was near the center of the old business district; while most of the surrounding areas had begun the long slide into decay, the brownstone stood amidst an oasis of greenery. Beautiful shade trees cast cool shadows on the lush, green lawn, and gardens full of hothouse flowers were in bloom throughout the grounds.

The sun beat down from a cloudless sky, vibrant and warm with early spring vigor. From outside of the pleasant plaza, the sound of a busy city reverberated from crumbling masonry.

A young woman hurried up the walk to the front door of the office building, her eyes resting briefly on the gold emblem painted upon the glass door. The stylized sword with oversized cross guard pointed downward appeared like a crucifix. In bold black lettering the words **CENTRAL COMMAND** underscored the gilt blade.

She pushed open the door open and burst noisily into the foyer. The guard/receptionist at the front desk came to alert with a start, then relaxed as he saw who was entering.

"Go on up, Miss," he said respectfully as he pressed the switch on the desk that opened the electric lock on the stairwell door. "Elevator's out again."

Without a look or word to acknowledge the man's existence, she continued briskly on her way, pushing the door open with a bang. At the foot of the stairs she paused, as much to catch her breath as to steel herself for the upcoming meeting.

She began her ascent, taking the risers two at a time; gradually, she slowed her pace as she became winded. It had been a long time since she had climbed such a flight of stairs, and the load in the saddlebag was heavy enough to add to the tiresome burden of climbing.

The suite of offices that she was destined for was, of course, on the top floor of the building. She stopped for a moment between the fifth and sixth floor, and sat heavily upon the dusty stairs. She pulled a canteen from her belt and helped herself to a mouthful of the tepid water. Wiping her mouth on the sleeve of her grimy jacket, she replaced the canteen and resumed her climb.

On the last flight of stairs before reaching the eighth story, she was challenged by a heavily armed, hulking guard. She spoke the password and he removed a key ring from his breast pocket. He fumbled for a moment getting the key into the latch, then quickly unlocked the door to let the woman through.

No sooner had she passed through the door than it was slammed shut behind her. She heard the key jingle as the door was locked, and she spun around. The door was featureless on her side—no doorknob, no handle—nothing. The only thing that broke the surface of the door was a peephole set at eye level. She made a rude gesture at the door with her middle finger, shrugged, and made her way down the richly carpeted hallway toward the only rooms on the entire floor. There was no use worrying about the door, anyway; she could not leave until her business was concluded.

She reached the end of the hall and knocked on the heavy door. The sound echoed down the hall, and from within she heard a muffled voice say, "Enter."

With the same slight hesitation she always felt whenever making a report, she turned the knob and walked into the huge inner office.

"Hello, my dear; how was your trip?" The man swung his swivel chair to face her. "You made very good time getting here."

"The trip was—fine," she replied in a monotone as she looked into the man's green eyes. He smiled, the crow's feet around his eyes wrinkling like tissue paper. He held out his hands for the saddlebag, and she passed it across the immaculate desk to him.

"You've brought me some helpful information this time, I trust," he said as a malicious smile touched his weasel-like features. "The packet you brought last time was woefully inadequate."

The woman snapped back, fire blazing in her emerald eyes, "Dammit, Dwight! I do the best that I can under the circumstances. What the hell do you expect?" She angrily pushed a stray wisp of auburn hair off of her forehead, and glared at the man before her.

Dwight Cochran smiled, but there was no warmth in the expression. "Mary, I only expect the best from—my daughter."

Mary Cochran sighed in defeat, and sat down. After a moment to collect her thoughts and to calm down, she began to make her report.

"Ready...aim...*FIRE!*" Greg Mitchell cringed slightly as the early afternoon air was shattered by the crack of a dozen rifles firing simultaneously—or nearly so.

The Great Meadow, a huge natural clearing which was several hundred yards east of the central plaza, was filled with a small crowd of serious young people, as well as several of the area's adults who had some free time.

Frank Post, after making sure that all the weapons had been put up, ran down to the targets at the far end of the clearing. He made some notes on a pad of paper, then ran down the field and nodded significantly to Greg.

"Okay, troops, let's try that again," Greg ordered. "Weapons ready...aim—hold it!" He looked at Frank as they both heard the siren that could only mean one thing—trouble.

Greg waved Frank on, and he ran in the direction of the central building. Greg turned to the small group of adults, and said, "Brian, Joe—I want you to take over. No more than twenty-five rounds each, okay?" Without waiting for an answer, he left the Meadow.

The weapons cracked again moments later, and from his observation post atop the administration building, Ben shook his head in dismay.

Jesse was the first to arrive at the council chambers, a large room on the ground floor of administration. He took the opportunity of his early arrival to make some preparations for the upcoming session that, he feared, would be as big a battle as the impending confrontation with Cencom.

Jesse moved silently around the chairs of the chamber; it was dark and empty now, but in a scant few minutes would be teeming with the conflicting shouts and angry grumbling of the discontented. The voting today might very well change the leadership of Paradise and irrevocably alter the course of the community's future; he was determined to avoid a loss if at all possible, and it was to this end that his present preparations were intended.

Gliding from one seat to another, Jesse stopped, squatted, and attached a small, flat box to the base of each seat. He made a few quick and precise adjustments, then moved on to the next. In less than fifteen minutes he was finished with his work.

Jesse had been contemplating this idea ever since Ben had first approached him with the real need to gain more support in Paradise; with the younger members of the council being either children of older members or newly-sworn members themselves, it was natural for a certain amount of dissent given the varied and unique make-up of the community's inhabitants.

Still, Jesse thought, there ought to be a way to control the violence with which these difference of opinion always seem to be infected. A pacifist at heart, Jesse disapproved the use of violence as anything but the last possible avenue.

It was only over the years since the founding of Paradise--working daily with his headstrong--brother that had served to alter his views in the least. Now, Jesse would trust violence as a means to an end; not the best one, certainly, but Jesse rarely shunned the employment of a useful tool.

Yes, Ben, Jesse thought with a grimace, *you'll be as surprised as the others when you see what I've cooked up for this meeting. If we don't succeed with our plans now, I don't know what else I can do.*

Jesse circled the room quickly, examining the walls for any listening devices, and found only one; fortunately, it was one that Ben had planted in order to keep a record of council meetings. Those records had proven useful in determining who held what opinions, and today would certainly be an occasion to remember.

His adjustments completed, Jesse stashed a remote control in his jacket, unlocked the door to the council chamber, and went to his seat near the head of the massive table. He lit a cigarette, put his feet up, and grinned.

"We'll win this one," he said with a trace of his brother's arrogance. His hand rested briefly on the remote control in his pocket, and his grin turned hard. "If not, then..."

Jesse removed his hand from the device, took a drag from his cigarette, and blew a dense cloud of smoke across the room.

"Boom," he whispered.

CHAPTER EIGHTEEN

"All right! Settle down back there or you'll be tossed out of here!" Ben pounded the gavel once more for effect, then stood mute as the council members slowly relaxed in a more dignified posture; he was patient because this day, of all days, he had to avoid making any new enemies.

When the council members had calmed down, Ben called the meeting to order.

"Because of the nature of this meeting," Ben said, "we will dispense with the reading of the minutes. Is there any new business?" He felt a chill as Carol Barton stood up.

"I think that it's time we elected a new leader," she said without hesitation, though she refused to meet Ben's eyes. "Ben has controlled things long enough, and not always with the approval of the council."

"Excuse me, Carol," Ben interrupted. "If you wish to make a motion, do so; otherwise, there will be no speeches today."

"Well! Then I move that we hold an election to replace Ben Walker and put someone in place who understands the needs of Paradise." *And a puppet that will do what the council dictates,* Ben thought bitterly.

"I second," Chad Davidson shouted. The council dissolved into uproar once more, and Isaac waited calmly for the commotion to die down before standing up. Ben nodded to him.

"Fellow council members; a point of order, please. According to the by-laws of Paradise, the leader may not be removed from office except by a sixty percent vote of confidence in full council session. Therefore, we must first vote to see if we wish to retain Ben, and only then will we be able to determine if a vote to elect a new leader is necessary. I would like to alter Carol's motion to read as such, then discuss the reasons why the motion was raised in the first place. We can hardly give Ben the boot without telling him why, can we?"

"That sounds reasonable," Greg Mitchell interjected.

"Are we in agreement, then?" Ben smiled his most charming smile, showing a confidence he did not feel for the benefit of the wavering council members. "Very well; let's try to keep this orderly, folks."

Chad Davidson was the first to speak; he was nineteen, and had been recruited just seven months earlier. He had proven to be a disruptive influence among the younger Paradisans, and was marked for early 'retirement' by the more conservative members of the council.

"I'll make this brief," Chad began with just a hint of nervousness. "Ben is a good enough leader for Paradise — but where is Paradise heading? Where are the new worlds to conquer? Why aren't we occupying greater areas of land and making the people pay taxes for our protection? With what we have here, we could be powerful beyond our wildest dreams!"

He sat down to a murmur of mixed reactions. The next member to be recognized was Len Tyllier, Chad's best friend and the husband of Linda Belker-Tyllier. Len, eighteen, was one of the Paradisans who chose work when he needed to eat, as opposed to his wife, who worked forty hours per week as one of the administrative staffers.

"I agree with Chad," Len drawled. "We have to grow faster, and the only way to do that is by being more aggressive. The small farmers and groups around here have no real hope of defending against us."

Jesse stifled an outburst of horrified anger at this war-promoting talk, while contemplating the different ways to torture both of the young men.

Len continued. "If we're going to outlast our enemies, we've got to expand; that's all I'm trying to say." He glanced at Ben with shifty eyes, and without speaking again, sat down.

That's two against, Ben tallied mentally. He recognized the next speaker, Linda Belker-Tyllier.

"I'm sorry, Len," she began with an apologetic glance at her lazy, ne'er do well husband, "but I don't agree. We have everything that we need right here in Paradise, and we are expanding. Why, I just saw the production figures for the methane plants and the stills the other day, and we are not only making enough for ourselves, we have enough to trade for goods produced outside of Paradise. We've got people from the outlying areas working for us, we're almost finished with the new library, and we haven't been attacked for over six months; I don't see how things could be any better." She smiled shyly at Ben. "I stand behind Ben all the way."

Two to one, Jesse thought as Len glared at his wife.

Doug Zimmerman, an older man who was a barber by trade but had shown an amazing facility in leather-working, cleared his throat. "I'm not sure what I think. Back — you know, before — things were different; however,

145

I can't say that they were any better. Until I see some changes either way, I withhold my vote."

Gene Volkmann and Sara McDougal both sounded against Ben, neither of them giving any reasons. Eddie Gordon, Sue Wildman, and Jack Barker remained neutral. Then came the most active attack yet: Carol Barton.

"I suppose that I should explain for the benefit of the council exactly why I oppose the continuing leadership of Ben Walker," she said in acid tones.

"My husband was a trusted friend and assistant to the Walkers; he was faithful and hard-working. He remained so until the day that Ben sent him out on his final 'scavenging' trip last fall — a mission that he should never have been sent on so soon after the attack by the Rovers. You'll recall that Ben had claimed that since we had sustained minimal damage — even as his own brother lay injured in the infirmary!--the raiders had no real strength, so were of no immediate danger.

"If that was so," Carol continued harshly, "why is it that Mike was found with a crossbow bolt through his chest?"

She wiped angry tears from her eyes and faced the council. "I want the Walkers out of power, before anyone else gets killed!"

Ben glanced at Jesse and grimaced. Jesse smiled faintly, his finger lightly brushing the stud on the remote control that would end the trouble of Carol Barton — forever. He restrained the impulse and turned to face the council.

Anna Graycloud stood. Smiling, first at Ben, then at Jesse, she stated simply, "Ben is our leader. What he wants, I want."

Jesse tallied the vote in his head. *Five against, four neutral, and two for us. Not good, but not over. The real vote is still to come.*

Frank Post stood and faced the council. "I think that under different circumstances I would back Ben, but maybe now *is* the time for a change. We're growing too slowly, we haven't increased our standard of living, and there are few allowances for children to advance in the community. We are, at present, a stale civilization, existing solely for ourselves. We could be a center of culture for most of the state — we owe it to the people to share what we have.

"And I think that this whole mess with the Central Command could have been avoided somehow," Frank concluded lamely with an apologetic glance at Ben.

Greg Mitchell said, "Sorry, Ben, but I agree with Frank." Both men sat back, relieved at having said their piece.

Ben maintained the frozen smile on his face. Now was the time for the real supporters.

Isaac stood up and slowly gazed around the table. He frowned, his brow furrowing, as he contemplated the members of the council.

"You know what I see when I look around this table? I see spoiled, incompetent, self-indulgent children who would have long since starved to death or been killed if it weren't for that man sitting over there." He gestured toward Ben.

"Many a time I've been with Jesse and Ben when there was a major decision to be made; often, they talked it out—more likely, Ben acted on his instincts. Sure, he's only human, but his instincts are more trustworthy than most people's researched decisions.

"Ben is our leader for two very good reasons. The first I've mentioned: his ability to make swift, sure decisions. The second is that he knows how to utilize human talent. Is there anyone here that is doing a job for Paradise that is something they are not supremely qualified to do? Is there anyone who has not been given a choice of what they want to do or be?

"Ben understands and uses a concept that most leaders fail to understand—delegation. He picks good people, and lets them do their jobs. We need a leader like Ben. We need his competence, his confidence, and his drive."

Isaac sat down quietly and surveyed the room. His eyes met Jesse's, and he shrugged as if to say, I did the best I could.

Jesse smiled. "I support Ben." He looked at Carol with an odd expression of mingled pity and disgust. "I wouldn't have been alive last year if it weren't for Ben. Sure, I took a bullet, but I had nine years of life between the Collapse and then that I might not have had. Carol," and Jesse almost whispered the last words, "Mike was my friend."

Carol broke eye contact with Jesse and turned to the council. In a shrill voice, almost as if she was afraid that if she hesitated she would change her mind, she screamed, "Put it to a vote—NOW!"

Ben pounded the gavel amidst the general hubbub that followed. "I believe that I have the right to speak on my own behalf, right?" He walked from the head of the table to the center of the right side; he now stood directly behind the active opposition.

"At first, we were primitive, but in the last ten years, despite the Collapse, we've added a few amenities: full electrical service, hot and cold running water, transportation, hydroponics' greenhouses, paved roads, a secure perimeter, a hospital, and the new research center.

"Most of these things were accomplished after the Collapse, although I had prepared for the possibility of much worse. When the economy collapsed, Jesse and I were ready—we had a functional, safe community capable of supporting nearly five hundred people as it was.

"We grew quickly after the Collapse; in just six months, we went from thirty-eight to one hundred and sixty people with scarcely a ripple in our day to day lives."

Ben's smile changed to an expression of contempt as he moved slowly about the room. "What did we ask of you when you joined? Did we take your belongings? No. We asked that you give twenty hours of your time to the community, each week, for projects that would benefit all. In return, you were provided with a home, food, clothing, medical care, and the freedom to live as you chose, subject to the good of the community as a whole.

"We have no taxes, no real economy; if you want something extra, you need only earn it through an arrangement with the person who has what you want." Ben paused and glanced at his audience—for the moment, spellbound—and his smile returned.

"Of course, the freedom we offered you was also the freedom to dissent—and the freedom to leave." Ben gazed with blank eyes at Carol Barton. He saw by the color of her face that his point had hit home.

"I sincerely hope that you decide to support me, because we are in deep trouble. Soon, the Central Command will be attacking. I estimate that as soon as the ground hardens, they'll be knocking on our gates. They'll be poorly armed, but will outnumber us, and because they are fanatics, they'll fight to the death. Our only hope is to fight—according to my plan—and win."

Gene Volkmann called out, "Why not just surrender? They'll leave us alone if they see we have nothing they need."

"That attitude is dangerous," Ben replied sternly. "Healthy pessimism never killed anyone, and can save your ass in a pinch. All I can add is that I have always functioned well under pressure, and no one knows Paradise or the surrounding area better than I."

He walked back to the head of the table and turned.

"Take your vote, if you must. Do what you think is right." He sat down and folded his hands on the table.

Jesse got up from his chair. "Before you take your vote, I have something I would like to show you...something that makes winning possible."

He walked purposefully to the light switches and turned them down, effectively throwing the room into darkness. He reached into his jacket and withdrew the small remote control and pressed the activator stud — carefully avoiding the row of tiny red buttons along one side of the case. He chuckled as he listened to the gasps of amazement as the realization of what was occurring dawned on the assemblage.

No longer were there sixteen people in the room; in their place was a montage of assorted northern plains foliage. Isaac was an oak tree; Anna, a slender pine. Ben was a large boulder, and Carol Barton a withered elm. Each of the council members was the image of something else. Jesse hoped that his choice of images for each of the councilors would not go unnoticed. His own choice of Ben's image was calculated to throw the council off-guard long enough to allow him to make his pitch.

"This is live-action holography," Jesse explained from within the holographic simulacrum of Ben. "You retain the appearance of the object on the projector's disk for about half an hour of battery life — longer, with the built-in solar cell charger. We can now hide in ambush safely. We can even go among our enemies cloaked in the visages of birds, gophers, fox, or anything else you can think of."

There was a general roar of shock from the councilors as they regained their aplomb. Jesse flipped the switch, and the council members regained their natural appearances. *I liked most of them better the other way,* Jesse thought.

The undecided votes of the discussion were looking very decided, and Jesse determined that now was the time. He rushed over to his brother's side, and shaking Ben from his daze, told him to call the question immediately.

Ben nodded absently, pounded the gavel, and called out, "We will now, by a show of hands, carry a vote of confidence. All those in favor of forcing my resignation, raise your hands." He counted as Carol, Sara, Gene, Chad, and Len slowly raised their hands. "Five against. Those in favor of my remaining in the post of leader, raise your hands."

Jesse immediately stood up and raised his hand. He turned to face the rest of the council and began to count. Ben needed nine more votes to remain in office.

Isaac: two. Anna, Linda, Jack—three, four, and five. *C'mon, Sue,* Jesse thought intently as he willed the woman to raise her hand. Yes! Eddie slowly raised his hand, his eyes shifting back and forth among the other councilors for their reaction. Seven. Frank and Greg looked at each other, smiled sheepishly at Ben, and raised their hands simultaneously. Eight and nine.

The only remaining votes to be cast were Doug's and Ben's. All eyes were riveted to the two men, and Doug began to sweat as he felt the pressure being mentally brought to bear by his peers. Ben seemed oblivious to the proceedings, his eyes focused upon the table before him.

Finally, hesitantly, Doug raised his hand. Ten. Jesse smiled and pressed another stud on the remote control; this one deactivated the tiny high-explosive charges that were nestled inside the holographic projectors. He breathed a sigh of relief as the tension of the past several hours ran out of him, leaving him drained but content. It had been a last-ditch effort, made in a desperate moment by a desperate man; still, Jesse was glad that he had been able to avoid killing anyone in order to gain this victory. He looked over at Ben, who was still sitting quietly.

"Well, Ben," he shouted, "you did it! *We* did it!"

Ben smiled faintly, but his mind was lost in thought.

BOOM! BOOOMM!

"What the hell is that?" Len Tyllier looked around the room with wide, fearful eyes.

"I think we've just received a calling card from the Central Command's advance force," Ben said calmly. "Everyone, grab a rifle from the cabinet and get to your assigned stations. Anna, sound the alert, then meet me in my office. Jesse, come with me."

The councilors left the chamber quickly, their recent adversarial roles forgotten as they ran outside for a quick look to assess any damage. Debris was scattered around and there was a lot of smoke, but not much real damage as far as Ben could tell. He and Jesse ignored the cannonade in the distance, being much more concerned with making it to the war room alive.

The red alert siren began braying, and shortly Anna met them in the lobby of the central building. As they ran up the stairs to Ben's office, Jesse shouted to Anna, "Have you seen Moira?"

As she reached the top of the staircase, Anna replied, "No. She left Paradise a couple of days ago on horseback. I don't think she was going to be gone long; she was only carrying a few days supplies in a single saddlebag, according to the sentry. She reported her destination as Tomahawk."

Jesse recalled Moira's plan to get a group of students from that area together, and hoped fervently that she was all right.

The trio reached Ben's office in double time, and as Ben opened the shaft that led to the nether regions, Jesse and Anna watched the attack from the main window. In the distance they could see the ragtag multitudes that served as the main army of the Central Command. If they were armed or even minimally trained, Paradise was in trouble. Fortunately, while it appeared that they had the strength of numbers, there were only a few sections that had heavy artillery of firearms of any sort. The normal weapons, which Jesse saw as he scanned the mob with a pair of field glasses, seemed to be clubs, knives, and farm implements.

"C'mon, you two," Ben cried from over by the central console. "You can watch the battle from below."

"Below what?" Anna's jaw dropped open in amazement as the central console split open, revealing a dark aperture. She turned to Ben. "What the hell is that?"

"No time to explain," Ben snapped. "Just follow me."

Anna cast a glance of entreaty at Jesse, but he just shrugged and ushered her into the shaft.

Ben slid down the ladder, followed tentatively by Anna. Jesse paused halfway down to make sure that the hatch was secured above them before descending the rest of the way down the shaft.

Ben had slipped into the chair in front of the main terminal, and swiveled to meet Jesse and Anna. Anna stared in wonder at the sight before her, but responded quickly and without question when Ben began giving orders. "Pull up a chair. I'll give you the two minute tour, Anna."

Ben explained in brief detail that each of the three stations controlled several weapons. All three stations had two reconnaissance drones at its disposal, quick little craft loaded with surveillance cameras. The drones had been fitted for carrying small air to surface missiles, but Ben had been unable to arm them before the attack occurred. The missiles were in a corner of the storage warehouse, sitting idle and doing them absolutely no good at all.

The stations were also in control of five remote tanks each to provide mobile attack and defense, and each of the main towers was armed with concealed automatic machine gun nests. Each control station had a keyboard, high-resolution color monitor, virtual reality goggles, and two joysticks; the right hand stick controlled the motion of the vehicles, and the left hand provided the direction of the firepower.

The tanks and airborne drones each had a sophisticated guidance system which would continue on previous course and modes when active control was centered on another vehicle, or the display could be split into as many as nine separate views from as many vehicles.

The central control station, where Ben was already activating his defensive weaponry, also included controls and view screens for each of the automated machine guns, as well as the operating controls for the single drone blimp. The blimp was set to hover at ten thousand feet to provide wide-area surveillance; Ben hoped that altitude would be beyond the notice and firepower of the Cencom army.

Ben completed his explanation abruptly as one of the machine guns signaled its activation. He turned to his console and activated the board, effectively putting him in touch with all of the automated devices and opening lines of communication to the twenty squads of combatants and the internal defenders — the Home Guard.

"Let's get busy," Ben ordered, then all was silent as the trio donned their headgear and familiarized themselves with the controls. Ben quickly took his drones out to the skirmish line, some two miles east of Paradise. He set them to fly circles and aim their cameras downward, then turned his attention with the touch of a button to the tanks. Scanning the forward lines through the camera array, he drove his lightly armored tanks into the enemy lines.

Sweat beaded his forehead as he saw the size of the force before his vehicles; he estimated the mob at roughly five thousand people. He tied in the view from the drone blimp, and gained some perspective on the size and position of the opposing forces. Examining the Cencom forces in the path of one of his tanks, Ben saw how poorly equipped they were, and many of the 'soldiers' looked malnourished and ill. Ben wondered just how bad off the Central Command really was.

He dispelled the tiny trace of pity he was feeling and with a light touch on the controls, he opened fire from the tanks. Ben watched in captivated horror as hundreds of bodies were literally torn apart by the steel-jacketed slugs of the .50 caliber machine guns. He automatically switched his display from one tank's vantage to another as rapidly as he could, hoping to demolish the front lines in one demoralizing barrage. Unfortunately, the tactic seemed to be having little or no effect on the steadily advancing horde.

He switched to communications and contacted the internal defense commander, Frank Post.

"Command to ID. Come in, ID." Ben fired another salvo into the mob as his listened to the crackle of static in his headset. He spoke again into the voice-activated mouthpiece, his voice cracking slightly. "ID, do you copy?"

"*ID here. I read you.*" In the background, Ben could hear sporadic gunfire, and Frank shouted out a couple of unintelligible commands before returning his attention to Ben.

"What is your situation, Frank?" Ben's voice was touched with concern, but it also held that indefinable note of command that had made and kept him leader for so long.

"*A small force broke through the perimeter south of the dam,*" Frank reported, his voice already hoarse and strained with fatigue, "*but we're holding our own. We have several serious injuries, but so far no fatalities. These kids are kicking butt out here!*"

"Hold on, Frank; I'll send some reinforcements to the dam and cut them off. Command, out." Ben swung his chair around to face Jesse, who was bent over his console in concentration.

"Jesse, where are your tanks?"

Jesse checked the coordinates printed on the top of the tanks' displays. "About half a mile northeast of tower two, Ben."

"Send two of them to the dam; Frank and the kids have a breakthrough over there, and they've already sustained some casualties."

Jesse punched in a few commands on his keyboard, and jiggled his joystick. "Done. ETA is two minutes." Jesse fell silent once more as he turned his attention to a large group of enemy troops who were blocking the route of his third tank. He closed his eyes for a moment, then with a grimace, activated the tank's targeting mechanism and pressed the Fire button. His eyes left the heads-up display as he directed the tank through the smoke and over the fallen bodies.

"How are you doing, Anna?" Ben spoke to her even as he directed one of his harmless drones to buzz a small group of attackers. They dispersed and dove to the ground, and Ben took the drone up and into a holding pattern again.

"I'm okay, Ben." Anna's voice was dry and raspy, and when Ben flipped up his visor to steal a quick glance at her, he saw tears and sweat mingling in streams on her mahogany face. "I'm firing on them with four tanks to keep them busy; I want to sneak the other one around behind and take out that cannon that they're shelling us with." Anna's fingers flew lightly over the controls as her features set into a cast of grim determination. Ben flipped his visor down and called up an aerial view of her maneuvers. He watched as three of her tanks fired at the mob, while the fourth suddenly blossomed into flames.

"Tank hit, Ben," Anna said in a distracted voice.

"Yeah," Ben replied as he reached onto his console for the self-destruct button for the tanks. "What number?" When Anna answered, Ben checked the screen, entered the number, and waited for the largest enemy concentration near the damaged tank. At the right moment, he pressed the button. In a burst of black-orange flame, the tank's fuel exploded, casting burning debris, charred body parts, and flaming diesel fuel for a hundred yards in every direction.

"Two tanks stationed at the dam site," Jesse reported, oblivious to anything but the view through his VR goggles. "Enemy troop movement appears to be slowing down, and the ID's are mopping up. Frank is having a crew slap a temporary patch on the perimeter fence."

"Good work, Jess." Ben returned his attention to the carnage he was, by necessity, creating. A wall of dead lay before the treads of his tanks, yet still they came—screaming, climbing over their fallen comrades, dying.

Fanaticism is a deadly thing, Ben thought bitterly.

Anna maneuvered her fifth tank behind the cannon with uncanny accuracy. In the general Chaos, the rumble of the diesel engines went unheeded until it was too late. She strafed the men manning the cannon with her machine guns and fired three high explosive shells directly at the big gun. The cannon exploded, and the store of ammunition soon followed. A piece of shrapnel must have struck the tank, because Anna abruptly lost the display from tank seven. "I've lost camera seven, Ben."

"How much ammo was left in the tank?" Ben's fingers hovered over the keyboard as he awaited Anna's reply.

"Uh, two shells and about fifty rounds in the machine gun," Anna read off of the display. Ben shrugged and pushed the self-destruct button. The concussion from the explosion was audible even in the war room, and all three of them jumped a little as dust filtered down from the ceiling.

Ben checked the area with one of the drones, zooming in on selected areas with the high-powered camera. He shuddered involuntarily at the carnage that came into view. Bodies were not evident...but body parts were.

Ben was suddenly alert. The camera had tracked across an area of fire, and Ben circled the drone back to get a coordinate fix on it. He activated the communications and contacted internal defense.

"Command to ID."

"*Go, Command.*" Frank sounded exhausted.

"You have a fire in the stand of trees just south of the garage and distillery. Get a crew over there, and activate the pumps that feed water into the stills from the Creek. We've got to get that fire under control now!"

"*Roger, Ben. I'll supervise myself. Out.*" Ben watched in his display as a small group of people ran from the defense station on Duenorth, and checked in with his other squads.

Anna had her tanks ranging around the eastern and southern perimeters of Paradise, the machine guns on automatic fire. Her drones were flying at about one thousand feet, roughly two miles east of the community. She attempted to get an estimate of the army's size, but it was difficult due to the distances involved as well as the clouds of smoke and cover provided by the surrounding woodlands. Her best guess was about six thousand, but it could have been as many as eight and as few as three thousand. No matter; they were outnumbered at least thirty to one!

Anna sighed, pushed back her headset, and looked at Ben. She respected him for his leadership ability, but it was for his confidence, his 'never say die' attitude that she treasured him. She welcomed a strong man like him after years of dealing with the men on the reservation; old and unwilling to change made them not men, but stubborn children in adult bodies. Ben was the sort to do what he pleased just for fun, because someone had forbidden it.

I hope we win this war, Ben, she thought with real yearning. *If we do, you and I will have a lifetime together.*

Jesse reveled in the remote control of his arsenal as the minutes turned into long hours; it divorced him from much of the damage he was doing, and allowed him to see it as a game. In this manner, he was able to perform with dispatch, cutting down the Cencom troops — if they could be called that — almost as fast as they came.

The attack at the dam had lessened after the tanks showed up, but Jesse was kept busy chasing down the soldiers who had already made it onto Paradisan soil. They were running scared now, and often he did not catch them before the ID's or perimeter guns mowed them down. He was so involved with the ground fighting that his drones were still in the hangars, unused and useless.

Hot damn! he thought as he chased down a pair of Cencom soldiers on motorcycles. So in touch with his machines was Jesse that he could almost smell the burning oil in the bikes' exhaust fumes. The cross hairs met the target, the tracking system flashed red, and he depressed the firing button. A sheet of lead sprang forward from the tank, a .50 caliber bolt of lightning, and the two men and their cycles dissolved under the deadly hail of bullets.

Jesse broke off from the battle, and slid his headset back. Abruptly he was in the war room once more, and he had to take a moment to reorient himself. He noticed that his body was soaked in sweat, and he pulled off his sodden shirt and threw it on the floor. He wiped his eyes, lit a cigarette, and turned to Ben.

"How are we doing, Ben?" Ben held up a hand to quiet Jesse, and listened intently to the incoming message on his headset. Ben's shoulders slumped imperceptibly, and he turned to Jesse. "I just got an updated report from all stations," Ben explained as he switched his visor to two-way viewing. "We have fifty-eight casualties, mostly women and children killed by the shelling and crossfire." Ben fell silent, then shouted, "Damn! I wasn't expecting an attack on the northern perimeter; I figured that they'd go for the defenseless southeast."

Jesse and Anna sat in silence. '58' did not seem like such a big number when you just thought about it or compared it with the numbers of the Cencom dead; however, fifty-eight dead Paradisans was over one quarter of their total population!

Women and children! The thought made Jesse shudder, and he had conflicting pictures rushing through his mind: In one scenario, he and Ben were being hung for war crimes by their own people. In the other, he envisioned a monument being erected to the honored dead. Of the two, Jesse much preferred the latter. His reverie was interrupted by a sound to his right. He turned in his chair and saw Anna sobbing quietly.

"Fifty-eight," she whispered. "Oh, God!" Her sobs became cries of grief and rage, and she slammed her fist down on the table. "God damn them!"

"Other than the casualties, what's our status?" Jesse turned to face his older brother, embarrassed by Anna's tears and more than a little ashamed that he could not yet share them.

"Estimated enemy casualties," Ben read from his display in a dead monotone, "two thousand plus. I think we've beaten them. Most stations report the enemy disengaging and retreating, without covering their asses or recovering their wounded."

"So, we've won," Jesse stated flatly without enthusiasm. He wanted to be happy about the outcome of the battle, but it seemed to him a Pyrrhic victory at best. He tried to smile, but the best he could do was a painful grimace. "You hear that, Anna? We've won."

Anna shook her head and stared through wide, red eyes at the two brothers. "Oh, my God—so we've won. But at what price?" She threw down her headset and stood.

Ben stood also, and blocked the path to the shaft. "I want you two to get out there and help with the clean-up. Anna, you can help coordinate the mopping up of any stragglers; Jesse, circulate and gauge the mood of the people. Help with the wounded—our wounded—and dispose of any Cencom wounded. Take no prisoners."

FROM THE ASHES: Paradise One   Jack Bandemer and Marat M. Bandemer, III

Jesse and Anna stood stunned by Ben's orders. "I have to contact their commander and negotiate terms of their surrender. Get moving!" Ben turned away from them, and resumed his seat at the console. He knew that both of them needed to keep busy, or they would fall into a state of despair. He, too, felt the stirrings of depression at the high cost of the battle—but he had plans to keep himself busy, too..

Dejectedly, Jesse and Anna climbed the ladder upward into the Hell that they had helped to create. Jesse cast a last glance back at his brother, who sat staring sightlessly at the desk. Jesse shook his head, and ascended.

CHAPTER NINETEEN

The door hissed softly above Ben as Jesse and Anna left the shaft. He turned back to the computer and hastily typed in a message for his brother; then, with a last glance around the war room, Ben ran crouching into the tunnel.

Heedless of the bumps and abrasions that he received as he sped down the dark tunnel, Ben veered into the left branch and continued at a breakneck pace for some three hundred yards until he reached the terminus of the tunnel. He checked the tell-tale light at the hatch, and when the light turned green, he opened the portal and climbed out of the dark nether region into the dimly lit aircraft hangar.

Ben ran to the wall and grabbed his flight suit from a hook, pulling it on with frantic haste. He fumbled beneath the insulated coverall for his belt holster, and finally managed to get it strapped on outside of the suit. He crossed the open space to the provisions locker and inserted his ID card into the electronic lock. He flung the door wide, grabbing dry rations, a sealed canteen, an AK47, and several loaded banana clips. He placed his supplies into the storage hold of the *Screamin' Eagle,* opened the hangar doors, and ran back to the plane.

As he strapped into the pilot's harness, Ben thought about what he was about to do. He had lied to Jesse and Anna, of course; had they any inkling of what he planned, they would never have allowed it.

According to Ben's intelligence reports, Dwight Cochran was monitoring the attack on Paradise from City Hall in what was once Dubuque, Iowa. He had moved there from his usual headquarters in St. Louis in order to be closer to the action—and, Ben supposed, to be in the vicinity to lay claim to Paradise in the event of a Cencom victory.

Ben planned to talk to Cochran in person; what he really looked forward to, however, was the surgery he planned to do afterward—a radical decapitation.

In order to carry out his plan of turning Paradise into an equal of her enemies, Ben needed to guarantee that the Central Command would never again attack his community. By disposing of Cochran, he would deprive the fanatical Cencoms of their figurehead, at least long enough for Paradise to regroup and consolidate their position. Soon enough, someone would make a bid for the top spot in the Central Command; power, Ben paraphrased silently, abhors a vacuum.

Ben realized with grim understanding that he was embarking on what would probably be a suicide mission. Even if he managed to kill Cochran, his chances of getting back to Paradise safely were slim to none. There might just be a power vacuum in Paradise soon, too, he thought bitterly. Such was the power of his dream, however, that even his own life held little importance for him when weighed against the survival of Paradise.

He heaved a sigh, put his card in the ignition slot, and pressed the starter. He allowed the twin engines to warm for a minute while he strived to clear his mind of all thoughts save one—killing Dwight Cochran.

Ben taxied the little plane down the tarmac runway and goosed the throttle. He was airborne in three hundred feet and climbing at a rate of one thousand feet per minute as he pumped power to the engines. He checked his compass as he leveled off at an altitude of five thousand feet, and corrected until he was at a heading of one hundred eighty-six degrees south-southwest. He locked the throttle and ailerons, and released the controls. Settling back in his harness, he allowed his weary body to relax; the trip would take about three hours if all went well, so he decided to try and get some rest. *This might be my last chance*, Ben mused without a trace of his earlier anxiety.

As the *Eagle* flew across the azure skies, Ben fell into a trance-like state. He reviewed the events of the last several days, and second-guessed his defense strategy again and again.

He had predicted that a strong enough show of force would cause a quick demoralization of the undisciplined troops that Cochran had mustered; the surprise was that it had happened so quickly. The first attack had come at 1040 hours; the battle had been nearly over by 1400. Here he was, flying through the peaceful skies some thirty miles from the site of the battle, and it was not even 1500 yet.

The flight was pleasant and relaxing. Ben found himself giving his complete attention to tiny details of the landscape and the sky that he normally would have ignored. He even found enjoyment in the way the wind rushed across his face, whipping his skin into a semblance of ruddy good health that almost, but not quite, covered the pallor of fear that his subconscious mind had imposed upon his features. He replayed happy memories, laughing aloud in a carefree, abandoned manner that would have embarrassed him had anyone been around to hear.

Ben thoroughly enjoyed the flight, his happiness made sharper by the thought of his impending fate.

When Ben saw the outskirts of Dubuque on the horizon, he dropped the plane to treetop level. Lowering the throttle to barely above stall speed, he wove between the trees, his wingtips nearly brushing branches and signs as he soared just a few feet above the pavement of the deserted streets. He cursed the fact that the ultra light was so noisy as he approached the downtown section; the few people he saw immediately stopped what they were doing to peer in amazed curiosity at the sight of his plane flying through the military-controlled town. Ben grimaced as he saw a patrol spot him, and he heard a couple of shots ring out as he approached his objective: City Hall.

He climbed rapidly to three hundred feet, heedless of the possibility of further gunfire so close to Cochran's office. He circled the brownstone building twice, evaluating his chances of landing on the roof.

The landing would be a tricky one. What Ben needed for a safe landing was a minimum of two hundred feet of relatively level ground; what he estimated he had on the roof of the building was about one hundred and forty feet, and that was broken up by heating and air conditioning vents and compressors. In order to negotiate a landing, therefore, Ben would have to hit the roof just past the retaining wall, then come to a stop in less than twenty-five yards.

Ben glanced down at the ground far below, and saw that more troops were converging on the area. With a ragged sigh, Ben grasped the controls firmly and went in for his approach. He would only have the one chance, and he sensed a cross-wind that was going to make the landing even trickier than he had anticipated. He adjusted his trajectory a few degrees to compensate.

He cut his throttle to one-eighth as he reached the edge of the building, pulling the nose up into a near-stall. As the front landing gear cleared the low wall with inches to spare, he killed the engine and pulled the nose up enough to create a full stall. He gritted his teeth as he heard the tail scrape across the wall, and relaxed as the plane dropped at fifteen miles per hour the last few feet to the roof with a bone-jarring thump.

I'll never do that again, Ben thought as he yanked open his harness, *even if it's a matter of life and death.* He stood on shaky feet, armed himself with a 9mm pistol, AK47 assault rifle, and six grenades, and set out to avenge himself upon the leader of the fanatical Central Command.

Ben shot off the lock on the rooftop fire exit and entered the dimly illuminated stairwell. A shot was fired at him from below, and the masonry cracked and flew away from a spot only inches from his head. Ben instantly dropped and rolled across the landing, firing several wild shots down the stairs to cover himself.

Cautiously, Ben peered over the edge of the stairs, pistol ready to return fire if necessary. He was gratified to see that one of his shots must have hit its mark, either directly or through ricocheting from the enameled brick. The guard, if such he was, lay prone on the landing below. His face — what was left of it — was shattered, and an expanding pool of blood was blackening the marble floor.

Ben padded quickly down the stairs on rubber soles, avoiding the slick of blood on the polished stone. He tried the door, and was not surprised to find it locked. With a grimace of distaste, Ben searched the fallen guard for a key ring. He ripped the ring free from the man's belt and put the single key into the lock. It turned freely, and in a moment Ben was on the other side of the door. He closed it with a soft click, and rapidly glanced up and down the corridor.

Guessing at the direction of what he hoped would be the old mayoral chambers, Ben ran down the hall, his footfalls echoing hollowly from the granite and marble walls. He held the pistol in his right hand and the pistol grip of the AK47 in his left, both loaded and ready to kill again if need be. He paused at the corner of the building and peered into the southern corridor. The hall was empty, and he checked his back once more before running down toward the offices at the end.

He was brought to an abrupt halt as one of the doors opened and someone stepped out. He fell to his belly on the floor, the rifle in both hands and the pistol laying an inch from his nose. He took aim, held his breath, and pulled lightly on the trigger. With a gasp of surprise, he let out his breath and released the trigger.

"Moira!" he shouted. "What the hell are you doing here?" He kept the rifle aimed at her chest, and his finger tickled the trigger.

The young woman jumped at the sound of Ben's voice, but she quickly regained her composure. "Ben! I was hoping someone would come, but I never thought it would be you. Hurry — follow me!" She moved to turn, but was brought to a stop by the tone of command and contempt in Ben's voice.

"Hold it right there! Why the hell should I trust you? I just flew cross-country to kill Cochran and put an end to the Cencom persecution of Paradise — and who do I find in the midst of the enemy's stronghold? Moira Doyle!" Ben stood slowly, the aim of the rifle never wavering from Moira's chest. "Why shouldn't I kill you now, traitor?" Ben spat at her feet, and raised the rifle to his shoulder.

Moira's eyes widened in terror as she remained motionless, not daring to move for fear that the madman before her would not hesitate to make good his threat.

"Ben, it isn't what you think," she stammered quietly. "P-please listen to me for a minute."

"One minute is all you have, bitch!" Ben relaxed his trigger finger for a moment, but his eyes still bored through her with the fire of unreasoning hatred.

"Thank you, Ben," Moira whispered. "I was on my way to Tomahawk, as you may know, to set up some school schedules with the Outsiders. I lost my way, and before I knew, it was dark. I found an old house to spend the night in, and decided to stop.

"I had just dismounted when two men showed up from nowhere. They were well-armed and insisted that I go with them. I couldn't do anything but comply, Ben," Moira pleaded. "They would have killed me. They were Cencom scouts."

Ben mulled over her story. It was just possible that her story was true; there had been Cencom scouts in the area. The note of entreaty in her voice, and the look of honesty in her eyes touched Ben. Before the echoes of her voice had faded from the hallway, his quick decisiveness had told him to trust her — for the time being.

"Okay," Ben said slowly. "You follow me. Do exactly as I say, or I'll fill you full of lead. I don't know why I trust you, or even why I should, but for now, I do. I'm here to kill Cochran — where is the bastard?"

Moira looked at Ben, her eyes showing surprise and, of all things, amusement. "Is that why you're here? If it is, then you're too late. Dwight died this morning when he got the first reports from his field officers. It seems that the strain of being defeated by Paradise was too much for him.

"They weren't expecting more than a token resistance; being fired upon by tanks and high output automatic weapons was more than they bargained for."

Ben swore under his breath, and he felt the adrenalin of fear and hatred dissipating. He took several deep breaths, lowered the rifle, and rubbed his beard.

"It seems like this trip was for nothing then," he mused aloud, then looked up and caught sight of Moira's eyes. "It's time to get the hell out of here, Moira; do you like flying?"

"Why? We don't have a — oh, that's how you got here! Of course!"

"Come with me." Ben shouldered the rifle, picked up the pistol, and unfastened two of grenades from his bandolier.   The two of them ran down the wide corridors to the single fire exit. Ben did not bother with the key this time, but blew the lock out of the door with two quick, accurate shots. He kicked the door open and listened carefully for a moment.

"Up the stairs and out the roof door, Moira — NOW!" He had heard the sound of booted feet coming up the stairs, and knew that they had only seconds before the patrol reached them. "Warm up the engines; my pass is in the ignition."   Moira ran past Ben, avoiding the gruesome sight on the landing. Ben waited until he saw the upper door close behind her, then positioned himself on the upper landing to wait.

He did not have to wait long; thirty seconds after he heard the plane start up, he looked down the stairwell and saw a half dozen soldiers running up the steps two flights down. He pulled the pins on the grenades, holding the triggering clips down firmly. He bided his time until all the soldiers were grouped on the floor below, and let the clips pop open. He counted to three, then dropped the explosives into the open stairwell.

The explosions rang out with a resounding, echoing roar, and Ben felt the heat and compression even as he flung himself against the far wall. The upper door and fire exit door were both blown off of their hinges, and through the smoke Ben could see late afternoon sunlight shining through the shattered rooftop portal. He paused, listening, to make sure that the patrol was no longer on the move, then stole a glance down the stairs.

A great hole had been ripped in the stairs, and there was little left of the soldiers except scraps of clothing, flesh, and pieces of their weapons. Flames flickered brightly in the now darkened stairway, and Ben turned away from the smoldering carnage. He ran lightly up the steps, tripping onto the top landing, and fumbled his way out to the roof.

Ben ran to the Eagle and without a word to Moira began to strip it down for the return flight. He tossed his spare flight suit to the woman, and topped off the fuel tanks from the extra cans on board. He tossed the cans aside, secured his weapons on the floor of the plane, motioned Moira into her sling seat, and clambered in after her.

"Ready?" Ben shouted over the roar of the engines. Moira gave him thumbs up, and he turned to his controls.

Ben took a deep breath, applied the throttle, and taxied the small plane into take-off position. There was only one way to do this—jump the wall at less than take-off speed, then gain flight speed in a dive. The only problem was that the dive could not be for more than sixty or seventy feet— the building was, at best, only one hundred feet high!

They sat in position for a minute or two as Ben steeled his nerves for the take-off. Finally, he gunned the engines. The *Eagle* gained speed as it rolled across the tarred roof toward the retaining wall and what seemed imminent disaster.

Just as it seemed that the plane was going to ram directly into the wall, Ben pulled back with all his might on the stick. The *Eagle*, true to its name, took flight—briefly. As the plane bounced over the wall, the left wingtip brushed a chimneystack, and the craft was flung into a partial spin.

Canted at an angle, the plane plummeted toward the pavement. Ben opened the throttle wide, kicked in the superchargers, and fought madly to pull the plane out of its spin while at the same time leveling off the dive.

Moira gave voice to a scream, but in the rush of air and the cry of the tortured engines, Ben was not conscious of anything but his battle to save their lives. Finally, after seconds that seemed hours long, the power of the little plane made the difference. The wing struts creaked and moaned, and the coated fabric of the wings snapped and crackled, but the *Eagle* leveled off just twenty feet from the ground and then soared skyward.

Ben kept the throttle on full as he turned to the northeast, unaware of the gunfire that was aimed in vain at the *Eagle*. He maintained full speed until the engine temperature and oil pressure were at redline; then, with a sigh of relief, he unclenched his hands from the controls where they had been glued, white-knuckled, since the take-off.

Ben turned in his seat to check on his passenger. Moira sat quite still, her face pale and drawn; however, the smile of relief and admiration on her face spoke volumes.

Ben loosened the collar on his flight suit, set the controls, and reached for his Thermos. The water was still icy, and he thought that nothing had ever tasted so good as that drink of water. He handed it reluctantly back over his shoulder to Moira, leaned back in his harness, and smiled.

"Get settled in," he yelled back. "It's a long flight home." *Home – to Paradise,* he thought.

Jesse moved cautiously about the battlefield, hoping to find Paradisan injured in time to help them. The Cencom wounded that he came upon, even though they pleaded and begged for help, he dispatched with impunity. Twice he had refilled the clip in his pistol; thirty times the gun had bucked in his hand, and thirty lives had been snuffed out.

He had found thirteen Paradisans on the field. Seven of them had been children, the other six adults. Of that number, three had been dead – all children. The rage that had swelled up in Jesse's breast had overwhelmed him, and the Cencom wounded did well to beg forgiveness and help from the half-crazed demon that stalked the battlefield. Jesse had retained enough presence of mind to call for transport for the Paradisan wounded; then, his mind filled with scarlet bloodlust, he had gone hunting.

The carnage was horrible, and the stench of burnt and mutilated bodies was overpowering. Jesse walked among the still smoldering wreckage and was about to turn back when he saw a small huddle of bodies near one of the destroyed drone tanks. He ran toward it, pistol cocked and ready, when something else froze him in his tracks.

Snapping out of his momentary trance, he stumbled over corpses already piled for disposal until he reached that which had caught his attention so fully. He stopped abruptly before the familiar shape.

He recognized the hair, the lines and curves of the twisted body, the clothing. Stunned, he knelt down, turned the limp body over, and stared through welling tears into the glazed, dead eyes.

"MOIRA!" Jesse screamed.

Those who heard that eerie cry in the early evening twilight felt the hairs on their necks rise, and gooseflesh crawled unbidden upon their skin.

CHAPTER TWENTY

The 9mm bucked in Jesse's hand, and the large brown rat that had been creeping along the opposite wall exploded, scattering juicy fragments across the empty, weather-beaten room. A soft breeze from the single glassless window quickly dispersed the blue cloud of cordite smoke that rose from the barrel of the pistol.

"Take that, you bastard," Jesse rasped hoarsely through cracked and bleeding lips. He reached into the breast pocket of his jacket and brought out a fresh clip. Releasing the spent clip, he allowed it to clatter unheeded to the floor as he rammed home the fresh cartridges. He carefully laid the pistol on his lap, and for the hundredth time in the twenty-four hours since the battle with Cencom, Jesse contemplated suicide.

His red-rimmed eyes, bleary with lack of sleep, stared at the weapon with a calm and deadly fascination; as he slowly raised his hand to grasp the pistol, he imagined how the chromed steel would taste when he finally mustered the courage to place the barrel between his teeth.

Dazedly, almost trance-like, Jesse fondled the pistol. He stroked the barrel lovingly and lightly caressed the trigger. He flipped the safety switch on, then off, on, and off again. He heard the scuffling sound of another rat arriving to feed upon its brother, and fired two wild shots in the general direction, scattering plaster and wood from the wall but missing the rat.

Jesse laid the pistol on his lap once again, and as he stared at the deadly thing, tears ran oily and wet down his grimy cheeks. A huge sob wracked his body, and it was only then that he realized he was crying. *Don't cry!* he shouted silently.

Jesse stood slowly, his knees popping like corn from being frozen in the same position for so long. Wearily, the pistol dangling from one hand, he staggered to the window frame. Squinting against the early morning sunlight, he looked without interest at the landscape spread before him.

In the distance, smoke rose into the clear blue sky, and Jesse's eyes hesitated to look more than once in that direction. Paradise lay there, and he was not yet ready to think too much about what had happened and what was more than likely still being dealt with today.

Unbidden, images of the battle with Cencom filtered up from the depths of his mind where he had carefully hidden them for the past two days.

Once again he was in the war room, only now, when he fired upon the invading forces, it did not seem like a game. In his mind's eye he saw the faces of each and every one of attackers as he dealt death among them. Though it was impossible both when it occurred as well as now in his memories, he imagined that he could hear the anguished screams of his victims as he dispassionately mowed them down.

Jesse savagely shook his head, flinging tears asunder, in order to clear his mind. His breathing was rapid and shallow, and he was dizzy, partly from fatigue and hunger, and partly from the force of his conscience.

And there was Moira. Her face peered around every unguarded corner of his mind, smiling sadly at him. Until he had come across her frail, battered body, Jesse had not realized the depth of his feelings for her. She had been a good and comfortable friend to him, and their sexual contact had been enjoyable—no strings attached. Her mind had been of particular interest to him; she was a kindred spirit, a seeker of knowledge for the sake of that knowledge alone, and she reveled in passing that learning on to her students.

Jesse heaved a ragged sigh and leaned heavily upon the weathered windowsill. He shifted the weight of the pistol from his right hand to his left, and glanced at the tumbledown outbuildings nearby.

For years this abandoned farm had been one of Jesse's special hideaways, one of the few places besides his project room where he could go to be totally alone. He had especially enjoyed his time at the farm, though the large house threatened to come crashing down about him each time he visited.

None of the windows had any glass remaining in them but one— through some miracle, or perhaps just some oversight on the part of vandals, a large picture window in the front room had remained unscathed. It was grimy with years of accumulated dust and flyspecks, but the glass itself was intact. Jesse had, in the past, considered cleaning the glass, but thought better of it each time the urge struck him. If the glass were clean, his reasoning went, a casual passer-by would know that someone had been in the house, and it would have lost all of its allure for Jesse if another had violated its threshold.

Jesse yawned, stretching his stiff back muscles, for the first time realizing how truly tired he was. It was not merely the feeling of wanting sleep, however; this fatigue reached clear into his soul. His despair was total, his lust for life was gone, and a death compulsion was growing stronger with each passing minute. Jesse was tired—tired of life.

"This would be a good place to die," Jesse whispered. He transferred the pistol to his right hand again and turned decisively from the window. He looked at the empty room around him, sighed, and slumped against one cracked and peeling wall. He slid down the wall, feeling the jagged edges of plaster clutching at the fabric of his jacket. He set the pistol on his lap as his rump hit the floor, and reached for his small canvas rucksack.

It took a few moments for Jesse to locate his objective: a pencil and a scrap of paper. He felt that he owed it to Ben and his friends to leave them some final message, an explanation for his action. He raised one knee and with shaking hands smoothed the paper flat.

After several minutes of staring at the blank sheet of paper, Jesse gave up his attempt to find something meaningful to write. He forced his hand to stop trembling, and with careful deliberation, he wrote one word at the top of the sheet: MOIRA. He set the paper and pencil on top of his pack, lowered his leg to the floor, and placed his hand on the cool metal of the pistol.

With a faint smile on his bearded face, Jesse took one long, last look around the lonely room. He spied the remains of the dead rat and chuckled quietly.

"Here's looking at you, kid," he said to the splattered rodent, and with a sound that was half sob, half laughter, he turned the gun toward himself. He stared for a moment into the black shark's eye of the barrel, feeling himself beginning to fall into a bottomless pit of despair that he would never be able to climb out of. Jesse closed his eyes slowly, and raised the pistol to his mouth.

It tastes cool and smooth, he thought, *just as I imagined.* The bitter, metallic tang was reminiscent of putting an empty fork into one's mouth. *But, oh, a fork never filled my mouth like this,* Jesse mused.

He fumbled for a moment to find the trigger, not daring to open his eyes lest he lose his resolve. He had made this decision, and he meant to follow through. . .

Even if it's the last thing I do. He laughed as it occurred to him that this was his intent.

Jesse took a deep breath, exhaled, and slowly applied pressure to the trigger.

According to Ben's watch, it was nearing midnight when he made his final approach to Paradise. He had radioed ahead, not only to let the community know who was coming, but also to get an update on the battle's aftermath. A lot could have happened in the hours that he had been gone — none of it good. He had spoken directly to Anna, since she was in charge of security in his absence.

"Where in God's name have you been? " Anna demanded to know. *"We've all been worried sick since you disappeared earlier today."* Ben heard the strain in her voice, and knew that she had been concerned; he had his doubts about the amount of concern forthcoming from other quarters.

"I'll explain when I get down, Anna," Ben soothed. "It isn't the kind of thing that I care to discuss on an open frequency." Ben glanced over his shoulder at Moira, and returned to the task at hand. "I'll be in my office in about ten minutes. Get Jesse and meet me there."

After a long pause, Ben keyed his microphone and repeated his request. Anna, her voice sounding even more strained than before, finally replied.

"Ben — no one has seen Jesse since about 1630. He went out with the cleanup crews, and was last seen running across the north fields toward the boat landing." She drew a ragged breath, then continued with her report.

"Jeff Barker was the one who saw Jesse. He was busy attending to our wounded at the time, and just assumed that Jesse was running down a straggler. Later, we found Jesse's AK47 near the site."

Ben applied more throttle, and the *Eagle* jumped forward. *Dammit, Jesse,* he thought savagely, *you had better not have gone and gotten yourself killed!* Ben felt Moira's body shaking behind him; he had forgotten that she would hear the radio, and her reaction convinced him that she was legitimate.

"Have you instituted a search for him yet? Do you have any idea where he may have gone, or what happened to him?"

"No idea, Ben," Anna replied regretfully. *"We've had our hands full just tending to the wounded. We've recovered all the — bodies, and Jesse wasn't among them, so I suppose that's something. I planned to get a search party out at first light. It's been damned hectic around here, Ben! You've got a lot of explaining to do."* Anna signed off abruptly.

Ben clenched his jaw and concentrated on his landing approach to take his mind off of the knot of worry gnawing in his chest. He held the controls white-knuckled as he made an approach and landing nearly as incautious as the Dubuque landing had been.

The small plane was still rolling along at about ten miles an hour when Ben un-strapped and jumped from the framework. He stumbled along for a moment, and then regained his footing on the asphalt landing strip. Running at his top speed, Ben left a bewildered Moira behind as he raced toward the administration building.

"Damn you...Jesse," he wheezed, "you had...better... be okay." The full moon shone on Ben's face as he ran, highlighting the puffing cheeks and the trickle of tears falling from the corners of his eyes.

Major Michael C. Mantey, USAF, Serial Number 356-79-9077, heard the first deafening thunder of artillery in midmorning. He immediately stiffened, and his battle-trained instincts went into survival mode. The siren that followed seconds later told him that the small community was prepared for an attack, and he relaxed somewhat.

His jailer, a youth of about nineteen, jumped up from his seat and grabbed a rifle from the rack behind the desk. He pulled open a drawer, withdrew a box of cartridges, and emptied them into his pockets. He then ran to the outer door.

"What's happening?" Mantey shouted. He was more than curious, for he had no desire to be caught sitting in this cage like a rat in a trap, unarmed and helpless.

The youth paused and turned to look at him, his eyes shifting nervously. "War," he said quietly, and slipped from the room.

War? Mantey thought. *Can it be that the Central Command has decided to attack this community?* He pulled on his full lower lip thoughtfully and tried to see what tactical advantage Cencom might realize in gaining control of this area. There was the obvious one, of course: if Cencom took control, then it would be that much harder for his provisional government to step in and regain their lost control. On the other hand...

Automatic gunfire in the distance upset the Major's train of thought, and he spent the next six hours trying desperately to tell by the ebb and flow of fighting just what the hell was going on.

Ben read the list through bleary eyes:

CASUALTIES:

Frederic Gillingham, Michael Johnson*, Eugene Martens*, Jack Barker, Marty Hawkins, Len Tyllier, Paul Anton+, Carol Barton, Gregory Mitchell, Suzanne Post*, Frank Post, Sally Zapranoff+, John Zapranoff, Dennis Stanton, James Shumaker*, Susan Wildman, Victor McGraw, Ernest McMahon, Alice Quade, Carl Knezel, Donald Isbell, Dana Isbell+, Jack Carlson*, Henry Club, Joseph Detra, Charles Devoe, Mark Engler, Robert Fargoh, Richard Fargoh, Barbra Ertel, Jenna Gerke*, David Hawthorne, William Hugo, Nathan Ingraham, Gina Bowers*, John Bussa, Kenneth Jones, Nancy Jones*, Kenneth Jones, Jr.*, Troy Kannel, Kurt Jorgensen, William Weaver, Nora Kamiski+, Richard Londo, Bette Little*, Kevin Mackey, Mitchell Flood*, Timothy Stone, Aba Mufat+, Michael Miller, Karen Mueller, Thomas McBride*, Francis O'Brian, Alan Novacek, Gregory Norris, Harold Pankow+, Bradley Renner, Vera St. John

*Denotes Children

+Denotes Noncombatants

Ben set the list down on the desk and rubbed his burning eyes. *So many names, so many faces.* He looked reluctantly at the haggard, pale face before him. "What else?" he asked.

"I think that covers it, Ben," Anna stated as she finished her update on the aftermath of the battle with Cencom. She had already been brought up to date by Ben concerning his activities in Dubuque; she had been relieved to hear of the demise of Dwight Cochran, but she still had many unanswered questions and unresolved doubts about Moira's involvement with the Cencom leader. "We have fifty-eight dead, eleven of them children, six other noncombatants. Twenty-one wounded, six of them in serious condition.

"Property losses were minimal, mostly confined to the dam and motor pool areas, with some fire damage to trees and crops. I've got a crew working on the dam right now, repairing the damage to the generators. We're running only emergency power right now, but I expect the main generators to be back online by late tomorrow.

"We lost the tower and supply depot on Duenorth—that was the first thing they hit. I've doubled ground patrols in that area pending erection of an emergency tower." Anna took a deep breath, handed another sheet to Ben with the figures on it, and stared wearily at him.

Ben pushed his hands through his hair, and let them drop to the desk.

He tried desperately to find in himself some way to justify the great loss of life among the Paradisans—his friends!--but the true realization of their losses would not truly hit home for some time to come. It would be several days before things were organized enough to get an accurate assessment of what was left of the population and where the greatest needs were. And it would take much longer than that to get used to the empty streets and fields where only yesterday the missing faces had walked, talked, loved, and played.

"Doc must be up to his neck in patients without Marty there to help out," Ben muttered, half to himself. He was silent for a moment, and allowed his burning eyes to drop shut once more. When he reopened them, some of his old spark of decisiveness and command gleamed from them, and he straightened in his chair.

"Anna, I want you to locate Jeff Barker and 'Rissa Peters and send them to Doc in the infirmary," Ben ordered. "Jeff will need something to keep his mind off the—loss—of his father, and he'll feel better with 'Rissa around. Both of them are old enough to be of some help, and if I recall correctly, both have taken the basic first aid and CPR courses.

"Once you have them settled, gather up a detail to begin preparations for a mass burial for our friends. Have Brian get the backhoe out of storage and begin digging a trench in the Great Meadow." He paused for a moment as he mulled over other problems.

"See if you can round up someone with religious training to perform a burial service. Yes, I know that you have the training, but this is too personal. I want someone who was not one of us to do this. I think there's an old preacher in Tomahawk that we may be able to convince to come here."

Anna scribbled some brief notes on her pad, then looked with hollow eyes at her beloved. When he did not continue, she cleared her throat and broached the subject that neither of them had mentioned since Ben's return.

"What about Jesse? We don't know that he's dead, and if he isn't, he may be out there somewhere, wounded and needing our help."

Ben's eyes flashed briefly, only to be replaced by weariness and despair. His voice still held the strength of command, however, and when he stood he appeared fresh and potent.

"I'm going to start combing the area at first light," he stated simply. "Until then, I have other details to take care of—what kind of leader would I be if I let personal preference dictate my actions?

"I want Isaac to take one of the ultralights to coordinate the search from the air. I'll need six horses, fully packed, and some of the older children to assist in the search. I'll be in the cargo hovercraft, just in case we need to transport Jesse back in a hurry." Ben smiled suddenly. "We'll find him, Anna, I know we will! He's my brother!"

"I'll arrange everything, Ben," Anna said gently. "Why don't you try to get some sleep? It's 0230 already, and dawn is at 0500."

"Sure, I'll get some shuteye. There are just a few more things that I have to do." Ben looked at Anna's red, bleary eyes. "I want you to get some sleep, too; you look like death warmed over. After you make those arrangements for me, okay?" he added apologetically. He walked over to Anna, kissed her lightly, and turned toward the central console. "See you at five."

Anna watched as Ben disappeared through the war room entrance, then turned to leave the office. As she reached the door, the full import of the previous day's events hit her like a train at full throttle, and she collapsed against the doorjamb, huge sobs wracking her body as she grieved for what they had lost that day in Paradise.

As soon as Ben hit the floor of the war room, he headed for the main computer console. Too tired to type, he keyed the voice recognition circuit and began to give instructions to the mainframe.

"Walker, Benjamin—Access One," he said clearly.

"RECOGNIZE ACCESS ONE," the computer responded in a monotone. "HELLO, BEN. READY FOR PROGRAM."

Ben thought furiously for a moment, then began. "Access tactical log: four-sixteen-two-oh-two-two. Run. Access personal log: 412022 through present. Run. Access security log: 4162022. Run." Ben waited for several seconds, his fingers drumming nervously on the desktop.

"ACCESS COMPLETE. WHAT NEXT, BEN?" The computer almost sounded anxious to continue, and Ben raised his eyebrows in suspicion. The computer had never before seemed so life-like. With a shrug that caused jolts of pain to shoot through his back and neck, he decided that it was just his mood carrying over to the machine, and he went on with his task.

"Cross-reference all log entries. Query: could loss of life been minimized through utilization of alternate tactics? Run." Ben held his breath as he awaited the computer's analysis. He stopped the twitching of his fingers, and closed his eyes.

"ANALYSIS COMPLETE," the computer stated, the voice startling Ben from a light doze.

"State analysis," Ben commanded, stifling a yawn.

"TACTICAL ANALYSIS CONFIRMS POSITIVE UTILIZATION OF AVAILABLE WEAPONRY AND MANPOWER IN SURPRISE ATTACK OF SIXTEEN APRIL TWO THOUSAND SEVENTEEN. CORRELATION OF PERSONAL AND SECURITY LOGS CONFIRM ANALYSIS.

"FACTORS CONTRIBUTING TO POSITIVE UTILIZATION ARE: EARLY TRAINING OF CITIZENRY; AVAILABILITY OF ADEQUATE WEAPONRY WITH EMPHASIS ON REMOTE CONTROL WEAPONS AND PERSONAL AUTOMATIC WEAPONS; USE OF HOLOGRAPHIC CAMOUFLAGE PROJECTORS.

"ESTIMATE PARADISE CASUALTIES AT FIFTY-THREE PLUS/MINUS TEN PERCENT. END ANALYSIS."

Ben sighed; the computer was accurate, but it was also unfeeling as it confirmed the deaths of so many. "Estimate casualties without use of holographic projectors. Run."

"ESTIMATE PARADISE CASUALTIES WITHOUT USE OF HOLOGRAPHIC PROJECTORS AT NINETY-SEVEN PLUS/MINUS TEN PERCENT."

"Estimate casualties without use of remote control weapons. Run."

"ESTIMATE PARADISE CASUALTIES WITHOUT REMOTE CONTROL WEAPONS AT ONE HUNDRED THIRTY-NINE PLUS/MINUS TEN PERCENT. ADDENDUM: LOSS OF PARADISE AUTONOMY EIGHTY-SEVEN PERCENT."

Ben whistled softly to himself, but not without a small measure of satisfaction. It seemed that his forethought had been of some use after all.

"Estimate losses without use of holographic projectors, remote control weapons, and personal automatic weapons. Run."

The computer was silent for nearly a minute, and Ben was about ready to rephrase his query when the machine spoke.

"ESTIMATE TOTAL LOSS OF PARADISE POPULATION PLUS/MINUS TEN PERCENT. ADDENDUM: DESTRUCTION OF PARADISE NINETY-FOUR PERCENT." Stated in the computer's flat tones, it did not sound like much of an epitaph.

Ben slumped back in his chair, his exhausted mind attempting to grasp the notion of his community barren and lifeless. Even worse was the thought of Paradise being perverted by a filthy mob of fanatical madmen.

"Print analysis. Run. Wake up 0430 today. Run. End program. Good night."

The laser printer hummed for several seconds, ejected a sheet of paper, and was still. "GOOD NIGHT, BEN. ALARM SET FOR 0430."

Ben grinned, closed his eyes, and was instantly asleep.

Jesse opened his eyes with a start, for a moment not sure where he was. After blinking his puffy eyelids to clear them, he looked about himself at the dingy, abandoned room. His rear-end was stiff and numb, and when he shifted his weight the tingle of blood rushing back into the starved tissue was exquisitely painful. He looked down at the floor and saw two things simultaneously: the 9mm pistol, and a small scrap of paper with the name MOIRA scrawled almost illegibly.

He gasped as a fresh wave of despair ran through him, and the memory of what he had been doing came back to him. *Am I dead?* he asked himself.

He could clearly remember bringing the pistol to his mouth, and thought that he could recall pulling the trigger. His mouth had a faintly metallic taste to it, and he turned his head and spat.

That was when he saw the rat. Huge and brown-black, it was at least eighteen inches long without the thick tail. It was squatting not three feet from Jesse, its whiskers quivering ever so slightly as its beady eyes stared into his.

"Damn!" Jesse shouted hoarsely, and he jumped to his feet and backed away from the rodent. The rat did not move, but continued to crouch against the baseboard and look hungrily at Jesse.

Jesse moved to pick up the pistol, stiffly bending over while keeping his eyes on the horrible creature. His hand was only inches from the gun when the rat turned and scurried out the door. Jesse scooped up the pistol, holstered it, and went to the window.

The sun was rising above the horizon east of him, and Jesse quickly deduced that he had been asleep for nearly sixteen hours. Smoke was still rising from the direction of Paradise, and he briefly wondered what was causing it. Was the community burning? Had the Cencoms returned to finish them off? Strangely enough, Jesse found that a part of him still cared.

His attention was caught by some noise closer by, and he turned his gaze in that direction. About a quarter of a mile away, he saw several figures on horseback riding slowly through the sparsely wooded area. He could make out green fatigues and rifles, but could not, at that distance, discern any faces.

Suddenly, he had the urge to leave the upstairs room. His feet seemed to move of their own accord, and he picked up his half-empty canteen as he left the room. He made his way carelessly down the rickety stairs that led to the ground floor. Here were the tattered remnants of furniture and belongings that had once been the pride and joy of some unknown farm family. He walked to the large picture window and wiped his sleeve against it, clearing a ragged streak of grime from the quarter-inch plate glass.

Somewhere in the back of his mind two conflicting ideas stirred, and he examined his motivations as he removed his heavy jacket. He emptied the pockets onto the floor and poured the contents of the canteen onto the dusty fabric.   One part of him wanted to clean the picture window as a way of making sure that his body would be found before the rats had a chance to devour it. This was the same part of him that kept silently screaming Moira's name like some heathen chant that corresponded to the beating of his heart. *moiraMoira**MOIRA*** it went, reminding him of the sound of war drums in an old Western.

The other half of his mind, in a more rational manner, justified his action as a method of ensuring that someone would find him before he killed himself. This part of him hoped fervently that it would be a Cencom patrol. He smiled grimly at that, and for the first time in his life, he actually looked forward to inflicting violence on another human being.

Jesse stirred from his reverie and saw that the entire inner surface of the glass was clean, the muddy residue covering his sodden jacket with a glistening wet paste.

He leisurely walked outside and went around the porch to the window. He squinted at the reflection of the sun in the glass and saw his own mirror image cast back to him in the glass. The sun must have been hitting him just right, because in the glass it appeared that he had a halo of brilliantly white hair—but that couldn't be, and in his foggy state of mind, he shrugged it off as an anomaly. He shook his head, looked at the glass, and ignored the face staring back at him.

A sign, he thought, *I need to leave some kind of sign.*

Jesse considered for a moment what type of message he could leave on the glass, then began to write in the dirt with his jacket wrapped around his hand. He had to jump to reach the higher portions of the window, but finally he was done.

He stepped back, wiped sweat from his face, and admired his handiwork. In rough, neat letters, the window read

JESSE WAS HERE

That ought to do it, he thought with a faint grin. He walked back into the house and, rather than climb back up the stairs, he sat on the floor beneath the window. He struggled with the holster for a moment, then got the pistol free.

I can wait a little longer to die.

"Come and get me," he whispered, but he wasn't sure who he wanted to come.

A loud roaring awakened Jesse, and he immediately hunched below the windowsill. He heard voices shouting nearby, but couldn't make out any words over the din.

Carefully, he raised his head just high enough to peer over the sill. He saw brush moving about a hundred yards from the house, but he still couldn't see anything.

Abruptly, the roaring ceased. Something about the noise was familiar, but Jesse dismissed any speculation as a shot rang out. He threw himself to the floor and began to inch his way across the moth-eaten carpet to the half-open door.

As he reached the open portal and looked outside, another shot was fired, and Jesse saw the muzzle flash less than a hundred feet away. He took hasty aim and fired two shots into the dense foliage. He was certain that the shots missed—initially, because the chance of hitting an unseen target at that range was slim to none; his belief was confirmed when several rounds shattered into the door above his head.

Jesse rolled away from the doorway and made an effort to control his breathing. The sound of his heart hammering in his ears gradually diminished, and he looked at the holes in the door with an almost complete lack of interest.

Several more shots slammed into the door as Jesse watched, and he heard someone shouting commands in the distance. The voice was distinctive and familiar, but he quickly dismissed that thought as wishful thinking. He surely didn't know any of the Cencoms, and would not recognize any of their voices at that distance even if he did.

It was strange. Jesse had never doubted that the group converging upon the farmhouse was Cencom soldiers; had he not been under so much strain, he may have noticed little details that would have made the next few hours easier to deal with. . .

Jesse sat quietly for several minutes, unsure of his next move. He was torn between running out the front door firing and sneaking out the back way.

He didn't get the chance to do either one. As he was sneaking a peek out of the window, he heard a scraping, slithering noise behind him. He ignored it, thinking that it was just another rat, not bothering to turn around until he heard the drawing of a bolt on the rifle aimed point-blank at his head.

He began to look around when a hoarse voice ordered him to freeze. "Drop your gun, dirt bag," the man rasped, "or I'll drop you right here and now." Jesse complied without delay, allowing the 9mm to clatter to the floor; he had heard the death in the man's voice. Frantically, his survival instincts temporarily overpowering his death wish, Jesse's mind raced to find a way out of his predicament.

"Stand up, put your hands behind your head, and turn around," the man ordered. Jesse began to rise from his knees to a crouch, picking up his canteen as his body shielded it from view.

Jesse was still bent double as he whirled, throwing the heavy canteen at his captor. He followed through with the turn, throwing himself out of the line of fire in the same motion.

The canteen struck the man square in the face, and the rifle discharged. Jesse felt the bullet whiz past his face and smelled burning hair as the muzzle flash singed his beard. He rolled across the floor away from his assailant, and went for the door. He was only inches from freedom when a new voice cried out, "Don't shoot! It's Jesse!"

At the sound of the woman's voice, Jesse froze. Slowly, he got to his feet and stood facing out the door, his eyes glazed and unseeing. Tears rolled down his dirty cheeks, and sobs shook his body as he stood framed in the open doorway. He didn't turn around, and he made no move to leave the house.

He was dimly aware of footsteps approaching him from behind, but ignored them until he was grasped roughly by one shoulder and spun around. Tears blurred his vision, and he looked down at his feet, blinking rapidly to clear his eyes.

"By God, it is you, Jess! We've been looking for you for the past two days!" The thick voice of the man shook with excitement, and Jesse was astonished when he was grabbed in a bear hug and swung off of his feet. He was set down moments later, and the man eyed him with suspicion. "Don't you recognize me, Jess?"

Jesse turned his gaze upon the other man, and for a moment was confused. The haggard, red-rimmed eyes and unkempt hair served to make his exhausted mind think that he was staring into a mirror, for that is how he imagined that he appeared. Then a dim spark of his old self flared up, and he whispered, "Ben?"

"It's me, Jesse," the older Walker said quietly.

Another figure walked out of the shadows to stand silently beside Ben for a minute.

"Me, too," Moira Doyle said.

As Jesse fainted Ben caught him and gently, carefully lowered him to the floor.

CHAPTER TWENTY-ONE

The hovercraft sped along Duewest Road in a cloud of dust, and the few who saw it pass could tell by the expression on Ben Walker's face that his search had been successful. A ragged cheer went up as the craft turned into the central plaza and headed for the infirmary.

Overhead, an ultra light circled in for a landing; its pilot, Isaac Peters, smiled brightly as he struggled to manage the controls of the tiny plane.

Ben brought the hovercraft to a halt in the yard outside the small hospital, and he and Moira hoisted the prostrate form of Jesse onto a stretcher and carried him through clouds of dust up the wooden ramp. As they entered the ward, Doc Riley bustled over to them and shot a questioning glance at Ben.

"I think he's okay, Doc," Ben said with a huge grin on his face. "He's exhausted, dirty, and suffering from shock, but other than that he's all right!"

"I'll be the judge of that, *Doctor* Walker," Doc snapped sarcastically. "Just let me be examining him now, and we'll see." The old doctor looked down at the prone figure on the stretcher, and his initial shock quickly passed.

Jesse's hair and beard — normally a dull, dark brown — were now totally white. He appeared to have lost a couple of pounds, though that could have been attributed to the stress fatigue of the last few days, and his face was haggard and lined. He had been gone just over two days, but Jesse appeared ten, maybe twenty years older than before his disappearance.

Doc completed his examination, jotted a brief note on his clipboard, and turned to Ben. "Well, Ben, it seems that your diagnosis was correct — but I'm thinking that you left out the most important part." Doc paused for a moment, frowning thoughtfully. "Look at your brother, Ben; do you not see anything amiss with his appearance?"

Ben looked critically at Jesse's unconscious form, and was shocked to see what he had not even noticed in his exultation at finding his brother alive.

"Jesus, Doc — what happened to him? Why is his hair white? What happened?" Ben looked ill and ready to faint himself, and the doctor and Moira guided him to an empty bed. Ben sat heavily on the edge of the mattress, and put his head in his hands.

Doc sat down next to Ben, and in soothing tones began trying to explain what he judged to be the cause of Jesse's remarkable metamorphosis.

"I've seen but one other case like this, Ben, and that was a veteran of the Vietnam war. 'Tis a kind of 'shell shock', a bizarre reaction to fear or extreme stress caused by an imbalance in the body's chemistry. It's rare enough, and the case I studied was permanent—but that's not what worries me the most. I need to know what caused such a shock of major proportions; there may have been permanent damage caused to the lad's mind."

"Are you trying to say that Jesse may have been driven mad?" Ben asked incredulously. "What could have been so bad?" Ben shook his head in disbelief, and look at his brother with deep concern.

What happened to you out there, Jesse? Is your mind intact, or are you lost to us forever? Ben frowned and turned his gaze upon the doctor for help.

"I canna say what it is that caused this, Ben," Reilly said, "but I'm thinking that it would be wise to keep Jesse sedated for a day or two—at least until he has regained his strength. I've a feeling that he'll be needing it to deal with whatever happened to him."

"No drugs, Doc," a hoarse voice whispered.

The three people assembled there turned as one. Jesse was propped up on one elbow, and his color looked much better. "No drugs," he repeated to the doctor, but his bloodshot eyes were riveted to Moira's face. "Water? Can I have a glass of water?"

"Marissa, get me a glass of water, and be quick about it!" Doc roared. He stood up and began to make his way over to Jesse, but his patient waved him away.

"Ben?" The older Walker rose unsteadily to his feet, walked over to Jesse, and squatted down next to the stretcher. He watched Jesse warily, as if expecting some manifestation of insanity to show itself at any moment.

"What can I do for you, Jess?"

Jesse's eyes finally left Moira's face, and he stared intently at Ben. "Is that really Moira?" he whispered. "She's not dead?"

Ben looked puzzled as he slowly turned to look at Moira. "It's her, Jess, and she's very much alive, of that I can assure you."

Jesse reached out and weakly grasped his brother's forearm. "Thanks, Ben." Jesse collapsed back onto the stretcher, and his eyes fell shut.

"Here's your water," Marissa said, and the three adults jumped.

"So, he's going to be all right then?" Anna's concern was real as she queried Ben, and she reached out to push a few stray hairs from her lover's forehead. Ben looked much better after a solid five hours of sleep, and she snuggled up to him, pulling the heavy blanket closer around her nude body.

"Doc says that he'll be up and about by tomorrow morning if he feels like it; however, we still don't know what caused the shock to his system that has changed his appearance so drastically. You'll be shocked when you see him, Anna; he looks like he's fifty or sixty years old!"

Ben sat up, positioning his head against the headboard and lighting a cigarette. "After Jesse fell asleep, Doc hooked him up to an IV to replenish his fluids, and snuck a sedative into it, just to help Jesse rest. God knows he looks like he could use it."

"You said that he asked about Moira—if she was dead?" Anna took the cigarette from Ben's fingers and puffed slowly as Ben nodded.

"The strange thing is," Anna continued, "I have several reports of others seeing her killed, but I dismissed them when I saw Moira arrive with you from your foray into Dubuque. Now, I wonder—somehow I can't see Jesse believing a report like that without checking it out for himself; he was assisting with the pickup detail just before he disappeared."

Ben sat bolt upright and shot out of the bed, pausing only long enough to pull on a pair of boxer shorts. He ran across the catwalk to his office, turned on his terminal, and entered a command. Within seconds, a list of names was printing on the screen, and he scanned it carefully as he felt Anna come up behind him.

"What are you looking for, Ben?"

"There—look!" Ben pointed at the list, and near the bottom was Moira's name.

"What list is that?" Anna asked. She didn't understand the significance of the reference, and looked to Ben for an explanation.

"This is the updated casualty list, Anna. Note that the total is fifty-nine, not fifty-eight. The additional name is Moira's, and it was just added yesterday." Ben punched in another command, and a short paragraph appeared on the screen:

ADDITION TO PARADISE CASUALTY LIST: MOIRA DOYLE

BODY LOCATED 4-17-2022 IN GROUP OF ENEMY CASUALTIES
POSITIVE I.D. MADE BY RILEY
INTERMENT ORDER: MASS BURIAL, 4-19-2022...END

"But—how can that be?" Anna asked with a frown. "She's here, and obviously very much alive!" She walked to the railing, leaned her elbows on it, and stared into the empty space above the living room below. "It would seem that we have a mystery on our hands."

"Yeah," Ben said grimly as he printed out the computer entry, "and I know where we can get the answers."

Moira felt a hand grasp her gently on the arm, and she roused from her slumber slowly. She opened her eyes, blinked to clear the sleep from them, and saw the creased and smiling face of Doc Riley looking down at her.

"Wake up, young lady," he said. "It's Ben wanting to see you, and he sent along an escort." He gestured with a nod in the direction of the door, and Moira followed his gaze.

Isaac stood in the doorway, his head almost touching the top of the jamb. He flashed a hesitant grin at Moira, and beckoned her over.

"Ben's in an awful rush this morning, what with the funeral and all, and he has everyone up early. I guess that you're no exception," he said apologetically.

Moira smoothed her auburn hair as she walked over to Isaac. She noticed with a frown that he was wearing a holstered .44 Magnum. She herself was unarmed, and had been since her arrival in Paradise three days earlier.

"Good morning, Isaac," she greeted him, deliberately trying to keep her voice light and cheerful. "I don't suppose that I have time to use the bathroom, do I?"

Isaac's laughter boomed through the hospital, and Doc looked up with an expression of disapproval at the noise. Isaac thumped Moira gently on the shoulder and smiled. "I guess you can take the time for that, Moira. Hell, even Ben himself can't mess with the call of Nature."

Moira walked down the hall to the bathroom, casting a last, longing glance at the sleeping form of Jesse. Her mind was awhirl with a thousand reasons why Ben would want to see her, but the unobtrusive use of Isaac as an armed escort narrowed the range of possibilities to just one.

How can I make them see the truth? I don't think that after what happened just a few days ago any of them will be willing to forgive and forget – even thought I had no part in it!

Damn Dwight Cochran! she swore silently.

Moira used the toilet, then looked in the mirror as she rinsed the sleep from her face. Her green eyes flashed back at her, not with the fear she felt but with the spiteful, evil gleam that she had seen in two sets of eyes for as long as she could remember: the eyes of her father, and those of her twin sister – Mary Doyle Cochran.

She took a deep breath, opened the door, and walked out to rejoin Isaac. She noticed with detachment that he was no longer smiling.

Jesse dreamed.

He moved cautiously about, searching through the victims of the battle, hoping to find injured Paradisans in time to save them.

The Cencoms he put out of their misery shot one in the head brains and blood spraying out Paradisans he had transported to the clinic too late for little Suzie her body torn and mangled could barely recognize it.

The carnage was horrible, and the stench of burnt and mutilated *Paul Anton roasted smelling of meat fuel the motor pool shelled* bodies was overpowering. Jesse was about to turn around when, in the distance, he saw something *NO!* that froze him in his tracks.

Snapping out of his trance he ran, stumbling over the corpses *slippery sticky* piled for disposal, until he arrived at his goal. Stopping suddenly, he saw *don't want to see DON'T WANT TO SEE* a familiar shape. He recognized the hair *her hair* , the shape of the body *her body* , the clothing. Stunned, he knelt down *blood on my KNEES!* , turned the body over *DON'T WANT TO SEE!* , and stared directly into the dead *noNoNO!* face of his love –

"MOIRA!" Jesse screamed, and Doc Riley ran over to the bed.

CHAPTER TWENTY-TWO

Ben sat stolidly behind his desk, staring blindly at the papers before him. They were the accumulated reports concerning the mysterious and disturbing activities of Moira Doyle and her deceased double. Although not incriminating in themselves, the reports did question her relationship to the Central Command.

Ben knew that the forthcoming interrogation would not be pleasant; however, he had to know the truth, and no matter how personally unpleasant that truth might be, he had to be prepared to make a decision based upon that information — and live with the consequences. There was no problem if Moira were found innocent of any complicity; the real crux of the matter lie in what to do if she was found guilty.

As Paradise's leader, Ben's loyalties should be with Paradise; as Jesse's brother, his loyalty lie with him, also. Ben shook his head in confused desperation. *How can I resolve this conflict? If Moira is guilty of consorting with the enemy, I could have her executed for treason. That could drive Jesse over the brink into insanity; however, if I don't have her executed, Paradise will probably vote to carry out that sentence anyway — with me added to the invitation list for that necktie party.*

Ben knew that the only possible solution was in deceit. If Moira was guilty of treason, Jesse would probably want nothing more to do with her, and the sentence could be carried out with impunity. If, however, Jesse still loved and wanted her, Ben could use his power to delay the execution long enough for the two of them to leave Paradise.

Ben sighed and reached across the cluttered desk for his bottle. Once only an infrequent drinker, the bottle was becoming his constant companion — he was drinking nearly a liter of liquor a day, and it showed in his mood swings and his present sluggish thinking processes. He drank down about three ounces without bothering with a glass, then replaced the cap. Glancing at his watch, he reminded himself that Isaac would be arriving soon with the object of his concern. He deliberately took another long pull on the bottle, then his it in a desk drawer. His brow furrowed as a thought occurred to him, and he activated his computer console.

"Walker, Benjamin — Access one."

"RECOGNIZE ACCESS ONE.   HELLO, BEN.   READY FOR PROGRAM."

"Access security log, special override code 7280906."   Ben waited patiently for the several seconds it took the computer to load the secure files.

"ACCESS CONFIRMED. READY FOR PROGRAM."

"Probability analysis," Ben instructed.   "Subject: Moira Doyle, Paradisan.   Analyze all information on file about subject; list possible explanations for subject activities as outlined during Cencom attack of sixteen April, two-oh-two-two.   Speculation on presence at Cencom headquarters. Order analysis by decreasing likelihood. Reject all answers with less than one percent probability. Hard copy. Run."

"UNDERSTOOD. PROCESSING ANALYSIS."

Ben lit a cigarette and waited.   The vocal circuits that Jesse had installed in the computer were a real time saver, and Ben was glad in retrospect that he had allowed his brother to have his way in regard to that bit of hardware. Jesse had argued that if you spoke to a machine nicely and treated it well, it would in turn perform better for you.   Although Ben privately felt that this bit of anthropomorphism was a bunch of nonsense, it was helpful to be able to program the computer without using the keyboard. It also made it handier to alter programming over the phone and even by radio in situations when a keyboard was neither available nor expedient.

The hum of the laser printer broke Ben's reverie. He watched in anticipation as three sheets passed quickly through the eject slot and into the tray. Reaching over the corner of his desk, Ben removed the printouts and dropped them on the desktop.

The first page was simply a copy of Ben's instructions, less codes. The second listed the parameters the computer had assumed within its pre-set limits. The final page—indeed, the last few lines—gave the meat of the issue. Ben read:

SUBJECT GUILTY OF COMPLICITY   92% +/- 3%

SUBJECT INNOCENT — DOUBLE GUILTY 61% +/- 3%

SUBJECT INNOCENT — COINCIDENCE   22% +/- 3%

SUBJECT FRAMED BY DOUBLE   9% +/- 1%

SUBJECT DECEASED — DOUBLE ALIVE   2% +/- 1%

CONCLUSION BASED UPON AVAILABLE DATA AS WELL AS

PSYCHOLOGICAL PROFILE OF SUBJECT IS AS FOLLOWS:

SUBJECT DOYLE GUILTY OF PRIOR KNOWLEDGE OF CENCOM ATTACK.

Ben re-read the final line several times before questioning the computer.

"Query: probability of certainty?"

"PROBABILITY NINETY-SIX POINT SEVEN PERCENT PLUS OR MINUS ZERO POINT NINE PERCENT."

Ben mulled that over. *Moira knew we were going to be hit!* Jesse would never believe that; in fact, Ben was having a hard time coming to grips with it himself.

"Query: probability of Moira Doyle being unable to communicate prior knowledge of Cencom attack to Paradise leaders sufficiently in advance of attack to allow for further preparations."

The computer, silent except for its cooling fans, said nothing for a moment. When it did speak, the abruptness of its tone startled Ben.

"PROBABILITY OF SUBJECT INABILITY TO COMMUNICATE WARNING NINETY-NINE POINT EIGHT SEVEN PERCENT. MARGIN OF ERROR NEGLIGIBLE."

Good, Ben thought with a measure of relief. *That means that although she knew, she couldn't tell us. Maybe there is a way to get her out of this mess intact.*

A knock on the door signaled Isaac's arrival with Moira. Ben buzzed to let them in, then called down to the lobby and ordered that he not be disturbed.

The door opened and Moira entered, followed a few paces behind by the imposing bulk of her escort. Although Isaac was not actually holding his big revolver, his hand was resting lightly on the butt of the massive .44 Magnum. He was alert and wary, and his brown eyes sent a questioning glance Ben's way. Ben shook his head almost imperceptibly, and Isaac relaxed a little.

"Do you want me to stick around, Ben?"

Ben shook his head in negation. "I think Moira and I will be all right, Ike, but if you'd wait outside I'd appreciate it."

"Whatever you say, Ben." Isaac exited the office with an almost pitying look at Moira, closed the door, and took a seat on the bench in the hall.

Ben took a few moments to study the woman before him. She was a slight, very attractive young lady, and Ben understood from the slight stirring in his loins what had attracted Jesse to her. She was of a pale complexion, and her freckles stood out on her milky skin. Her copper-colored hair hung in loose, soft waves about her almond-shaped face, and her emerald green eyes pierced Ben with a return look of appraisal. As she took her seat, Ben noticed the slender waist, taut thighs, and shapeliness of her calves before they were hidden behind the edge of the desk, and a faint smile played briefly upon his lips. His eyes returned to her face, and the look of resignation that those pretty features wore. It was as if she knew that she had lost control of her destiny, and that her fate was in his hands. It was sad to see such a desolate look in one so young and attractive, but Ben knew that he must be even harsher than she could expect before they had seen this crisis through.

"Get comfortable," Ben said, his voice turning a normal politeness into something just less than a command. He waited while Moira fidgeted in her seat, taking the brief respite to clear some of the clutter from his desk. He turned on his conference recorder, and turned to face Moira.

"I'm going to get right down to business," Ben began quietly. "You were in the Cencom attack headquarters during the thwarted invasion of Paradise, apparently without guard and for no discernible reason.

"A woman who could be your double — who was mistaken for you — was killed in the attack, fighting on the side of the Cencom forces.

"You are hereby formally accused of treason and espionage; of having foreknowledge of the attack; of withholding said information from the leaders of Paradise, thereby indirectly causing the deaths of over fifty of our citizens.

"As the leader of the Paradise council, my duty is clear: If you are found guilty of these charges, I will appoint a squad to execute you for treason under the rules of war. Have you anything to say in your own behalf?"

Moira's pallor heightened, and beads of sweat appeared on her forehead. She looked terrified, as well she might; Ben had just pronounced her death sentence if she could not convince him of her innocence.

"B-ben," she stammered hoarsely, "I know that the circumstances all point to what you've accused me of, but I am not the enemy. I love Paradise, and I love your brother! How can you even think that I would betray you?"

"Then why did you take a chance that Cencom would destroy us? Why did you keep information from us that would have kept fifty-eight people — my friends — from dying?"

Moira took a deep breath, and allowed her eyes to fall shut with more than physical fatigue. "I can explain," she whispered, "but it will be more than you can believe."

"Try me," Ben said gruffly.

"When I came to Paradise last year, I was a fugitive from the Central Command. It was hard for me to live with them chasing and hounding me day and night. You see, I was — valuable to them.

"I thought that if I went in with you and Jesse that I would be safe from them.

"A couple of weeks ago, I went out for a ride — I needed some time away to think, mostly about Jesse. I was waylaid by a couple of Cencom scouts who took my horse and provisions, and arranged for my transport to Dubuque.

"While I was gone, they substituted my double, hoping to get a line on the soft spots in Paradise. She was working directly under Cochran — " Moira spat the name " — as a spy. Her assignment was to be me, and to use my standing in the community not only to search out our weaknesses, but to kill you and Jesse if possible.

"Cochran must have felt that you were the only ones here capable of leading Paradise into battle with any chance of success."

Moira paused, then asked meekly for something to drink. Ben got up and went to his small icebox, getting out a jar of cider for Moira and a beer for himself. He returned to his chair and passed the jar across the desk to Moira. She murmured her thanks, and after a long drink, continued with her story.

"The spy managed to get a message through to Cochran; she used the pretense of going to Tomahawk to set up the exchange school, and was met by a helicopter just north of Paradise. The information that she brought to Dubuque convinced him that you would be an easy target. He ordered the attack to commence immediately, and the rest you know. One thing I'd like to know Ben; how did you manage to defeat Cencom when you were outnumbered so greatly?"

Ben gave her a stern look. "Because we were able to keep some secrets, despite having a spy among us.

"I'm not sure that I believe your story, Moira. I'd like to ask you a few questions for clarification.

"First, why were you not a prisoner in Dubuque if you were so important to them?

"Second, who is the so-called 'double'? The spy?

"And finally, how do you know so much about Cencom and Dwight Cochran?"

Moira smiled tightly and told him.

"I wasn't locked up because there was nowhere to go. I was, however, under 'house arrest', and a guard was assigned to me ensure that I didn't try to leave or get a message out to you somehow.

"You see, Cochran didn't trust me; he thought that I had been corrupted by the temptations of freedom while I was here. He wouldn't do anything to me, though; I was still important to him in a small way.

"The woman—my double—that you found among the Cencom dead was a special agent for Cencom named Mary Cochran. . . Dwight Cochran's daughter." Ben's eyes widened in dawning comprehension, but he kept his peace as Moira continued.

"The reason that I know so much about Cencom and Cochran, and the reason I was so important to them is because the woman that was killed was my sister—my twin sister.

"My full name is Moira Doyle *Cochran* ."

Moira fell silent and looked directly into Ben's stunned and disbelieving eyes. "Well, Ben, you're in charge; do you kill me, or will you get someone else to do the dirty deed?" She straightened defiantly in her seat, though her face was still pale.

Ben's mind raced as he stared at the woman before him. *Cochran's daughter?* In his mind, there was no capital offense here; technically, all she was guilty of was a poor choice of father, something that he could not blame her for. The people of Paradise, he feared, would consider that enough to justify a lynch mob. Ben took a deep breath and came to a hasty, though reasoned, decision, and he turned away from Moira as he activated the computer.

"Access One—Walker, Benjamin. Null salutation. Access tactical analysis for battle of April sixteen, two-oh-two-two. Access prior computations regarding subject Moira Doyle; add datum: action or inaction of subject during battle.

"Instructions: correlate all related information and estimate loss of life to Paradise assuming subject was able to communicate Cencom battle plans to Paradise. Run."

Seconds later: "ESTIMATE CASUALTIES WITH FOREKNOWLEDGE OF ATTACK AT SEVENTY-ONE PLUS OR MINUS TEN PERCENT."

Ben raised his eyebrows in surprise. *If we had known ahead of time, we would have lost more?* He looked at Moira's astonished expression, and allowed a small, quick smile to cross his face.

"Computer, query: could prior knowledge of attack have in any way altered the casualty ratio positively?"

"NEGATIVE. OPTIMAL RESULTS ACHIEVED PLUS OR MINUS THREE POINT NINE THREE PERCENT."

Another thought occurred to Ben. "Query: what is the likely outcome of a vote of confidence taking place within the next seventy-two hours?"

"NINE COUNCIL MEMBERS REMAIN. VOTE OUTCOME: NINE FOR, ZERO AGAINST."

"Query: add datum—subject Doyle's past revealed, and judged innocent by Benjamin Walker. New vote."

"VOTE OUTCOME: FIVE FOR, FOUR AGAINST. DEADLOCK." Moira gasped, and Ben was momentarily distracted.

"Um—query: what action can Benjamin Walker take to ensure a minimum of six votes in a vote-of-confidence scenario?"

The computer was silent except for a slight hum from the speaker recessed into the desk. The seconds seemed like hours until it finally answered.

"THERE ARE FOUR POSSIBLE COURSES OF ACTION:

"ONE: FIND SUBJECT GUILTY IN PUBLIC TRIAL AND EXECUTE.

"TWO: GIVE POPULACE A HERO TO DISTRACT THEIR NEED TO BLAME SOMEONE.

"THREE: HAVE JESSE WALKER ANNOUNCE HIS CONTINUING SUPPORT OF SUBJECT DOYLE.

"FOUR: SAY NOTHING."

"End query," Ben said after a minute or two had gone by in silence. "Recording mode on; active mode off."

"RECORDING. GOOD NIGHT, BEN."

Ben turned to Moira with a smile on his face. "Well, you heard that. It seems to me that the best course of action is a mixed course—I can say nothing, and Jesse will be declared a hero along with the rest of the wounded." His smile faded, and he stared intently at Moira.

"Or we could proclaim Jesse a hero and still toss you out of here on your ear. What do you think?"

Moira sat motionless as tears began to run down her cheeks.

"You mean you aren't going to have me executed?"

"Hell no! You're guilty of being Cochran's daughter, but the worst thing that you're guilty of is not letting us know that in the first place—and I don't think that being Dwight's kid is something that I'd brag about. Paradise law respects a person's right to privacy, so in a sense this is mine and Jesse's fault—we wrote the rules."

Ben stood. "Anyway, you'll live; I'll see to that."

"Ben—will Jesse believe me?"

The older man frowned. "I don't know, Moira. I hope he will, but he's still recovering from his shock. The biggest problem facing us right now is how we're going to reconcile your standing in Paradise. Only a few people saw your double's body, and with all of the Cencom bodies having been either burned or buried, it's their word against ours. We can't rely on Jesse's support right now, so we'll play up the 'hero' angle to take peoples' minds off of revenge."

Ben paused to take a sip of his now tepid beer, grimacing at the full-bodied flavor of the homemade brew. "The council is almost sure to convene in the next couple of days, and the major issue on the agenda is going to be the battle. If I'm going to do anything, it has to be before then." Ben smiled a crooked grin, and gazed at Moira. "I don't suppose that you and Jesse have ever talked about marriage, have you?"

Moira was taken aback by the abrupt turn of the conversation, and blushed. "We haven't talked about it, Ben; Jesse always seems to be too busy or preoccupied to make a commitment, and I never felt the need to pressure him. He's always been an attentive lover, and a good friend. For now," Moira smiled sadly, "that's enough."

"I was just wondering..." Ben said in a wistful tone.

"What?"

"Well, if you and Jesse were to be married, that would solve all of our present problems. I could still make him a hero, and as a hero's wife, you would be forgiven any imagined transgressions." Ben shrugged. "I suppose that it all hinges on what Jesse thinks. We'll have to find out what that is soon, though." Ben looked at Moira, and his expression told her that it would be up to her to discern what Jesse's intentions were.

"One thing that's been on my mind since you told me that Dwight was your father, Moira," Ben said. "Cochran wasn't a handsome man by any stretch of the imagination—where do you get your looks from?"

Moira reddened at the thinly veiled compliment, then smiled a genuine smile for the first time since entering Ben's office.

"My mother was a pure Irish red-head," she explained. "She was my father's—Cochran's—mistress for several years. He was good to her, in his way, even after their relationship was over, and she always spoke highly of him to my sister and myself.

"When I was eleven, she and Dwight seemed to rekindle their old romance, and we saw a lot of him. Then, when I was fifteen—just before the Collapse—she disappeared without a trace. I haven't heard anything from her since then." Moira looked unbearably sad for a moment, then her expression turned hard.

"Dwight took over our upbringing at that point; he kept us in a large home outside of St. Louis, and we had the best of everything. My sister became one of his aides at about the same time, but I always felt that he was responsible somehow for my mother's departure. I could never thereafter be comfortable around him, and when the country went to hell, I left.

"You know the rest of the story."

Ben nodded slightly; the story was a familiar one to him, though not from experience. It sounded like a typical Hollywood or Washington story, and he understood the bitterness that a 'love child' could feel under the same circumstance.

Suddenly, Ben sprang from his chair, startling Moira. He went to the door, swung it open, and stepped into the hall. As the door closed behind him, Isaac turned in his seat.

"Is anything wrong, Ben?" He seemed concerned, not only for his friend but for Moira, too.

Ben held up a placating hand. "No, Ike, everything's fine. You can take off if you'd like; I know that you probably have a million things that you could be doing besides cooling your heels outside of my office. I'll stop by later and let you know what's going on."

"Whatever you say, Boss," Isaac said with a shrug. "Do you want me to have dinner ready?"

"Sure, Ike; but make it for two."

Isaac's eyebrows rose at this last comment. It was rare for Ben to take dinner with anyone, although he had sat through a couple of dinner meetings with Jesse upon occasion; however, with Jesse laid up in the hospital, Isaac was understandably curious about Ben's choice of dinner partner.

"Two?"

"Yeah. Moira and I will be dining together after we visit Jesse. Is there a problem?" Ben was instantly on the defensive.

Isaac shook his head with a faint grin. "Um, no problem, Ben. About 2100?"

"Fine," Ben replied, mollified by Isaac's ready acceptance. "See you then. Have a bottle of wine chilled, okay?"

Isaac nodded, and without another word, went down the stairs. He was troubled, but as always, kept it to himself.

He seems less than pleased , Ben thought bitterly. *I hope that this doesn't lessen his support of me in council.* Another thought occurred to him.

If Jesse's okay, he'll help keep Isaac in line.

Ben returned to the office and faced Moira. "Let's go see my brother." He indicated the door with a sweeping gesture.

Moira smiled hesitantly, stepped in front of Ben, and left the room. Ben locked up behind them, and they walked together down the stairs.

As the unlikely pair stepped out into the late morning sunshine, the few people who were about the plaza stared and made hushed comments to one another. *Perhaps they wonder why I walk with this newly mysterious woman* , Ben thought. *Well, tough shit! I'm still in charge around here, and I plan to stay that way! I can do anything I want to...*Ben's thoughts trailed off as he realized that he was falling into the trap of **POWER**. He inwardly chuckled at himself as the two walked arm in arm toward the clinic. They engaged in small talk to ease the tension of their earlier conversation; Ben in particular felt bad about the way that he had been forced to act. In the months that his brother had been seeing Moira, the two of them had not exchanged more than a few words, and for their first real talk to be under circumstances like this —

Ben cast a sideways glance at Moira when she was not looking. He had to admit — privately — that Moira Doyle was a fine woman. "Moira," Ben said as an idea came to mind, "I've been thinking. If we let Paradise know your real name, they'll never let you stay. Therefore, I've decided that your name is now officially Moira Doyle — period. I'll see to it that it's changed in all of the records, especially Security." He wondered whether Anna had stumbled across the record yet, and what her reaction would be.

Moira smiled brightly, and gave Ben's arm a squeeze. "I don't know how I can ever repay you, Ben. You've been so fair and understanding."

"Don't mention it — *ever*," Ben mumbled as they walked up the stairs and into the domain of Doc Riley. "Don't mention it at all."

FROM THE ASHES: Paradise One   Jack Bandemer and Marat M. Bandemer, III

CHAPTER TWENTY-THREE

Doc Riley looked up as Ben and Moira walked into his small office. He had been writing up the reports on his patients, sorely missing the clerical skills of his late assistant, Marty.

Of those seven patients, three had broken bones, two were suffering from bullet wounds, one had a serious infection from a knife wound, and Jesse Walker was still recovering from his ordeal.

The doctor greeted his guests with a perfunctory wave, and kept on writing. "I'll be with you in a minute, Ben. It's these charts that have me so busy."

Ben motioned Moira to sit, and Ben himself took a seat with its back to the wall and in clear sight of the door. Since Moira's revelation that her double had been sent to kill him, he had been apprehensive. Who else might be a spy or assassin if someone who he thought he could trust had really been a killer?

They sat in silence, waiting for Doc to finish. Out of the corner of his eye, Ben saw Anna at the door, and he got to his feet. "I'll be right back."

Anna led Ben by the arm out onto the porch. "What have you found out about Moira?" she asked tersely. "Is she really a spy? I was reading the security report   on her a little while ago when the screen blanked. I tried to access the file again, but my codes wouldn't work. What the hell is going on?"

"Shh..." Ben put his finger to Anna's lips. "First things first." Ben grabbed Anna in a strong embrace, and she melted into his arms as he planted a passionate kiss on her full, soft lips. "It's been a long time."

Anna smiled, but her eyes remained hard and inquisitive. "It has been a long time, Ben, but don't think that you can put me off the trail that easily. Something's going on around here, and I'm going to get to the bottom of it if I have to tear that damned computer apart chip by chip!"

"Calm down, woman," Ben snapped. "I'll talk!" He proceeded to outline the story as Moira had told it, omitting the parts that she had no need to know. He could see her growing angrier with every word, and when he got to the end of his explanation, braced himself for the inevitable explosion.

"You've got to be kidding!" Anna shouted. "The council will never

197

buy that story, and I can't say that I blame them. You'll wind up with another vote-of-confidence, and this time, you'll lose."

"No, Anna," Ben replied in measured tones. "Three of the four council members who opposed me are dead. The remaining nine are, for the most part, still picking up the pieces of their lives. If I call an emergency session soon, I figure that I can carry at least seven of the nine votes.

"After all, I was right about the attack, and it was my planning — far in advance of the actual event — that allowed most of us to live through it. And as far as the Moira Doyle incident goes, right now it's strictly rumor; if no one pushes it," and he glared significantly at Anna, "chances are that it will never become an issue.

"I'll carry a vote-of-confidence, don't you worry."

The elderly doctor appeared at the front door, and cleared his throat. "Ben, I can see you now."

"Anna," Ben said, turning away from her, "I have to get going now. If you'll meet me at the cabin around ten, I'll explain more then."

"What are you doing that's so important until then?" Anna's voice dripped acid, and Ben inwardly cringed.

"Business." He turned, opened the door, and walked into the clinic, leaving a bewildered and furious woman standing on the porch.

Ben and Riley walked into the office, and the doctor asked Ben to sit.

"Ben, m'boy, it's good news that I've got for you. Jesse's recovered enough to tell me what happened. It seems that he found a body that bore a remarkable resemblance to this young lady here. Unfortunately," and Riley frowned, "the lady was dead, and the misidentification threw your brother into a state of profound shock. It seems to me that he must care deeply for the lass, Ben."

"How about his physical health, Doc?" asked Ben, more to give him time to digest the doctor's report than for the information.

"Oh, nothing he'll not live through," the old doctor replied. "A bruised rib, a cut or three, and a score of insect bites were the worst of it, plus the fact that he's hungry as a horse. Give him a couple days rest and he'll be back to normal."

Moira, who had been sitting quietly throughout the doctor's report, finally spoke up. "What about his mental health, Doc? Will that be back to 'normal', too?"

Riley sat back in his chair and looked at the two pair of expectant eyes staring back at him.

Yes, I'm certain that he'll recover with no permanent damage—in time. Just go slow with the lad and don't burden him with questions about the time he was missing. It may take him quite a long time before he'll be able to relive that portion of his life without reliving the pain and shock, also."

Doc returned the hesitant smiles that the pair gave him at this news, but his eyes were full of concern as they fell upon Ben's haggard countenance. "And what of you, lad? This has all been hard on you, too; is the strain getting to be a bit much?"

Ben barked out a laugh. "Don't worry about me, Doc; I'm a survivor. When the day comes that I'm ready to give up, bury me—I'm already dead!" Even as the words came from his mouth, Ben winced; he had forgotten for the moment that the funeral for the Paradisan dead was still forthcoming.

"Still, you might try to get some sleep once in a while, Ben. I like the people responsible for the keeping safe of this old bag o' bones to be in tip-top condition. It leaves less worrying for me t'do, and lets me relax. I know it can be hard, but do try to get some sleep. Doctor's orders!"

The old man smiled at Ben and Moira. "You can go in and see Jesse now. Shoo—I've got work that needs doing!"

Ben saw Moira out of the office, then hung back in order to speak privately with the doctor. "Say, Doc? Just one thing: pretend that you never heard Jesse mention a 'look-alike' for Moira, okay? It's a sensitive security matter, and the less people who know about it the better."

The doctor nodded slowly. "I can understand the need for secrecy, I think. I'll keep my peace, but I canna speak for your brother. He may find it necessary to talk about it with someone, and I would na' want to try and stop him. Do you understand?"

Ben smiled. "I understand. I wouldn't do anything to keep Jesse from healing; I just don't want to exert any more pressure on him than he already has. Thanks, Doc."

Ben turned on his heel and left the office, leaving a bewildered but determined man behind him.

Moira rushed to Jesse's side, hesitating as she reached the bed. Jesse looked at her warily for a moment before reaching a tentative hand out to touch her cheek.

"Moira?" his strained voice whispered. "Moira, is that really you?"

The young woman smiled, and laid a gentle hand on Jesse's. She nodded, and her smile broadened as she felt Jesse's hand grip hers, squeezing slightly as he did when feeling affectionate.

"My God, Moira—I thought you were dead!"

Jesse turned away from Moira as Ben walked up. "Ben, Moira, do you realize how close I came to k-killing myself in that old farm house? I-I put the barrel of the pistol in my mouth, and actually started to p-pull the trigger! I still don't know what stopped me." He closed his eyes for a moment, then continued as if choosing the next words with great care. He looked deep into Moira's eyes as he spoke.

"I love you, Mo'; I realized that when I thought I saw you—dead. I love you!"

Moira slowly bent and kissed Jesse gently but thoroughly on the lips. "I love you, too," she whispered.

Ben's laughter broke them from their admissions of love. "I hate to break this up, but I have to run. Jesse, I'm going to let you and Moira get caught up," and he gave Moira a significant look. "Moira, don't forget our appointment later—be sure to explain to Jesse what's going on." Ben reached down and gave Jesse's shoulder a gentle squeeze. "You and I can talk later. I'll be back tomorrow, Jess."

Ben turned to go, and Moira hurried to him.

"Ben? Thank you for everything." She reached up on tiptoe to kiss his cheek and Ben, flustered, muttered a 'your welcome' and rushed from the room.

Ben turned down the corridor toward the general clinic, his thoughts confused. He knew that he was doing the right thing, but at what personal cost? *Have I alienated Anna by helping my brother?* he wondered. *And what of Jesse? He just doesn't seem the same!* Ben realized that he was scowling as he reached the main ward, and quickly rearranged his features into something he hoped looked more pleasant and upbeat.

As he pushed through the double doors that led into the hospital, he braced himself for what could easily become a shouting match. It was quite likely that the injured Paradisans would blame him for their condition, and Ben could not wholly deny that it was his fault.

Great was his surprise, then, when he entered the room and was greeted by six cheering patients. He was nonplussed; he had expected, at best, resignation. The morale of these few, however, was far better than he could have hoped.

"Good afternoon, folks," he said with a smile. "How you doin', Dave? Karen! How in hell did you manage to break your leg? Steve, how's the shoulder?"

He slowly went through the ward, speaking personally to each patient, showing a knowledge of their conditions and of their family status, if any. He commiserated with those who had lost loved ones, and joked with those who seemed depressed or just plain bored. It was an example of Ben's capability as a leader; he demonstrated to the wounded that he knew them, and cared about them as individuals – not from some altruistic idealism, but because they were his, and he theirs.

When he had finished, it was nearly 1700 hours. He hurried home for a quick nap, remembering at the last minute to set the computer for a wake-up call at 2000 hours. He had a dinner date to keep, after all.

In Jesse's private room at the clinic, he and Moira were still doing their 'catching up'. Moira had decided that honesty was the best policy, and she told Jesse everything that she had told Ben, including her unsavory lineage.

As she stumbled through her story, her greatest fear was that Jesse would turn away from her in contempt; however, she was even more fearful of what should happen if she was not completely honest and Jesse came upon the truth through some other means at a later date.

To her surprise, Jesse took the news well.

"I suppose a part of me knew that it wasn't you that died on that field, Mo'; my inner suspicions were confirmed when I saw you with Ben –

when you found me." Jesse smiled faintly and tenderly gripped Moira's hand.

"Does that mean that you don't mind who—what—I am?"

"I can't blame you for who your—" Jesse stopped and shook his head. "Do you love me?"

"Oh, Jesse; yes!" Moira's eyes filled with tears as she looked at the older, harder man before her.

"Then nothing else matters," Jesse stated with a faint grin, the most that he would allow himself.

Moira slid into bed next to Jesse, and slowly wrapped her arms around him. "I'm so happy, Jesse. I love you so much!"

"Me, too," Jesse mumbled as he hesitantly returned her embrace.

The two reunited lovers lay still and quiet for a long time, Moira lost in her love for Jesse, and Jesse wondering how he could ever reconcile his feelings for Moira. He knew that it would be a long time before he would ever truly be able to feel anything but horror when he faced her; he also knew that, if only for her sake, he had to try to be the same Jesse with whom she had fallen in love.

If only she knew that I am not that man, Jesse thought. *Part of me died that day, and nothing I do can ever make that cold, dead feeling flee from my heart. Nothing.*

Jesse held Moira tighter, and forced himself to caress her hair and kiss her cheek. She did not notice the silent tears that rolled down his cheeks and onto the pillow.

Ben sat at the bar, drinking some of Isaac's latest brew—a fermented apple liquor that he figured had to run at least one hundred and twenty proof. Ben was grateful for the kick; he needed something to calm his nerves, and he knew that in spite of Doc's admonishment, a good night's sleep was far off.

"Hey, Josslyn, tell your husband that this stuff is almost adequate," he quipped.

"I heard that, Walker," Isaac's voice boomed from the kitchen. He came through the door, brandishing a meat cleaver in mock outrage. "That stuff took a long time to perfect. Don't complain, just give it a chance to kick in." He glared at Ben, his features ferocious but his eyes sparkling.

"Whoa, big fella; I was just kidding," Ben laughed as he backed away from the bar. "I take it back — it is adequate!"

Isaac roared with laughter and slapped the bar. "That's better, Ben. Dinner's almost ready; you're not being stood up by your 'date', are you?" His eyes scanned the late night crowd, then returned with a questioning look to Ben.

"No, but I expect her any time now," Ben replied as he bellied up to the bar again. "I imagine that she and Jesse had a lot to talk about. Set up another drink, and keep the food warm."

"She does the drinks tonight," Isaac said as he pointed at his wife. "It's my turn to cook. Finally, the customers will get something edible." He dodged the bar rag that Josslyn threw at him, and ran back to the kitchen, his booming laughter echoing after him.

Ben returned the laughter until he saw Josslyn giving him the 'evil eye'. He abruptly forced his amusement back down, and hastened to soothe Josslyn. "Hey, everyone knows you're the best cook in these parts. Can't a couple of guys have some fun?" He could feel the effect of the apple brandy, and to cover his embarrassment, he sipped slowly at the refilled glass before him.

"Just be sure that you're kidding, Ben," Josslyn chided him, "or the next time you want dinner, I'll be sure to make it one that you'll never forget." She smiled icily, winked, and walked down the bar to wait on another customer.

Moira chose that moment to enter the tavern. As the door swung shut behind her, eyes turned from all corners of the smoke-filled room to watch her. *The rumor mill has been running overtime, I see,* thought Ben. He noted the angry glares, the puzzled looks, and the unspoken accusations in some eyes, and rose to greet his guest.

"Moira, glad you could make it. Let's grab a booth and I'll have Isaac bring our food to us. Would you like something to drink?" Moira shook her head, and Ben picked up his drink from the bar. "First, however, I want to make a little announcement."

Moira stared at him in horror. "Not about me, Ben; please, don't." Her pleading whisper fell on deaf, or at least numb, ears.

Ben stood in the center of the floor, weaving ever so slightly. In his most stentorian voice, he addressed Isaac's patrons.

"Listen up!" he boomed. "This is an official proclamation from me as leader of Paradise. Rumors have been circulating about the involvement of this young woman regarding the Cencom attack. An investigation, headed by myself, has cleared her of all suspicion. She is to be treated with the respect that you would like to be treated with; anything else, and you'll answer to me—or my brother." He took another sip of his drink, and slowly met the eyes of each person present.

"Any questions?" He waited for a long moment as the warmth from the liquor spread through his body. "I didn't think so. Pass the word." Ben quickly ushered a blushing and innocent looking Moira to their booth, just glad that he had made it through his little speech without slurring any words. *Potent stuff, Ike,* he thought with a grin.

Dinner went well; Isaac saw to it that their service was at its best, and the two strangers had a pleasant time.

When the night was nearly over, and Moira had recounted her conversation with Jesse, she looked at Ben, her brow creased in a frown. "Did you notice anything—different—about Jesse?"

"'Different'?" Ben repeated. "How do you mean?"

"He seems distant and distracted," Moira said. "Almost as if he was playing a role, and not trying too hard to get it right."

"I haven't had much time with him since we found him, but Doc said he was going to need just that—time. Maybe that's all it is." Ben smiled and patted her hand. "Don't worry, Moira; things will be just fine." *I hope.*

"Thanks, Ben. You've been so kind and understanding through this whole mess, and you've made it possible for me to stay here with the man I love. I know I can never repay you—thank you!"

"Just be good to my little brother, Moira; that's all I ask." Ben stood up, stretched, and rubbed his numb rear-end. "Time for me to go., I have another, um, date."

"Thanks for the dinner, Ben. G'night."

"'Night, Moira."

The two walked from the tavern, turning their separate ways as they went out the door.

Anna arrived early at Ben's, wanting to be there when he got home. She made herself a sandwich, tidied up a bit, then paced incessantly around the house for an hour.

There were many things that she and Ben had to work out, not the least of which was their opposing views concerning the Doyle woman. Anna was convinced that Moira was not all she appeared to be, but without the security files available to her, she was at a loss to prove anything.

Anna slowly worked herself into a frenzy. *Ben has allowed himself to be taken in by that bitch's looks,* she thought. *He's ignored the facts, and it was probably him who put the new codes on the files.* She threw a pillow across the room, and kicked the old sofa. He was even seen having dinner with her at Isaac's!

Anna tried to tell herself that she wasn't jealous, but she had hoped that on this, the first night that they could be alone in many, they would have been.

A rattle from the front door shook her out of her reverie.   "Anna! Are you here yet?" Anna looked at the wall clock; he was twenty minutes early. She fought back the urge to make a nasty comment, and called out as calmly as she could.

"I'm in the living room, Ben."

Ben walked into the center of the house and took Anna in his arms. "God, it's good to see you, babe!"

Anna's anger overcame her common sense, and she pushed herself away from her lover. "You could have seen me earlier if you hadn't been out with that traitorous bitch!"

Ben stared at her. "What did you say?"

"I heard that you took Moira to Isaac's. I want to know why!"

Ben's face clouded over, and he turned away from Anna and made his way across the room. At the bar, he silently poured himself a tall shot of whiskey, took a sip, and slowly replied.

"Moira Doyle is not guilty of anything but being captured by an advance party of Cencom scouts," he intoned through clenched teeth. "She has various ways of proving this, which she has — to me. I gave her my word that she would have to undergo no further interrogation, and I intend to see that my word is law.

"All that matters is that I am convinced, and that because of her return, Jesse is recovering."

He lit a cigarette and glowered at Anna. "Would you like to push for more, or are you satisfied?"

"I don't like her," Anna snapped, "or trust her!"

"Will you fight me in council over this?"

"Maybe," Anna said quietly. "Maybe I will. Sometimes I get tired of you pushing your weight around here like you're some sort of god. Well, I've got news for you, Ben Walker—you're not!" Her eyes closed until they were mere slits, and she jammed home the barb.

"A lot of good people died here because of you, you son of a bitch!"

To her surprise, Ben laughed. "What makes you think it was because of me?"

"It's obvious to everyone but you. You wanted a fight, and by God, you got one. I can't see how you ever got to be our. . ."

"That's enough!" Ben roared. His face was scarlet with fury, but he controlled his temper enough to pull some sheets of fanfold paper from his pocket. Thrusting them blindly at Anna, he turned away. "Read that, damn you!"

Anna slowly read through the computer assessment of the battle with Cencom, and her anger dissolved into discomfiture.

"Is this true?" she asked, her face pale and voice hushed.

"Yes, it is. I did what was possible given the circumstances, and according to the computer, got optimal results—meaning the fewest Paradisan deaths possible for the safety of Paradise as a whole—including your ungrateful ass!

"Had I done any differently, the funeral would be for a hell of a lot more; had I not planned as well as I did, there would have been no funeral— there would have been no one left alive to administer the ritual." Ben stood before Anna, his rage dwindling as he saw her acceptance of the truth.

"My God," Anna whispered. "I had no idea that it could have been so much worse." She looked up at Ben with tears welling up in her eyes. "I'm so sorry, Ben. Can you ever forgive me for being so ignorant?"

"What about Moira? Will you let that lie, or will you still fight me?" Ben's smile was crooked, but Anna was relieved to see any sort of smile after her verbal attack of him.

"Are you truly satisfied with her story, Ben?"

"Yes, and the computer confirms it. That's good enough for me, although the fact that my brother would never have fallen for someone who was less than 'okay' has a lot to do with it, too. I sometimes doubt my judgment, but when Jesse and I agree upon something, we're seldom wrong."

Anna tried a laugh, and it sounded right; it also brought an answering grin of relief to Ben's careworn features. "I know," Anna said. "You two are so much alike, but your differences are what make your partnership unique. If you agree on something that strongly — well, all right, I'm wrong again. I'll back you and Moira, if it comes to that."

Ben reached over and pulled Anna's lips to his. "Now that's the Anna I love."

"Sure, whenever I agree with you."

Ben chuckled. "Yep. I do seem to like being in control. Tell you what; you can take charge tonight. But first, I'm going to take a shower. It's been a long couple of days."

"Skip the shower, Ben. I love a man that smells like a man. Besides, I'm in a hurry. Fighting with you has me all riled up, and I can't wait to make it up to you." She smiled coyly, but Ben read something else in the expression as well.

"To bed with you, Mr. Walker; you said that I could be in charge."

Ben paused only long enough to program the computer with some selections from the CD library stored in its banks. As they entered the loft, the strains of Ravel's *Bolero* could be heard from below, softly wending into the night.

As the sounds of passion came down from the loft, a soft, mechanical chuckle could be heard issuing from the computer's voice speaker. Ben had, once again, forgotten to put the machine to sleep.

CHAPTER TWENTY-FOUR

The Journal of Ben Walker: April 19, 2022

Today we held the funeral service for the fifty-eight men, women and children who were lost in the battle with Cencom.

We don't have a resident minister in Paradise, but many of the family members expressed a desire for a proper burial, so I instituted a quick search of my files for a preacher known to live in the surrounding area. Denise Howard, formerly of Tomahawk, aided my search when she remembered an uncle—a retired minister—who lived near her when she left some two years ago. She and I took one of the hovercrafts to the area this morning and looked him up.

The preacher's name is the Reverend Douglas Bormann. He's eighty years old if he's a day, but when we explained the situation, he was eager to come with us. In the course of our conversation on the return trip, the old man asked if we were in need of a full-time minister. I avoided a direct answer.

Jesse and I have discussed this subject many times over the years; we had come to a decision that Paradise as a community should not have any formal stand on religious beliefs; in that way, we could maintain the rights of our people to freedom of choice. However, with Paradise reeling in the aftermath of such a tragedy, I felt that Jesse would understand—and the people had exercised their right to choose by requesting a preacher in the first place.

Just before we reached home, I offered Bormann the position of community chaplain.

Bormann insisted that he be taken to visit the injured in the clinic as soon as we arrived in Paradise. I agreed, and he went about ministering to the living while several volunteers and I took the small Bobcat bulldozer out of mothballs and went about the grisly task of preparing the mass grave for our comrades.

At sunset—an appropriate time for a funeral, I think—we gathered on the edge of the Great Meadow. I had decided that this tranquil spot should house our cemetery so that the dead, no matter what their ultimate

DESTINATION, COULD FOREVER REMAIN IN PARADISE.

AS THE THRONG GATHERED, FIFTY-EIGHT LESS THAN JUST A FEW DAYS AGO, I WATCHED THE FACES OF MY FRIENDS AS THEY MOURNED THE LOSS OF THEIR LOVED ONES. IT SEEMS UNFAIR TO ME THAT WE SHOULD SUFFER SO MUCH FOR TRYING TO DO THE BEST THAT WE'RE ABLE; JESSE AND I WANTED NOTHING MORE THAN A SAFE HAVEN FOR OURSELVES AND THOSE AROUND US. INSTEAD, PARADISE HAS BECOME A PLACE FOR PEOPLE TO DIE!

THE LOSS OF MIKE BARTON LAST FALL HURT ME DEEPLY; HE WAS A GOOD FRIEND FOR MANY YEARS, AND A LOYAL COMRADE-IN-ARMS. THE LOSS OF THE FIFTY-EIGHT NUMBED ME; SOME OF THEM I NEVER REALLY KNEW.

THE MOST PAINFUL LOSS, HOWEVER, WAS THAT OF THE CHILDREN. ELEVEN KIDS, TWO FROM JESSE'S KINDERGARTEN CLASS! THEY HAD BEEN GIVEN NO CHANCE TO LIVE; THEY WERE GIVEN NO CHOICES! SOMETHING IN THE DEATH OF THOSE CHILDREN HAS LEFT ME WITH A STRANGE FEELING OF EMPTINESS, A LOSS OF SOME PART OF ME THAT I DIDN'T KNOW BEFORE. MAYBE I'M IN MOURNING FOR THAT LOST PART OF MYSELF, AND MAYBE IT'S JUST THE REALIZATION OF MY MORTALITY HAMMERED HOME BY THE FACT THAT IF CHILDREN CAN DIE, SO CAN I....

Pastor Bormann waited until the crowd had quieted down before he began to speak. Looking out over the sea of strange, sad faces, he felt again the freshness of his calling; he had not felt the presence of his God so strongly in many, many years.

Ben had briefed him on some things that he wanted said, and had expressed a desire to speak afterward as the secular leader of Paradise. *Strange one,* Bormann thought idly. *Odd mixture of faith and denial, that Ben Walker.*

Bormann cleared his throat, took a sip of water from the glass next to his hand, and in a deep, resonant voice only slightly weakened by age, began:

"Friends and neighbors, we are gathered here this evening to bid farewell to your loved ones, fallen comrades, and children—those who were lost to you fighting to keep Paradise—" the pastor hesitated on the word "—free.

"Many of you are probably asking yourselves about God's plan right now—or if he even has a plan. How can God care what happens when he allows children to die? Do we really matter to Him?

"The answer is 'Yes', God does care. He cares about all of us—the good, the bad, the indifferent.

"But why does he take our loved ones from us? No one among us can read the mind of God; however, I say that God takes those whose time has come."

The crowd muttered, a low and dangerous sound; however, Pastor Bormann ignored it and continued.

"God never causes a death out of its time; Man, however, can take the lives of his fellows without God's intervention. That is called 'free will'.

"It has been said that funerals are for the living, and this is true, for it is we who have to continue on with our lives missing the company and love of those we've lost. More importantly, though, we must continue on so that we may continue to cherish our loved ones, and keep their memories alive. That memory must be the messenger that daily helps us to prevent any more needless suffering and death, by our hands or those of others. We must learn a lesson from our loss, and teach it to others by carrying it into our actions every day of our lives."

He removed a shining crucifix from his vestments, held it high, and called out:

"In the name of our Lord, Jesus Christ, I commend these fallen souls to your care. Help those among us who feel loss, sadness, or despair to take comfort in the fact that their loved ones are in Your perfect care, and will have everlasting life. Amen." A hushed echo of 'amen' came from the crowd, some of whom were totally unfamiliar with the Christian rites.

Bormann walked to the huge mound that marked the common grave, and made the sign of the cross over it. As he faded into the crowd, Ben took his place at center stage.

"Friends!

"Today is a sad day for all of us, but in the midst of that sadness, there is also a reason for rejoicing. While we have lost many of those near and dear to us, we have also saved many who otherwise might have died. Thanks to the bravery and sacrifice of all of you, the vast armies of the Central Command were held at bay, and then driven off like a pack of wild dogs.

"Some among you probably feel like curling up in a corner and pretending that the whole thing never happened. You may; I will not stop you. But for those of you who want to go on living—who will not hide with your heads in the sand like frightened ostriches—I must remind you that we have only begun to fight our battles. We still have enemies, as long as we have what others want. Unfortunately, the provisional United States government is one such group who covets what we have built here." Ben scanned the crowd of stunned faces, and saw the beginnings of bewilderment and anger growing there.

"Those who died did so fighting for a cause—that of freedom. Can we do less? Can we tell our dead comrades that we got scared and quit, after they gave their lives in the same cause?" The contempt for such an attitude was clear in Ben's voice.

"Think about it, people. Let's make damned sure that we don't have to bury any more of our people after today!" Although the mood was one of mourning, a subdued ripple of applause spread through the one hundred sixty-seven people who were present. Far to the rear of the crowd, Ben was surprised to see the argent beacon of Jesse's hair. Their eyes met briefly, and Jesse gave Ben a faint smile, nodding his approval. Ben moved into the crowd, and except for a few who chose to stay at the side of the grave, the surviving Paradisans followed in his wake, beginning the slow walk through the deepening twilight—and to home.

PART THREE: SPRING/SUMMER 2022

Trouble in Paradise

His bike had broken down, and to make matters worse, Jo had his tool kit in one of her saddlebags. The day was hot, he was miles from the nearest town, and he was thirsty. This was not one of Frank's better days, but just when he thought that things had gotten as bad as they could get, things got worse.

From *Riders*, Jesse Walker (2007)

CHAPTER TWENTY-FIVE

Major Michael Mantey of the provisional United States government sat disconsolately on his bunk. The cell he was in was small, but clean and well-furnished. He had a small desk and a supply of writing materials; there was a tiny icebox; a sink, toilet, and shower — even two comfortable easy chairs. He had been in worse situations before, and the conditions here were luxurious by comparison. However, his mood grew darker with each passing day.

It had been nearly a week since the Cencom attack, and in all that time he had seen no one but his guards. He still did not understand the little night trip that he had been taken on soon after his capture; he had been treated well, if brusquely, until his return to Paradise in the early morning hours before dawn.

The guards who brought his meals were young, but their faces were serious and their silence was that of mature adults. That, more than anything, was getting to him; he was, by nature, a gregarious individual, and he was getting lonely. He wanted, more than anything, for someone to talk to.

I wonder if they're doing this to me deliberately, he mused. Maybe they think that if I miss having company it will soften me up to the point where I will give up my secrets. Are they that ignorant? Or are they just busy? Mantey walked to the small barred window on one wall and gazed out at what he could see of the tiny community.

I have no idea how they fared against Cochran and his minions. That I am still getting regular meals is a good sign, I suppose. It's too bad that we've plans to annex them, he thought with a measure of real regret. They've accomplished more here with less resources than most of my country — and I admire the fact that they stood fast against the Central Command forces.

Mantey went to the sink and poured himself a glass of tepid water. As he drank it (the day was unseasonably warm for late April), he took stock of his position. *At least it doesn't seem that they'll be executing me. If they were going to do it, they would have done so already. Maybe their leader is competent enough to realize that my death can only bring ruin upon his little village.*

Footsteps in the corridor jarred him from his reflections, and he glanced at his watch. What? It's way too early for lunch — maybe I was wrong about their decision; maybe they were just too busy too...

A figure rounded the corner abruptly, and Mantey studied him through the tiny window in the cell door. He saw a man in his late thirties or early forties, walking with the easy self-confidence of a man accustomed to leadership. He was nearly two meters tall and roughly ninety kilograms of toned muscle, with salt and pepper hair and beard, both neatly trimmed. He wore a clean but threadbare flannel shirt, faded straight leg jeans, boots, and a gleaming 9mm handgun slung low on one hip. He had piercing brown eyes that exhibited a deep intelligence but little patience. Here was a man who would not be taken in, and would not surrender to a purely logical argument. Mantey decided that this was a man of strong passions—someone to be reckoned with.

"Major Mantey? I'm Ben Walker, leader of the Paradise community council. I'm sure that you have many questions for me, as I do for you. Therefore, I am prepared to spend the entire afternoon discussing matters of import to both of us. I'd also enjoy it very much if you would join me for lunch."

Mantey scowled as he contemplated the thought of another meal in his cell. "The honor would be mine, Mr. Walker. Will we be eating here?"

"No, Major; we'll be partaking of the finest meal our little town has to offer, namely lunch at Isaac's Inn. The menu includes almost anything you might like, and all of the cooking is done by Isaac's wife—best cook in town. Also, you are free to sample some of Isaac's alcoholic beverages; he is a talented brewer, and I highly recommend his 'Paradise Punch'." Ben seethed inwardly at the necessity for overt politeness but realized that if he was to get anywhere with the Major, he had best try to cajole it from him with friendly overtures. *Dammit, Jesse, this is more your line!*

Ben called for the guard, and soon the pair was on the way to the Inn, discreetly tailed by one of the security guards.

"Mr. Walker…"

"Call me Ben; I don't believe in formality here. Our lives are based upon mutual respect for one another. What can I do for you?" A little propaganda never hurts.

"I know that you were attacked a week ago," Mantey said, "probably by the Central Command. How did you fare?"

"The bastards attacked with roughly eight to ten thousand troops, although as a professional soldier I doubt that you would class them as such.

We took an estimated thirty-nine percent. We lost twenty-seven percent. It was close."

Mantey lost his composure for a moment.

"Close! My God, man, you took almost four thousand of theirs with what, a couple hundred of yours?"

Ben's voice remained calm and in control, but his eyes flashed fire. "No, Major. We did it with fifty-eight of ours, eleven of whom were children. Fifty-eight of my people died because a fanatic decided to play power games." Ben smiled, but it was not a pretty sight. "When I play games, I win. That son of a bitch is dead, now."

Cochran is dead? Mantey mulled over this development, as well as the veiled innuendo made by this Walker fellow. *I'd better watch my step here,* he thought, *or I may end up in deep shit.*

The two men walked in silence for a while, until they arrived at the Inn.

"Come, Major," Ben said affably, "let's delay any further business discussion until we've eaten."

Isaac greeted them at the door as they entered, and Ben nodded his thanks when he saw that the dining area was clear of other patrons. Ben had requested this in order to avoid any unwanted interruptions.

Ben and the Major sat at the bar while the Paradisan introduced his friend. "Major, this is Dr. Isaac Peters, retired Colonel in the Special Forces and bartender *extraordinaire*. Ike, Major Michael Mantey of the Provisional United States Army."

The Major's eyes widened as recognition came to him. "Sir, are you the specialist that they called 'Iodine Ike'?"

Isaac boomed out a laugh. "That's me, Major. The army gave me the tools, and I made whatever was necessary to get the job done. Cut my teeth in Desert Storm, and after seeing what gas bombs could do, made chemicals my specialty." He tipped his head toward the well-stocked shelves behind the bar. "Of course, the chemicals I deal in now are a little safer than the ones I made for the Army."

"That's what you claim, my friend," Ben said with a chuckle. "Major, sample his wares with caution."

The Major and Isaac swapped a few more stories as Isaac readied their drinks, then Ben and Mantey followed Isaac to a corner table near the end of the long room. The security guard sat down unobtrusively at an adjoining table, and rested his M16 against an empty chair.

Ben suggested to Mantey that he let Isaac choose their meal, and the Major agreed. They sat back in their seats and relaxed, slowly sipping their drinks.

"Tell me, Major," Ben asked, "what sort of politics do you and the Provos support?"

Mantey riled at the use of the derogatory term 'Provos', but was too disciplined to show his ire.

"We, as a nation, support the ideals of Democratic Socialism. We feel that it is the right and responsibility of the government to look out for those who cannot do it themselves. We have programs to help the poor, to cure the ill, to educate the ignorant..."

Ben broke in. "In other words, you want to perpetuate the same form of government that got us into this mess in the first place. Who decides who is able to 'look out for themselves'?"

"The people decide, of course. We've amended the Constitution so that human rights are guaranteed by law; there is no discrimination against any group, and everyone has the same rights as everybody else."

"But I'll be willing to bet there is plenty of discrimination against individuals who don't fit into your little dream world, eh, Mantey? What about people who just want to live in peace and be left alone? What about people who want to decide for themselves without the benefit of government's benign influence?" Ben spied Isaac heading toward their table; he took a deep breath, composed his features, and smiled at Mantey.

"Enough of that for now; our lunch is here. Just think it over while you eat."

The meal was superb. A salad with hothouse vegetables, crisp pickles, and fresh wheat bread with churn butter made up the first course; later, Isaac brought the main course: venison steaks sautéed in a mushroom and chive sauce; young, tender asparagus spears in butter; baked potatoes with sour cream; and for dessert, blueberry pie—a favorite of Ben's.

The two foes ate in an atmosphere of truce, and when they were finally done, Ben tossed his napkin on the table, sat back, and called out to Josslyn.

"Joss, you're the best cook in the Midwest, but this time you've outdone yourself. Thank you!"

"You're welcome, Ben," Josslyn said with a blush as she hurried into the kitchen.

"Isaac!" Ben yelled.

The big man turned from the bar. "Yeah, Ben? What do you need?"

"Would you grab us a pitcher of your best brew and drag your ugly carcass over here? We need to talk."

"Coming right up." Isaac pulled a battered aluminum pitcher from beneath the bar, filled it from one of the taps, and ambled over to the table.

"It looks like regular beer, Major," Ben whispered conspiratorially, " but be careful—it packs a hell of a punch." Ben watched as the officer carefully sipped some of the amber liquid, and smiled at the man's pleased expression.

"Nothing succeeds like excess, I always say," Isaac stated with a satisfied grin.

"Let's talk shop, Major," Ben said, his tone all business. "Isaac is the military advisor for Paradise, although some sixty percent of our members have some military experience.

"What do you—does your government—want?"

Mantey sat completely still as he considered his chances of making an escape at that moment. He decided that his chances were slim to none, what with Ben on his left, Isaac on his right, and an armed and wary guard at the next table. Slowly, he relaxed tense muscles and looked at Ben.

As if sensing the soldier's thoughts, Ben said with a smile, "I wouldn't try it. Isaac is a martial arts expert, and I have my pistol aimed somewhere near your family jewels as well. And if you got past us, our silent friend at the next table would still be waiting."

Mantey slumped in his chair, trying to make it look as if he were simply making himself comfortable after so large a meal. He asked for a smoke, and Ben passed him one of his own hand-rolled cigarettes. The Major muttered his thanks as he lit it, taking the opportunity to marshal his thoughts and his courage before beginning.

"The provisional U. S. government has been expanding their territory over the past five years or so, ever since we got the lights back on, so to speak.

"We began with seven of the eastern seaboard states, and have now reclaimed almost all of the states east of the Mississippi. We plan to move against Wisconsin, and soon.

"Our attack was going to be against the Central Command first, but it seems that they are going to be less of a threat to us now that you've dispensed with Cochran. I suppose that the main thrust of our operations will center on Wisconsin now — mainly you, I'm afraid."

Isaac grimaced, but kept his peace.

"Continue," Ben urged.

"We have a list of communities that have shown signs of becoming organized enough to resist a takeover with military strength; yours was at the top of the list, and it was decided that after Paradise is annexed, the rest will follow suit."

"Why are you telling us this, you bastard?" Isaac interjected. "We can kill you and prepare for the attack. We'll beat you Provos at your own game!"

"Not without a lot more than you have here, Colonel Peters, in spite of Ben's statement that when he plays games, he wins."

Ben's interest was piqued. "How so?"

"The provisional government has a functioning army and air force, including limited nuclear capability. I hardly suppose you can defend against that." The Major smiled at Ben's expression.

"I suppose that you thought we were nothing more than a group of die-hards, Walker? Well, think again."

Ben spoke slowly and deliberately. "We cannot fend off an attack of that magnitude, Major; however, I don't believe that the Provos can afford to mount that sort of attack, either." Ben looked at the man's gaunt frame, noting again the slight stretch marks and sagging skin of a man once used to a more affluent lifestyle.

"It does the Provos no good to nuke us when what they need most is arable farmland. Almost all of what you say you have 'reclaimed' is over-industrialized wasteland.

"A starving people will not sit idly by and watch you destroy their one possible source of food."

Ben's conclusion hit the mark, and Mantey leaned forward as he slammed his glass to the table. "Damn you! You sit here, complacent, eating more in one meal than the President gets in a day! And you flaunt your wealth! I see what you have, your high standard of living. Rooms as spacious and well-appointed as the cell you keep me in would cost a month's pay just a couple of hundred miles east of here.

"What gave you the right to survive so well? We were prepared for war, we were ready for plague, famine, and chemical poisons. How could we have known that all our preparations depended upon a world economy that collapsed beneath us?"

He stubbed out the last remains of his cigarette and swore softly. "God damn you."

Isaac looked at Ben, who nodded. Isaac stood, walked around behind the Major's chair, and helped the man to his feet. The guard and Isaac then escorted the officer out of the Inn and back to his cell.

Ben lit a cigarette, took a sip of his beer, and leaned back. Poor guy, he thought. He's hungry, and jealousy is his only motivation. The Provos are all hungry.

It was something to keep in mind.

CHAPTER TWENTY-SIX

Jesse roamed around the familiar confines of the classroom as his students watched in anxious silence. *It seems like it's been such a long, long time,* he thought.   Now that he was recovering from his experience and the immediate threat of all-out war had been abated, he felt that regular class schedules should resume. As soon as he had set the school bell to ringing almost all of the surviving school-age children had come running with delight to the schoolhouse.

Jesse sat down at his desk, leaned back in the comfortable chair, and gazed out at the eager young faces that filled the room. He was determined to make it as normal a school day as possible, but he could not help but wince inwardly as he read the roll—skipping over the names of those who were not, and never again would be, present.

Jesse was a sensitive man—some would say too sensitive—and the thought of his kids dying appalled and saddened him. He could still see their faces, and thought he would miss them forever.

The room darkened abruptly as a dark cloud crossed before the sun; Jesse reached up to pull the cord that would illuminate the three one hundred watt automobile bulbs that provided scant lighting for the classroom.   The switch clicked as the cord went taut, and Jesse hastened to shade his eyes from the brilliant light that shone down from the ceiling.   To the muffled laughter of his students, Jesse looked up through squinted eyes.

Instead of the three bright but narrowly focused headlights, the room was now evenly lit by a series of standard-sized light bulbs in rows above the desks. Jesse estimated that there were more than twenty of the lights, all at least seventy-five watts or more. It gave the classroom a whole new look.

"Look at Teacher's hair!" a young voice cried out. Jesse smiled faintly as he imagined the bright light reflecting off of his snow-white hair, and shook his head.

"It's something, isn't it, Jenny?" he said gently. "Looks like I got old overnight, doesn't it?" The classes laughed, tentatively at first, then with more abandon.

The door at the back of the classroom opened, and the source of the new lights entered with a big grin on his bearded face.

Jesse stood as Ben walked up the center aisle. "Class, say 'hello' to my brother Ben — and a big 'thank you' for the new lights."

The class responded in typical fashion. "HI, BEN! THANK YOU FOR THE LIGHTS!" The windows rattled with the force of their voices.

Jesse shook his brother's hand, and led him to the desk. "Thanks, Ben."

"You're all very welcome," Ben responded, directing his comment toward the class. He turned to his brother. "As soon as we had the time, I had the shop turn out some stuff for the schoolhouse; wiring and light bulbs, mostly. Like it? We have almost five hundred more bulbs in back stock. Of course, they won't last like the General Electric ones we have, but *we* made them! They've been lasting anywhere from one hundred to three hundred hours in shop tests."

Jesse frowned. "How are you getting the extra power for the higher voltage?" Jesse knew that most of the electrical current for Paradise was provided by twelve volt generators, since he had installed them at the dam himself.

"Easy," Ben replied. "We liberated some fifty kilowatt generators from an abandoned factory near Rhinelander back before the battle with Cencom. It was a bitch getting those monstrosities here, but now we can produce all the power we'll ever need from the dam. Those home-made jobs of yours were adequate, but we outgrew them a long time ago."

Jesse's lips curled in a slight grin. "Thanks again, Ben; it was a nice surprise."

"No problem, Bro'. I'll let you get back to your job now — the natives are getting restless." Ben clapped Jesse on the shoulder and spun about. His long strides took him out the door, leaving behind a grateful and bemused Jesse to teach Paradise's children.

One thought kept running through Jesse's mind throughout the day: *Where had Ben found the time?*

Anna Graycloud, Paradise's security chief and its leader's mistress, walked provocatively across the loft bedroom. Ben lay in bed watching as Anna slowly removed her clothing, her lithe body gyrating sensually. Ben smiled in appreciation as she undid her brassiere and let her well-formed breasts out into the open. Her erect nipples were crinkled with excitement, and Ben began to show his own reaction as the 'tent' went up.

Anna allowed her panties to fall to the floor, and the dark thatch of her pubic hair showed faintly in the even darker shadows of the room. She went to him in a rush, and shortly the room was filled with the sounds of their passion.

Ben awoke from a gentle doze as he felt Anna stir beside him. "Will you marry me?" he asked softly.

Anna rolled over, her breasts warm against his chest, and she murmured softly. Suddenly, abruptly awake, she sat bolt upright.

"What?"

Ben smiled in the dim light. "I asked you to marry me."

"Are you serious, Ben?" Anna peered at her lover in the murky darkness of the bedroom, trying to read the expression on his face. "Do you really want to marry me?" Anna shook her head and pinched herself, certain that she was dreaming.

"Yeah. I guess that I've been afraid of commitment for too long, dear. I can't be afraid any longer." Ben hugged her, pulling her down on top of his body and squeezing her rear cheeks gently. "I can't think of anyone I'd rather be with than you."

"Do you love me?" Anna asked.

"Yes, Anna," Ben replied softly. "I love you."

"Yes."

"'Yes', what?"

"Yes, I'll marry you. Oh, I love you, Ben Walker!" Anna wiped tears of happiness from her eyes as she gazed into those of her lover. "When?"

"How about tomorrow? As the saying goes, 'Twere best done quickly. Pastor Bormann can still wield a mean marriage ceremony, if you don't have any objections. Otherwise, Jesse has the legal authority as my second in command to do it. Of course, we really only need to announce that we're married, but I thought you might want to do it proper-like."

"That would be nice, Ben," Anna considered. "Pastor Bormann would be fine for the ceremony. I lost my love for religion, not my faith. Who will be your best man—as if I need to ask?"

"Jesse, of course; who else could be?" Ben frowned. "What about you? Who could be your maid of honor?"

It was Anna's turn to frown. "I don't know, Ben. I really don't have any close, female friends; most of them resent me either because of my authority or because I have you. Any suggestions?"

"Just one," Ben mused out loud, "but only if you promise me that you won't get pissed off."

"Not Moira, Ben; you can't be serious!" Several thoughts flashed through Anna's mind, the least of which was the idea of strangling her fresh, new fiancé.

"I am serious. Moira's a nice girl, despite what you may think, and she's Jesse's girlfriend. You two could be friends, too, if you'd give her half a chance. Well, here's the chance!"

Anna heaved a sigh, and relented. "Okay, beloved. I'll trust you on this one."

Ben squeezed her tight with an inward wish for his prediction to come true. It was important to him that things were patched up between Anna and Moira, if not for their sake, then for that of his brother.

The two lay awake for a long, lazy time, holding one another and softly caressing each other until the wee hours of the morning.

BRRRRING! Ben reached over Anna's prone form and grabbed the phone from the shelf near his bed. Speaking quietly into the mouthpiece, he slid out of bed.

"What is it?"

"*Sir, Phil Towers, at the jail. I—I just came on duty at 0600, and found Eddie Gilbert, the night guard...well, he's dead! He's in the Major's cell, and the Major is gone!*"

"Damn!" Ben had been afraid that something like this might happen.

"What is it, Ben?" Anna asked sleepily from under the blankets.

Ignoring her, Ben fired off a string of commands. "Towers, take the top twelve men from the roster and three hovercrafts. Mantey will be heading east to southeast, probably toward the Green Bay area. Check the garage and the stables—if he's on foot, we've got him! Arm the men, and shoot to kill—I repeat, shoot to kill. I want his body brought back here. Keep me posted on security channel five every thirty minutes. Any questions?"

"None, Ben," Towers replied. *"We'll get the bastard!"*

"What's going on, Ben?" Anna was standing next to him, the bed sheet draped carelessly around her.

"That son of a bitch Mantey escaped last night, killing Eddie Gilbert on his way out." Ben outlined the instructions that he had given Towers. "Once the sun is a little higher, I'll dispatch a couple of the ultralights to assist in the search."

"What harm can he do? He's only one man," Anna pointed out, "and we never told him anything he could use against us."

"He told *us*, though. He can warn the Provos that we will be prepared, so they'll hit us soon and with everything they've got. Shit! I thought that the fighting was over."

Anna wrapped her arms around Ben's tense shoulders and held him close. "It will be, Ben, if we get Mantey before he reports."

"That's a big 'if', doll."

George Stanton contacted Ben by radio shortly after eight o'clock that morning. *"Good news, Ben. The prisoner has been terminated, with no chance to contact his superiors. Over."*

"How can you be sure of that, George? Over."

"We checked the area that he was in, just west of Silver Lake, and we have the only functioning radios in the area—and there are no phones. He couldn't have possibly gone as far as Tomahawk on foot and still made it to where we found him. I think we can be certain that he made no contact. Over."

Ben heaved a sigh of relief. "Good work, George. Express my gratitude to all of the men. C'mon home—and don't forget the body. Paradise, out."

Ben was satisfied with the result of the search, although he thought that, given different circumstances, he could have called Mantey 'friend'. The twinge of regret passed quickly, however; Ben had done what he must to protect Paradise, as well as to avenge the death of young Eddie.

There must never be any regrets, he chided himself. *Regret is a sign of weakness, which is dangerous to decision and leadership.* The voice in his head reminded him of his father, and he shuddered at the notion that he was beginning to think like the man who brought him into the world.

Ben turned to the task of arranging for both a funeral and his wedding, and never thought of the major again.

The community center was decorated in bright colors for the wedding; it was only the third formal wedding to take place in Paradise, as most couples preferred to cohabitate without artificial constraints. Ben and Anna, however, wanted to be bound by more than just complementary genitalia; they wanted to be married in the traditional sense of the word: commitment.

Jesse had dredged up some old suits from the warehouse, which had to be aired of their cedar and mothball fragrance before wearing. Jesse's was a summer suit of light gray with baggy pants and a white T-shirt; Ben's was of a more conservative cut: a charcoal pinstripe with matching vest. The bride wore a simply cut cream-colored dress that accentuated her figure, white being out of the question as Paradise did not have, nor would they use, chemical bleaching agents to lighten the natural color of the cotton fibers. Moira, the maid of honor, wore a Kelly green dress to match her eyes.

Pastor Bormann gazed down from his makeshift pulpit with a grin on his leathery countenance. "'Bout time," he chuckled quietly so that only the wedding party could hear. "And when are you two," he said, pointing a bony finger at Jesse and Moira, "going to tie the knot?"

Jesse flushed uncomfortably, and Moira looked at her lover in embarrassed confusion. "Someday, babe," Jesse whispered with a slight grin, but the expression did not reach his sad, cold eyes.

The pastor began the traditional wedding service, complete with 'love, honor, and obey'; Ben had insisted on leaving that in the vows, much to the amused chagrin of Anna. After they had been pronounced husband and wife, kissed, and walked through a receiving line of all the Paradisans, the crowd lost all sense of decorum and a loud cheer erupted.

Ben and Anna waved to the throng and clambered aboard the waiting *Screamin' Eagle,* already loaded with their supplies.

"Jess," Ben called out, "take good care of this place."

"Don't worry about it," Jesse replied with a crooked grin. "Just have fun!"

The little craft roared into life and sped along the pavement of Duesouth Road. Soon, sent on its way with the waves of their comrades, the *Eagle* was a mere speck on the horizon.

Then it was gone.

Jesse called the council meeting to order. He remembered the last meeting in this chamber, and a shudder passed through him as if he could feel the ghosts of the dead councilors there with him.

"I've called you here to discuss, in Ben's absence, a plan to save us from future attacks." He allowed a moment for that to sink in before continuing.

"We must find other communities to ally ourselves with — perhaps as a loose confederation — so that we will have the strength to defend against even enemies as large as the Provisional United States. What I envision is sending an envoy — an ambassador, if you will — to the outlying areas and convening a conference of the inhabitants to work out some sort of trade and defense agreement. You've all had a few minutes to read over the draft of the agreement that I gave you before we convened; are there any comments?"

"Yes, Jesse; I have one."

"Go ahead, Deb."

"Does Ben know about this idea?"

Jesse sighed. "We've discussed it many times in private, but he never showed much interest; however, that was before the battle with Cencom and the Provo threat."

"Well, I like the idea," Deb said. "We could use a few new faces around here, and the trade will only serve to generate good will and communication with the Outsiders."

"Any other comments?" Jesse waited tensely for a moment, and looked over the room full of expectant faces.

"Okay, let's put it to a vote. Since Ben is away I will, as always, vote his proxy. Anna has also given me her proxy.

"In order to maintain a sense of good will, I have installed voting pads on your seats. Press the 'yes' button for acceptance of this idea, and the 'no' button for rejection of the plan. The tally will show up on the board behind me. All in favor?" Jesse pressed his button three times, and three red LED's glowed on the tally board. He watched as the remaining ten lights lit, and smiled faintly. "All opposed?" The lights did not change.

"The motion, by unanimous vote, is carried. Are there any nominations for the post of ambassador?"

Moira spoke up shyly; she was the newest member of the council. "I nominate Isaac Peters."

A murmur of approval circulated through the room, much to Isaac's dismay. "I can't go," he pleaded. "I have a business to run, and besides, there may still be some folks out there who still don't care for people of my color."

"Isaac, my friend," Jesse responded, "I think that you're the best qualified of any of us to do this thing—in spite of your 'color'. It may be best for the poor country folks around here to see that someone like you can rise up to such a high station." Jesse grinned to show that he, too, saw the way that things might be.

"Oh, shit," Isaac said as he shook his head and threw up his arms in mock defeat. "Take the vote."

Jesse called, "All in favor?" The board lit up.

"All opposed?" One light shone in the negative column. "I guess that the motion is carried.

"Well, Mr. Ambassador, here's what you need to do. Take a few men—no more than ten—for an 'honor guard', and any equipment that you think you might need. We want to impress the Outsiders without depressing them. Some trade goods would be a nice door opener—food and medicines, especially.

"We need to multiply our effective strength a hundred-fold, and augment our interior population by at least two hundred. Do some recruiting for residents while you're out there.

"Any questions, Ike?"

"Yeah," the big man said as he leaned forward and peered intently at his younger friend. "Do I have to?" This caused a ripple of laughter among the councilors.

"'Fraid so, old friend. Why don't you come back to my place before you go, and I'll go over the trade agreement in detail with you."

"Good luck, Isaac," Moira said, and the sentiment was echoed by all of those present.

"Don't worry about me; I'll do just fine, I guess. I'll get what we need, one way or another. There is just one thing that I'm worried about..."

"What?" Jesse held his breath in anticipation, but he thought he knew what Isaac was about to say.

Isaac's ever-present smile faded. "Ben's going to be really pissed off when he finds out."

Jesse chuckled. "Yeah, probably; however, he's going to be off getting laid for the next week or two, so there's plenty of time to worry about that. Let's just present him with a *fait accompli*, and he'll have to accept it."

"You're the boss," Isaac said with a broad smile. He stood up, nodded to his peers, and exited with a jaunty step from the council chambers.

"If there is no further business, I call this meeting adjourned," Jesse said with a bang of the gavel.

Far to the north of Paradise, among the Apostle Islands, a couple ran hand-in-hand along the shore of Lake Superior. Her dark hair, unbound, floated behind her in the breeze, exposing her burnished copper complexion. The man loped easily beside her, his muscles rippling beneath his paler skin.

From a distance they seemed like children, so happy and carefree did they appear. From water to sand to trees they romped, heedless of their surroundings.

Their small camp was some two miles up the beach. Their ultra light was idle, camouflaged in a copse of pines, awaiting the time that it would be needed once more. It was here that they spent their nights, locked in passionate embrace. It was here, among the rocks, that they spent their days, roaming the rough shoreline like a pair of beachcombers.

For five days they played; it was a time of revelry for them, for too soon they would have to come face to face with reality again. For now, however, they had their fantasy time; they were the only people in a world with no cares.

Everything happens as it will; life and death are not subject to the whims of mortal man.

At least, life is not.

A shadowy figure dropped his binoculars to his chest with satisfaction as the couple frolicked, unaware that they were no longer alone; unaware that the world was about to intrude upon them.

The figure—stout in his dark green fatigues—quietly turned and walked to the waiting men assembled in the sand dunes above the shore. Gun bolts clicked into place and safety switches snapped off as the men read the expression of their leader.

"It's time," he said.

CHAPTER TWENTY-SEVEN

Isaac Peters rolled into Paradise four days after leaving on his mission of good will, and he brought with him several surprises.

Jesse was sitting on the balcony above the central office, taking simple pleasure in the heat of the sun, when he heard an uproar from the southeastern corner of Paradise. Seconds later, he was summoned to the telephone in the office below. He slid down the brass pole and hurried to the desk.

"Jesse here," he answered abruptly as he picked up the receiver. "What the hell is going on out there?" Jesse's look of consternation slowly faded, and was replaced by an almost happy expression. He continued to listen to the telephone for several minutes, then thanked the caller and replaced the phone gently in its cradle.

"Well, I'll be damned," Jesse muttered. He lit a cigarette, ran a hand through his white hair, and walked out of the office to greet his homecoming ambassador.

As Jesse walked casually down the road toward the southeast tower, he examined the faces of those who were headed in the same direction. On most faces he saw nothing but simple curiosity; however, there was an even smattering of fear and hostility evident, too. To those people, especially, Jesse flashed his biggest and best smile. *To hell with them if they can't deal with reality,* Jesse thought bitterly. He continued to saunter toward the tower, his trek taking him into the relative quiet of the shady lane known as Downright Road.

The closer he came to the tower, the louder the din from the growing crowd became. As Jesse reached the edge of the throng, he tried to see over the heads in front of him what the attraction was, but was unable to catch even a glimpse. The assembly reluctantly parted to let him pass, his long, white hair acting as a beacon to announce his presence. Still smiling broadly (though feeling like it was more of a grimace), Jesse made an attempt to compose his features into an expression at once both dignified and powerful; whoever Isaac had brought back with him would be expecting to see one of the leaders of Paradise, and Jesse did not want to disappoint them.

When he finally reached the other side of the crowd milling around the base of the guard tower, Jesse's carefully composed expression faltered for an instant. He took a deep breath as he saw what awaited him on the other side of the eight-foot high fence, and slowly turned to face his fellow Paradisans. He held up his hands and waited for an uneasy silence to fall over the assembly. Looking into the eyes of those who would meet his, he addressed his comrades.

"Hey, folks! Calm down and listen to me for a minute," he began tentatively. From the rear of the crowd, Jesse heard a muffled catcall, but the surrounding people promptly hushed it, so he ignored the disturbance..

"What you see before you is not an invasion force, so you can put away your weapons." He caught the eyes of a few of the more heavily armed and trigger-happy citizens, and waited until they lowered their guns. "The people on the other side of the fence are peaceful, and have been led here by our very own Isaac Peters." Jesse turned his back to the Paradisans, and faced what lay beyond the metal fence. "Take a bow, Isaac!"

The big black man waved from the front of the group of Outsiders, and with recognition, the assembled Paradisans let out a cheer. Jesse smiled faintly as he beckoned to Phil Towers, the on-duty sentinel and Anna's deputy security chief. In low voices, he and Jesse discussed the security arrangements for the coming meeting, and Jesse asked Phil to arrange the opening and airing of one of the two singles dormitories to house the refugees from outside their borders.

Having made all the plans possible until he spoke with Isaac, Jesse dismissed Phil and walked not without a trace of nervousness toward the gate. He sought out Isaac, and at the ecstatic look on his friend's face, Jesse gained more confidence and approached the strangers with a look that radiated considerably more self-assurance than he felt. *Dammit, Ben, why can't you be here to handle this?* Jesse thought, then chuckled silently. He knew that this meeting would probably not be taking place if Ben were here, and he felt a strange sense of power surge through him as he realized what he was about to accomplish without his brother there to oversee every detail.

Jesse walked through the opening in the tall Cyclone fence, and with his hand out, approached the leader of the ragtag band of Outsiders that stood before the gates of Paradise.

While Jesse was greeting the Outsiders, the young radio operator for the Paradise community was in the radio room of the central complex, wishing fervently that he wasn't. He knew that Jesse was not in Ben's office, and with both Ben and Anna gone, he had nothing to worry about if he was a little lax in his duties. With a deep sigh, the youngster swung his feet up onto the edge of the radio table and clasped his hands behind his head. The soft hiss of static from the equipment lulled him into a light sleep, so he was not fully awake when the short wave radio came to life.

"Mayday….mayday….Graycloud calling Paradise…"

The message was interrupted by a loud burst of noise that sounded suspiciously like gunfire, then resumed with a burst of static.

"Graycloud and Walker…under fire by…force…position Apostle Islands…Sand Island…mayday…" The signal faded as it was overcome by static.

The radio operator-- now fully awake--reached out to grab his mike. He attempted to raise the Walkers for several minutes, with no success. Sweating, more from fear of reprisals for his slow reactions than his horror at what Anna had said, the young man hurried to scribble down a transcript of the transmission.

He called the main office for a replacement at his post, and waited impatiently the several minutes it took her to arrive. When she finally came in, he ran from the office in search of Jesse.

"So, Damon, we're in agreement about the use of the land? I want to stress the fact that we want to clear as much as possible, both for homesteading and for farming." Jesse gazed expectantly at the older man, the nominal leader of the envoy from the Merrill area.

Damon Kane rubbed his grizzled upper lip in an automatic gesture and glanced significantly at Isaac. His thick, silver eyebrows rose ever so slightly, and his piercing blue eyes shifted to regard Jesse with a mixed look of gratitude and mistrust.

"What you're saying, Jesse, is that we would deed the rights to all of what used to be Lincoln County, and in return we would become probationary members of Paradise, with rights to goods, services, and protection? Isaac explained the terms of such an agreement, and I believe that he said a seat on your ruling council might go along with it?" Damon waited with a sense of his own importance running through his mind; the thought of what an alliance with the rich Paradise community would mean to his own status pushed aside the needs of his friends and family — no matter that his own comrades had been starving for years — and made him easily able to justify giving up the vast area of land that Jesse so obviously desired. This was a chance for him to gain power!

"All of that, and more," Jesse smiled. "But the protection is mutual — I'm sure that Isaac told you what happened in our battle against the Central Command." Damon nodded with a carefully orchestrated look of commiseration on his deeply lined face.

"And I know," Jesse continued, choosing his words with the utmost care, "that you were not left unscathed by the influx of troops into this area. What I envision is added security for all of us, if we can only consolidate our resources. Paradise has the technology and know-how to provide for a vast number of people, and you can provide the people and land that we need so desperately to protect us all."

Damon nodded slowly as he mulled over what the younger man had said. He remained silent for a moment, then stood. "If I may have a few minutes alone with my people," he said with a small bow, "I'm sure that we can come to some sort of agreement."

Jesse nodded his assent, and he and Isaac exited the room. As they left, they saw Damon and three of his compatriots in a huddle around the table, and the murmur of their voices rose and fell with their discussion.

Once outside, Jesse turned to Isaac. "Well, Ike, what do you think our chances are? Do you think that they'll try and hold out for more than we're offering, or will they be reasonable and accept what we've outlined? They have to know that they'll be better off with that than with the little or nothing they've got now." Jesse watched the other man's face as he wiped sweat from his forehead.

Isaac looked pensively at his friend for a moment, his face brightening. "Jesse, I think that we can be pretty confident that they'll accept our terms; after all, what have they got to lose? They have land and materials that they can't hope to utilize without our help, and in the meantime, their people are starving to death. I think this one's in the bag, Jess." Isaac smiled broadly as he reached into the small pack that he had carried with him since his return. He withdrew a sheaf of neatly typed papers, and handed them to Jesse. "Read these," he suggested.

Jesse began to read through the papers as Isaac rattled off a verbal explanation of what he was reading. "What you have there, my friend, is what I've been calling the Treaty of Lincoln County. I drafted it after two days of talks—not just with Kane and those 'associates' of his, but with most of the common folk, too. I got an idea of what they want and need, and if it didn't go against our interests, I incorporated it into the deal." Isaac paused, and his tone held a serious note.

"I don't think that any of us have realized just how hard things have been for these folks, Jess. Sure, we knew that they needed some of the things that we have, like medicine and fuel—and we've traded some of that away on a limited basis. What weren't clear were those things that they were either too proud or ignorant to ask for—food, for instance. They've lost over a hundred people to starvation and starvation-related illnesses in the last two years alone, simply because they would not admit their need. And," Isaac said sadly, "I've seen the place where they burned and buried their dead during the Plague."

"Why didn't they farm the land?" Jesse asked without looking up from the document. "They must have had seed, and they damned sure have the land and people."

"Yeah, they have all of that," Isaac agreed," but they didn't have the equipment or fuel to run it. For some reason, they refused to use 'people power' to farm. They've been living off of canned foods and whatever forage they could find in the woods and abandoned farms for years.

"Most of the people who are left in the Merrill area are middle-aged or older, and carry with them strong memories of how things were before the Collapse. They remember what it was like when the government handed out 'free' supplies, and what it cost them in the eyes of their neighbors. To them," Isaac explained, "'charity' is a four letter word, and the last thing they want is a hand-out."

"That explains the wording of the treaty, then," Jesse said in sincere appreciation. "The way you've written it, it seems that they're giving up a lot of property for the simple right of calling themselves 'Paradisans', when in actuality they are losing nothing but land that they could not, or would not, use. In return, they'll have a fighting chance to better themselves faster, and at less actual cost to them, that would have been possible without this agreement. So everyone saves face, and everyone benefits." Jesse smiled, and reached up to thump the big man on the shoulder. "If I didn't know any better, I'd think that you were taking lessons from Ben on how to sell Arizona ocean-front property."

Both men chuckled at the old joke, and Jesse was re-reading the treaty when a breathless and flushed young man came running up to him.

"Jesse," he puffed, "I'm glad that I finally found you! I have an urgent message from Anna Graycloud—I mean, Walker—that came in on the short-wave about fifteen minutes ago. I tried to reach her after her transmission, but all I got was static. I think I might have heard gun shots in the background."

Jesse stared at the youngster (*Peter?*) and tried to assimilate what he'd been told. "Do you have a transcript of the message, Peter, or am I supposed to guess at what she said?" The boy handed the hastily scrawled slip of paper to Jesse, and waited in uncomfortable silence for the acting head of Paradise to read it.

Jesse looked up from the paper, glared at the young radioman, and handed both the message and the treaty draft to Isaac. "Come with me, Peter," he ordered. "No, Isaac—you stay here and make my apologies to Damon. I'll be back ASAP." He turned to run at top speed toward the central complex. "Let's go!" he shouted at Peter as the boy hesitated.

Isaac shook his head sadly, and wondered what kind of trouble Ben had managed to get into—and on his honeymoon, at that! He leaned against the outer wall of the dormitory and tried in vain to keep his mind settled on the business of the treaty negotiations, while he kept wondering if his friend Ben and his new bride were all right.

Ben was just getting dressed as Anna went out of the tent and into the cool mist of the morning air. She was only gone a moment when Ben heard the report of gunfire, followed by a cry of pain from Anna.

Ben rushed from the tent with his M16 in hand, and was met by his wife stumbling toward him, her chest torn and bloody. She tried to speak, but could not seem to form the words; however, the pain in her eyes was enough for Ben. He thrust her into the tent, and turned to meet whatever threat waited in the woods.

Ben fired a burst into the trees that was promptly answered with return fire from several directions. Ben threw himself to the ground behind a fallen tree, and heard Anna's laboring voice speaking into the radio in the tent.

Good girl, he thought as he carefully took aim and fired the remaining rounds in the banana clip at his unseen enemies. He ran to the tent, grabbed Anna by the arm, and dragged the semi-conscious woman to the *Screamin' Eagle*.

Bullets tore up the sand inches behind his feet as he tore the camouflage from the small plane and thrust Anna into her seat. He gasped as he strapped her harness; he had not realized the extent of her injuries until this moment, and tears threatened to blind him even as he strapped himself in, reloaded his carbine, and started the plane's engine. Surely Anna's only chance for survival lay in the speed and power that Ben had incorporated into the *Eagle*; her wounds were serious, if not immediately fatal, and Ben prayed that the modified ultra light would be up to the task he was setting for it. "Hang on, Anna; we'll be home soon!" *If only it will be soon enough,* Ben thought in silent prayer.

Ben applied the throttle and turned the plane away from the direction of the gunfire even as another hail of bullets rained down around the plane. The *Eagle* sped down the beach, her soft tires floating on the wet sand. Ben eased the stick back, and the little plane jumped into the sky. Ben looked over his shoulder and saw their assailants emerging from the scrub pine bordering the dunes. There were at least twenty professional-looking soldiers, and they took aim and fired as they saw the plane fly above them.

Ben rammed the rudder stick back and forth, and the plane zigzagged through the sky. He felt a shudder as bullets tore into the under-carriage and wings; his right arm dropped from the rudder with a painful burning sensation as a copper-jacketed slug ripped through his elbow. He quickly switched hands as another fiery burst of lead hit the plane and the *Eagle* dropped in altitude. Ben pressed the pedal that would initiate the supercharger, and with a leap, the plane shot forward and was out of range of the enemy gunfire in seconds.

Ben took a second to glance at his ruined right arm, then turned to check on Anna. To his surprise, she was conscious.

"Ben..." Her voice gurgled as blood trickled down her chin. "I...got through."

Ben nodded, doing his level best to keep the fear from his face. "I know, Babe; hang on — we're on our way."

Anna smiled faintly, and Ben could tell from the expression on her ashen face that she knew there was no chance for her. "I — I love you, Ben," she gasped over the roar of the engine.

Ben's voice cracked as he replied, "I love you, too."

Anna lapsed back into unconsciousness, and Ben had to spend increasingly more attention to the flight of the badly damaged craft. The wings were badly holed and providing little lift, so he pushed the supercharger to the limit to gain air speed. Even so, he realized that it was a long shot; the plane was slowly losing altitude, and their best chance was to get as far as possible before going down.

"Don't worry, Babe!" he shouted over his shoulder as he struggled with his good arm to hold the stubborn *Eagle* on course. The small plane roared with the effort of trying to compensate for its damaged port wing surface by overpowering the propeller. The engine, while supercharged, had never been intended to remain in that mode for extended periods of time. Ben stole a glance at the gauges, and saw that the engine temperature as well as the oil pressure were both dangerously high.

He throttled down a hair, and the plane skidded to the side, throwing both pilot and passenger against the safety straps. Ben gritted his teeth to stave off the pain from his arm, and from behind him he heard a faint moan from Anna.

"Damn!" he hissed. He fought to regain a southward course, and re-applied full throttle. His airspeed indicator was set at fifty-five knots, and Ben had to take a second look to make sure that he hadn't misread it.

Fifty-five. At full, supercharged speed, the plane should have been doing closer to ninety knots. Ben checked the other gauges, and saw that the oil pressure and temperature were now way above redline. The engine temperature was up to two hundred and seventy degrees, and steadily climbing. Ben realized with a sick feeling in his chest that it would not be long before something had to give.

As if on cue, a scream of tortured metal came from over Ben's head as the supercharger ground to halt, its bearings burned out and seized. The plane lost speed with a violent lurch, and began to go into a steep, curving dive. Ben struggled in vain to slow the dive, and he reached forward with his nearly useless right arm to try and level out the craft. He applied as much pressure as possible to the foot pedals that controlled the lift surfaces, and the plane began to level off, though it continued to crab sideways.

Ben forced the rudder full to starboard, and the plane lurched and stalled. Ben swore as he smelled burning oil, and he looked above him to see black smoke and oil spraying from the engine housing. He pushed the starter button, but only the whine of the starter motor sounded; the engine itself was dead. The *Eagle* began to spiral downward with steadily increasing speed, and Ben watched in futile frustration as the altimeter registered their descent.

As he alternated between watching the trees rushing up and the reading on the altimeter, Ben began to laugh—at first, it was just a chuckle, but soon he was whooping with uncontrollable hysterics. "I love you, Anna," he cried above the roar of the wind and flapping wings, and turned to look at his wife for the last time.

Anna hung limply in her harness, and Ben struggled to reach her. Just as his hand touched her cold, pale cheek, the *Eagle* landed.

Ben heard the gear shear off and one of the wings snap before he was torn from his harness.

A sensation of flying.

Blackness.

"Jeff, fuel up two of the ultralights, and strap on extra tanks; I want those planes ready ten minutes ago!" Jesse turned to Peter, and barked out more orders. "Run over to the armory and break out four AK47's and about five hundred rounds each—and get me another pilot on your way past Security."

"I know how to fly one of these," a quiet voice said from behind Jesse, and he whirled to face the speaker, coming face-to-face with Damon Kane. Isaac was shuffling his feet on the tarmac a few feet away.

"Why is he here?" Jesse demanded of Isaac with a nod in Damon's direction. "You know that only authorized personnel—Paradisans—are allowed in this area!" Jesse put his hands on his hips and glared at Isaac.

"Please, Jesse, do not be too hard on your friend," Damon said calmly. "When I asked him about your abrupt absence, he was hesitant to reply; I couldn't understand what was of such importance that it could tear you away from such a crucial meeting. I'm afraid that I pressured him into telling me what has happened."

The older man gazed at Jesse with a cold look of appraisal. "Of course, I understand your concern for your brother and his wife. That is why I offered to assist in any way I can, both as a gesture of goodwill, and because

I feel that it is the duty of all men to assist one another whenever possible." Damon paused, thinking: *Power play number one. Get in good with the leader's family.* Damon smiled as he saw Jesse wavering from his outraged stance. "When I return will be soon enough to sign the treaty."

Jesse nodded, and Damon continued. "But, first things first. We must be on our way to find your brother and his bride. I hope that you'll allow me to be of assistance in this matter; I have not only flown craft of this design before, but am something of a marksman, too."

Jesse took a deep breath and allowed a slight, sheepish smile to cross his stern features. "How can I refuse?" He turned to the hangar and called, "Jeff, are those planes ready yet?"

"Two minutes, Jesse," came the muffled reply. Jesse nodded, then turned to face his new ally.

"I don't suppose that you're at all familiar with the Apostle Islands, are you?"

"I went on a couple fishing trips up that way before the Collapse," replied Damon. "It will be different going there by air, but we should have enough landmarks to get us there."

Jesse pulled out a map, and showed Damon the last known location of his brother and Anna. The two conferred for a moment, then the map was put away as the men watched a sweating and grease-stained Jeff Barker walk toward them from the hangar.

"They're ready," he announced. "Full tanks, and twenty extra gallons of fuel for each plane. I strapped on first aid kits and a couple of ration packs, just in case you need them. The planes are going to be a little sluggish with all the extra weight, but that's a self-correcting problem. Is there anything else you need?" Jeff's eagerness and obvious effort to please made Jesse smile. Damon made a mental note of the boy's loyalty.

"That's great, Jeff; good work. We can wheel them out to the runway. Why don't you run down to the Pond and get cleaned up, then go see that young lady of yours?" Jesse smiled at the young man and waved him off.

Jeff beamed at Jesse, nodded to Damon, and looked for approval at his soon-to-be father-in-law. Isaac laughed heartily, and sent Jeff on his way. He ran from the hangar area, and all three men heaved a sigh.

"Isn't young love grand?" Damon said with a chuckle. Isaac and Jesse both nodded, and they turned as one to the task of moving the planes into position.

"Where the hell is Peter with those guns?" Jesse asked of no one in particular.

Ben regained consciousness slowly, fighting his way up from the depths of a warm, comfortable darkness into a twilight level of awareness where the first thing that he felt was pain. As he came to his senses, his first thought was that his right arm must be asleep; no matter how hard he tried, he could not move it. He struggled to open his eyes, and blinked rapidly to clear the film that had settled over them while he was out.

Trees hung low over his head, and he smelled the spicy scent of pine in his nostrils, mingled with the acrid odors of oil and methanol. With a start, he attempted to sit upright—that was when he became aware of his right arm once again.

A sharp, excruciating bolt of pain shot from his arm up to his head, and he slumped onto his back as he desperately tried to deal with the agony. Carefully, he rolled onto his left side; as his right arm flopped painfully, uselessly onto his chest, he saw the ragged, seeping wound just above the elbow. White bone protruded from the flesh that the bullet had torn, but the bleeding had slowed to a steady oozing of blood. Clenching his teeth, he made an effort to move the wounded arm, but as hard as he tried, he could get no more than a slight jerking motion from it that only served to intensify the pain.

Quickly he took stock of the rest of his body; he was bruised all over, and there was a nasty gash on his left leg, but otherwise he was in fair shape. He looked up from his inventory, and saw the tattered remnants of a nylon wing surface crumpled beneath a tree some ten meters away.

All thought of his own pain and injuries fled from his mind, and he struggled to his feet. "ANNA!" he cried in anguish as he hurried to the wreck of the *Screamin' Eagle.*

He stopped short when he reached the remains of the aircraft, and fell to his knees. Anna lay motionless among the tangled framework, her skin a dusky gray. Ben looked in disbelief at her, and saw the makeshift bandage that he had applied to her chest dangling, exposing the mangled flesh of the bullet wounds piercing her chest. The blood had stopped flowing, and flies buzzed angrily around her, fighting over the rich blood. Her head hung at a strange, jaunty angle, and Ben saw a trickle of drying blood seeping from her ear. Her eyes were open and staring, the pupils glazed a milky white.

With unrelenting force, a wave of grief and horror swept over Ben. He began to sob, quietly at first, then with spasms that wracked his entire body. No tears fell from his eyes, for they were too tightly shut for anything to escape — or for anything to get in.

Several hours later, Ben sat smoking a cigarette as he watched the *Eagle* and his wife burst into flames. Outwardly calm, he followed the trail of black oily smoke that arose from the wreckage; then, with a flash, the fuel tanks ruptured, and a brilliant cloud of orange and blue flame conveyed skyward whatever soul, if any, Anna had possessed.

Ben was still sitting with a cigarette when Jesse and Damon landed their ultralights in a clearing several hundred yards from the fire. Jesse rushed over, weapon ready, and frantically sought out Ben.

"Thank God, Ben; I thought we'd lost you! If it weren't for your beacon..." Jesse trailed off as he realized that his brother had not heard a word he'd said. He followed his brother's dazed stare to the still smoldering wreckage, and felt a shudder run through him. He looked about for Anna, and felt a wave of compassion for his brother even as he felt a chill that took him back to the day of the Cencom battle.

Jesse looked down at Ben with tears stinging his eyes, but when he would have touched Ben's shoulder, the older of the two brothers stood shakily.

"Let's get the hell out of here, Jesse," Ben rasped through clenched teeth, and he walked slowly, shakily away from the love that he had so recently found — and so tragically soon had lost. He held his shoulders straight, though his right arm hung limply at his side, and walked toward the way home.

Jesse paused to turn toward the glowing embers of the fire that was starting to spread into the surrounding brush.

"Good-bye, Anna," he whispered as he, too, made his way toward the waiting planes.

CHAPTER TWENTY-EIGHT

By mid-June of 2022, Paradise had settled down to some semblance of what it had been before the attack by the forces of the Central Command, and the loss of their comrades, while not forgotten, was no longer uppermost in the minds of the Paradisans.

What damage the dam had sustained had been repaired, at the cost of one new generator, a quantity of wire, and the sweat and toil of several able-bodied men and women. Old Harry, who had somehow survived the shelling, acted as foreman for the job; he amazed everyone by actually getting down and slogging in the mud with the others to keep an eye on the rebuilding and repair work. When questioned about his part in the repairs, he just muttered, "She's my baby," and walked away. His part in supplying the Angels had not been brought up since Ben and Jesse had discovered it—but neither of them had forgotten.

A direct hit on the main hangar had seriously damaged several of the ultralights as well as one of the hovercrafts, but more tragically, had claimed the lives of Paul Anton and Jack Barker. Paul's grease-stained face and his skill with machinery were sorely missed for a long time, and the loss that Jack's son had sustained hit him hard. Jeff Barker had poured his grief into almost endless study sessions as he tried to fill the vacancy left by his father's death. After too many fourteen to sixteen hour days poring over technical manuals, during which he managed to rebuild all of the damaged machinery, he went through a physical and mental collapse from which he had to be slowly nursed. With the help of Doc Riley and Marissa Peters, he was soon up and around, and did not show his grief to the outside world again. It was evident, however, by the quiet weeping he did in his sleep for months afterward.

Repair work along the perimeter had, perhaps, been the most difficult. While large stocks of Cyclone fence had been laid in during the initial construction, it was hardly enough to replace those sections of fence bent, torn and twisted during the attack. Several scavenging parties had been sent out, one of them going as far as Eau Claire. It was a patchwork but thorough job, and had taken the better part of six weeks to finish.

The tower at Upright had been a total loss, and as a stopgap measure, the Paradisans had reconstructed one of the original thirty-foot towers in its stead. It was sufficient for the foreseeable future, and was better than no tower at all.

In the Great Meadow, grass had finally begun to grow over the mass grave of the fifty-eight casualties of the attack. Few of the survivors had erected markers for their loved ones since there had, as yet, been little time or energy to spare for such a project. Near the center of the ever-expanding cemetery, however, there sat a large boulder that had been transported from a site several miles up-river by a group led by Isaac Peters and Damon Kane. Mounted on the massive stone was a bronze plaque cast by Josslyn Peters; it bore the names of each of the lost Paradisans.

An undercurrent of excitement ran in Paradise all through that Spring and early Summer, as more and more of the Merrill area refugees — known as Outsiders — filtered into the community to take up housekeeping. As part of the Lincoln County Treaty, the homes and belongings of the deceased Paradisans that had not already been claimed were made available to qualifying newcomers. Single people were encouraged to stay in one of the two large dormitories until such a time that land could be cleared and new homes erected. Damon Kane and Bonita Drew had been voted onto the council, with the grudging approval of both Ben and Jesse.

Ben's mind ran over these things as he stared from the tower balcony above his office. *So many new faces, and so much to do.* He sighed deeply and squinted as he turned his face toward the sun.

That feels good, he thought as the heat of the noonday sun baked his tanned forehead and high cheekbones. He stepped closer to the railing, and the heat eased the ache in his right arm. The nearly healed bullet wound was now nothing more than an angry pink pucker above his elbow, but the knitting bones in his arm still throbbed incessantly. *The sun can't ease the pain in my heart*, he mused, and shook his head to clear it of such sentimental thoughts. *No time for that shit!*

The chirping of the newly installed phone system interrupted his reverie. He turned reluctantly from the railing, wrapped his left arm around the brass pole, and slid awkwardly down to his office. He hurried to the desk and picked up the phone on the fourth ring.

"Walker, here," he said. He grimaced at the amount of static on the line, and pressed the receiver closer to his ear.

"*Doc Riley, Ben,*" came a faint, faraway voice. It reminded Ben of an overseas call that he had made in another time, another place. He realized that the doctor was still talking, and strained to hear.

"—*wants to see you. He's at my office, and seems rather agitated about something. He insisted that I call you. Can you come over right away, Ben?*" The doctor paused, awaiting Ben's reply.

Ben had obviously missed part of Doc's message. "Sorry, Doc, but we've got a lousy connection. Who wants to see me?"

"*It's Jesse, Ben,*" Doc repeated. "*He was here for a check-up, and I gave him a clean bill of health. He told me to call you, and when I asked him why, he wouldna' say. If it's not too much trouble, could you swing by? I'll take a look at your arm while you're here.*"

"My arm's fine, Doc," Ben replied vacantly. He frowned, wondering what could be so urgent that Jesse needed to see him now.

Jesse had been in a near-invalid condition for several days after the Cencom attack—a combination of shell shock, dehydration, and depression. He had bounced back from it with remarkable swiftness, and his health had, if anything, been better than ever. Ben knew that Jesse had been weight training in his spare time (of which there seemed to be little enough these days), and the improvement was evident. Jesse's once lithe, supple frame now sported stronger, heavier muscles than before.

Ben had notice other changes in his younger brother over the past several weeks, too; he did not smile as often as he once had, if he smiled at all. The usually ever-present twinkle was gone from his eyes, and had been replaced by a hard, flinty stare. Lines had been etched deeply into his face beneath the still shocking crown of long, white hair. Jesse rarely spoke, and when he did, he talked matter-of-factly, without humor or wit. He seemed withdrawn into a shell, a world of his own, and Ben avoided seeing him unless it was absolutely necessary; it was as if Jesse were a stranger.

Often, Jesse would get a lost, harrowing look in his eyes, as if he were seeing things just beyond the sight of others. Most disturbing to Ben, though, was the way that Jesse carried himself. He was twitchy and nervous, walking the perimeter of Paradise daily like a caged animal. Ben had seen his brother like this on only one other occasion—just before Jesse had left home on a cross-country hiking trip in 2001. Ben had not seen or heard anything from his brother until late in 2002, and when he finally returned, Jesse had been changed.

What frightened Ben the most was how much Jesse reminded him of their father.

Ben had a sneaking suspicion that he knew what Jesse wanted, and he took a deep, ragged breath.

"Are you still there, Ben?" Doc Riley asked faintly from the telephone.

Ben looked at the receiver as if it were an alien creature, then put it back to his ear. "Yeah, I'm here; just wool-gathering. Tell Jesse I'll see him, but that he'll have to meet me at my office. I'm too swamped with paperwork to get away, and I prefer to talk with him in private."

Ben heard Doc relay the message, and when they said their 'good-byes', the doctor sounded upset. *If the old man wasn't such a gossip...*Ben stopped the angry thought short. *I'll go by and apologize later.*

While he waited for Jesse to arrive at his office, Ben went over to his 'secret' cabinet and took out two glasses and a bottle of Peter's No. 8, a brew that Ben grudgingly admitted was almost as smooth as his dwindling supply of Crown Royal. He poured three fingers into a glass, slumped heavily into his chair, and closed his eyes.

Jesse's long strides carried him with swift purpose toward the central complex and his brother's office. He hadn't expected Ben to come to the infirmary, but he was still angry at being treated like an underling.

He responded to shouted greetings with curt nods, but did not waver from his course nor stop to speak with anyone.

In the distance he could hear the cries of the children as they enjoyed a brief respite from their studies. Two weeks ago, Moira (*MOIRA!?* The name brought gooseflesh to his body, and he shook his head to clear it) had taken over his duties at the school at his insistence, and 'Rissa Peters was training as her assistant. A slight, sad smile flickered over Jesse's somber face when he remembered that 'Rissa and Jeff were to be married in July. *Too bad that I'll miss their wedding,* he thought with real regret, then dismissed the thought from his mind. *I've got to keep a clear head now,* he reminded himself.

Jesse shook his head in the light breeze, and his mane of snowy hair bristled and crackled around him like St. Elmo's fire. Normally he would have worn his hair tied back in a ponytail at this time of year, but he took a certain morbid fascination at the response his altered appearance elicited from people. He could sympathize with their reactions; each morning when he looked in the mirror, he felt for an instant that it was some stranger's visage that was staring out at him from the glass. It often bewildered him, but lately pleased him to no end, that he had gained this unusual, distinguishing feature.

He smiled a tight little smile, and quickened his pace. After all, he couldn't keep Ben waiting.

The heavy door thundered in its frame, then swung open with a bang against the wall. Ben sat up abruptly, startled into instant alertness by the shadowy figure in the doorway. He saw the frizzy white hair of his brother, and relaxed—but just a little.

He stood up and met Jesse halfway across the floor. "How's it going, Jess? Doc said that you wanted to see me?" Ben looked for some sign in Jesse's eyes, but quickly averted his own when he saw the icy expression in his brother's.

"I'm fine, Ben," Jesse replied in a calm, even tone as he strode to his customary seat in front of the desk. Ben noted with uneasiness that Jesse sat erect and rigid, rather than his usual feet on the desk, slouching position. Ben followed his brother to the desk and slowly situated himself behind it in the large leather armchair.

So he wants a formal meeting, Ben thought bitterly. He did not feel at all comfortable with this 'new' Jesse, and the term *iceman* kept creeping into his mind.

Ben forced a smile and gestured at the glasses of amber whiskey. "Drink, Jess? It's some of Isaac's best." Ben lifted his own glass, forcing himself to sip at it as he watched Jesse take his glass and cradle it in his hands without drinking.

Jesse took a deep breath, letting it out in a rush before speaking. "Let's get down to it, Ben. You've probably noticed that I'm not quite the man I was—before," Jesse began with a nasty chuckle that sent shivers down his brother's spine. "It's not something that I can get a grip on, but Doc says that I'm as sane as I ever was, so...anyway, the reason that I wanted to see you is two-fold: I want to requisition some supplies; and I wanted you to be the first to know that I'm leaving Paradise."

The words hung in the palpable silence between the two brothers for a long moment, and Ben sat with his eyes heavy-lidded and a lump in his throat. Despite himself, he drained his glass of whiskey in one swallow, and gingerly set the tumbler down on the desk. He stared intently at the thin film of whiskey as it drained down the sides of the glass, then sighed and looked at his brother.

"I guess I'm really not surprised, Jess. I know that you haven't been happy for some time, and recently I've noticed that it's been more difficult for you to deal effectively with others. When I look out of my window, I've seen you pacing the grounds like a caged animal," Ben admitted, "and I knew that you'd have to get out soon." Ben produced a wan smile and reached out to pour himself another drink. He noted in passing that Jesse had still not touched his own glass.

"Tell me what you want," Ben said in a bitter, resigned tone of voice, "and I'll try to accommodate you."

For the first time in weeks, the old Jesse seemed to peer out of the eyes of this 'new and improved' Jesse; he smiled faintly, set his glass on the desk, and lit a cigarette.

So the Iceman still has a vice, Ben thought with amused bitterness.

"Ben, try to understand what I'm going through," Jesse said softly. "It's not Paradise that I'm dissatisfied with; rather, it's more my place here and what's happened in the past few months that make me feel trapped.

"I've thought this through, and the only way that I can objectively deal with everything is to distance myself—to get away." Jesse sat back a little easier, and puffed on his cigarette. "I know that things haven't been easy for you—I miss Anna, too—but you've always been tougher when it really counts than I'll ever be. You can handle anything that comes your way; I guess I can't, or I wouldn't be running away. I suppose that before the Collapse, I'd be a candidate for therapy, but things are different now. I have to give myself the therapy, and leaving Paradise is the prescription.

"I'm not going to ask for much—I'd like two pack horses, an AK47, five hundred rounds of ammo, and a couple of weeks provisions. The rest of what I need I already have."

Ben nodded absently as he jotted down Jesse's list, and decided to be generous to this stranger who was his brother. Resigned now to Jesse's decision, and with a clearer understanding of how Jesse felt, Ben smiled.

"I'll throw in that sawed-off twenty gauge that you like so much, and a couple hundred shells, and whatever else you decided you need. All I ask is that you do me a favor in return—keep in touch. I'll give you one of the portable short wave transceivers and a solar charger, just in case you run into more trouble than you can handle. But first, I have a couple of questions for you.

"One," Ben began, putting up his index finger. "Who will run the school while you're gone?"

"Two: who do you designate to hold your council proxy?"

"Three: what do you propose to do about Moira?"

"And four," Ben finished, "when will I see you again?"

Jesse jumped to his feet and stamped out his cigarette in the desk's green marble ashtray. He looked down at his older brother, and noticed distantly how tired Ben seemed. Jesse picked up his glass of whiskey, flashed Ben a surprising wink, and tossed it back. Putting his glass down, he turned; for a moment, Ben thought he was going to leave. Instead, Jesse began to pace restlessly up and down the length of the office as he considered Ben's questions.

"Ben, M-moira and 'Rissa are doing just fine without me at the school, and have been for a couple of weeks. I think that they can hold down the fort without me a while longer. Besides," and Jesse laughed harshly, "some of the kids are afraid of me.

"As far as the proxy goes, I think that I'd like Isaac to vote it for me. He's fair, honest, and popular, and that's what you're going to need to hold together this new alliance with the Outsiders. Let Ike be your front man for a while; he'll do a good job, and frankly, I'm sick to death of it.

"As far as — Moira — is concerned, she is welcome to use my house for as long as she wants to. The rest is strictly personal and none of your fucking business." Ben was shocked at the cold note of power that crept into Jesse's voice at that point, and decided that there was absolutely no way that he would interfere with Jesse's personal life at this point.

Jesse stopped in front of the desk and looked directly into Ben's eyes. "As for your last question, Ben — I wish I knew. I don't know how long I'll be gone, where I'm going, or even if I'll be back. I just know that right now it's leave here--or stay and end up a basket case." Ben glanced sharply at Jesse, and the younger Walker nodded.

"Yeah, Ben; it's that bad. I feel like a gallon jug of gasoline, and there's a burning match out there somewhere just waiting to set me on fire. I'm afraid that if I stay here, that match may turn up, and I'll hurt someone I care about. I'd rather take it elsewhere, someplace where—maybe—I can vent it safely."

Ben sipped at his drink, set it down, and asked Jesse for a cigarette. As he lit it, Ben stared at a picture on his desk. The photo was of Jesse and himself, taken the day that they closed the deal for the land that was eventually to become Paradise. His eyes darted from the picture, to Jesse, and back again; he finally realized how much of a stranger Jesse had become to him over the years—accentuated by the changes in the past few weeks. No longer was he the happy-go-lucky tinker, always ready with a fresh, young approach—an outlook that began with good humor and ended with a workable solution to the human equation involved. No, that Jesse was gone, and in his place was this tense, cold, *old* man.

At times—since Anna's death—Ben had felt as if he, and not Jesse, were the younger of the two; at other times, he could see himself mirrored in his brother. More often of late, Ben took into account the people affected by his decisions rather than just the end results. It was almost as if he and Jesse had magically traded places, swapping their souls in some devilish deal that neither of them would have chosen to make had they known the cost.

These thoughts made it easier for Ben to sign an open requisition form and hand it to Jesse. With a brief word of thanks and the handshake of a businessman concluding a successful deal, Jesse exited the office, leaving Ben sitting behind the desk in the suddenly very empty office.

"Good-bye, Jess," Ben whispered to the barren room.

CHAPTER TWENTY-NINE

The next morning dawned clear and cool, but the dampness in the air held the promise of the warm, muggy day ahead. Early risers were in the fields, quietly going about the business of planting, weeding, and irrigating the young crops. The morning stillness was occasionally broken by the roar of a tractor, the barking of a dog, or a birdcall, but even these seemed parts of the natural whole.

Behind Isaac's Inn, muffled noises came from the stables: the snort of horses awakening; the clomping of an iron-shod hoof; the metallic tinkle of a saddle harness as it was cinched tight. A light breeze stirred through the courtyard, bringing with it the mingled odors of hay, horse manure, and the bone-dry smell of the dust raised by the wind.

Inside the stable, the air was already hot and sticky with humidity, and the smell of hay and manure was overlaid by the tang of horse sweat and old leather. A horse whinnied softly, its tail brushing the stall door as it whisked away flies with a rhythmic motion.

Jesse Walker, dressed in baggy, faded black denims, mountain boots, and a light blue chambray shirt was casually inspecting the harness of his lead horse, a gentle young mare named Dolly. Behind her stood an older mare loaded down with several saddlebags, packs, and water skins. She had her head bent low over a steel pail of oats that Jesse had placed on the floor before her. Jesse finished his inspection, checked the holsters that carried the AK47 and the shotgun, and patted Dolly on the neck.

"Looks like we're about ready, girl," he murmured gently to the beast. He checked the leather lead strap that joined the two horses, and mounted with a single fluid movement. With a nudge to her flanks, Dolly moved forward, the older and more experienced pack horse reluctantly leaving her breakfast of oats and falling into step behind Jesse's steed.

As Jesse drove his team from the stable and into the yard, he saw Isaac coming out of the back door of the Inn. In the big man's hands were several large wineskins, so full that they threatened to burst. Jesse brought the horses to a halt, and Isaac walked silently past him and lashed the skins to the packhorse. Then he stepped back, his massive arms hanging despondently at his sides.

Jesse looked at his friend and felt a burst of compassion for this man who had been one of his closest companions for years. He wanted to say something that would take away the pain on Isaac's face, but could think of nothing appropriate. The silence hung palpably between the two men like a wall—unseen, but felt, nonetheless, by them both. Finally, Isaac broke the silence.

"So you're really leaving? I didn't think you would," he muttered to himself. "You take good care of yourself, my friend, and think of me whenever you take a drink of that whiskey, okay?" Isaac's usually thunderous voice was hushed and hoarse, and tears welled up in his eyes as he turned away.

"I will, Ike; I will," Jesse assured his old friend. He reached down from the saddle and gave Isaac's iron-hard shoulder a squeeze, then kicked gently at Dolly's flanks and trotted from the courtyard.

Isaac stood and watched sadly as Jesse moved down the road to parts unknown. He had an awful, sinking feeling that he would never see his friend again.

His broad shoulders slumped, and he turned toward the Inn and the long day's work ahead.

As Jesse moved down the streets of the quiet, sleeping town, he felt an overpowering urge to go past the schoolhouse where he had spent so much of the past ten years. *Who knows when—or if—I'll ever see it again*, he thought. He reined in the horses as he approached the schoolyard and sat silently, sadly admiring the little schoolhouse that he had built. His outward appearance did not betray the poignant wash of emotions that rushed over and through him as he recalled the past ten years in an instant.

With a gentle nudge at Dolly's flanks, he started to move past the school; suddenly, a familiar voice called his name. He brought his team to a halt again—reluctantly—and slowly turned in the saddle.

"Wait, Jesse," Moira cried out as she ran toward him down the road. Jesse had been hoping to avoid a confrontation with her, but now it was too late. He steeled himself for what could prove to be an unpleasant experience.

When Moira caught up to him she was out of breath. The rise and fall of her breasts coupled with the flush on her face stirred old longings within Jesse, which he quickly dispelled.

Moira leaned against Dolly as she regained her composure, and her arm lightly brushed Jesse's leg. He flinched as if from a hot iron, and while Moira appeared not to have noticed, she felt a stab of pain wrench her heart.

"You weren't going to leave without saying good-bye, were you?" she asked Jesse. "Ben told me you were going on a trip, and I wanted to see you before you left." She gazed up at her lover, green eyes brimming with tears, and thought, *I don't think I'll ever see you again, my love. I don't know why, but I get the feeling that this is our last good-bye.*

Jesse averted his eyes and stared intently at the school. "I'm going to be gone for quite a while, and it's sort of a secret mission," he lied easily. "I don't know how long I'll be gone, so keep the school running for me, okay?" His deception spoken, he could now look directly at Moira.

You're lying to me, Jesse. "I'll miss you, Jesse," Moira said softly. "Come back soon." *Come back to me!*

"As soon as I can," Jesse replied. He looked down into the young woman's face, into those emerald green eyes, and for an instant he wanted more than anything to reach out and touch her, to brush the stray wisps of hair from her forehead, to wipe the tears from her cheeks. His hand began to move toward her almost of its own accord, and he had to make a conscious effort to halt it. He turned the motion into what even he saw as a feeble wave, and began to move slowly down the road. Moira paced him for a while, then stopped.

"I love you, Jesse Walker!" she shouted.

"I love you, too, M-moira," Jesse said faintly, hesitating over her name as he had since his return to Paradise after the Cencom attack. He waved once more, and Moira waved back.

Jesse turned his back on Moira, and moved the horses into a slow trot.

Ben sat in the new tower at Upright and watched as Jesse came up the road. Everything that could be said had been said, and the two brothers had not spoken since their meeting the previous afternoon.

When Jesse reached the gate, Ben buzzed it open for him without either of them uttering a word. They exchanged waves, and Jesse made his way out of Paradise without looking back.

"I hope you find whatever it is you're looking for, little brother," Ben whispered. For just a moment, he was sorely tempted to chase after Jesse, or at least call him on the radio that he had insisted Jesse take with him. The urge passed quickly, however; he knew in his heart that this was something Jesse must do on his own. He had no right to interfere.

As he made his way down the ladder from the tower — still favoring his injured right arm — Ben thought about everything that still had to be done today, and he almost wished he were riding away with his brother.

Almost.

CHAPTER THIRTY

Ben pondered the events of the past several weeks as he waited for Isaac to come to his office.

Damon Kane, the leader of the Merrill faction and one of the newest council members, had been stirring up mischief. Nothing overt, just muttering about how things were better in the old days and comments about how Paradise had kept its wealth to itself out of greed. Nothing that was truly out of line, since freedom of speech was still the rule. Nonetheless, it was disturbing.

Ben balked at putting a lid on Kane because the town needed people in order to grow. The Damon Kanes of the world would just have to be endured and adapted to.

Although Ben did not have a formal source of intelligence, he *did* have ways of finding things out. He knew, for example, that Damon had been spending an inordinate amount of time speaking to the young--especially those who would be of voting age come next election. It looked like a play for the top spot—Ben's position—and Ben was none too sanguine about his ability to hold on to the leadership, whether or not Jesse was here to help him win.

At the thought of Jesse, Ben's mind took a turn. *I wonder where you are, bro'*, he thought. Jesse had been gone for three weeks, and out of respect for his privacy, Ben had not inquired where he was bound.

It had been a curious separation for both of them; Ben had come to rely on Jesse's easy-going nature as counterpoint to his own often strong-armed tactics. Of late, though, Jesse had not been the same man. A cold, cunning, and dispassionate apparition had taken over the body of the fun loving and even-tempered Jesse Walker, leaving something almost sinister in his place.

Perhaps it was partly the long, unkempt shock of pure white hair that had become a trademark of the younger man, or maybe the cloak and accouterments he wore; there was now something about Jesse that made even his closest friends shy away from him. The odd thing was that Jesse didn't seem to care if anyone liked him or not. *This is the same Jesse*, Ben remembered, *who used to cry on the playground when another kid would leave him out of a game.*

Their parting had been neutral. Ben had not really wanted him to go, but Jesse claimed that he had been on the edge of a collapse since the attack — a claim that Ben could well believe from his brother's altered demeanor and bearing. *Maybe Jesse was right*, Ben thought bitterly. *Maybe I am stronger.*

A knock on the door brought Ben's attention back to the here and now. "Come in."

"Hi, Ben," Isaac's deep voice thundered as he appeared around the central pillar. "How are thing's going?"

"Fine, Ike. I was just wool-gathering. Do you have some news for me?"

"Not *good* news, unfortunately," Isaac replied with a sad shake of his massive head. "The youngsters are solidly behind Kane; they're obviously ready for a change."

"What does he have up his sleeve?" Ben thought about the reports that his 'eyes' and 'ears' had sent him, and fumed at their almost deliberately vague contents.

Isaac cleared his throat and attempted to answer Ben's rhetorical question. "Kane's biggest gripe is that we have not volunteered to rebuild Merrill. I told him that you felt that Paradise's responsibility was not for that area, but that as resources became available an increasing amount of them *could* be funneled into the surrounding area.

"He claims that we want his people to work on Paradise so that when we have what we want we can tell them to 'piss off' — his words — when they've been used up."

"Dammit!" Ben exclaimed. "I told Kane exactly what the schedule was, and that Merrill would be getting its first supplies within a month or two. He has to understand that we just got through fighting a war, and we have to ensure the continuation of Paradise *first*. How can he expect us to weaken ourselves any more at this time?"

"Calm down, Ben, and let me tell you the worst. He's got a majority of the youths — those who will be voting in the next election — siding with him. Pipe dreams and promises, Ben; that's all he's offering, and they're swallowing it hook, line, and sinker!"

Ben smiled a mirthless smile. "Hell, Ike, if that's all you're worried about, I can just put a delay on the elections with an emergency clause like I did the last time."

Isaac shook his head. "Not this time, Ben. Kane has enough backing in the council itself to overturn any emergency power clause that you could possibly invoke. There's no way to block him, short of drastic measures that could have even more serious repercussions. Even with me voting Jesse's proxy as well as my own, we'll fall several votes short of a majority, let alone the sixty percent needed to carry the vote."

"Then what can I do? Has Kane given any intimation that he might be willing to compromise?" Ben lit a cigarette and waited for Isaac's reply. Even now, he held out a small shred of hope that this particular fat could be pulled from the fire.

"No such luck. He said that the only thing that will keep him from leading his faction against you is your voluntary abdication."

Ben's eyes blazed. "He can rot in Hell before he'll get that!"

"That's pretty much what I told him you'd say," Isaac said with a quiet chuckle. "He said that his offer stands until the end of this week; after that, he's pulling out all the stops. Ben, I'm afraid that he isn't going to wait until the September elections for you to be removed from office." Isaac stared mournfully at his friend and leader before he continued. "I wish that Jesse were here to help out. Not that he'd be able to fix this; it just seems that we need him to complete the team."

"I know what you mean, big guy." The two men shared a moment of companionable silence, each of them remembering in his own way the many times when Jesse's simple brand of wisdom had cut through the murk to solve the apparently insoluble.

"If Kane is going to get the youngsters against us," Isaac said, breaking the silence, "the most we can do is fight back with the older Paradisans. Not everyone has forgotten what led to the Collapse, Ben. Maybe we can gain some more support, maybe not. We have to try, right?" Isaac's lopsided grin forced an answering smile to Ben's countenance. "Besides, it'll give you a chance to kick some more ass."

Ben stamped out his cigarette with a harsh laugh. Suddenly decisive, he spoke in a voice that was all business. "This is what I want you to do, Ike. Take a few of my backers—you know who they are—and work on the original citizens. Concentrate on those who are over twenty-five; chances are, they'll have the strongest memories of the Collapse, as well as the more established homesteads here in Paradise. In the meantime, I'll be working on a plan of my own."

"All right. I'll get started during the lunch rush at the Inn. What better time to talk politics than over lunch and a beer?" Isaac lifted his huge frame from the chair and smiled at Ben. "We'll do it, Ben; don't you worry." He walked from the office, humming tunelessly.

Ben sat back and lit another cigarette. Exhibiting outwardly a tranquility that he did not feel inside, he slowly poured a Texas shot of Crown Royal from his next to last bottle. Sipping slowly, he started to think.

Jeff Barker and Marissa Peters were deeply in love. Because Jeff's duties kept him working more and more of the time, 'Rissa had taken to joining him in the hangar after she was done at the school. In fact, she was becoming a capable assistant to her young man.

When Ben came through the open door of the hangar, he saw the two of them huddled under the hood of one of the hovercrafts. His footsteps echoed on the smooth cement floor of the building, and Jeff looked up. "Hi, Ben! What can I do for you?" Marissa peered shyly from behind the craft's fan blades at her 'uncle'. "Hi, Ben."

"Howdy," Ben said with a smile. "If you have the time, Jeff, I'd like you to make a few modifications to two of the ultralights for me — quietly."

Jeff's expression turned serious as he took a battered and grease-stained note pad and pencil from a pocket of his coveralls. "Just tell me what you need, and it's good as done."

"Take numbers two and six," Ben said. "They have the least time on them. In locker twelve-forty in warehouse one you'll find two large crates; each one contains a five hundred pound thrust jet-assisted take-off unit. I want one JATO mounted on each plane under the fuselage. Trigger them with buttons on the throttle sticks.

"The JATOs must be partially camouflaged; I don't want them conspicuous to a casual observer. I also want them to have their own fifty-pound fuel tanks. That will be enough for about a half hour's operation." Ben paused and looked at the two teens.

"Add structural supports to the wings, skids, and nose. Add the winterized fiberglass body panels to enclose the cockpit area so that it's as airtight as possible. Install two full twenty-pound air tanks behind the seats of each plane.

"Spray fiber resin on the wing surfaces, then paint both planes flat sky blue. On each skid support, I want two remote control mounts for bomb release; each mount holding five grenade bombs to be released as a group. I'll get you a sample five-pounder from the ordnance shack in a day or two. Then, the two most important things...

"First, seal off the luggage area. Then, I want both short wave and CB radios installed—put the antennae against the leading edge of the tails. Finally, I want to take two engines from other planes so that we have twin-engine ultralights with shared supercharging. Tweak them until you get two hundred and fifty horsepower from the pair.

"I want you to test the structures yourself, and bench test the engines; when you're satisfied, dismount the wings, and load both planes onto the trailer. Hook it up to one of the hovercrafts, and give me a call." Ben surveyed the looks of disbelief on both Jeff's and Marissa's faces, but also noted with pleasure that Jeff had taken copious notes. "Okay?"

Jeff was already planning his steps. "How soon do you need them, Ben? I'll probably want a blanket requisition for all of the material, and some help moving crates over here."

"Isaac will help you with the heavy work, Jeff. The requisition is already on its way. As far as when I need them—is yesterday too soon?"

Jeff smiled. "Yesterday it is, Ben. Anything else?"

"Two things," Ben said as he held up two fingers. "One—Damon Kane is *not* to enter the back half of the hangar while you are working on the planes; and two—I want a name painted on the number two plane.

"In silver letters, eight inches high, paint the name *Phoenix*."

Moira Doyle was busy, as only the teacher of a classroom full of little children can be. The school's total enrollment, now that it was open to the outlying areas, was nearly one hundred. Because of this, classes ran in shifts, with several teachers from the Merrill area lending a hand whenever possible.

Marissa shared the duties with Moira, but seldom had a class of her own. The onus of teaching kindergarten through third grade levels was Moira's; it was getting to be a big job, and she missed—at times like these more than almost any other—the adept hand of Jesse.

She managed to run the school with a minimum of conflict, but the 'Outsiders' seemed unable to accept her authority. It was as if they thought that the school was rightfully theirs just because they had more students and teachers than did the Paradisans. Moira had briefly considered going to Ben with the problem, but had quickly discarded the idea. Ben had his own problems these days, and Moira had a much deeper reason for not bothering him. She was always reminded of Jesse whenever she saw his older brother.

Although five years older than Jesse, Ben was very similar in voice and mannerisms to his brother. Though he wore his hair shorter and was of a heavier build, Moira only had to close her eyes when she heard Ben speak, and she was able to pretend that it was Jesse. The way that made her feel shocked her, because it was *Jesse* that she loved, not Ben. But still, the similarities were there, and so for that reason, too, she shied away from Ben.

She now regretted being harsh with Jesse the night that he told her that he was going on his 'trip'. She felt that her words of entreaty—to be honest, her *begging*—had been the determining factor in Jesse's decision to leave Paradise. She constantly blamed herself for that, and now that Jesse had been gone for several weeks, she wondered if he was on a mission, or if he had simply up and left. The rumor mill, always busy in such a small community, said that he was gone for good. Moira hoped with all her heart that such was not the case.

The jangling bell, signifying the end of another school day, startled her from her musings. She stood, packed her case, and began the long, dreary walk to the single's dormitory where she was staying now that Jesse was— gone.

Ben had spent a free five minutes staring out over the peaceful waters of the stream-fed pond, simply enjoying the silence and serenity that the sight gave him. Finally, thoughts that he would rather not deal with began to intrude, and he turned away from the placid scene. Ben casually strolled down the dirt path that led from the Pond to Jesse's house.

I hope you don't mind, Jess, Ben thought, *because I'm going to have to break into your inner sanctum and grab a few aces for my game with Damon Kane.*

He approached the front door, and it opened to his touch. Knowing how trusting Jesse was, he was not surprised to find the door unlocked. He entered and set about looking for the tools with which to break into his brothers project room. He located a toolbox in Jesse's study; when he opened the box, an envelope dropped out.

Curious, Ben picked up the yellow envelope and turned it over. His name was inscribed on the front, so he had no qualms about tearing it open.

Ben (it read)— —

If you read this, I suspect things are not going too well and you probably want access to my Project Room and the tricks therein. Leave the tools alone! You won't need them. If you are still in the study, go to the far left end of the long bookcase. Pull out the volume that deals with eccentric PhDs. Behind it is a sensor pad keyed to your index finger. Hold your right index finger there for three seconds, and the way will open for you. Close the doors when you leave — —were you born in a barn? Good luck.

Jesse

With a grunt of thanks to his absent brother, Ben followed the instructions on the note. He pulled out the book indicated (his own collection of essays, *The Not-So-Mad Professor*), and located the pad. He held his finger there until he heard a click, and jumped back when the bookcase began to swing away from the wall. Ben laughed with amazement at his brother's ingenuity, and hurried down the short ladder that led to the subterranean passage.

His first stop upon entering the project room was Jesse's file cabinet. He flipped through the disarray until he found a manila folder labeled 'HOLOS'. He pulled the file and searched the listings for the specific images he would need—he would not have time for improvisation.

Ben grabbed the disks from the storage closet, put them and two projectors into his rucksack, and ran down the tunnel to the exit. As he left the underground mini-complex, the doors silently swung shut behind him; he *had* forgotten to close them.

Isaac Peters, innkeeper and finest (and only) distiller in Paradise, sat despondently at the bar, scowling at the scant handful of customers — mostly Outsiders — who sat there drinking and lounging.

Isaac seldom saw his old customers any more; at least, not in the bar. They still came to him for the varieties of distilled liquors he had concocted, but it was obvious that the 'marriage' of Merrill and Paradise would not be a happy one.

He poured himself a tall shot of his best grain vodka, ignoring the glare that Josslyn shot in his direction. She was a confirmed non-drinker, and did not wholly approve of his drinking or of his support of other peoples' habits. She was, however, tolerant enough to not make an issue of it when so much else weighed upon her husband's mind.

Damned foreigners! Isaac thought. Everything had been all right — even the War — until Jesse had begun his project to consolidate the area's resources — and Isaac had gone along with it. Any man with half a brain could have foretold the conflict between the 'rich' producers and the 'poor' non-producers. It was a classic dialectic of Marxism. *The only thing old Karl ever got right,* Isaac thought with a bitter chuckle.

Isaac sighed. The Inn used to see at least forty or fifty people every night, all Paradisans. Now, with twice the population, the 'crowds' were hovering around twenty — all Outsiders.

Isaac hated the Outside. It had tried to take his family away from him. It had very nearly taken his adopted home away from him, as it was again threatening to do. And the Outside, years ago, had nearly denied him his doctoral dissertation because of his race.

Yes, thought Isaac, *it always boils down to prejudice.* Isaac had made a tough decision when he chose not to tell Ben about some of the racist mutterings he and others had overheard amongst the Outsiders; they had enough trouble without stirring up any embers in *that* fire.

Old habits die hard, Isaac mused, *but after years of being a second-class citizen, this black man, Isaac Randall Peters, is going to do his best to just be a good man. Not black or white — just a* man.

Isaac gulped down the remainder of his drink and followed Josslyn into the kitchen where Nate was already starting the evening meal. *Life goes on,* Isaac sighed, as he turned his attention to the task ahead.

Damon Kane, the newest council member, relished the thought of being in charge. He'd been in nominal control of the Merrill area for several years with the help of a select group of 'assistants', and being in charge of Paradise would be a real feather in his cap. He was not by nature a mean-spirited man, nor and evil one; he just had the all-too-common power lust that so many men seek to sate once they have become accustomed to power.

The power he felt in Paradise was incredible. He marveled at the resourcefulness and shrewdness that had caused the Walker brothers to build this place. Thinking of the power and relative wealth that would be at his command if he were in charge nearly overwhelmed him. He felt an almost sexual tension when he thought about wielding that potential.

He knew, however, that Ben Walker was a force to be reckoned with. That was why he decided to hit early and hard, then hope for the best. Damon was not certain what means Ben had at his disposal, but he was *sure* that whatever they were, they would be formidable. It was evident that Ben had a network of informants, and that the older citizens were fiercely loyal to him. *They'll just have to be dealt with,* Damon thought with a sly smile.

Not so apparent was the way the younger kids respected the man. It was because of that reverence that Damon had decided to subvert the youngsters — it was their votes that would count much in future elections.

Damon smiled grimly, anticipating the upcoming battle with confident satisfaction. He realized that no matter who won in the end, the better man would win.

And Damon knew who *that* was.

In the bluffs surrounding Eau Claire, there is a valley about ten miles long filled with conifers, fresh air, and the sense that humanity has never been there. A cloaked figure plodded through the early morning mists, his shrouded form showing no clue to his identity. His very stance, however, exuded an aura of calm strength.

As the figure reached a small tent, a sudden breeze blew the hood of his cloak aside, exposing the face of the mysterious mist-walker.

Jesse calmly reached up and replaced the hood, but strands of argent hair shone from beneath it in the hazy light of dawn.

CHAPTER THIRTY-ONE

SECURITY CODE: ACCESS ZERO

TRANSMISSION TO: ACCESS ONE

June 19, 2022

Ben—

I don't know what I'll find while I'm away from Paradise. I know that I'm not superhuman—far from it!--and that the world that I am entering holds many dangers for the unwary. I will do my best to keep on my toes; however, if something *should* happen, I want you to know where I've been, and more importantly, what I have seen and learned.

So...I will keep a journal.

When we met this afternoon, I don't think you fully understood the turmoil going on inside of me—and I'm sorry if I hurt you. But I know that you carry your scars of pain like an old soldier: they remind you of old battles and of lessons learned, but like all scar tissue, they're numb and can hurt you no longer. It's unfortunate that my leaving comes so soon after Anna's death, but I didn't plan that tragedy.

You are stronger than I am, Ben; however, I think that you could occasionally benefit from an outburst of weakness. Don't be afraid to let your shield down, even if it means getting hurt again—and again...

I find that I already miss seeing you more than I thought I would. For the better part of ten years, we have spoken every day, and now that I am preparing to go off alone, I feel the need to tell you some things. I could wait a few days and use the short-wave, or I could stop at your place before I go. The things I need to say, though, are things best left to the neutral tones of a letter.

To you, most of all, I owe some explanations. I want you to understand, or at least *accept*, how I feel and why I consider it necessary to leave Paradise.

I know you've always wondered where I went and what I did when I 'vanished' back in '01--and I think that you've never forgiven me for not being there when Mom and Dad had their accident. Believe me, had I known, I would have been there! I know that ignorance is no excuse, but it's the only one I have.

The reason that I left was because Dad and I were not getting along. The reason I stayed away was, of course, because of a woman.

I headed north into Canada, and spent a few weeks getting my bearings, then applied for a work-permit visa. I soon found seasonal work as a cook at a logging camp. On one of my few days off I went into town with a few of the other new men; it was there I met Jackie in a quiet little saloon.

We hit it off from the very first—love at first sight, if you will. She was a beautiful woman with dusky blonde hair, gray-green eyes, and a fine figure. One thing led to another, and in a few weeks, we set up housekeeping.

I continued to work for the lumber camp until the end of summer, when I was forced to look for another job. Jackie arranged for me to work at the tavern as a short order cook, and she was promoted to bartender. Things were great!

That fall, Jackie got pregnant. At first I was terrified; we weren't in any position to raise a child, but with Canada's socialized medicine, we decided that we might just squeak by on what we were bringing home. And there was no denying the look of joy in Jackie's eyes when she spoke of the baby.

I married Jackie three weeks after we got the news; shortly thereafter, I applied for Canadian citizenship.

I was very happy during those few months, as only an expectant father can be. I watched her belly swell with the growth of our child, and the day that I first felt that new life stir within her, I knew I wanted that baby as much as she did.

Jackie was in her eighth month when things started to go wrong. She was in pain all of the time. Then she began to hemorrhage.

Jackie died just forty-five minutes after our son.

After the funeral I went on a binge that lasted as long as I had money—about two weeks, I think. I spent the remainder of my time away roaming the back roads of Ontario and Alberta, sleeping under the stars and trying to find a reason to go on living.

When I was once more whole and healed, I returned to Wisconsin and the news of what had happened to our parents. Somehow, after what had happened in Canada, I was able to handle the loss of Mom and Dad with little grief. I haven't given them much thought since then—until today. I guess that I never missed them that much. Does that sound heartless?

I suppose that this comes as something of a shock to you, but you know what they say: "No one truly knows anyone else." While we *have* been close, I've had my secrets.

All of this is my roundabout way of getting to the reason I left Paradise: Moira.

I've tried, with little success, to come to grips with my feelings for her; however, since the battle, whenever I look at her, touch her, I get a quick flash of her (or should I say Mary?) lying dead on the battlefield. My predominant emotion at that time is grief, coupled with revulsion. It's like being a necrophiliac, or like being in love with a tragic memory.

On a conscious level, I know that Moira is not dead. Deep down in my subconscious, however, she *is* dead. I can't seem to make the connection between the two halves of my self, and therein lies the trauma. I truly believed her to be gone, and that conviction overwhelmed me. At the same time, it forced me to admit just how much I love her. I don't know how to change the way I feel, and I can't forget what happened. I only know that it's driven a wedge between Moira and me, and her puzzlement and my confusion preclude any relationship between us—at least for the time being.

The rage I felt in the days following the Cencom attack is still with me; it was with me even before the battle. We have lost many friends in the past ten years, but it the apparent loss of Moira to bring it out like squeezing pus from a festering wound. I don't ever want to become inured to the loss of comrades.

My rage is a cold-hot current within me that I can often sense bubbling deep inside; I know that if I ever lose my grip on it, it will rush out in a torrent of destructive energy. For that reason, if for no other, it is best that I am not around Paradise. If I am forced to vent my feelings, better that I should do it among strangers. I don't want to hurt anyone, least of all those I hold dear.

I consider myself to be a pretty shrewd judge of character, Ben, and after all these years, I can read you like a book. I know that you aren't at all pleased with the changes that have occurred in me over the past couple of months. You may be surprised to hear this, but I am fully aware of how I've changed, and I'm not entirely happy about it myself.

I've looked in the mirror every morning for the past two months, and I am shocked, bewildered, and aghast at the outward change in my appearance. What *you* don't realize is that the changes are much more than skin-deep. I find myself shunning old friends, keeping to myself, and running away from all that I care about. Is that the Jesse you know?

I often get the feeling that I'm just along for the ride in the head of a stranger who, while he has my name and position, is *not* me. I find myself doing or saying things that would not normally be in character for me—almost as if I have lost a measure of conscious control over my actions. It's appalling to feel so detached, so cold. I wish you could understand that, given a choice, I would not be as I am today.

When you acquiesced to my request to leave, it was as if a great weight was lifted from my spirit, and for the first time in what seemed like forever, I felt whole.

Maybe it's for the best, these changes in me. I feel stronger than I ever have, and perhaps a little more mature. I've denied my feelings for a long time, and look upon my journey as a way of coming to terms with who and what I am.

I'm running away—but not from myself.

I think that I'm finally growing up, Ben. I suppose that it's about time.

Thanks for catching me when I've needed a steady hand, Ben, as you have so many times throughout my life. You are, above all else, my big brother.

A word to the wise: *Watch out for Kane.* He is shrewd, crafty, and quite capable, or he wouldn't have been able to control and hold together the Merrill area for so long. Nevertheless, I don't trust him; he may just be a force to be reckoned with when it comes time for the fall elections. Watch your back, Ben.

Jesse

Ben stared at the screen after he finished reading the letter from Jesse for the tenth time in three weeks. Once again, he ran the gamut of emotions as he scanned back through the pages; anger, compassion, sympathy, and even fear all melded at once into what Ben assumed Jesse had hoped to gain by the letter: understanding. So many things were clear to Ben, and he felt a load lift from his shoulders. *Jesse's going to be all right,* he thought with a smile. Ben scanned to the last page of the letter, and Jesse's final words jumped out of the screen at him.

Watch out for Kane, Jesse had written. *Watch your back, Ben.* While Jesse had invited the snake into their midst, at least he had the wisdom to see Kane for what he was. Ben thought it unfortunate, however, that Jesse had no other words of advice for him—such as how to turn Kane's ambitions to the side of Paradise. The warning was appreciated, though; it confirmed Ben's suspicions, and decided his course of action.

Ben stored the letter in his personal file, and turned off the terminal. He stood, straightened his shoulders, and walked from the office.

He strode confidently into the central plaza several minutes later as if he owned the place—which, of course, he did. Rumor had it that it was here that Damon Kane had been holding the public meetings that had been corrupting the minds of the younger Paradisans. Ben had decided once and for all to see first-hand what the ruckus was about.

Ben was dismayed when he saw the small crowd of youngsters gathered in the plaza. They were cheering and shouting, and he was determined to find out just what it was that they were applauding.

Kane stood on a crudely constructed platform of rough log splits. His gray hair and broad shoulders contrasted sharply with the rough, homespun fabric of his clothing. He looked dignified, and to Ben's trained eye, dangerous. He was flanked by two of his assistants—henchmen—and was speaking in calm, unhurried tones to the gathering of teens. It was obvious from the glares of some of them as Ben approached that Kane had been turning them away from him, and that wasn't good. Not good at all.

The elder Walker stopped near the back of the crowd and hunched down to remain out of Kane's view. He listened intently to the refugee from Merrill, now a leading council member in Paradise.

"My young friends, I tell you that you have no future here unless you make it yourselves," the older man intoned. "Ben Walker and his team of do-nothing conservatives are determined that their lives be easy, but do they care a whit about yours?

"Paradise is ten years old now. Some of you were born here, and all of you have called Paradise 'Home' for most of your lives. How many young people are on the council? None! Out of the thirteen council members required by the Paradise Charter, none of them is under the age of twenty-three. Yet the sixteen to twenty-five year olds make up nearly thirty-five percent of the voting population.

"I say that it is time that you used the voting power you have at your disposal, and wipe the slate clean—get the Walker's and their followers off of the council!"

Kane paused for a moment to let this idea settle in, noting the few in the crowd who seemed shocked by the idea of ousting the Walkers.

"You must make your demands known," he continued in hushed tones that carried across the plaza. "The first demand must be fair representation on the council. Then, Paradise must build more single homes, more industry, and must freely associate with the outlying areas in a spirit of free trade."

So that's his game, Ben thought. *He's out to get what he wants, and he's using my people to get it!*

"How, you may ask, will you become wealthy if you have no paying job? How will you help to rebuild America if you can't work for American money? Ben Walker strictly refuses to accept American dollars at the trading post—why is that? Is he afraid that by accepting good money that he will be sapping the strength of his little prison colony?" Several of the older children gasped at Kane's veiled accusation; others cheered him.

Kane stared at the captivated eyes before him. "Yes, my young friends. Ben may not admit it, but he's running a prison camp here, not a town. He is the warden, the final authority, and he uses the council as a tool to step on anyone who steps out of line or exercises a little free will. You can't leave Paradise without checking with a guard—and if you do leave without permission, the charter allows for stiff punishment.

"If you stockpile necessary supplies for your own use, you are branded a hoarder and can be exiled. Is this freedom?"

"NO!" came the shouted reply.

"You must stand up for yourselves and demand your rights as human beings and as citizens of Paradise, U.S.A.!" Kane concluded with a small smile of triumph touching his lips as the crowd gave him a standing ovation.

Ben turned away and quietly made his way behind the platform, his mind seething with fury at the way that Kane had twisted the Charter's guidelines to his own nefarious purpose. He grasped the butt of his pistol reflexively as he approached Kane's rear.

Damon was speaking to a small knot of teens, and Ben waited as they slowly dispersed before confronting his rival.

"What do *you* want?" Kane asked in an openly hostile tone as he turned to face Ben. "Did you catch my little speech?"

Ben searched out the location of Kane's thugs, and was relieved to see them across the plaza with the main group of kids. "I'd like to discuss it with you — *now*," Ben said through clenched teeth.

"Sorry, but I'm all booked up today, Walker," Kane quipped. He turned to go, but was brought up short as Ben grasped him by the shirt collar.

"We'll discuss it now," Ben growled.

Kane laughed. "If you start anything here, the kids may not wait until the election to boot your ass out. Why don't you just go and do what you do best: go have a drink." Kane tried in vain to shrug out of Ben's hold, but stopped when he felt the barrel of Ben's 9mm pressed against his ribs.

"Is there any way that I can convince you that we really do have to talk? Maybe a bullet in the belly would be more persuasive?" Ben smiled sweetly as he turned Kane to face the administrative building.

"I guess you aren't kidding, eh?" Kane said with bravado made false by the pallor in his face. "Where are you taking me?" He looked around frantically for his bodyguards, and his shoulders slumped slightly when he saw that they were too far away to be of any immediate help.

"Admin," Ben ordered. "Slow march. If anyone tries to speak to us, we'll ignore him and keep on walking. Just two rivals having a chat. Got it?"

Kane slowly nodded, then at Ben's urging, headed for the administrative building.

"All right, Kane—why are you gunning for me? What the hell do you want?" Ben challenged the older man sitting across the desk from him.

Kane sat rigidly and looked at Ben through steely eyes. "I want to be the leader of Paradise. I want what you have. It's that simple, Walker."

"Do you really think that you could take Paradise away from me that easily. I'm fairly popular around her, y'know."

"Sure, with the older folks and your circle of friends," Kane replied. "But the majority of the people here don't give a damn about you. They want leadership that they can trust to give them 'bread and circuses.' You know that as well as I do."

Ben stared at Kane. "Look, the only reason you're here with your fellow refugees is because my brother took pity on you. Don't abuse the privilege of being here; I went along with this plan for my brother's sake, and I can change my mind at any time!"

Kane smiled. "I've been told that your own brother can't even stand it here."

Ben briefly considered strangling the man, but reason won out by a hair. "Jesse left to do some recon for me. Anything else you've heard is pure fiction."

"Bullshit, Ben! Jesse left because he couldn't stand to watch you fuck up everything that he's worked so hard at over the past decade."

The accusation smote sharply on Ben's already tense nerves, and something inside him snapped. Without thinking about what he was doing, and with no other movement, his right hand swept up from his waist, and he fired three closely spaced shots.

Kane started incredulously at the holes that blossomed in his chest. He looked at Ben in surprise for a few seconds before his eyes glazed over and he toppled forward to the floor.

Ben stood, his eyes dull and pain throbbing through his still-healing right arm as he stared down at the body of his erstwhile nemesis lying in an expanding pool of blood. He set the still-smoking pistol on the desktop, and calmly poured a glass of whiskey from the ever-present decanter.

The intercom beeped, and Ben jumped to answer it. *"Is everything okay, Ben?"* his secretary asked. *"I thought I heard shots."*

Ben assured her that it had been simply an accident while reloading, though he wasn't sure how convincing he'd been.

He clicked off the intercom with a sigh of relief, and then picked up his glass. He slammed the remaining whiskey down quickly, then bent to the grisly task of disposing of Kane's still warm corpse.

He dragged the body over to the central column and pressed a button that would allow him voice command of the computer.

"Computer—emergency override, code seven two two nine zero four. Access override, code five eight one. Command: Paradise is not yet lost."

With a hiss of air and the hum of electric motors, the central column swung away to reveal the shaft that led down to the 'War Room.' Ben dragged the body into the shaft; then, struggling with the effort, he slung it over his shoulders in a fireman's carry, and started down the ladder. Twice he stopped on his descent to shift his burden. Soon sweat was pouring freely from him and mingling with the blood of the corpse.

He was still nearly ten feet from the bottom of the shaft when Kane's body slid from his shoulders and fell to the floor below with a meaty thump. Ben cursed and slid down the rest of the way down the ladder, gingerly stepping over the fallen body.

"Code five eight one ay," Ben said, "Command: And the air is still as sweet." He sighed as the ventilators came on, the slight breeze cooling him as well as taking away the hot, rancid smell of blood. Ben did his best to ignore the sticky feeling of his clothes as he went across the subterranean room to one of the two emergency tunnels and opened the hatch.

He switched on a spotlight just within the tunnel, and immediately the interior of the concrete tube was illuminated for a distance of sixty or seventy feet. He turned to the console behind him, and pressed a button to summon one of the small remotely controlled cars.

One of Jesse's brainstorms, Ben thought with distracted appreciation. The tiny car was about the size of a mechanic's creeper; it was mounted on independently powered canted wheels that rode in the cylindrical tunnel system smoothly. A high-efficiency battery powered it, and a whip antenna rose from a tiny circuit board that controlled the car's movement with direction from the main computer.

The car arrived with a chirping alarm, and Ben lifted the body of his dead foe onto the platform of the small vehicle. He had to bend Kane's legs nearly double to make them fit, and when he was finished, the body was in an ungainly posture that even a contortionist might find uncomfortable. Kane, however, registered no complaint.

Ben lifted the light steel side rails into place, locked them, and closed the tunnel hatch. Turning to the main console, he flicked the switch for manual override, and a small joystick popped out of the casing.

"Command: Display tunnel grid, magnification two," he told the computer. The main screen lit up with a three-dimensional display of the tunnel system. He applied forward thrust to the car's electric motors, steering it through the maze of tunnels as he followed its progress on the screen. When the car reached the lime pit under the distillery, Ben stopped the car. He went to the hatch, opened the door, and ran slouching through the tunnels until he reached the car and its gruesome load.

In the dim light that shone from the spot far behind him, Ben fumbled with the side rails. He finally pulled Kane's body from the car, wincing as one of the arms flopped up and smacked him painfully across his face. In a near panic, Ben pushed the body into the pit, and moved back to avoid the cloud of powder that came up from the pit.

His task accomplished, Ben hopped onto the tiny car, grabbed the little control stick, and drove it quickly to the hatch.

Ben spent the next half hour cleaning up the floor, the car, and himself. When he was finished, dressed in clean clothes, and seated at the computer console, there was no trace remaining of what has recently transpired.

"Computer," Ben said wearily, "Data entry: Councilor Damon Kane has been murdered. Analysis mode. One: election results if subject Kane's death is announced. Two: election results if subject Kane's death is kept secret. Three: election results if Ben Walker is found to be responsible for subject Kane's death. Vocal and hard copy. End program. Run."

"WORKING, BEN. RESULTS PRINTING." The quiet hum of the laser printer began as the voice of the computer coldly read the results of its computations.

"ANALYSIS COMPLETE. ONE: IF SUBJECT KANE'S DEATH IS ANNOUNCED AND BEN WALKER IS NOT SHOWN TO BE RESPONSIBLE, THE CHANCE OF BEN WALKER WINNING THE ELECTION IS ELEVEN PERCENT.

"TWO: IF SUBJECT KANE'S DEATH IS NOT ANNOUNCED, CHANCE OF BEN WALKER WINNING THE ELECTION IS NINE PERCENT.

"THREE: IF BEN WALKER ASSUMES GUILT FOR SUBJECT KANE'S DEATH, CHANCE OF BEN WALKER WINNING THE ELECTION IS ZERO PERCENT.

"ADDITIONAL ASSUMPTION: GIVEN RESULTS OF ANALYSIS THREE, SURVIVAL CHANCE FOR BEN WALKER IN THE TWENTY-FOUR HOUR PERIOD FOLLOWING ADMISSION OF GUILT IS SEVEN PERCENT."

Ben felt his throat constrict in panic. "New program, analysis mode. Assume Jesse Walker present. Assume death announced as assassination by outside force. Estimate election results. End. Run."

"WORKING, BEN. GIVEN ASSUMPTIONS, CHANCE OF BEN WALKER WINNING THE ELECTION IS THIRTY-SIX PERCENT."

"Analysis. Conjecture. Query: what can Ben Walker to guarantee that either he or Jesse Walker maintain leadership of Paradise? End. Run."

"WORKING."

Ben lit a cigarette and poured a drink. His chances looked ominously poor unless the computer could come up with a miracle answer for him. He gulped the whisky from a glass that trembled in his hand, and watched the screen for telltale signs that the analysis was nearing completion.

It was unusual for the machine to take such a long time given the computer's enormous resources. The seven main processing units were tied together in a network run by a super-conducting server, giving the computer unbelievable speed. Conjecture mode, however, required the computer to emulate human thought processes, and was still the biggest roadblock the computer faced.

"ANALYSIS COMPLETE. IT IS UNLIKELY THAT CHANCES OF ELECTORAL SUCCESS FOR EITHER BEN OR JESSE WALKER CAN BE INCREASED TO OVER FORTY-FOUR PERCENT BY HONEST MEANS."

Forty-four percent, Ben thought. *What I'd give for a fifty-fifty shot...*

"Computer. Define 'honest means'."

"HONEST MEANS: THOSE METHODS CONSISTENT WITH THE FRAMEWORK OF MORAL ACCEPTABILITY, ETHICAL RESPONSIBILITY, AND LEGAL DEFINITION."

"Detail. Conjecture. Methods not falling under the category of honest means. Parameters: success chance for election and survival no less than seventy-five percent. Print results. End. Run."

"WORKING. PRINTING RESULTS."

Ben walked to the printer and waited, a cloud of smoke billowing around his head as he puffed furiously on another cigarette. Soon the laser printer hummed and ejected a single sheet of paper.

On the sheet, Ben read his options:

BANISH ALL OUTSIDERS—CLOSE EMIGRATION	93%
Note: Chance of winning ensuing war	81%
FIX THE ELECTION	87%
Note: Chance of exposure	97%·
BRIBE THE COUNCIL MEMBERS—BUY SUPPORT	77%
Note: How do you keep their support?	

CONCLUSION:

YOUR CALL. "YOU PAYS YOUR MONEY AND YOU TAKES YOUR CHANCES."

Ben stared at the printout for a long time. He spent the rest of the day doing some serious drinking...and thinking.

CHAPTER THIRTY-TWO

Jesse was glad that the weather was holding up. He had been on the road for three days, and the clear blue skies and mild temperatures had made the beginning of his journey pleasant. The somewhat chilly nights, while not nearly as enjoyable, served to make him feel more alive than he had in a long time—how could he deny his existence when his body was shivering underneath a woolen blanket in the bone-chilling cold of night?

He had not been sleeping much; the cold kept him awake and restless, and he spent a lot of time dozing in the saddle during the day. Dolly had proven to be a fine choice as his steed, with an easy, rolling gait and a gentle disposition.

The roads he had been traveling upon were in poor condition, due more to forces of Nature than anything else. He was staying on secondary roads to avoid any traffic and to keep the horses within easy reach of fodder in the wild fields.

Earlier that day, Jesse had passed trough a small, apparently deserted town. He had no idea what the name of the abandoned town was, and not for the first time, Jesse wished he had brought maps with him.

At the edge of the town, he came upon a huge jumble of rusting and wrecked cars, tractors, and other less identifiable machinery. The blockade crossed the road and stretched for nearly a quarter of a mile to either side, tainting the overgrown cornfields with scrap metal and leaking oil. Jesse had heard of such blockades being erected by towns during the Year of the Plague, but this was the first time he had actually seen one. He detoured his team around the wreckage, fully alert and wary of ambush. Almost without thinking he made sure that both of his weapons were within easy reach, but as it turned out, the precaution was unnecessary. The town *was* empty, and Jesse did not see even the stirring of a wild dog to alarm him.

He was slowly working his way west, in the general direction of the city of Eau Claire. After his nervous passage through the small, anonymous town, Jesse decided to skirt the smaller communities; they held nothing of interest for him, and if he had to detour around similar roadblocks every few miles, it would cause delays that he could well do without.

Eau Claire—both according to rumor and the infrequent forays that Paradisans had made on scavenging trips—still maintained a substantial population, and Jesse wanted nothing more than to talk to the people, find out how they lived, and how they saw the world of 2022 A.D.

We've been too sheltered for a long time, Jesse thought as he rode down the road at a leisurely pace, and we really don't have a true picture of what is going on outside our borders. We've looked at the outside world as nothing more than a giant warehouse, a place to go when we need supplies. Jesse frowned in contemplation. There are people living out here — people who just might resent our careless acquisition of their resources.

Jesse's thoughts ran to the Provos, and the possible threat they represented. I need to find out what opinions, if any, people hold about the Provos. Good, bad, or indifferent, I have the suspicion that if it means a little more food in their bellies, the majority will jump back on the old bandwagon. Disorganized as it must be, the Provisional United States government could still muster more resources than Paradise could ever hope to acquire. *But at what price?* Jesse wondered.

As the sun fell into the western sky, Jesse cast about for a good place to bed down for the night. The sky was growing overcast, and the cooling wind held the threat of rain. Jesse located a basically intact shed, and after checking for vermin, decided it would be sufficient shelter for the night. He tended to the horses' needs before setting them free to forage, and made his camp.

His third day on the road came to a close.

Three days later, on June twenty-sixth, Jesse was in the city of Eau Claire. He spent the first couple of days there getting his bearings and talking to people. From his conversations, Jesse got the feeling that there were disturbing developments in this once beautiful city — something that annoyed, dismayed, and frightened him.

Eau Claire still maintained a sizeable population of roughly fifteen thousand people. It was rather daunting to Jesse, since the largest assemblage he'd seen in years (other than the attacking Cencom hordes) was less than three hundred people. The inhabitants of Eau Claire were so spread out, though, that he rarely saw more than a few dozen at any one time.

The townspeople were concentrated along the waterfront, though from information Jesse gleaned, there were isolated pockets of loners scattered throughout the city's interior as well. It was among these 'lowers' that Jesse concentrated his activities.

There was a form of government at work in Eau Claire, a tyrannical dictatorship that held control of all the local trade and river traffic in the area. A young man named Timothy told Jesse that the 'Uppers' — the people in control — were seldom seen, but they had hired bands of mercenaries to enforce their control. Timothy also informed Jesse that the 'Lowers', who comprised the bulk of the population, were totally dependent upon the 'Uppers' for all services and distribution of goods within the city.

Among the loners, Jesse found that the main source of income was farming. Whole neighborhoods had been razed to make room for the planting of wheat, corn, barley, and potatoes; the dilapidated shells of homes still stood in the middle of many of the fields like misplaced monoliths.

The condition of the people physically was much better than Jesse expected to find, although nearly everyone still showed signs of teetering on the brink of starvation. They glanced furtively around themselves through sunken eyes as if they expected something evil and nasty to spring out from the shadows.

Jesse found out soon enough that, at least in Eau Claire, it often did.

The late morning sun beat down on Jesse as he walked through the waterfront area of the city. The horses were in tow, and he was talking with a wizened little man of Oriental ancestry named Jim Tozai.

Jim was an animated little fellow with black hair shading to silver, a wrinkled monkey face, and an exuberance that belied his age. There was a glimmer in his black eyes below the epicanthic folds that indicated a ready wit, and Jesse found him to be well-educated and eloquent.

Jesse had met Jim the previous night as he was looking for a place to bed down. Jim ambled by on his way back from the market and immediately hustled Jesse back to his home, a small house and shed in the center of about three square blocks of former residential district. The land had been cleared and fields planted with wheat, corn, and potatoes. The 'farm' was within walking distance of the old downtown section, and about the same distance from the waterfront markets where Jim traded his crops for necessities.

After helping Jesse see to the needs of the horses, Jim invited Jesse to stay the night. Jesse accepted gratefully, and spent the evening entertaining Jim and his little family with stories of his travels and what he knew of the outside world.

The following morning at daybreak, Jesse went out to the shed behind the house and began to tinker with the ancient Toro lawn tractor that was stored there. Soon enough, Jesse had the machine started with the help of a pint of Jim's carefully stored gasohol; it started with a roar of unmuffled engine and a cloud of dense black smoke that brought Jim and his family running.

"Jesse," Jim cried, "I don't know how to thank you! That infernal machine hasn't run for years!" The children stood well back from the smoking tractor, their eyes wide with awe. "I can use it in the fields for plowing and harvesting my crops."

Jesse smiled and shrugged his shoulders. "It's the least I could do to repay your hospitality, Jim." Jesse went on to mention his plan to go down to the waterfront to seek work.

Jim became agitated, and shook his head. "You can't do that, Jesse; *they've* been known to shoot strangers and ask questions later. Unless..."

"'Unless' what?"

"Unless you had an escort," Jim explained. "It would be safer for you to travel the waterfront if you were with a familiar face—like mine." Jim's face wrinkled as he grinned broadly.

Jesse started to ask Jim why he needed an escort, and who *they* were, but Jim waved off the questions. He simply insisted that he accompany Jesse, and if the truth were known, Jesse was glad of the offer.

The next morning, they had shared a breakfast of hoarded baked beans, boiled potatoes, and some jerky that Jesse dug from his pack. They left as soon as the meal was over, with Jim's wife watching their retreat in worried silence.

They had been walking along the quiet streets for perhaps half an hour when the warehouses and wharves slowly began to make way for an area of relative opulence. Fairly new and attractive apartment buildings sprawled for blocks along the water; the gray-sided, modern buildings stretched along the river with lush, well-tended lawns and tree-lined paths winding between them. It was obvious to Jesse that this had once been an exclusive condominium complex, and he soon discovered that it was even more exclusive now than it had ever been before.

Jesse's packhorse, evidently starved for fresh greenery, pulled loose from his grip and made a beeline for the verdant growth. Jim cried out, and

Jesse rushed to grab the bridle. As he struggled to restrain the old mare six heavily-armed men in uniforms approached them from the nearest building.

As Jesse gained control of the horse, he noticed that the men were wearing dark green military fatigues—clothing matching the description that Ben had given him of the attackers who killed Anna. Jesse's thoughts were interrupted by the clatter of automatic weapons being cocked and trained on him. He glanced at Jim with several unspoken questions in his eyes, but the old man just whispered, "Ignore them, and keep on moving."

Though he was puzzled and not at all happy about turning his back to the hostile gunmen, Jesse complied. The pair had not gone ten feet when they were brought up short by a shout.

"HALT!" a hoarse voice ordered.

Jim frowned and cast a concerned look in Jesse's direction. They stopped and turned to face the soldiers. Jesse glanced nervously at Dolly's saddle where the AK47 was holstered just out of reach. He sighed and faced the armed men.

"Who's dat wit' you, ol' Jim?" a heavyset, hairy brute asked. Jesse noticed that the man's face was badly scarred by pockmarks, and above a scraggly beard his oily face glistened in the sun. "He a stranger? You know we don't like too many strangers 'round here, Jim."

Jesse moved to speak, but Jim shook his head imperceptibly and laid his hand lightly on Jesse's arm. He cast his eyes downward, and in a humble and subservient tone addressed the soldier.

"Sergeant Asher, I'd like to introduce my brother-in-law, Fred Morgan," Jim lied skillfully. "He's traveling through here on his way to the Twin Cities to look for work."

Asher scrutinized Jim for a moment through small, pig-like eyes, then turned his attention to Jesse.

"Fred, where you from?" he demanded.

Jesse looked the soldier straight in the eye as he hastened to come up with a cover story. "I'm from a small town upstate called Glidden," he lied, "Uh--Sir. I decided to take my skills on the road after my wife died, and I'm always looking for an honest day's work."

Asher grinned around filthy yellow teeth and glanced at his cronies. "If you be lookin' for fer work, Fred, dis is da place. We got all kinda work to be done. If you do a good job," he continued in a voice heavily laced with sarcasm, "we might even let you keep dose nags 'a yers. What you do fer a livin'?"

"I'm a tinker—a mechanic," Jesse elaborated as he saw a lack of comprehension on Asher's troglodyte features. "If it's broken, I can fix it." Jesse noticed out of the corner of his eye that Jim had faded against one of the horses and was slowly pulling one of the saddle blankets down to cover his rifle.

Jesse briefly considered pulling his 9mm pistol and taking out the goons, bit figured his chances of killing all six men were slim to none. Besides, who knew how many more of these 'soldiers' were in the surrounding buildings? He decided to play out this little game, but stack a few of the cards in his favor.

"Sergeant Asher, if you will allow me to return to Jim's place, I can get my tools and be back here in less than an hour. I really am eager to get to work—I've been on the road since early spring, and feel the need to get settled down once more. That is," Jesse prompted, "if you can use my skills." He gave the soldier a sunny smile and waited for the man's pea brain to accept his suggestion.

Asher scowled as he thought over Jesse's proposal, his sloping brow furrowing with the force of his concentration. Finally, he nodded to Jesse, though not without a certain suspicion.

"Okay, Fred. If you ain't back in one hour," Asher stated in a calm tone that was somehow more threatening than his shouts, "you know we be lookin' fer you. Right, boys?" The other soldiers nodded agreement with varying degrees of sadistic pleasure showing in their sullen eyes. Jesse knew that they hoped he would *not* show up.

"We don't like workin' any harder than we has to," Asher confided in a stage whisper, "and huntin' down strangers is too much like real work." He chuckled, and was echoed by his sidekicks.

"No problem, Sergeant," Jesse said affably. "I can easily make it to Jim's and back in that time." He waited for some comment, but Asher and his troops just stared dully back at him.

"Well, get movin', Fred," Asher commanded. "Don't keep us waitin'." He shooed them away with a gesture, then he and his chums headed back for the buildings. Jesse got astride Dolly and motioned for Jim to climb aboard the packhorse. He scrambled up, and the two of them trotted down the street toward Jim's house.

Jesse had no intention of remaining in Eau Claire any longer than was necessary to ensure the safety of Jim and his family; he knew that if he didn't show up in the promised hour, Asher and his men would make things rough on the old farmer.

When Jesse made it clear that he was going to leave, Jim became frantic. He tried to convince Jesse to stay, his face pale and voice shaking. Jesse had to give the old man credit; his concern seemed equally divided between Jesse's welfare and that of his family. He explained to Jesse that Asher and his crew enjoyed hunting down fugitives — especially those who didn't keep their promises.

Jesse made it clear to Jim that he could not stay any longer, and had no desire to become 'slave' labor for the Uppers. Jim silently took offense at the word 'slave', since he was in thrall to the Uppers as much as anyone in the area, but kept his peace in deference to the friendly stranger.

Out of gratitude for his help and hospitality, and as a way of appeasing Asher when he came looking for him, Jesse left Jim with some of his provisions, including one of the skins of Isaac's whiskey and the twenty-gauge shotgun (less shells — Jesse had no intention of being fired upon by his own weapon). Jim calmed down sufficiently to allow Jesse to bid a hasty farewell to the family; then, with a wave, Jesse spurred the horses to a trot and headed south as fast as his team could carry him.

As he once more entered the rural areas, Jesse began to mull over what he had seen in Eau Claire. The situation that most of the people were in — a kind of serfdom — was disturbing enough; what really gave Jesse pause was the fact that there seemed to be a strong military force backing up the position of the 'Uppers'.

Is it possible that the Provos are behind this? Jesse thought. *And if so, who is really in control of their government?*

They were good questions — Jesse just wished that he had some answers to match.

CHAPTER THIRTY-THREE

Jesse spent several days finding his way to a relatively safe haven in which to regroup and plan his further travels. He headed southwest on state road 85, a serviceable and unsettled stretch of blacktop. Since any pursuit would assume that he was heading in the direction of Madison, he felt reasonably secure and did not push his animals beyond their endurance. He did, however, exercise some caution, and did not approach any farms or homesteads too closely.

As he traveled down the unfamiliar highway, Jesse wished once again that he had thought to bring maps with him. He found it disconcerting to be going through strange country with little or no indication of where he was or where he was bound.

Jesse made camp his second night out of Eau Claire in an abandoned restaurant on the outskirts of a town called Durand. The restaurant was situated at the crossroads of Highways 10 and 85, with a clear view to the east and west along Highway 10. Jesse looked with longing along the eastern route, but knew that it was too soon for him to head back to the interstate — any pursuit would more than likely follow that route since he had told Jim that he intended to go to Madison.

It did not matter in the least that Jesse had not chosen that way — on the morning of June 30, as he was hitching the horses in preparation to leave Durand, he heard the unmistakable sound of motorcycles heading in his direction from the north.

Jesse quickly unhitched the horses and led them into the large garage behind the restaurant. He ran back outside to get the saddles, and the roar of the cycle engines was noticeably closer. Panting for air and in a state of near-panic, Jesse threw the saddles to the floor, pulled the garage door down to about a foot off the ground, and readied his AK47.

He laid belly-down on the dusty, oil-stained floor, positioned so that he had a clear view from the north, south, and east. The restaurant building itself obstructed the western view, and Jesse noticed with some relief just how ramshackle and neglected it really appeared.

The neon sign that had once proclaimed brightly that this was *Betty's Place* hung askew from a single iron hook, swaying back and forth with faint scraping sounds in the early morning breeze. The building itself was virtually without windows; the only whole panes remaining were in the tiny windows of the kitchen area. The paint, once a cerulean blue with white borders, was now gray with age and peeling off of the wood siding in dry, brittle sheets like a shed snakeskin.

Jesse could hear the individual sounds of the approaching motorcycles as their drivers alternately downshifted and applied the throttle as they wound their way down the cluttered and broken streets of Durand. He checked the rifle, clicked off the safety, and placed another full banana clip beside him in the shadow of the door. He took several deep breaths, exhaled slowly, and rubbed his eyes to clear them. He waited, finger lightly caressing the trigger of his weapon, as his heart thudded in his chest and sweat beaded his forehead. He was at once exhilarated and terrified, and had to exert all his willpower to calm his shaking hands. Finally, just as Jesse was sure that he was imagining the sounds, the riders came into view.

In their dark green uniforms, Jesse had no trouble identifying the riders of the hodge-podge collection of cycles—it had to be Asher and his crew. Although Jesse could not make out any of their features, the bikes were another story.

The low, throbbing drone of an out-of-tune Harley is a sound that is recognizable to any mechanic, and to Jesse, it was unmistakable. There were at least two of those monstrosities in the pack, and their rumble was underscored by the high-pitched clatter of two-stroke dirt bikes. Jesse was amazed that such a group of ill-tended machinery had made it this far—it was obvious that they were running on a poor gasohol mixture, and one of the bikes was casting out huge clouds of blue-black smoke as it burned nearly as much oil as it did fuel.

The cycles rounded the corner on Highway 85, disregarding the rusted stop sign as they began to roll past Betty's on Highway 10. For a moment, Jesse relaxed when it appeared they were going to drive on by. He tensed up again rather quickly, however, as the tail rider tooted his horn and shouted something unintelligible. He slowed his bike, veering off the road and into the gravel parking lot maybe twenty feet from the garage where Jesse was concealed. As the other bikes turned back into the lot, he saw what had caught their attention.

Near the edge of the lot, close to the rear door of the eatery, was an old hand-powered water pump. The tail rider pulled up beside it and killed the engine on the aging Harley with a splatter of backfiring. He pulled his stout frame stiffly from the saddle and removed his hat and goggles. As he turned to watch the others park their cycles, Jesse recognized the hairy features of Asher. He was still as ugly as ever; only now Jesse saw no trace of the humor that he had seen when they had last met. Asher's pocked face held a set expression of mingled anger and irritation.

Asher motioned to one of the other men to start pumping water, and with a hideous squeal, he began to move the handle up and down. Jesse breathed a sigh of relief when he thought what would have happened had he not used a similar pump that was inside the restaurant's kitchen rather than the outdoor pump.

Water, orange with rust, began to trickle from the spout as the soldier pumped harder and faster. Soon it ran clear, and Asher pushed the man rudely to the side and doused his head under the flow of icy water. His hair dripped and rivulets ran down his craggy face as he cupped his hands under the water and took a deep drink. His thirst momentarily sated, he waved for the others to go ahead, and leaned back against the bike.

Asher's eyes roamed back and forth across the lot and overgrown yard looking for signs of inhabitants. Jesse had been careful to allow the horses to graze only in the tangled fields of wild wheat and grasses across the road, so he was not overly concerned with any possible sign of his brief habitation of the area.

Jesse was not sure whether it was a keen sense of smell or some sixth sense, or simply brute curiosity that drew Asher from his reclined stance and toward the garage, but the soldier slowly rose and began to amble toward where Jesse hid. The man was not carrying a rifle, but he had a heavy semi auto pistol holstered on his belt. As he neared the garage, he unsnapped the holster and pulled out the weapon. He carried it lightly, and Jesse sensed that he was up against a master of arms. Jesse tensed and slowly put Asher's chest in the crosshairs of his telescopic sight.

One of the other men called out to Asher, who half-turned to answer. He did not get a chance to get a word out of his mouth before Jesse took the offensive.

Switching his weapon to fully automatic, Jesse let fly a burst of lead into Asher's side and back, even as he rolled to fire at the other three men. He hit one of them in the leg, and the man went down writhing and screaming in the dirt. The other two ran for their motorcycles, unslinging their weapons as they ran. They fell behind the bikes and began firing at the partially open garage door.

Jesse was no longer there. He ran across the concrete floor to the broken side window facing the restaurant. He picked up a tattered blanket and threw it in the doorway to rivet the attention of his adversaries, then took careful aim out the window.

His first shot struck dead center in the fuel tank of one of the Harleys, and the metal screamed as the tank exploded in a mushroom of blue-orange flame and black smoke. One of the men rolled out from behind the burning wreck, his clothes and skin aflame. The other man, further from the explosion, lay prone, his feet dancing a ragged tattoo on the ground for a moment before he lay still.

Jesse aimed and fired a shot at the man whom he had shot in the leg, and he abruptly stopped screaming as his head burst like an overripe melon. Cautiously, Jesse approached the garage door and slid it up on its rollers.

A shot ripped into the frame just inches from Jesse's head, and he ducked back into the shadows. Miraculously, Asher was still alive, but his weakened condition and the strength of the pistol's recoil had caused his shot to go wild. Jesse walked casually over to where the man lay and kicked the gun away from where Asher had dropped it.

The big man was breathing with wet, raspy snuffles, blood bubbling from his mouth and down his chin with each breath. He was bleeding freely from at least half a dozen wounds that Jesse could see as he knelt beside his opponent.

"Hello, Asher," Jesse said coldly, and the soldier glared up at him through glazed eyes filled with hatred and pain. "I guess this means we won't be working together, right?" Jesse smiled faintly, and shook the man as his eyes slowly closed.

"I want to ask you some questions before you — leave," Jesse said sternly, and when Asher shook his head, he nudged the fallen man in the ribs with the butt of his rifle.

Asher cringed at the pain, and his breathing stopped. For an instant, Jesse feared that the man had died, but then Asher's eyes opened, and the underwater sound of his breathing resumed.

"What...do...you...want?" Asher asked in a thick voice.

"I want to know who you work for, and who is in charge of this country." Jesse demanded. "Something just doesn't ring true about you — you acted like a stupid, local heavy, but it's obvious that you have some real military training."

Asher looked at Jesse, and a glint of his sense of humor flickered through the agonized glaze of his eyes. "Provos...pay me," he whispered, stopping when a spasm of pain wracked him. When he continued, his voice was stronger, but Jesse could tell by the pallor of his face that Asher didn't have long to live. "But...I work for...Uppers...old guy...named St. John...owns the Provos..." Asher trailed off, and his eyes closed against the pain.

Jesse struggled to make some sense of what Asher was telling him. "You mean to tell me that one man runs the Provisional U.S. Government?"

Asher shook his head imperceptibly. "St. John...*is* the government," he gasped. "Who are...you? Why do you...want to know?" He feebly grabbed the front of Jesse's cloak and stared intently into the younger man's eyes.

"I am Jesse Walker, of Paradise," he surprised himself by saying, his voice full of pride. "I don't like the Provos, and I sure as hell don't like what's going on in Eau Claire."

"Get used to it...Walker," Asher said quietly with a faint smile on his bloodstained lips. "The same...everywhere..." He sighed, let go of Jesse's cloak, and fell back, lifeless.

Jesse squatted beside Asher's body for a long time, his mind racing at full speed as the sun crossed the summer sky. Asher's answers had only served to give Jesse the beginning of more questions, but he no longer had anyone to ask them of — except, of course, himself.

CHAPTER THIRTY-FOUR

After several days travel, Jesse found himself circling back through Durand, though he gave *Betty's* a wide berth. The rain that had been falling for the past three days had finally stopped, only to give way to a cold front that brought with it unseasonably frosty temperatures — just above freezing, Jesse estimated by the frost on the trees.

Jesse pitched camp in an old wayside, erecting his little tent in the lee of the outhouse to give him some shelter from the chill wind that was beginning to whip down from the north. After gathering up enough green wood to keep his fire going through the night, Jesse cooked a meager meal of Dinty Moore Chicken Stew that he had liberated from an abandoned farmhouse. Washing it down with a slug of Isaac's whiskey — more to warm his bones than to quench his thirst — Jesse leaned back against a tree stump and lit a cigarette.

As he sat in the night watching the fire and listening to the howling of the wind, Jesse realized that for the first time since leaving Paradise he was lonely. Frowning, he flicked his cigarette into the fire and reached into his battered knapsack for the little short-wave transceiver that Ben had given him.

He extended the antenna to its full four-foot length, propped it on the gutter of the outhouse roof, and uncoiled the cable. Once the lead was plugged securely into the jack on the radio, Jesse turned on the set and tuned to the Paradise frequency.

With mingled excitement and trepidation, Jesse thumbed the send button and spoke clearly into the microphone. "Prodigal Son to Fatted Calf...Prodigal Son to Fatted Calf...do you read me?"

He released the button and listened carefully to the static hissing from the tiny speaker. He checked his watch to make sure the frequency would be monitored, and saw that it was nearly ten o'clock — the time that Ben had set aside for any transmissions from Jesse. "Prodigal Son to Fatted Calf," he repeated. *Maybe Ben thinks I'm dead,* Jesse thought whimsically. *It's been nearly three weeks without a word.*

Suddenly the speaker gave a loud squeal and the hum of a broadcast came on the air.

"Prodigal Son, this is Fatted Calf," a voice said clearly. *"Jesse, where the*

hell are you?" Ben's voice was ragged and hoarse, but still recognizable over the miles.

"Near as I can tell," Jesse replied, "about twenty miles southwest of Eau Claire. It's nice to hear your voice, too." Jesse chuckled and returned the frequency to Ben.

"Yeah, yeah," Ben replied irritably. *"The shit's hit the fan, Jess. Can you get back in a couple of days?"*

Jesse's brow furrowed. "There's no way I could, Ben, even if I wanted to. What's the problem? Is it the Provos?"

"I can't tell you on an open frequency — dammit, Jess, I need you!"

Jesse sighed, suddenly filled with misgivings and an icy finger of dread touched his heart. He took stock of his personal aches and pains, looked at the worn out horses dozing just inside the circle of firelight, and turned to the radio.

"I'll be there," he said reluctantly.

Jesse sat down heavily and lit another cigarette. He'd taken his time putting away the radio in order to give himself some time to think.

Not only had Ben *never* come begging to him for help before, he knew why Jesse had left Paradise in the first place. So for him to ask this of Jesse was a last ditch effort to deal with a major problem.

Shit, Jesse mused. *Two tired horses, one tired me. How am I going to get back in time to help?*

With resignation born of utter fatigue, Jesse stood up, pulling his cloak tightly about him to keep out the worst of the chill wind. He considered repacking everything, but decided that the precious moments list in striking his tent would be better spent on the road.

What's the name of the farmer who has all the horses? he wondered, trying to recall the brief reference he had picked up in Eau Claire. *Meyers? Yeah, that's it.* But would fresh horses help?

As Jesse pondered his situation, he weeded out the supplies that were expendable and threw them into the tent. Some other wayfarer might be able to make use of them, but to Jesse they were so much dead weight. Suddenly, he stood up and shouted, "YES!"

His hosts of a few evenings before had mentioned that there was a

Provo airbase in St. Paul. They ran a regular schedule of supply flights to Chicago every three or four hours, with air drops over Green Bay and Milwaukee.

If I can get on one of those planes, Jesse thought with a thrill of excitement, *they can air drop me, too.*

As Jesse mounted Dolly and spurred her into an easy canter, he reviewed what he had learned of the Provisional United States.

The Provos had regained most of the eastern states — in fact, all of those east of the Mississippi except for Wisconsin and Michigan. None of the western states were as yet part of Provo territory, but most did cooperate freely. Minnesota was one of them, and now that Cochran had been deposed, Iowa and Missouri were teetering on the brink of joining the provisional republic.

That was fine with Jesse. Flying home meant that he could make it in time to be of some good to Ben without being exhausted from 'round the clock horseback riding to get there.

He was a little anxious about skydiving, having only done it once before; however, if it meant getting back in one day instead of two, it would be worth it. With the trade goods her was carrying, he should be able to 'buy' a ticket on one of those flights. The liquor and sugar alone were worth a veritable gold mine, and if they weren't enough, he had a tiny cache of *real* gold in reserve.

His mind made up, Jesse spurred Dolly into a full gallop and bent low over her neck. He resolved to trade in his horses for new ones *tonight*, then get to the Twin Cities as early the next day as possible. With luck, he'd be back in Paradise for supper.

Jesse made excellent time getting to St. Paul. The horse-trading went smoothly, although Mr. Meyers did not appreciate being awakened in the wee hours of the morning. Jesse's persuasiveness, coupled with the quality of the horses that he had to trade, quickly brightened the mood of the horseman from El Paso, Wisconsin.

Jesse did not do as well in the trade, however; the horses he acquired were, in all honesty, nags. They were rested and well-fed, though, and in the long run that made all the difference.

He rode the horses hard through the night, switching off between the two when the one he was on became tired. In this manner, he made it to the outskirts of St. Paul shortly after dawn the next day. It took only an additional hour to locate the airfield by following the flight paths of numerous ultra lights, small planes, and large cargo craft.

The airport was set up much as it always had been, although tickets and transport passes were arranged for at the main gates rather than in the terminal — because the terminal was a fire-gutted ruin. Jesse managed to trade nearly all his goods, including the horses, for passage on an airplane that was passing over Wausau. With some additional haggling (and two one-ounce ingots of pure gold), he also received a thermal flight suit and a glider parachute.

After checking the loading of the parachute, Jesse settled down in the shadow of a hangar to await his plane.

The plane was an old four-engine jet, but Jesse's inspection of it as it taxied from the hangar gave him no cause for alarm. The engines seemed to be running smoothly, and the fuselage was shiny and apparently intact. As he entered the cargo bay, he saw bolt holes that ran the length of the plane; obviously, some enterprising people had converted it from its original use of ferrying passengers into its present cargo-carrying capacity. The bulk of the interior was filled with enigmatic crates, and the walls of the bay had a series of fold-down benches for the infrequent passenger. Jesse sat down on one of these, set his parachute and knapsack beside him, and nervously awaited take-off.

A crewman dressed in the green fatigues of the Provos came down from the cockpit to check on the hatches. He asked Jesse how he was doing.

"Fine, thanks," Jesse replied. "I'm a bit nervous about the jump, though. I've done several from five thousand, but I've never attempted one from thirty thousand."

The man shrugged in sympathy. "I know I wouldn't want to do it. The air is thin up there, and weather reports say that the temperature is about twenty below at that altitude." He glanced at Jesse's flight suit. "Are you going to be warm enough in that? The wind chill is going to be about a hundred below as you're falling, and still around minus-forty when the chute opens."

"Yeah, I think so. The suit is lined with two-fifty Thinsulate, and so are the gloves." Jesse frowned as he thought of something he'd forgotten. "I forgot about goggles, though; I don't suppose — "

The crewman reached into a pocket of his flight suit and extracted a pair of leather-rimmed goggles. "I thought you might need these."

Jesse grinned his thanks. "I wasn't relishing the prospect of my eyes freezing on the way down--and I sure as hell wasn't going to keep them shut falling at that speed. Thanks."

Jesse offered the man a cigarette, and the two smoked in silence while waiting for the ground crew to finish preparations for take-off. The intercom crackled finally, calling the crew to their stations, and announcing take-off in two minutes.

"See you," Jesse called out, "and thanks again." He watched the man climb up into the cockpit and breathed a sigh of relief when the hatch was dogged shut.

He felt the throb as the igniters fired up the four jets and idly wondered what the plane was using for fuel. *Probably alcohol,* he decided. *It should burn well in jet engines.*

His thoughts were chopped off as the plane began to make its long takeoff run. Jesse felt every imperfection in the runway as they jostled and vibrated their way down the tarmac.

Shortly, he heard the whine of electric motors as the landing gear was folded into the undercarriage of the giant plane, and the ride smoothed out. *In an hour, I'm going to jump out of a plane flying almost six miles up,* Jesse thought. *Am I crazy?*

The plane's roar was loud in the cargo bay, and already the temperature was dropping; Jesse anticipated that the noise would drop in proportion to the lessening of the temperature as they reached cruising altitude.

He turned his thoughts to Ben and whatever the trouble might be. *Why does everything have to fall apart now?* he wondered. For nearly ten years, he had lived, worked, and dreamed of nothing else but Paradise; then, in the space of a few months, along comes Dwight Cochran and his fanatical hordes, Major Mantey and his talk of 'reunification', and a score of other problems.

Ben and Anna—newlyweds—had been attacked by a group of marauders—Provos, by the description--while on their honeymoon, and the result of that skirmish had been the death of Anna Graycloud.

Jesse fervently hoped that whatever the new problem was, he could help Ben with it—but he held out little hope. The way things were going, the Walkers would soon be just a memory in Paradise.

The click of the intercom jolted Jesse from his pensive state. *"Five minutes to drop time,"* the pilot said. *"Altitude is twenty-eight thousand feet, airspeed at one-thirty knots – held down for passenger convenience in disembarking."* A chuckle made it through the mike before the pilot's thumb released the send button.

Jesse stood up, donned his parachute, gloves, and goggles, and checked the seal on his suit. He glanced at the compass strapped to his wrist and made sure that the knapsack tied around his waist was within easy reach.

"Three minutes."

He walked to the exit hatch. Peering out of the port, he could see the cloud layer below, and beyond that, the patchwork quilt of ground five and one-half miles beneath his feet. It was an immensely beautiful sight, and Jesse became so caught up in it that he nearly missed the drop call.

"One minute. Stand by for hatch release."

Jesse grabbed the overhead rail in a death grip, clipped his ripcord to the lanyard, and looked on as the door slammed open in the hurricane-force wind that immediately whipped at the dust and tarpaulins in the cargo bay.

Jesse took several rapid and deep breaths to enrich his blood with remnants of pressurized air; it was a long way down with nearly no oxygen for the first several thousand feet.

"Drop."

Jesse took one final breath, held it, and with a silent prayer and a thought for the helpful airman, he stepped out into the empty air more than five miles high.

Ben struggled to his feet as the short-wave came to life. He had drunk so much that he had a terrible hangover – something unusual for him. With his hands clasped tightly to his throbbing temples, he staggered to the transceiver.

"Prodigal Son to Fatted Calf. Come in, Fatted Calf," he heard Jesse's voice say faintly. It sounded as though he was speaking from inside a tornado.

Ben picked up the microphone. "This is Fatted Calf. Where are you, Jess?"

The whistling sound nearly drowned out the younger Walker as her replied. *"I'm at about eight thousand feet, Ben. I'll be grounding just south of Wausau in a few minutes. Do you want to send someone to pick me up, or do I start walking?"*

Ben keyed the mike. "We'll pick you up, Jess." He looked at his watch. "It'll be about an hour or so. Start sending up signals at eleven thirty."

"Roger that, Ben," Jesse said. *"Prodigal Son, out."*

Ben placed the microphone back on its hook, then reached for the telephone and dialed the three-digit number for the hangar. Jeff would be there, and Ben wanted to know if the 'Phoenix' was ready to take wing.

Jeff answered on the second ring. *"Hangar. Barker here."*

"Jeff, this is Ben. Is my bird ready to fly?"

"All done, sir," Jeff replied respectfully. *"I just finished applying the final clear coat of acrylic."*

Ben chuckled. "You must have stayed up all night!"

Jeff answered slowly. *"Well, 'Rissa helped me with some of it, and I finished the rest this morning."* The youngster stifled a yawn. *"I could use some sleep, though."*

"Tell you what, Jeff. Fuel her up, warm up the engines, and open the hangar doors. I'll be over in fifteen minutes to take her out. *Then,* you can knock off and get some sleep." A thought occurred to Ben. "You'd better begin work on the other one like it as soon as possible, Jeff—like later today?" It was phrased as a question, but Jeff interpreted it differently.

"The Phoenix will be ready, Ben. I'll get started on the other one later this afternoon, all right?" The connection broke, and Ben dialed the number for the Inn.

When Isaac answered, Ben explained that he was going to be making a test flight. "I'll be gone most of the day, so you're in charge."

"Hell, Ben; you don't sound like you're in any shape to go flying. Can't it wait? "

"No, Ike. I've built a new screamer to take the place of the 'Eagle' and I'm itching to try it out." *And I want Jesse back here as soon as possible, old friend.* Ben hated to keep Isaac in the dark, but the fewer people who knew Jesse was back, the better.

"*All right, Ben. I'll hold down the fort until you get back.*" He paused, and then abruptly changed the subject. "*I haven't seen Kane all day – any ideas where the weasel is hiding out?* "

Ben knew very well where Kane was, but kept control of his voice as he replied. "No, Ike, I haven't seen him either. Why?"

"*I just like to keep track of my enemies, Ben. Stop by here when you get back, okay?* "

"You bet, Ike. Later." Ben hung up the phone slowly in its cradle. *I'm glad to hear that I'm not the only one who couldn't stomach Kane,* he thought with a grimace. He quickly washed and changed into his flight suit, even though it wasn't necessary in the enclosed cockpit of '*Phoenix*'.

He grabbed a cup of black coffee from the ever-ready pot on the stove and slammed its searing contents down before sprinting off toward the hangar.

Here I come, Jess – ready or not.

Jesse neglected to pay close enough attention to his angle of descent, and as a result, his left ankle was a little sore from landing on it the wrong way. *Probably sprained it,* he thought ruefully as he rubbed the bruised joint.

He divested himself of the chute and crawled out of the heavy canvas and Thinsulate jumpsuit. He rolled the chute into a ball and placed it next to him on the ground. The jumpsuit he folded carefully, placing goggles and gloves atop it.

He opened his knapsack and withdrew a folded garment from within. Shaking it out, he smoothed the fabric and donned his cloak. Brushing his platinum hair out of his eyes, he settled down on the rolled up parachute and lit a smoke.

The mid-morning sun felt good on Jesse's back as he bent to the task of building a signal fire. He gathered up a small pile of leaves and twigs from around him, and with the butt end of his cigarette set fire to it. He quickly scoured the area for green branches and soon had a small but smoky fire going. He picked out another pile of limbs to keep the blaze fed and sat down next to it.

They ought to see that, he thought as he watched the pillar of white smoke drift upward into the calm blue sky. He resumed his seat atop his parachute cushion, wrapping his cloak tightly around his chilled body.

Something was nagging at the back of his mind—something to do with the attack on Anna. Ben had mentioned that the attackers had all worn dark green uniforms. What was it about that which bothered him? Jesse knew that somewhere in his memory was buried the answer to who had killed his brother's wife.

As he bent to pull a burning branch from the fire to light another cigarette, the memory clicked into place. Several nights earlier, while stopped at a small farm near Sparta, Jesse had held a conversation with an old farmer. The man—Harold Jaeger—had commented on how "the woods aren't safe any more, what with the Death Squads."

The kindly old gent had gone on to explain that the Squads were the strong arm of the provisional U.S. government; not really a part of it—they were mercenaries used to 'reduce dissent' among the fiercely independent people of Wisconsin. Part of their image, setting them apart from the regular troops, was the forest green jumpsuits they wore, as compared to the regular olive drab of the typical Provo soldier.

Ben will want to hear this! Jesse thought. *The damned Provos must want us badly if they will kill rather then negotiate. Wisconsin must be a real thorn in their sides – the only state east of the Mississippi besides Michigan able to resist them with any success.*

As Jesse completed the thought, he heard a high-pitched wail from the north. Looking up, he saw the silhouette of a small plane, but could make out no details. *Must be from Paradise,* he concluded. *They made good time.* As the plane circled his smoke signal, Jesse prudently ran for cover in the nearby bushes, keeping his eyes on the plane as he tried to make out any identifying marks.

The sun glinted off the side of the plane as it swung down towards the ground. It was a sleek craft with an enclosed cockpit and souped-up engine, but it was indisputable that it was an ultra light of some sort. *I wonder who it is?* Jesse mused. *It sure as hell isn't one of* ours.

The plane swept low on its final descent. It dropped rapidly, and Jesse thought for a moment that the pilot had misjudged the altitude. At the last possible instant, the plane went into a stall—a mere yard from the ground—and settled heavily on its landing gear.

Jesse peered cautiously from behind the bush, eager and anxiously waiting for the pilot to get out.

The red leather flight suit was a dead giveaway. Jesse stepped out from behind the undergrowth and hailed the familiar figure. "Over here, Ben!"

The older man turned and ran toward Jesse. "How the hell are you, Bro'?" he shouted as he grabbed his brother in a bear hug. "It's great to see you. We have a mess at home—there's trouble in Paradise, for sure!"

The *'we'* was not lost on Jesse. "What's up?"

Ben stepped back and grinned at Jesse. "We'll discuss it when we get back—I'd like to have Isaac in on this, too."

He ushered his younger brother over to the plane. "Let's get going, Jess. The sooner the better."

Jesse eyed his brother with misgiving, but the mechanic in him took over as he approached the plane. "Nice," he murmured, his voice holding a barely concealed note of envy. "Where'd this come from?"

"Jeff," Ben replied. "He worked day and night on the modifications for me—" he noticed Jesse's glare "—and he's doing up one for you, too."

Jesse smiled, nodding his approval as they boarded.

Ben fired up the engine and called out to Jesse in the rear compartment. "Strap in and hang on, Jess!"

Jesse smiled and nodded, knowing his brother was always a showoff when it came to new toys.

"Here we go!" Ben shouted. He hit the button igniting the JATO and opened the throttle at the same moment. The tiny craft shot forward, pushing both men against their seats as the jets flung the plane forward. In less than a hundred feet they were airborne and climbing at a forty-five degree angle.

Awesome, Jesse gasped silently as he swallowed his heart.

Ben swung the plane around to the north, set the controls, and headed for home.

CHAPTER THIRTY-FIVE

Ben and Jesse spent the flight getting caught up with each other. Jesse handed Ben his concise travel journal, and Ben skimmed through it.

"Dammit, Jess," Ben raged over the roar of the engines, "if the Provos are 'owned' by some big shot, how can we stop them?"

Jesse shrugged. "I don't know. I do know, however, that I don't like the way those people are being forced to work for the Uppers," he exclaimed. "I thought that slavery was abolished back in eighteen sixty-five, but you wouldn't know it to see the conditions in Eau Claire." Jesse took a savage drag from his cigarette and glared at the back of his brother's head. "What *do* we do?"

Ben leaned his head back against the rest and closed his eyes. "I have no idea, Jess, but we may find out sooner than we want to," he muttered enigmatically. Jesse attempted to get a further explanation out of him, but Ben made a pretense of checking the instruments.

"Hell," Jesse rumbled, "I might just as well get some sleep." He crushed out his cigarette in the armrest ashtray, propped his head on his hand, and was instantly asleep.

After what seemed only seconds, Ben shook his brother gently. "Wake up, Jesse." Jesse's eyes flew open, and for a moment he was disoriented. As he blinked his eyes against the sunlight, he saw Ben's form seated in front of him in the plane's cockpit.

"What's up, Ben?" Jesse asked groggily. He straightened in his seat, adjusted the restraints, and ran a hand through his frizzy white hair.

Ben turned around to face his brother. "Do you remember that abandoned airfield just west of Lake Mohawksin?" Jesse nodded. "We're going to land there, stash the 'Phoenix', and hike the rest of the way to Paradise after sunset."

Jesse raised an eyebrow and frowned. "Are things so bad in Paradise that we have to sneak back like a pair of fugitives? I know *I* haven't done anything wrong—have *you?*" Jesse watched his brother carefully, and saw his face close up like a slamming door.

"No, it's not like that," Ben lied as he glanced away from his brother. "I just don't want anyone to know that we're back yet." Ben's eyes flicked nervously at Jesse and he smiled. "Besides, we've got a lot of work to get done before morning."

Ben turned back to the controls, as much to stifle any further inquiry as to prepare for landing. The plane banked sharply in response to his guidance, and they spiraled down toward the little airstrip.

Ben and Jesse held their packs overhead as they made their way out of the river. The chill night air struck them like a winter frost, and both men shivered as they stood on the riverbank east of Harry's place.

Jesse shed his shirt, squeezed it until it was no longer dripping wet, and tied it about his slim waist. Ben, seeing what he had done, followed suit. After removing his cloak from his pack, Jesse donned it over his bare torso. Ben pulled on a dry black sweatshirt; this, combined with his wet black jeans, made him nearly invisible. Jesse covered his glowing mane of hair with the hood of his cloak, affording himself the same camouflage.

Ben pulled on his backpack and gestured for Jesse to do the same. Then, as one, the two men quickly and quietly made their way down the riverbank towards the glowing lights of the Paradise dam. Their feet made squelching noises in the slippery mud, and once Ben nearly fell, caught in the nick of time by his brother. Ben nodded his thanks, and they resumed their trek.

Suddenly, Ben dropped to his knees, reaching out an arm to pull Jesse down. Silhouetted by the night-lights, a shadowy form was walking across the top of the dam. A wisp of bluish smoke rose from the man, and the glowing tip of a cigarette arced out over the water to be extinguished a second later with an audible hiss. The man glanced up and down the river, and then slowly walked from the dam to the house. Out of view of the two brothers, a door squeaked open, and then slammed shut.

Both men heaved a sigh of relief. "That was close," Ben whispered. Jesse nodded, unsure whether Ben saw him or not, and the pair got to their feet. With only slightly exaggerated stealth, they walked to the base of the dam.

Ben opened a concealed hatch with a slight inrush of gurgling water, and clattered into the tunnel. He motioned Jesse to follow, and after some hesitation, the younger man entered the darkened maw. Ben reached around Jesse and pulled the hatch shut, activating the tunnel lighting at the same time. In the dim orange light, Jesse saw that two of his electric carts were waiting for them.

Ben grinned at Jesse. "Brother, your 'chariot' awaits."

A short time later, the entrance to the War Room opened, and a damp and bedraggled pair walked through the doorway. Jesse quickly peeled out of his clothes and pulled a dry sweatshirt and jeans from his pack. Ben did likewise, and the two men changed in silence. Jesse shot a curious glance at his brother as he rolled up his wet clothes.

"What was that odd smell in the tunnel, Ben?" Jesse asked, breaking the silence. "I thought you told me nothing could get into the tunnels, but it sure smelled like something crawled in there and died..." Jesse trailed off as a look of dismay crossed his brother's face.

Ben walked over to the computer console and sat down with a sigh. "Something did crawl in here, Jess—and it *did* die," Ben began. "But it was *you* who allowed it to get in here in the first place!" Ben's eyes snapped up to meet Jesse's, but the younger man's face held an expression of confusion.

"What the hell are you talking about? I haven't even been near those damned tunnels since we went out to Harry's!" Jesse was beginning to get angry—a good, healthy emotion he had not felt in a long time. "I sure as hell didn't allow anything or anyone in—" Jesse stopped abruptly. "Oh, shit."

"You didn't let anything into the tunnels," Ben spat, his face red with rage, "but you sure as hell let a rat into Paradise!" When Jesse continued to look puzzled, he snapped, "Damon Kane!"

Jesse's face fell into an expression of exhausted defeat, and he joined Ben by the console. "Are you trying to tell me that Kane is—dead?" He uttered the word hesitantly, as if by saying it he would make it so.

"That's exactly what I'm saying, dammit! The sonofabitch pushed me too far, and I shot him!" Ben took several deep breaths to regain his composure, and then went on.

"It was bad enough when he started to badmouth the way that we've been running things in Paradise, and I couldn't stop him from campaigning for a seat on the council; when he began to run for *my* seat, and accused me of bungling the battle with Cencom, well—let's just say he forced a confrontation, and lost." Ben settled back in his chair and wished mightily that he kept a bottle of liquor in the computer room. He watched as what he said sank into his brother's mind, and prepared himself for the worst.

"Well," Jesse began slowly, "I was afraid that Kane couldn't be trusted; however, I think that *I* might have handled things with a bit less-- finality." Jesse lit a cigarette and offered one to Ben with a faint smile on his lips. "But we can't bring him back, so we'd better find a way out of this. Have you consulted the computer?"

Ben handed Jesse the printouts of his earlier computations, and as Jesse read through the results, he whistled softly.

"Doesn't look too good, does it?" he muttered. "There's definitely trouble in Paradise." He turned toward the console, glanced at Ben, and reached out to activate the voice recognition circuits.

"Walker, Jesse. Access Zero."

"ACCESS ZERO ACCEPTED.   HI, JESSE.   HOW ARE YOU TONIGHT?"

Ben stared in amazement at Jesse; he had never heard the computer sound so animated, and did not realize it was even programmed to respond to Jesse.

"I'm just fine, thank you — hold," Jesse said as he noted the expression of bewilderment on Ben's face.

"Sorry about that, Ben, but when you asked me to install the voice circuits, I couldn't do it without being able to get it to respond to my voice, too. You weren't around when I did it, so I didn't bother to tell you."

"What else haven't you told me?" Ben asked in hushed tones.

"Uh — I didn't think you'd mind, so I installed a Turing program that I modified for my personal computer a couple of years ago.   With this computer's larger capacity, I was able to expand it considerably." Jesse grinned proudly. "That's why it can respond so readily to voice commands. It 'thinks' almost like a human, so it can talk like one better.   And," Jesse hesitated, "I beefed up some of your security codes."

Ben nearly exploded out of his seat. "You did *what!?*"

"Just what I said," Jesse replied defensively. "I didn't need to change much. You had a good programmer on this beast." Jesse grinned, knowing that Ben had done nearly all of the original programming.

"Okay, you've made your point," Ben said, mollified. "Now, what were you going to ask the computer?"

"Oh yeah—computer, resume. Analysis mode. Given the fact that Ben and Jesse Walker are forced to vacate the Paradise area, what do you outline as the next logical step, given the fact that the Provisional United States Government is gaining an increasing hold over the Midwest? Entering data for scan." Jesse pulled out his journal and slowly fed pages into the laser reader. When the last page had been entered, he ordered the computer to correlate all the data.

"Vocalize analysis: compute optimum course for the Walkers to maintain survival, with ultimate goal of fulfilling and honoring original Paradise goals, sub file nine-oh-nine-ay."

The room was silent, and the two brothers watched each other for several minutes. Finally, the computer broke the tense silence.

"JESSE, FIRST ASSUMPTION BASED UPON EARLIER CONSULTATION WITH BEN WALKER IS THAT BOTH BEN AND JESSE WALKER ARE ABLE TO LEAVE PARADISE UNDETECTED. CHANCES, MINIMAL."

"SECOND ASSUMPTION IS THAT BOTH BEN AND JESSE WALKER CHOOSE TO STAY TOGETHER."

"FINAL ASSUMPTION IS THAT BOTH BEN AND JESSE WALKER HAVE THE SAME GOAL IN MIND: THE PRESERVATION OF PARADISE AS PER SUBFILE NINE-OH-NINE-AY."

"AWAITING VERIFICATION OF ASSUMPTIONS."

Ben and Jesse exchanged glances, and both nodded, their faces grim.

"All assumptions true," Jesse stated flatly.

"IF ALL ASSUMPTIONS ARE TRUE, THE OPTIMUM COURSE IS AS FOLLOWS:

"ONE: CONSOLIDATE STANDING AND POWER IN PARADISE WITH ISAAC PETERS AND JEFFREY BARKER. BOTH MEN WILL CONTINUE TO HOLD SUBSTANTIAL POWER FOR THE NEXT SIX TO TEN YEARS. THE POWER OF MR. PETERS WILL WANE AS MR. BARKER'S STRENGTH SLOWLY GROWS."

"TWO: DO NOT ANNOUNCE THE DEATH OF COUNCILOR KANE. IF THE GENERAL POPULACE DOES NOT HAVE PROOF OF GUILT, THE FUTURE POSITION OF THE WALKERS IN PARADISE WILL BE MORE SECURE."

"THREE: LEAVE PARADISE UNANNOUNCED."

"FOUR: MAINTAIN CONTROL OF MAIN COMPUTER. THIS MAY BE DONE VIA SHORTWAVE LINKUPS, WITH THE MAIN TRANSCEIVER BASED IN THE CONTROL ROOM AND PERSONAL TRANSCEIVERS CARRIED BY BOTH BEN AND JESSE WALKER. PLANS FOR BOTH ARE PRINTING OUT NOW."

Ben and Jesse both jumped as the laser printer began to hum.

"FIVE: AFTER LEAVING PARADISE, CUT COMPUTER CONTROL OF ELECTRICAL AND COMMUNICATION SYSTEMS FOR A PERIOD OF TWO HOURS. THIS WILL CAUSE CONFUSION AND WILL DELAY ANY POSSIBLE PURSUIT."

"SIX: GO TO CHICAGO. IT IS THE CAPITOL OF THE NEW AMERICAN REGIME. FOMENT DISCONTENT AMONG THE GENERAL POPULACE."

"FINAL ANALYSIS OF OPTIMUM COURSE OF ACTION: START A REVOLUTION."

Both men were absolutely silent for several minutes as they absorbed the computer's directives. Finally, Jesse cleared his throat. "Thank you, computer. Good night."

"GOOD NIGHT, JESSE. YOU TOO, BEN."

Ben looked sharply at Jesse, who shook his head and shrugged. Both men began to laugh, and soon tears were streaming down their faces.

Jesse was still laughing as he pulled the plans for the transceivers from the printer and got to work.

Jesse left quietly from the rear of the administration building, pulling the hood of his cloak around his head. His white hair, while at other times an advantage, acted now as a disadvantage. He did not want to be seen or recognized, and in the dark, his hair served as a beacon.

With reflexes born of instinct, Jesse made his way through the trees and over obstacles, and hurried across the silent streets whenever they could not be avoided. An automatic rifle swung from his shoulder, and he carried a knife in his right hand. He was wary ready for trouble.

At long last he reached his home on DueEast Road, and furtively approached the attached mobile home that he had converted into his workshop. He opened the light screen door with a screech of infrequently oiled hinges, and walked through the shadowy structure. With careful steps he walked down the familiar hallway and entered the back room. Here, he pulled out a flashlight and aimed its narrow beacon at the back wall.

Pulling on the vise attached securely to the workbench, Jesse opened the concealed door to his personal underground complex. Securing the door behind him, he turned on the single dim bulb that lit the shaft and made his way down the short ladder.

Several minutes later, Jesse exited by the same route, his arms and pack laden with electronic components and holographic projectors. He had just closed the door and turned to leave the building when he heard a well-known sound.

Ralph, his faithful dog, was just outside the mobile home, and barking wildly. Jeff Barker had been watching the canine during Jesse's absence, and he felt a stab of guilt as he thought of the friendly mutt. Jesse had given the dog little thought during his travels, and nearly no affection or attention in the weeks prior to his leaving.

Suddenly, a strange voice shouted, "Shut that goddam dog up!" and a shot rang out. Jesse heard a strangled yelp from Ralph, then the sound of heavy footfalls approaching the trailer. He ran toward the rear door, which as he reached it, swung inward, knocking him off his feet. He barely had time to register the sight of the rifle butt sweeping down before a brief flash of pain exploded his world into oblivion.

Where the hell is Jesse? Ben thought as he looked at his watch in irritation. He had completed the reprogramming that would enable the computer to accept short-wave broadcasts as well as remote systems shutdown; all that was needed was to finish assembling the hardware—and Jesse had gone to pick up the parts.

Ben fidgeted restlessly for several more minutes, then spoke to the computer.

"Ben Walker, Access One. Conjecture. What are the chances that Jesse Walker has been apprehended while outside of the computer complex, given the fact that the Merrill populace is concerned over the disappearance of Damon Kane? Run."

The computer hummed quietly as it worked. "CONJECTURE IS UNNECESSARY. JESSE WALKER IS UNDER DETENTION IN JAIL CELL BEE. DETENTION LOGGED INTO SECURITY CONSOLE THREE MINUTES NINE SECONDS PRIOR TO ACTIVATION OF CONJECTURE MODE."

Ben swore loudly. "Thank you, computer. End."

"GOOD NIGHT, BEN."

Ben picked up the telephone and hastily punched Isaac's number. The phone rang several times before it was answered. A sleepy voice came over the line.

"*This is Isaac,*" the big man yawned. "*What the hell are you calling at this hour for? It better be good.*"

"Ike, this is Ben. I have to see you *now!*" Ben paused to collect his wits, and continued, "Jesse's in jail, and I don't know what else is going on— can you meet me at admin in ten minutes?" Ben waited impatiently for his friend to reply.

"*Yeah,*" Isaac said slowly, "*I can be there. I think I know what this is all about, and you're not going to like it.*"

"I already don't! Just get over her ASAP." Ben hung up the phone, lit one of Jesse's cigarettes, and began to pace the floor.

A few minutes later, when he heard the door buzzer, Ben climbed the ladder and entered his office. He pushed the button that unlocked the lower entrance to the building and waited for Isaac to arrive.

He did not have to wait long. Isaac's heavy footsteps thundered up the stairs, and he stormed into Ben's office. Ben noticed again how Isaac's presence seemed to fill the room. He also made note of the fact that the usually peace loving Isaac Peters was wearing a sidearm.

Ben motioned Isaac to sit down, and barely waited for him to be seated before he began speaking.

"If you know something I don't, spill it," he said as he paced the room in anger. "I can't think of any reason for Jesse to be in jail—unless being my brother has become a crime!" Ben slammed his fist down on the desk and glowered at Isaac.

"Calm down, Ben; this has nothing to do with you, or the fact that Jesse's your brother," Isaac explained. "He's in jail because he's a prime suspect in the disappearance of Damon Kane."

The words hung in the air, and Ben shook his head. "Jesse? Damon?" Ben walked to his chair and sat down heavily. He continued to shake his head, and began laughing. He continued to do so, tears rolling out of his eyes, until Isaac growled at him to stop.

"What's so damned funny? They're going to try your brother for murder, and you sit there and laugh?" Isaac shot daggers at Ben, and the older Walker made an attempt to control his hysteria.

"It's not funny, Ike; what *is* funny is that Jesse just got back into Paradise tonight—with me. Besides," and Ben's tone grew serious, "they have the wrong man."

"You mean you know who did it? Why didn't you say something to me earlier? I could have stopped this nonsense." Isaac watched Ben with an appraising eye, and slowly came to a conclusion. His jaw dropped open and his hand unconsciously fell to his pistol.

"You didn't—I mean—shit, Ben—did *you* kill Kane?" The accusation made, the two men stared at each other warily. Isaac's hand twitched closer to his pistol, and Ben spoke sharply.

"Don't do it, Ike. I wouldn't want to have to shoot you," he warned, "with this." Ben raised his right hand from under the desk and showed Isaac the nine-millimeter pistol.

"Can we talk reasonably," he asked, "or do we have a shootout?"

Isaac slowly dropped his hand away from the holster and Ben lowered the pistol to the desk. "That's better, old friend. Ike, I'm not going to give you any explanations; however, I'm going to ask you a favor, based on our years of friendship.

"I'm leaving Paradise, and I want to take Jesse with me. I don't plan to get hung for killing that son of a bitch Kane, and I won't let my brother take the rap, either. All I ask is that you keep this under your hat until after we're gone. Then you can take charge of this zoo. Fair enough?"

Isaac looked intently at Ben for some time, deep in thought. He wondered what was happening here that he was not aware of, but he couldn't put a finger on it. He heaved a great sigh, leaned forward, and his eyes searched Ben's.

"Okay, Ben," he said slowly, his deep voice carrying a note of sadness. "I want you to know that I'm going to have to brand both of you outlaws in order to keep the peace. And I know," he pointed out, "that there are several people—all from Merrill—who will enjoy tracking you down and killing you. Not out of love for Kane, of course; just for the sport of it."

Ben nodded. "Let them; we both know how to defend ourselves." Isaac grimaced as Ben continued.

"Can you arrange for Jesse to be released, or do I have to do it the hard way?"

Isaac shook his head. "I won't even try, Ben. I have a wife and kids to look out for. Besides," he chuckled as he went on in a spiteful tone of voice, "you're still the leader, so it's *your* problem." With that said, Isaac stood and walked from the room.

Ben sat inertly for a long while, and then picked up the pistol from his desk. He ejected the clip from the weapon, and it clattered as it fell, empty, before him. He opened a drawer and pulled out a handful of shiny brass cartridges and began to refill the magazine he'd emptied before meeting with Isaac.

Jesse roused painfully, and when he attempted to sit up, a red haze blurred his vision. He carefully laid his head back and tentatively opened his eyes.

He was unsure of his surroundings in the gloom, but as his eyes adjusted, he recognized one of the jail cells. Sluggishly, the memory of the night's encounter returned to him. He vaguely recalled being carried roughly from his trailer; after that, he drew a blank.

He sat up abruptly, ignoring the jolt of pain that shot from the wound on his forehead. "Ralph," he said sadly, and felt a wave of sorrow run through him. He silently vowed to deal with the person who had killed his dog in a very personal and unpleasant manner.

Jesse peered across the cell and through the barred door to the desk that lay beyond. There was no guard posted, but he thought he could make out the silhouette of someone outside the window.

Jesse glanced down at his wrist to check the time, and noticed with anger that someone had removed his trusty Timex. By the light in the streets and the color of the sky, Jesse estimated that it was about midnight. He lay back on the hard mattress, wincing as pain sliced through his head again. He reached up to touch the sticky, ragged laceration that was still oozing blood. Closing his eyes, Jesse drifted off to an uneasy nap.

Suddenly alerted by an unusual noise, Jesse opened his eyes. He slowly turned his head to the side to see the drainage grate in the floor swing down. As it disappeared, a head shot up with a shushing motion.

CHAPTER THIRTY-SIX

Jesse smiled at his brother.

"And what took you so long? Those bastards were going to hang Kane's death on *me!*"

Ben chuckled softly. "Yeah? They still have to find the *corpus delecti* — in the lime pit and decayed as hell by now. Let's get out of here. We've got work to do, 'cause we're leaving Paradise tonight."

Ben turned and slipped down the shaft. Jesse, taking a last glance at his cell, followed him after delaying only long enough to slide the grate back into place and secure it. Ben's light was a few yards ahead in the western tunnel.

"Ben," Jesse called, "wait up!" He scurried like an ant through the dimly lit and moistly glistening concrete tubing that served so many purposes for himself and his brother.

When he finally caught up with Ben, they were almost to the central intersection. "Where to?" Jesse panted, out of breath.

"Take a break, Jess," Ben replied. He handed Jesse a cigarette and they both lit up. "I haven't planned our next move yet; I just wanted to get you out of jail."

Jesse mulled over the situation. "Ben — you said that you want to leave tonight, right?"

"Yeah, that's the plan."

"I was thinking — believe it or not — that if we're going out into the cold, cruel world, we should go as prepared as we possibly can. Trade goods, bribes, and all that."

Ben looked sharply at his brother's argent haired countenance. "So?"

"Remember what I told you about Harry's 'secret' stash of goodies? Let's raid it, load what we can, and split." Another thought occurred to Jesse. "Is there any chance my plane will be ready before dawn?"

Ben frowned. "I'll have to check — Jeff assured me it would be, but he may have run into problems. As far as raiding Harry's place, doesn't he keep a close watch on the dam area? We aren't exactly in a position to take it by storm, especially considering that you're going to be a fugitive as soon as they discover that you're missing. We'll have to sneak in, take what we can carry, and sneak out again—then make it to the airfield in one piece."

"Ben, if I didn't know you better, I'd swear you were losing your nerve. Whatever happened to the 'no guts, no glory' Ben that I used to know?"

Ben's face flushed in anger for a second, only to be replaced by an expression of unbearable sadness. "I guess that Anna's death made me doubly appreciative of my own life. I never truly thought about life until hers was taken from me."

Jesse looked at his big brother in sympathy. "I'm sorry, Ben; I know that Anna meant a lot to you." He suddenly stood, cracking his head against the roof of the tunnel. "Ben! I almost forgot about this—the goons let me keep it." He handed Ben a little plastic case about the size of a pack of cigarettes. A small silver button was recessed into one end.

Ben turned it over and looked at it curiously. "What is it?"

"Press the button, big brother."

Jesse watched Ben's face closely as his brother sought out the switch. Out of the opposite end of the case sprang an image—a holographic likeness of Anna Graycloud-Walker. Jesse had fashioned it for Ben as a wedding present, but had never had the opportunity to give it to him.

"Anna!" Ben gasped. He turned away, but not before Jesse saw the soft glow of a teardrop coursing down his cheek. Jesse lit another cigarette and smoked it in silence.

Several minutes later, the image of Anna snapped off, and Ben turned around to smile at Jesse. "Thanks, Bro," he said hoarsely. "Let's go."

Not another word was exchanged until the two approached the portal of the underground passage that was closest to Harry's. Ben doused the flashlight and allowed the phosphorescent glow of the inner hatch to illuminate them.

Ben turned to the task at hand. He grasped the hatch bolt, pulled it out, and swung the door out over the water. Peeking out of the opening, he whispered, "Looks clear. More water than usual; Harry must have opened the sluice gates."

The two men climbed out of the tunnel, grabbing the loose soil above them for support as they mounted the steep bank of the flowage. Ben reached the summit first and cautiously surveyed the area. When Jesse arrived and they had both ascertained that it was safe, they ran for the building that housed Harry's treasure trove.

They rounded the power plant, knowing that the low roar of the five thousand watt generators would drown out any noise they made. Ben paused, rifle cocked and ready, to glance through the single window of that building.

"He's not in here, Jess," Ben whispered. "What time is it?"

Jesse, who had always had a keen time sense, made his best guess. "One, maybe one-fifteen," he said. "Harry'll be sleeping."

Ben motioned Jesse to follow, and the pair ran swiftly to the double doors of the warehouse. Ben grabbed the door handles and shook them in frustration. "Damn things are locked," he muttered. "What the hell do we do now?"

Jesse smiled faintly, reached down to the ground, and lifted a fist-sized rock. "This might help," he said.

"You can't break in with that," Ben said in consternation. "You'll have all of Paradise down on us with the noise."

Jesse fumbled with the rock for a moment, and then held out a shiny silver key. "Who said anything about breaking in, Ben? You're not the only one who thinks ahead." He unlocked the doors and replaced the key in the stone, carelessly tossing it to one side. The doors opened smoothly inward on freshly oiled hinges, and they went inside.

Ben closed the doors behind them, then turned on his flashlight and panned its beam back and forth across the large room that adjoined Harry's house.

"Holy shit," Ben exclaimed in a stunned voice. "Where'd he get all of this?"

Jesse didn't reply, for he, too, was stunned.

There were cases of Spam, macaroni and cheese, and Campbell's soups; pallets full of catsup and mustard, pickles, olives, and coffee; boxes full of cigarettes, liquor, toilet paper, and medicines. The list went on and on— thousands of cases of items that had not been seen in Paradise for a long, long time.

Ben's sharp eyes found a case. "Jess," he hissed, "look at this!"

Jesse followed his brother across the crowded floor to the case, half-hidden under a box of Alka Seltzer. *Mickey's Malt Liquor*, it read.

"Mickey's Big Mouths?" Jesse said in awe, his eyes lighting up. He had always been more of a beer drinker than one of hard liquor, but the local beers were suitable only for watering the lawn, so he had long ago given up any hope of having his favorite brew again. "I wonder if it's still good?"

Ben smiled at his brother. "I'd like to find out, too," he said in sympathy, "but we haven't the room for it. Grab about fifty pounds of canned meats, chocolate, liquors, and medicine. Anything else that you think is valuable and lightweight is okay, but the planes will only handle about two hundred pounds of cargo.

"We'll have to drop off this stuff and go to the armory — my personal one, that is. Decide what you want for weapons, and we'll pick that up, too."

Jesse sighed, cast a last longing glance at the Mickey's, and nodded. A cold, calculating part of him thrilled at the prospect of creating havoc.

For nearly twenty minutes they worked silently, packing goods with utmost care into four nylon mesh bags that Ben found hanging just inside the doors. They were almost finished when they heard heavy footsteps approaching the door that connected the warehouse to the house-proper.

The connecting door swung open with a crash, and Harry Miller's form filled the opening. "Hey," his voice boomed, "what the hell are you two doin' here?" Harry scowled at the two intruders down the double barrels of his twelve gauge 'rat buster'.

Jesse cleared his throat nervously. "Hi, Harry. We were just inspecting..."

"'Inspecting', hell!" Harry shook his head and grinned maliciously. "Jesse Walker and his infamous brother. I heard that you were s'posed to be strung up today, Jesse — how'd you manage to get out?" He swung the shotgun around to aim at Ben, who had been slowly edging toward the stack of boxes against the near wall. "Freeze, Walker!"

Harry glared at them through angry, blazing eyes. "I don't know whether I should shoot you or sound the alarm. Ah, hell," he decided, and scuttled back to the door and reached for a button on the wall. Ben sprang forward, drawing Harry's attention from Jesse. The gun roared in the confines of the storeroom seconds before Jesse reached Harry, pushed the weapon aside, and slid eight inches of cold steel into the man's chest. Harry

313

slid to the floor with an expression of surprise on his weathered face, his hand still reaching in vain for the alarm button. Finally, his hand dropped to the floor, and with a perplexed look in his dying eyes, he slumped over.

Jesse turned away and saw Ben leaning against some crates, his hands bloody and his face pale. Jesse ran lightly over to him.

"Are you okay, Ben?"

Ben cursed. "Lucky for me the bastard was loading buckshot instead of slugs, Jesse," he said between pressed lips. "I got nailed, but I think I'll live. I guess we're going to have to visit the doctor before we leave."

"Can you walk?"

Ben's eyes flashed. "Of course! I got shot in the arm and the ass, not my legs. It hurts like hell, and it's a bloody mess, but I'll manage."

Ben shouldered two of the four bags of booty, wincing as he slung the carry straps over his wounded arm, and limped out the door. Jesse picked up the other bags, and paused over Harry's body.

"Damn you, old man," he swore, "I thought we were friends." He ran to catch up with his brother, and followed him in sliding down the loose riverbank.

Excerpt from The Journal of Ben Walker—July 11, 2022

TODAY IS MY LAST DAY IN PARADISE, AND I'M OVERCOME WITH A SENSE OF FAILURE—OF DEFEAT. I BUILT THIS PLACE, FOUGHT FOR IT, AND LIVED EVERY DAY FOR IT—YET NOW I AM BEING CAST OUT LIKE A PIECE OF MAGGOT-INFESTED MEAT! DAMMIT! I WISH I COULD GO BACK AND FIGHT FOR WHAT IS RIGHTFULLY MINE, BUT ALL THAT WOULD ACCOMPLISH NOW IS TO GET BOTH JESSE AND ME KILLED.

BETTER TO WAIT, TO COME BACK PREPARED TO TAKE PARADISE FROM THESE USURPERS. SOMEDAY, I'LL BE ABLE TO RECLAIM PARADISE AS MY OWN—NOT SOON, BUT SOMEDAY.

I'M IN THE PROCESS OF WAGING AN INTERNAL WAR OF EMOTIONS, AND I SEEM TO BE LOSING! THE DEATH OF MY DEAR ANNA, AND THE LOSS OF PARADISE—BOTH POINT TO THE EPHEMERAL QUALITY OF LIFE, AND THE LITTLE TIME THAT WE ARE GIVEN TO ENJOY IT.

I MUST BE UPSET—I DON'T OFTEN WAX PHILOSOPHICAL THIS EARLY IN THE DAY. I'VE OFTEN TOLD JESSE THAT THE REASON HE CAN'T WRITE GOOD POETRY IS BECAUSE HE ISN'T DEPRESSED OFTEN ENOUGH.

JESSE GAVE ME A GIFT TODAY THAT I'LL TREASURE FOREVER: A LIFE-SIZE HOLOGRAM OF ANNA. I WEPT, THERE IN THE DARK TUNNELS. I DIDN'T LET JESSE SEE, HOWEVER; I TAKE GREAT PAINS TO BE THE STRONG OLDER BROTHER—I ALWAYS HAVE—SO IT'S HARD TO LET ANY OF THE WEAKER EMOTIONS SHOW.

RAIDED HARRY'S PLACE. HARRY IS DEAD, BY JESSE'S HAND, NOT MINE. I WAS SHOCKED BY THE RUTHLESS MANNER WITH WHICH MY BROTHER DISPATCHED THE MAN HE USED TO CALL 'FRIEND'; ALL I CAN SAY IS, BETTER HARRY THAN ME. AS IT WAS, I TOOK SOME BUCKSHOT IN MY SIDE, ARM, AND RIGHT CHEEK.

WHAT A PAIN IN THE ASS.

Jesse followed Ben, who was scrambling through the tunnels along at what seemed to be a breakneck pace for someone with lumps of lead in his rear. Only once did Ben stumble, but Jesse was close enough to right him before he fell.

They exited from the subterranean byway just outside the airplane hangar north of the boundary of Paradise. Jesse asked Ben who was on patrol.

"One of the Merrillites," Ben responded in a voice tinged with fatigue. "Rob Tulliger, I think."

"Is he going to be a problem?"

Ben laughed. "No...I took the liberty of spiking his coffee. He'll sleep through most of his shift, by which time we'll have been gone for long while." *I hope*, Ben added silently.

The two men hefted their loads out of the tunnel and made their way into the hangar. Jesse gasped as he saw the plane sitting in the center of the hangar floor. "It's beautiful," he whispered in admiration.

A voice startled both of them from their reverie. "I'm glad you think so," Jeff Barker yawned, hastily holding up both arms to ward off the nearly imminent attack as the Walkers spun around, ready for combat. "Hold on, guys; I didn't mean to scare you."

Jesse grinned as he re-sheathed his knife. "No problem, Jeff. Is it ready?"

Jeff smiled crookedly. "As ready as it'll ever be. I'm not even going to ask what's going on, guys — but good luck." He shook hands with both Ben and Jesse, then without another word turned to the back room of the hangar and the cot that awaited him with its promise of uninterrupted sleep.

Jesse glanced at Ben. "How in the hell are we going to get this out of here without waking up the whole town?"

"Easy," Ben replied. "We push it."

Jesse shook his head with a wry chuckle. "'Easy', he says. Why don't we get you to Doc's first, Ben? You're starting to look a little green around the gills." Jesse was, in fact, concerned by the gray cast of Ben's pallor and the beads of sweat that were pouring down his brother's face in the cool air of very early morning. The thought of pushing even a lightweight plane several miles along pitted roads was less than appealing; doing so with his brother injured was — well, it was insanity!

"No, Jess. First we get the plane out, and then load up yours and the *Phoenix*; then we hit my place for weapons; *then* we go to Doc's."

Ben's tone was forceful and stubborn enough to keep Jesse from arguing, though the word 'insanity' continued to echo in his mind. "You're the boss, Ben. I just hope you know what you're doing." He carelessly tossed the bags of supplies into the fuselage of the plane and bent to the task of folding the wings vertically as Ben kept watch by the door.

"Ready," Jesse announced a few minutes later as he pushed the plane toward the door. He was gratified to note that it rolled smoothly along on its oversized balloon tires. *Maybe this won't be so bad after all.*

Two hours later, as they were making their way back to Paradise, Jesse revised his earlier assumption. He was drenched in sweat, his cloak long since removed and tied around his waist along with his shirt. Ben, stoic as ever, plodded along in the final throes of fatigue and near shock — but he pushed on.

316

Once inside the borders of Paradise again, they turned to the overgrown path that led to Ben's home. The cozy little A-frame was rarely used; it was a retreat for those few times when the burden of running the community got to Ben. He had not been there since Anna's death.

They entered through the front door, and Jesse walked across the room and poured drinks for both of them—a shot for himself, and three fingers of bourbon for his brother. "To Paradise," Jesse said as he handed the glass to Ben.

Ben gratefully accepted his, and drank it with relish as he rummaged through the gun cabinet in his study. When he finally returned to the living room, the glass was gone; it had been replaced by a double armload of weapons that he let fall to the sofa with a clatter.

Ben sorted out those armaments that he wanted, letting Jesse pick among the rest. Ben's choices made it clear that he was serious about defending himself: a Taurus 9mm automatic; Ruger .44 Magnum with laser sight; an M16 with grenade launcher and a bandolier of six grenades; three throwing knives; and a Kevlar flak jacket to complete the list.

Jesse's choices were simpler—he picked up a twenty-gauge shotgun, another 9mm pistol, and an M1 carbine. "Got a hacksaw, Ben? This shotgun is just a little too long for me."

Ben motioned distractedly to the tool cupboard as he collected ammunition for the weapons into a large canvas bag. "Five hundred rounds gonna be enough for the M1, Jess?"

"Yeah," Jesse responded as he clamped the shotgun carefully into a vise. "About the same for the shotgun, if you have it; if not, I've got some stashed at my place."

"Not a good idea, Jess; your house is probably staked out. I've got enough here, I think." Ben turned to the gun cabinet, and his steps faltered.

The barrel of the twenty-gauge fell to the floor with a clank, and Jesse walked over to his brother, gun in one hand and a piece of emery cloth in the other. As he began to smooth out the end of the sawed-off barrel, he eyed his brother critically.

"Time to go to Doc's, Ben," Jesse said in a tone that sent chills down his brother's spine. Rarely—if ever—had Ben heard a command given in such a light yet forceful tone. Almost without thinking, Ben lashed up the weapons, handed Jesse the bag of ammo, and headed for the door.

"Wait," Ben said as he reached for the knob. He thumbed a switch on the intercom and spoke distinctly into the speaker. "Computer. Access One. Security procedure four-eight-two-gee-aitch. House shutdown. Run."

The speaker hissed with the response. "SHUTDOWN ACKNOWLEDGED. CHARGES AND SENSORS ON STANDBY ALERT. THIRTY SECONDS TO INITIATION. TWENTY-NINE...TWENTY-EIGHT..."

Ben grimaced with pain, then looked at Jesse as he ushered him out the door and turned the key. From inside the cabin, the voice of the computer continued counting down the seconds. "No one can get in here unless they force their way in," Ben explained. "If the door or window sensors are disturbed, the computer will activate a twenty second fuse coupled to one hundred pounds of thermite nitroglycerine charges. Anyone in the house or within five hundred feet will be blown to Hell — literally. The ultimate burglar deterrent."

"Nasty," Jesse said with a grimace of appreciation.

They crept through the wooded areas as they circled north to the infirmary. The thick, overgrown field that Doc called a yard afforded them ample cover as they made their way the last hundred feet to the hospital.

Jesse arrived at the back door first and knocked quietly. "Doc, are you in there?" he called out. He knocked again, his eyes nervously scanning the compound in the dim light of false dawn.

A muffled voice came from within the log building. "Who is it? Don't ye know what time it is?"

"It's Jesse, Doc. Open up — Ben's hurt!"

The door opened, and the lined, sleepy face of Doc Riley peered out into the darkness. "Come in, lads; come in."

Jesse smiled as he clasped the hand of his old friend. "Sorry to have to wake you, Doc, but Ben's been shot and we need to get him patched up."

"Right away, Jesse," Doc said as he bustled about the infirmary for supplies. "And might I say that you're a sight for sore eyes, boyo. What brings you back?"

Jesse gave the doctor a sidelong glance. "I'm *not* back, as far as you're concerned, Doc. If anyone asks, you haven't seen me."

The old man nodded, fully understanding the need for discretion in the unsettled times. "Aye, I'd heard that you were on the blacklist —

something about killing that Kane fellow? Figured you'd be long gone by now."

"We would have been," Ben winced as the doctor removed a piece of buckshot from his posterior, "but I got in the way of a—OUCH! --trigger-happy son of a bitch."

"Well, now, I'll be sad to see you go, but if I were only twenty years younger, I'd be hitting the high road with you. Paradise is a mighty pretty place, but the blight has settled with us in the form of those folks from Merrill. We don't owe them anything, and here they are making their demands!"

Ben looked at his brother and smiled. They had heard Doc go on tirades before; usually the bee in his bonnet was the IRA. Riley was not one to withhold his opinion just because someone might not agree; instead, the old man would shout it from the rooftops and dare anyone to prove him wrong.

Doc finished up his 'repair' work, and took Jesse's hand in his gnarled, bony ones. "May fortune smile upon you, my friends," he said sadly as Ben painfully pulled on his pants. "And the luck of the Irish be with ye!" He smiled, tears brimming in his tired eyes, as he waved them out the door.

"I'm going to miss that guy, Ben," Jesse remarked as they entered the cover of darkness. "I hope we see him again."

"We will, Jess. We will."

CHAPTER THIRTY-SEVEN

Excerpt from *A History of the Provisional United States: A Twenty-First Century Business*, By Andrew Wellerman, Ph. D.

...can be clearly shown that the economic collapse of the Western world in the early twenty-first century, and the succeeding breakdown of political cohesiveness world-wide, can be attributed to one man.

Raymond St. John, born Robert Elias Kane, built a financial empire that spanned the entire North American continent, as well as reaching tendrils into the rest of the world. It was through his efforts to attain total control of the world's precious gem and metal markets that he managed, quite ably, to bring the world markets to their knees and dissolve the strongest and most widespread capitalist system the world had ever known.

His greed, stemming from a poor childhood in north-central Wisconsin, is the root cause for his actions later in life. He left his home in 1961 (A.D.) at the age of sixteen to pursue his future in business, leaving behind him his parents, an older sister, and an infant brother (see **Damon Kane**, Ch. 17, pp. 337-349).

In 1976 he changed his name to 'Raymond St. John' as part of his merger with St. John Fabrications, Inc. From that point on, his was one of the most meteoric financial climbs in history.

...in 2012 [he] attempted the greatest coup of all time— and failed. He did not lose, however; his plans had taken into account the possibility of such a defeat. He instituted a class system in the urban areas of the eastern seaboard that would eventually change the face of the United States, and in time, the world.

...in a reincarnation of Social Darwinism [St. John] decided that if a person was not a billionaire, then he had no useful purpose; therefore, minimal effort should be expended in keeping him alive. Since, by these parameters only about two hundred people were of any use, the remainder slipped into abject poverty.

St. John coined the term 'Lowers' to describe anyone who was not of his class. He gave the Lowers a minimum of food and medicine, and their average lifespan dropped over a period of less than a decade from seventy-three to the mid thirties.

The 'Uppers'—those of St. John's peer group--on the other hand, were living life spans that were virtually unlimited. With the finest in medical facilities to draw upon and a vast fund of people willing to sell their organs in exchange for food or favors, the Uppers had nearly total control of their world.

The appearance of the cities changed as the new order settled into place. Chicago became the standard by which all other major metropolises were judged, and became the seat of the St. John empire—and consequently, the capital of the provisional United States government. Tremendous bridges and suspended parkways spanned and filled in the gaps between the buildings that housed the Uppers and their minions, cutting the Lowers off from even the birthright of all men—the Sun.

Escapes to the countryside were, at first, commonplace; but as the average food ration dropped, so did the energy level of the citizenry, making journeys of more than a few blocks more than all but the hardiest traveler could endure. Of little help were the rural communities, who jealously guarded and protected the little that they had managed to keep during the years of the Collapse and the Plague.

St. John knew that the only thing that would put an end to his power was the forlorn hope of a revolution—and the people were too tired, too worn out from their daily struggle to survive, to fight among themselves, let alone take on the might of the Uppers.

The only hope for the majority of the country's people lie in the outside chance that a force from a distant place would take enough interest in the inhumane conditions in the cities to do something about it.

It was an empty hope, but rumors constantly circulated through the Lower sections of the cities about a 'savior' that would fly into the cities, free the people, and defeat the Uppers.

A foolish hope, of course. Who would be crazy enough to leave the relatively safe haven of the countryside to engage the dangers of the cities?

The war room was just as Ben had left it; he was not surprised, since he and Jesse were the only people aware of its existence. He sat gingerly at one of the consoles, gesturing to Jesse to do likewise. The clock above the board read 3:57. Ben did not know how much longer the guard, Tulliger, would remain out, but he was not too concerned about an alarm being raised immediately. Rob would not admit that he had slept through most of his shift, especially with the situation in Paradise what it was.

Still, Ben thought, *best that we be on our way by sunrise.* He knew that the changing of the guard at the jail would cause a town-wide alarm to be sounded.

"Pour a couple of stiff drinks, Jess. I have a few things to finalize with the computer."

Jesse fetched the drinks, lit a smoke, and sat down to watch.

"Computer. Access One." Ben paused, and took a deep breath. "Security procedure zero-zero-zero-four-ell-zero. Run."

"ACKNOWLEDGED. SECURITY SYSTEMS AND INTERLOCKS IN PLACE. ALL EMERGENCY OVERRIDES IN PLACE. SHORTWAVE TRANSCEIVERS ACTIVATED. BACKUP TRANSCEIVERS READY."

"Addition to program," Ben stated. "At 0430 hours today, cut off all electricity except the line to the infirmary. Resume normal operations at 0700.

"At 0430 hours today, cut current and connections to all telephone lines within Paradise, as well as all lines to outside terminus.

"At 0430 hours today, institute all-band interference with any attempted radio transmissions except that occurring at 650.22 megahertz. Continue interference until 0700 hours.

"Block computer access to the following files, except upon verification of codes Access One or Access Zero: Access One, Access Zero, Top Gun, War Games, Special File Octagon, Security.

"Repeat, verify, and acknowledge."

Ben lit a smoke and sipped his drink as he waited. His haggard, red-rimmed eyes darted around the room as if trying to remember something—this would be his last chance for some time to do anything in Paradise.

The computer listed the program changes Ben had made, and verified acknowledgment. "END OF LIST. ALL SYSTEMS VERIFIED. COMMUNICATION ON 650.22 MEGAHERTZ ONLY. VOICE CHECK REQUESTED FOR ACCESS ONE AND ACCESS ZERO."

Jesse perked up. "Jesse Walker. Access Zero."

"CONFIRMED."

"Ben Walker. Access One."

"CONFIRMED. ALL PROGRAM PARAMETERS RUNNING. EIGHTEEN MINUTES UNTIL INITIAL ORDERS BEGIN."

Ben thought for a moment, and then said, "Addendum. Any attempted access to the computer chamber by unauthorized personnel is to be met with full retaliatory measures. Automated disposal approved. Ventilate if necessary. Authorized personnel are listed in file oh-four-ay. Paraphrase and acknowledge."

"FULL ANTI-ACCESS MEASURES, INCLUDING RETALIATION AND DISPOSAL. ACKNOWLEDGED."

Ben sat back, stubbed out his cigarette, and sighed. "Begin SecZero now." He turned to Jesse.

"*Now* I think we're covered. We have the entire history of Paradise, its secrets, and its people on file in this room. It needs protection. In the meantime, we can still partially control Paradise, through the computer, from wherever we are. Our transceivers, hooked into the planes' power supplies, should easily give us a five hundred mile range."

Jesse sipped his drink slowly and looked at the clock. *0418,* it read. "Let's hope that no one discovers this chamber, though; I like to think that Paradise, and the Paradisans, will live on until we can return."

"Amen to that." Ben sat forward, his eyes also on the clock. "Computer. Security addendum. Full authorization and discretion to use force to defend the physical attributes of Paradise and the all citizens on the manifest as of thirty April, two-oh-two-two. All defense systems, including Top Gun and War Games, at computer command. End." He switched off the terminal, knowing that the computer had stored his commands in its memory.

Ben looked at the clock and stood stiffly. "Today — *now* — we leave Paradise. Tomorrow — who knows?"

Ben and Jesse drained their glasses in silence, gathered up their last minute supplies, and entered the tunnel.

As they both turned to take one final look at the war room, the disembodied voice of the computer spoke.

"GOOD LUCK, BEN AND JESSE WALKER."

CHAPTER THIRTY-EIGHT

The two ultralights were right where they had left them, a few miles east of Paradise on the runway of the tiny airfield. The *Phoenix*, Ben's sky-blue and white craft, glistened in the early dawn sunlight. Jesse's craft, as yet unnamed, was a flat black, sleek looking craft. Both had similar modifications for quicker, more maneuverable flight.

"Give me a hand with these guns, Jess," Ben wheezed as he struggled with the bulk of their arsenal. Jesse packed the weapons into the storage compartments of the planes as Ben handed them to him.

The guns stowed away, Jesse brushed a stray lock of white hair from his sweaty forehead. "What's the range of the planes now?"

"Well, Jess, if we stick to cruising speed at about four thousand feet, we should have about eighteen hundred miles of fuel; however, if we go at full power for any amount of time—"

Jesse cut him short. "Christ, Ben, can't you just answer the question?"

A look of anger flashed over Ben's face, to be quickly replaced by a sheepish expression. "Sorry. I just get caught up in details. I know you don't really give a shit."

Jesse laid a hand on his brother's arm. "No, Ben; *I'm* sorry. I shouldn't have snapped at you." He smiled. "What have we got for communications?"

"FM transceivers are built into the planes, but they're only good for about a half mile—maybe more, airborne. Anything farther than that, and we have to risk using the short-wave."

Jesse secured the sawed-off shotgun under his cloak, and swung it up a few times to get the feel of it. "Any in-flight weapons?"

Ben grinned. "Do you think I'd forget that? Each plane is equipped with .30 caliber machine guns, with a five hundred round magazine. Just line up the nose at your target, and push the fire button on the stick.

"We've also got twelve hand-loaded grenades wing-mounted. Releasing them pulls the pin, and they have ten second fuses. Be sure to pull up after releasing, or you'll blow your ass out of the sky!"

Jesse sighed. "Just once I'd like to catch you unprepared. Why didn't you seem this devious when we were kids?"

"I hadn't dealt with thousands of morons then."

Jesse chuckled as he pulled out the old, battered pocket watch that he had liberated from Ben's desk. "It's nearly five, Ben. We'd better get going; I'm sure all Hell is breaking loose in Paradise by now."

Ben nodded agreement, donned his flight suit, and climbed into the cockpit of the *Phoenix*. Jesse folded his cloak around him, adjusted the shotgun, and followed Ben's example.

Both men fastened down the cockpit covers of their planes, and inserted their key cards in the ignitions. They fired up their engines, the racket especially loud in the calm stillness of dawn. Ben throttled down enough to ensure that Jesse's plane was running, and put on his headset.

"Phoenix to –" Ben stopped, unsure of what to call his partner. *"What's the name of your bird?"*

Jesse finished securing his headset in place and thought for a second, picturing the black craft flying through a moonless sky. *"Nighthawk ,"* he responded.

"Phoenix to Nighthawk. Ready to fly? " Ben's voice was clear in Jesse's ears.

"Roger, Phoenix. Let's roll."

"First stop, Appleton. Phoenix, out. "

The *Phoenix* began its takeoff roll, bounding down the rough and makeshift runway. Ben pulled sharply back on the stick as he reached speed, and cleared the trees at the end by several yards. Jesse, a more sedate flier, veered away from the trees and took flight to one side.

When the pair had climbed to several hundred feet, Ben banked west and headed for the distant scattered buildings of Paradise.

"Phoenix to Nighthawk."

"I copy."

"Let's say a fond farewell to Paradise, shall we? Follow me. Over." Ben put his plane into a sharp dive, kicking in the supercharger with a banshee whine. Jesse flew right on his tail, and the two men laughed as people began to run from their homes.

The planes did large, sweeping dives, swooping down as low as thirty feet, then climbing again. Ben saw Isaac standing in the center of the compound, and made a low, slow pass at nearly ground level to salute his friend and ally.

Isaac waved, an incredulous expression on his face as Ben's madly grinning countenance flashed by. The two planes rolled upward in a steep ascent, and then banked to the southeast.

Jesse and Ben flew their craft wingtip to wingtip, and in twenty minutes they had left Paradise—home—far behind them.

Flight Log of the *Phoenix*: July 11, 2022:

JESSE AND I ARE FLYING AT ABOUT FIVE THOUSAND FEET AT A CRUISING SPEED OF ROUGHLY EIGHTY KNOTS. OUR IMMEDIATE DESTINATION, FOR FUEL AND INFORMATION, IS THE CITY OF APPLETON.

I WONDER ABOUT THESE PLACES THAT WE USED TO FREQUENT—WHAT IS LEFT OF THEM, WHO LIVES THERE, AND IF I CAN STILL FIND MY WAY AROUND.

APPLETON, THE BEAUTIFUL CITY AT THE NORTH END OF LAKE WINNEBAGO. FOND DU LAC, 'FIRST ON THE LAKE', AT THE SOUTH END OF THE LAKE. EVENTUALLY, INTO SUBURBAN MILWAUKEE AND THE CITY ITSELF.

WHAT WILL WE FIND THERE? WILL THE PEOPLE BE LIKE US, OR WILL THEY HAVE ADOPTED ENTIRELY DIFFERENT VALUES AND ETHICS?

JESSE'S STORIES ABOUT THE UPPERS AND LOWERS OF EAU CLAIRE HAVE ME WORRIED. IT SPEAKS OF A HIGHLY ORGANIZED SOCIETAL STRUCTURE; IF THINGS ARE LIKE THAT EVERYWHERE, THE MASSES ARE AS GOOD AS GONE. THIS ST. JOHN FELLOW—WHAT A MAN HE MUST BE TO HOLD SUCH ABSOLUTE POWER OVER SO MANY. HAS THAT POWER CORRUPTED HIM AS MUCH AS IT SEEMS IT SHOULD? WE'LL JUST HAVE TO LOOK HIM UP AND SEE.

I'M HOPING THAT BECAUSE WE HAVE TRADE GOODS TO USE AS BRIBES THAT WE WON'T HAVE ANY REASON TO FIGHT. I CAN'T ADMIT TO JESSE THAT THIS TRIP WORRIES—NO, FRIGHTENS—ME. I HAVE THIS NEW AND IRRITATING FEAR OF THE UNKNOWN. PARADISE I CAN DEAL WITH, IN ALL HER MANY PHASES. THESE WARRENS THAT THE PROVOS CALL 'CITIES' I DON'T UNDERSTAND. I FEAR WHAT THEY REPRESENT.

WHAT I FEAR MOST OF ALL IS THAT WE MAY NOT SURVIVE TO DO ANYTHING

ABOUT THE PROVOS. AFTER ALL, WE'RE GOING INTO DECIDEDLY HOSTILE TERRITORY, AND THERE ARE JUST THE TWO OF US. CONFRONTING THOSE IN CHARGE MAY WELL PROVE TO BE RISKY BUSINESS, AT BEST.

OH WELL—IT'S A LONG FLIGHT, AND I NEED TO RELAX. I'LL SET THE HOLOGRAM OF ANNA ON THE DASH, AND REMEMBER...

Jesse watched the checkerboard ground sweep below him through the lightly scattered clouds as they sped on a southeasterly heading. They had been airborne for a little over an hour, and the sun was well above the horizon.

Jesse donned a pair of flight glasses and became absorbed in the waning spectacle of sunrise, the brilliant orb of the sun lightening to white-yellow as the pink and crimson clouds turned to fluffy white. He was flushed with anticipation, but his new emotional outlook did not allow any room for fear. Rather, he was filled with the thrill of adventure.

In just a few weeks, Ben will turn forty, he thought. *Have to remember to save a bottle for the occasion.*

A flash of light off to his right snapped him from his pleasant reverie.

"Nighthawk to Phoenix. Come in, Ben."

"Phoenix, roger. Did you see it, too?"

"Yeah. What do you suppose it was? It was too bright for a reflection."

Ben was silent, weighing the possibilities. *"Can't say for sure, but it looked an awful lot like an explosion. Look carefully, Jess – is that a plume of smoke?"*

Jesse scanned the area. *"Might be. Do you want to take a look?"*

"Yes," Ben responded. *"It might be something important. Lead the way, Jess, and keep an open mike."*

Jesse banked steeply and veered west, dropping sharply to about two thousand feet. Ben flew several hundred feet behind his brother, ready to cover him with a barrage of gunfire if need be. They soon reached the area where they had seen the blast, and they dropped altitude to just over one thousand feet. As they flew over a large, water-filled quarry, Jesse let out a yell.

"Ben! To your left!"

Ben banked in the indicated direction to afford himself a better view. Below him, scattered all over the upper levels of the quarry, were all types of heavy equipment. Several of the machines appeared to be enlarging a cleft in the cliff face, and a steel framework of supports surrounded the heavy construction.

"Looks like they — whoever they may be--are putting up some sort of building," Ben said. "And a lot of that equipment is Army issue."

"Ben, I'm going to fly this thing into that pit and take a closer look," Jesse said decisively. "I'll keep in touch."

Ben watched in helpless frustration as the *Nighthawk* plummeted into the quarry, pulled out of the dive, and leveled off just fifty feet over the water. Several flashes of light came from the wall of the dig.

"Jesse, get the Hell out of there!" Ben cried. "Someone's shooting at you!"

He kicked at the lever that would load a magazine into his machine gun, and dove straight for the cliff wall.

As he neared the area from which the gunfire had come, he pushed the trigger button, went into a slow spin, and let fly a spiraling cone of steel-jacketed lead into the wall. He leveled off and pulled back on the stick just short of the rock face, and climbed to two thousand feet.

Jesse was already circling the quarry at that altitude, and Ben's radio snapped to life. "'Bout time, Ben. Gave 'em what for, eh?"

"You bet, Jess. Are you all right?"

"Not a scratch. How about you? You dove in a helluva lot closer than I did."

Ben laughed. "I shot about a hundred rounds into the wall. Probably scared them to death, and made a lot of racket, but I don't think I hit anyone. Couldn't take time to look," he added apologetically. "That wall came up too damned fast."

"I saw all I needed to..."

"Well?" Ben demanded. "Who was it? Some private group, or maybe a Cencom outpost?"

"No, Ben. They had to be Provos. Same uniforms, military hardware — who else?"

Ben whistled softly. *"Damn. Provos in central Wisconsin. I suppose they're out to regain the farmlands. Paradise can't have too much time before they get up there."*

"I wonder what they're building," Jesse mused aloud. *"It didn't look like a normal building — more like a fortress, or..."*

"'Or', what?"

"Or a castle!" Jesse exclaimed. *"It looked like a goddam castle!"*

Ben mulled that over, then filed the information away for later study. *"Do you want to go back for another look, and maybe a piece of lead? Or do you want to get keep heading for Appleton?"*

"Appleton, I guess," Jesse replied reluctantly. *"We're only about an hour or so away."*

The two planes dipped back to their southeastern heading, and they flew, wingtips just meters apart, above the outwardly bucolic scenery.

Ben and Jesse arrived outside Appleton just past eight o'clock that morning. The early morning mists were already dissipating, and the day promised to be clear, calm, and warm.

Ben contacted Jesse on the radio and suggested that they land a mile or two west of the city to rest and catch a bite to eat.

"Sounds like a great plan," Jesse remarked. *"I'm starving, and my eyes feel like they're about ready to fall out of my head."*

The *Nighthawk* banked into a steep dive that took it toward a relatively remote stretch of farm road. The tiny plane bounced twice before settling down to a short taxi down the rough asphalt road. The *Phoenix* touched down just seconds later, taxiing to where Jesse had stopped the *Nighthawk*.

Ben opened the canopy and called out to Jesse. "Before you get busy, let's call Paradise and get the 'news'. Want to listen in?" Jesse nodded vehemently, and trotted over to the *Phoenix*.

Ben flicked on the short-wave and entered in the digits **650.22** on the frequency keypad. A burst of static poured from the tiny speaker, and he picked up the mike.

"Ben Walker, Access One. Activate voice command circuits."

Dead air hissed for a moment, then a familiar voice responded.

"ACCESS ONE, CONFIRMED. GO AHEAD, BEN."

Ben smiled at his brother, who nodded in appreciation.

"Access sealed security logs ay-ay-one-oh-one," Ben commanded. "Scan data from 0430 hours through present, July eleven, two-oh-two-two. Correlate data, analyze, and paraphrase report. Run."

Several seconds ensued while the computer complied with the orders. It was necessary for it to access the security videos, as well as recordings of radio communications throughout Paradise for the time period that Ben had specified — that morning, to be exact. As part of its programming, it was also capable of extracting information from patterns of movement among the population and deducing reasons for those patterns. It was not one hundred percent accurate, but it would give the Walkers some idea of what was going on in their erstwhile home.

"PARAPHRASED REPORT READY."

"Run report," Ben ordered.

"A STATE OF CONFUSION AND GENERAL PANIC AMONG THE MAJORITY OF THE PARADISAN POPULACE BEGAN AT 0438 HOURS, WHEN IT BECAME APPARENT THAT MOST PUBLIC SERVICES WERE NON-FUNCTIONAL.

"AT 0517 HOURS, SECURITY LOGS REVEAL THAT JESSE WALKER HAD ESCAPED FROM THE PARADISE JAIL.

"AT 0526 HOURS, ROBERT TULLIGER, ACTING AS SENIOR SECURITY OFFICER, ISSUED ARREST AND APPREHENSION WARRANTS FOR JESSE WALKER ON CHARGES OF SUSPICION OF HOMICIDE AND JAIL-BREAKING; WARRANTS WERE ALSO ISSUED FOR BENJAMIN WALKER, ON CHARGES OF DISRUPTING PUBLIC UTILITIES, CONSORTING WITH A HOMICIDE SUSPECT, AND INCITEMENT TO RIOT.

"GENERAL SERVICES RESUMED AT 0730 HOURS. SEARCH AND CAPTURE TEAMS WERE DISPATCHED INTO THE OUTLYING AREAS TO APPREHEND THE WALKERS, BUT REPORTS FROM SEARCH TEAMS HAVE BEEN NEGATIVE."

Ben sat back and lit a cigarette. "Looks like they want to play rough. Lucky for us we decided to go on vacation, eh?"

Jesse chuckled deep in his throat, an evil sound that chilled Ben despite the warm sunshine streaming into the plane. "We should call that bastard Tulliger and tell them that the whole place is booby-trapped with thermite bombs set to go off on our signal. Give the son of a bitch something to do...a wild goose chase of the best kind."

"You've got some nasty ideas, Bro'," Ben said with a smile.

"Comes from living with you so long," Jesse quipped through clenched teeth.

Ben toyed briefly with Jesse's suggestion, then dismissed it as *too* nasty; people might end up getting hurt—the wrong people. "Computer. File report. Continue to upgrade file every twelve hours, and store permanent daily log in Access One files. End." He turned off the transceiver, and climbed out of the plane with a grimace of pain. He rubbed his rump with a wry grin at his brother, stretched, and yawned.

"Let's grab some chow, then hike into Appleton."

Jesse raised his eyebrows, then nodded. "All right. Sandwiches and coffee okay?"

Ben's mouth began to water. "Yeah. Lots of coffee. I wish Harry had shared that with us earlier; chicory is adequate, but only just." He yawned again, his jaws popping as they stretched wide. Rubbing a hand through his bristly beard, he leaned back against the *Phoenix*.

Jesse whipped up some sandwiches, and started a small, hot fire to brew coffee over.

The meal passed in relative silence, the only interruptions coming from the chirping of birds and the occasional rustling of small animals drawn from the underbrush by the smell of their food.

The two men sat companionably smoking after their meal, each with a hot cup of coffee steaming in his hand. They finally grew restless, cleaned up their camp, and put out their fire. Pairing up, they moved the planes off of the road and onto the gravel shoulder, camouflaging them with broken tree limbs. After each had packed trade goods into their knapsacks, they began the long walk down the dusty road to Appleton.

CHAPTER THIRTY-NINE

"Hold on a minute, Ben," Jesse cried out as he turned and ran back to the *Nighthawk*. Ben watched in exasperation as his brother crawled under the brush camouflaging the plane with muffled grunts. He heard the clatter of items being hastily rummaged through, and a loud snap as the door of the storage compartment was slammed shut. Jesse clambered out from the tangled branches, replacing them with his free hand. He flashed Ben a brief smile as he ran up the road.

"What was that all about?" Ben asked tersely as he cocked an eyebrow at his younger brother. "What's in the case? You didn't go to all that trouble for a pack of cigarettes, did you?"

Jesse looked down at the small leather case in his hand; when he looked back up at Ben, his face held a mischievous grin. He tossed the case to Ben, who caught it with an expression of surprise at its unexpected weight.

"Go ahead — open it," Jesse said as he fumbled with his hair. The day was already much too warm for his thick, white mane, and as he struggled to tie it back, he wondered once more why he bothered to keep it long.

Meanwhile, Ben was unfastening the heavy snaps set into the case. About five inches long, three inches wide, and a little over an inch deep, it *did* bear strong resemblance to a cigarette case — hence Ben's erroneous assumption. As the last snap gave way, Ben pulled open the flap and glanced at the contents.

Unmistakable, the dull sheen of twenty or so small, gold ingots shone up at Ben. With a sharp look at Jesse, Ben removed one of the tiny slabs of precious metal and held it in the light for closer inspection. He noticed a small, raised inscription below a relief of an eagle, and moved it closer to his eyes to read:

PARADISE FREE COMMUNITY
ONE TROY OUNCE
.999 FINE

Carefully, frowning with intense concentration, Ben replaced the gold and refastened the snaps. He reached into his pocket for a cigarette, and made a show of lighting it with a stick match. He smoked in silence for a moment, then his eyes met Jesse's.

"I wasn't aware," he said slowly, "that Paradise had a mint."

"They don't, Ben—at least, not anymore." Jesse relaxed, lowering himself to sit cross-legged in the middle of the asphalt, and continued with his explanation.

"You asked me once what I had done with my share of the lottery money, and I'm afraid that I was rather evasive. I accounted to you for a little over four million, what with the dam, the hydroelectrics, and a fair share of the buildings. However, I figured that since *you* weren't giving me a rundown of your expenses, I didn't owe you a full accounting.

"Well," Jesse sighed, "here's my accounting. Other than the money you know about, I spent several hundred thousand on the modifications to my place, including the project room and my private library—a library, you'll be pleased to know, is nearly as well stocked as the research center library.

"I compiled as many paper-bound books as I could store, and backed up most of them on DVD's. I also collected several thousand music CD's, and an entire library of classic movies on disc.

"And I spent quite a lot on other things." Jesse lit a cigarette, and Ben noted in passing that his brother's hands shook almost as if he were afraid of what he was saying.

"I guess now that we've been booted from Paradise, this is as good a time as any to tell you that I did not put all of my 'eggs' in one basket. Paradise is *not,* and has *never* been, my only concern." Jesse waited, his eyes watching Ben warily, for the expected reaction from the older man.

"What are you talking about?" Ben demanded. "What have you been up to?" Ben forced himself to calm down, but his eyes were ablaze as he stared at Jesse.

"You've heard of Pacifica, the survivalist community in Michigan?" Ben nodded sternly, and Jesse continued. "Well, it's no accident that they're running things the way they are; you see, they're following a charter that was outlined by their present leader and myself—just before I deeded the land that they claim to him. *I* am one of the founders of Pacifica!"

Ben shook his head in bewilderment, his anger and stupefaction blurring his thought processes. *Jesse, founder of* another *community?* Ben could not bring himself to believe it, and with his typical 'Doubting Thomas' mentality, demanded proof from his brother.

"How can that be? It must have cost millions of dollars to set Pacifica up, and you couldn't have possibly come up with that kind of money. Who's running the show over there? Is it someone you can trust?" Ben realized that he had just admitted that he believed Jesse—in a roundabout way—and he hastily backed up his train of thought.

"What did it cost?"

Jesse took a deep breath. "My investment came to about two and a half million dollars, but that was mostly in hardware and, of course, the land itself. There were other investors, and the total price tag came to something on the order of twenty million—but I was the largest single investor." Jesse paused to light another cigarette as Ben stamped out his own in the dirt.

Jesse blew out a cloud of blue-gray smoke, and went on with his story.

"Pacifica was never intended to be wholly self-sufficient, as Paradise was. Pacifica has ties, no matter how tenuous, with the Provos, and regularly trades with their outposts for necessary goods." Jesse held up his hands to forestall another outburst from Ben.

"Before you ask, let me make one thing clear: to the best of my knowledge, Pacifica had no dealings with the Cencoms, although I've been out of touch with them for nearly two years—at their leader's request.

"It seems that my continued interest in Pacifica's operations were becoming a nuisance to their council, and the inhabitants were coming to resent the fact that their leaders were 'puppets' for some far-flung stranger—your's truly.

"So, in April of '20, I turned over full control of Pacifica to their on-site leader. He's someone that I've known all my life, and who you would approve of, even though you were sorely disappointed when he refused to join us in Paradise."

Ben cast his thoughts back to the beginnings of Paradise, trying to come up with a name for Jesse's mystery man. Ben had asked many to join him, and few had refused that he really wanted except—

"Uncle John?" Ben shouted as the memory clicked into place. "Pacifica is run by John?" Ben had risen to his feet, and stood over Jesse in a threatening posture of mingled rage and surprise.

"Yeah," Jesse affirmed, "Uncle John. You and he are like two peas in a pod, and I used a little foresight to predict that, sooner or later, the two of you would come to a parting of the ways if you were both in Paradise. It was I who convinced him to refuse your offer.

"It helped when I told him that I would stake him to a claim of his own, *if* he agreed to run the show according to a compromise plan that we hashed out together.

"For several years that's how things stood.

"Then, when his own people became disaffected, I stepped out of the picture. As far as I know, Pacifica is still thriving."

Ben sat silently, pensive, for a moment. "So, John is alive," he mused. "I had assumed that he died in the Collapse or during the Plague Year. But now, to find out that he's alive, and very much in power, well…"

"I'm sorry, Ben. I meant no treason toward you or Paradise. I just thought that it would be best if we hedged out bets against a future I hoped would never happen—like our expulsion from Paradise, for instance." Jesse smiled ruefully and stood next to Ben.

"I hope you understand. What I spent on Pacifica could not, in any way, have changed what has happened. Money would not, and could not, have saved any of the lives lost; it would have, at best, prolonged the agony." Jesse brightened. "And now we have a place where, I hope, we'll find a welcome."

Ben stood quietly digesting everything for several minutes, then held up the case of gold. "What about this? Where did the gold come from?"

A smile flickered across Jesse's bewhiskered face, and he was privately pleased at the change of subject. "I told you that there used to be a mint in Paradise, and there was—in my project room. Do you remember when I got that shipment of 'construction materials' back in June of '11? Maybe you don't.

"One of the crates contained two hundred and forty pounds of gold bullion—all that I could get at eight hundred dollars an ounce. I melted it down, and put about fifty pounds of it into one ounce ingots like those you have there. The rest of the gold is hidden in my cabin."

"What do you mean 'hidden'?" Ben inquired. "You must realize that your cabin will be used by someone else now that you've achieved fugitive status. Somebody's bound to find that much gold?" *And use it against us,* Ben thought bitterly.

"Not to worry, big brother. It won't be found, even if the cabin is torn down. Who would think to look *inside* solid granite foundation stones for gold?

"I molded crushed granite around five thirty-eight pound ingots, and scattered the 'stones' throughout the foundation. Only my records and an obscure file in the main computer have the location. No one will find them." Jesse smiled at the puzzled expression on his brother's face. "In the meantime, we have about twenty-five pounds of one ounce ingots in the plane—just in case we need to barter with something other than trade goods."

Ben shook his head slowly back and forth, and for the first time in his life, respected his brother for more than his humanitarian ideals. Ben struggled with the realization that he did not have a premium on foresight; in fact, in many ways Jesse's preparations rivaled and surpassed his own accomplishments.

Ben grasped Jesse's shoulder and gave it a squeeze, then bent to pick up his backpack.

"You've given me an awful lot to think about, Jess; but I can tell you one thing," he said, his face flushed with embarrassed honesty. "I'm proud of you." Ben turned away, and began to amble down the dusty blacktop.

Jesse stared at Ben's back for a moment, amazed and glowing with his brother's praise. Finally, he pocketed the gold, picked up his own sack, and ran to catch up with Ben.

Ben looked at his brother as they walked side by side down the road. "Tell me everything you know about Pacifica," he said.

John Walker threw the letter onto his desk with an expression of angry disgust, and sat back in his chair. *Damn them* , he thought. *I haven't worked my ass off for ten years only to have someone come along and tell me that all I've accomplished was for naught!*

With a heavy sigh, the leader of Pacifica leaned forward and re-read the letter.

12 July 2022

To: John Walker, Leader

    Pacifica Community

    Hiawatha National Forest

    Upper Michigan, Central

From: Raymond St. John, Executive Director

    Control Industries Conglomerate

    Central Provisional United States Headquarters

    Chicago

Mr. Walker:

In regard to your last communication, dated 30 June, 2022--the answer is NO.

I thought that I had made our position clear on this point. I have a commission from the Provisional United States Government to provide a complete, ready-to use base to house military personnel and their families. While CIC could build from the ground up, financial constraints make that prohibitively expensive.

In communicating my concerns to President-General Lewiston, he assured me that a writ of eminent domain would be issued should a suitable site be found that already provided the necessary utilities and other facilities.

Let me digress. Eminent domain states that while title to land may rest in private hands, in time of need the government may, with fair compensation, rescind the right of private ownership in favor of the needs of the State. This is now the case with the Hiawatha National Forest Preserve area, some of which you now hold deed and title to.

Enclosed you will find a copy of the present writ, empowering CIC to take possession of the lands listed as of 1 September, 2022. We will make every reasonable effort to assist in the relocation of the present inhabitants, as well as fair compensation for all properties.

Let me add that, should you fail to comply with the writ, a division of Provisional U.S. Forces will be dispatched to escort you from the premises; in such a case, expenses for this will be deducted from any compensation due you or your people, as well as possible crimin al charges levied against you and the members of your council.

I urge you to comply. If you have any questions, one of my representatives will be in your area on or around the 15th of this month.

Cordially,

Raymond St. John

Raymond St. John

John set the paper on his desk, then thought better of it. He picked up the letter along with the copy of the writ between two fingers as if they were something foul, and stood up. His massive frame loomed over the desk like an angry bear as he stomped over to the battered filing cabinet across the room. He pulled open the top drawer and thumbed through the folders until he found the one marked **MISC**. He thrust the papers into it and angrily slammed the drawer shut.

"Dammit!" he roared. "How the hell do I get out of this?" For an instant eh had a feeling of *deja vu* — as if he had been through this before. From somewhere deep in his subconscious, a mental picture of his nephews, Ben and Jesse, swam into his mind.

"Now what made me think of them?" he muttered. "Is it possible that *they* could be in the same boat?" With the decisiveness that had kept him in the top seat of Pacifica for a decade, John walked from his office and across the hall into the radio room. Seating himself at the dusty old short-wave set, John brushed a stray lock of silvery-gray hair from his creased and sun-tanned brow, and bent over the controls.

He hadn't used the radio since the last time he and Jesse had spoken — could it be two years? He quickly warmed up the radio and dialed in the frequency that he and Jesse had long ago agreed upon. His forehead beaded with sweat as he attempted to contact the last remaining members of his brother's family.

For several minutes John tried, without success, to raise Paradise. Finally, his patience was rewarded by a tired, surly voice from among the static.

"Paradise, here. Identify yourself, and state your business."

John was immediately suspicious; a Paradisan operator had never treated him with such a lack of respect and courtesy. They tended to be a friendly lot, and for the most part enjoyed hearing from the outside world. *It has been two years,* John thought solicitously. *A lot can change in that time.*

"This is Pacifica, Michigan, calling Paradise. I would like to speak with Jesse or Ben Walker. It's urgent. Over."

There was a lengthy pause, and John imagined that he could hear voices in the background. A new voice came on the radio, and the man's tone was, if anything, harsher than that of the original operator.

"Why do you wish to speak with Jesse Walker? He is an outlaw and fugitive from justice. Do you know where he is?" The voice continued impatiently. *"If you know where he or his brother Ben are, we'd appreciate the information. Over."*

Ben and Jesse — outlaws? "Can you tell me what they are wanted for? I was under the impression that they were among the leaders of Paradise." John hoped that he sounded as puzzled as he was; it would tend to calm any suspicions on the part of the person on the other end. "To whom am I speaking?"

"This is Robert Tulliger, acting Chief of Security. Who are you?"

"My name isn't important," John said sternly. "Can I speak to whoever *is* in charge?"

"You'll talk to me first; I'll decide whether or not to bother Mr. Peters with your message." Tulliger spoke with a tone that said he was overly conscious of his place in the community, and it was obvious to John — even over the radio — that this man enjoyed wielding his petty power. *I'd call him a pissant ,* John thought with a grimace.

"No thank you, Mr. Tulliger. I'll speak to Isaac, or to no one at all." *Put that in your pipe and smoke it!*

The reply came almost immediately. *"Very well."* Suddenly, John was listening to dead air.

"I'll be damned," John swore. "The bastard hung up on me."

John sat at the console, absently rubbing his grizzled face, and wondered what kind of trouble his kin had gotten themselves into. *Fugitives? For what crimes? And could it be true that they had been deposed from the leadership of their own community?*

He could scarcely believe it. Ben was his father's son, and Ben Sr. had never been one to let something like this happen. Besides, John had great faith in the ingenuity of both his nephews.

If they've been given the boot, John mused, *I'll bet even money that they'll be back.* The thought gave him shudders; he knew how ruthless Ben could be.

A terrible thought came to mind. *If it can happen to them, it can happen to me!*

John jumped to his feet and ran back to his office. He locked the door behind him, and sat rigidly behind the desk. Plans would have to be made— and made *soon.*

John was about to have a long and sleepless night.

The stench assailed the brother's nostrils as they crossed Highway 45, and they shot each other looks of disgust. The wave of hot, heavy air was blowing from the south, and with it came the mingled odors of wood smoke, sweat, and manure. Ben cocked an eyebrow at Jesse, and the two of them unholstered their pistols and took them off safety. Jesse replaced his 9mm, swung his sawed-off twenty-gauge from under his cloak, and checked the loads. Satisfied, he allowed it to drop back, where it was concealed, slung from a leather strap, beneath his cloak.

Both men stooped down on the shoulder of the roadway and began the task of becoming road-weary travelers. They rubbed dust onto their faces and garments, and scuffed their sturdy boots in the gravel and grass. Jesse unfastened his ponytail and poured water from his canteen over his head; then, with a grimace, he proceeded to mess and dirty his usually well-groomed locks.

Ben, with his brush-cut hair, did not have the option of messing it up like his brother. Instead, he dug into his pack and pulled out a battered felt fedora. After dusting it thoroughly, he placed it on his head with the wide brim shading his eyes.

Ben looked over at his transformed brother, and noticed that Jesse was giving his M16 a meaningful stare.

"I'm not ditching the gun, if that's what you're thinking," Ben protested. "If we get into any trouble, this will get us out of it in a hurry."

"True enough, Ben," Jesse agreed. "But do you think it's just possible that it could get us into trouble in the first place?" Jesse grinned to take the sting out of his words, but the icy hardness in his eyes told Ben that he meant what he said.

Ben sighed. "You're right, Jess; however, I seriously doubt that *anyone* travels unarmed these days. How about if I put it in the case?" As he spoke, Ben was already going through his pack for the nylon gun case he had fashioned for the carbine. He held it up for Jesse's inspection when he was through packing the weapon, and the younger man nodded.

"I guess that'll do. Just try not to start anything, will you?" Jesse smiled, and Ben laughed.

"You ready, Bro?" Ben asked as he slung the case over his shoulder.

"Ready as I'll ever be," Jesse replied. He squinted ahead of them, wrinkling his nose as a stray zephyr brought a wave of fresh—or not-so-fresh—odors their way. "What do you think is up there?"

"From the smell, I'd say some sort of farm, or maybe even a stockyard." Ben, too, made a face, then straightened. "Let's not stand here all day speculating; let's find out!"

He resumed walking south, and Jesse matched his stride. Their boots crunched loudly in the gravel along the weathered stretch of road as they went forth to the unknown.

In its heyday, the Fox River Mall had been a place of wonder for people of all ages. One of the largest shopping malls in Wisconsin, it had held over one hundred stores, eateries, and attractions. In the aftermath of the Collapse, however, many of the shops had been forced to close as a dwindling supply of goods, looters, and a lack of currency both hard and electronic left them with little or no incentive to stay open.

People have a hard time changing old habits, though, and the old mall was still a source of attraction for many of the remaining local populace. Though much of its window glass was gone and many of the walls bore the scars of graffiti, fire, and bullets, it had become a center for much of the area's trade. Many of the smaller shops on the ground level had been altered to serve as stables for livestock, while others had been utilized as spaces from which to hawk the meager grains, vegetables, and fruits grown in the outlying fields.

Even in the early morning hours the mall was bustling with activity as the traders geared up for a day of frenzied barter that rivaled any bazaar of the Middle East. Farmers, dressed in rough homespun fabrics or threadbare dungarees displayed their goods on tables formed by laying planks over the tops of barrels or milk cans. They kept a wary, watchful eye on the passers-by to ensure that none of their precious produce walked away without being purchased.

Horse traders, their boots or bare feet splattered with dung and their eyes heavy-lidded against the brilliant morning sun, leaned against the walls near their livestock, picking and choosing among the crowd to find someone who appeared affluent enough to give them the price they asked for their animals. Occasionally, one of the traders would rouse himself and call out to someone in the crowd, and the dickering would commence.

Once or twice an hour, someone would get into an argument; if it became heated, green-clad soldiers armed with automatic weapons would appear from the shadows and put an end to the disagreement with a well-aimed blow of a rifle butt or a fist across the transgressor's face. In each instance, a short, very stout man would bustle in behind them, speak to the trader in hushed tones, and then have the man sign a receipt for goods owed for protection. The heavy-set man would then return to a central booth where he could recline upon a luxurious divan eating ripe fruits and nodding off in the steamy heat.

As Ben and Jesse entered the mall, the over-powering stench of unwashed bodies nearly drowned out the less unpleasant odor of animal dung. After a few minutes of wide-eyed wandering about the compound, though, their noses became accustomed — out of self-defense — to the generally overwhelming smell, and only the worst of the localized odors reached their more civilized olfactory senses.

The Moderator — for such was the title of the over-fed man in the booth — made note of the newcomers. One of his talents, extremely useful for a man in his position, was an eye for faces and details. He knew nearly all of the several thousand local citizens by sight, and these two were not in his memory—until he saw them. He noticed that although the strangers appeared to be unkempt and road-weary, their clothing was relatively new and well-mended. Their boots, in particular, were of a style and state of repair that the Moderator had not seen outside of the Upper enclaves in at least five or six years.

The larger of the two men, he saw, carried a weapon of some sort in a case slung over one shoulder. A slight bulge in his jacket indicated the presence of a handgun, but neither was too uncommon for a traveler. The slighter of the two, his tangled mane of white hair glowing in the morning sun, carried a pistol in a holster that swung outside his long, dusty cloak. He had no other weapons in evidence, but that cloak could conceal a multitude of sins. Both men wore back packs, old and much used.

The Moderator reached over to the small table next to his couch and lifted a walkie-talkie from it. Keeping his eyes on the strangers, he keyed the talk button.

"B-Group, this is the Moderator. Come in, B-Group Leader." He released the button and listened to static for several seconds before being answered.

"Moderator, this is B-Group Leader. What's up?" The man's voice held more than a hint of boredom, and a trace of irritation.

"Strangers have entered the mall," the Moderator stated flatly. "Two men, possibly mid- to late thirties. One is wearing a hat, the other has long, white hair. They are both armed. They are approaching your sector. Keep an eye on them; they may be trouble—and I don't want any trouble." He ended his transmission with a tone of command, and when the group leader responded, it was in a more subservient voice.

"I have them spotted, Moderator," he replied. *"Do you want them pulled in for questioning?"*

"Do not interfere with them *yet* ," the Moderator ordered. "Let's see what they're up to; we can always pick them up later." His orders given, the Moderator set the radio down, put the two strangers out of his mind, and turned his attention back to the plums resting in the bowl before him.

"Nice place, eh?" Jesse muttered sarcastically to Ben as they ambled through the booths and stalls of the open-air market. "The old mall just isn't the same, is it?" Jesse indicated a steaming pile of manure in front of them, just in time to allow Ben to avoid stepping in it.

"Yeah, it's just great. It *is* gratifying, to an extent, to see at least this amount of trade being maintained," Ben said. "It looks like they're doing quite a bit of farming and animal husbandry, if not as advanced as before the Collapse." Ben scanned the stalls as they continued to walk among the traders until his attention was caught by a movement in the shadows of the far wall.

"Jesse," he whispered, "look carefully to your right, and tell me what you see."

Jesse allowed his gaze to shift ever so slightly, and his breath came shallow and quick as he saw what Ben had seen.

"Provos!" he hissed, his right arm twitching as he tensed to draw his shotgun.

"That's what I thought, from your description of the Eau Claire contingent," Ben agreed, his voice lowered. "I thought that this place was just a little too good to be true." He made note of his brother's state of readiness, and lightly placed a hand on Jesse's arm. "Not here, not now, Jess."

"So, do we leave, or do we stay?" Jesse asked quietly. He felt the comforting weight of the 9mm, and his hand rested lightly on the small, rounded butt of his shotgun where it nestled under his cloak.

"Smile, Jesse," Ben commanded. "We're here for the duration. I want to get some information, and if possible I want to get into the Lawrence University Library — assuming it still exists."

Jesse thought of a comment, but bit it off before he could utter it. "Okay, Ben, you're calling the shots. But let's be damned careful."

Ben nodded, and made his way over to a stand that displayed a few bushels of tiny, worm-eaten apples.

"How much?" he asked the proprietor, a man who had once been fat. His flesh now hung on his body like a sagging elephant skin, wrinkled and gray with a mixture of fatigue and malnutrition. The man turned to face Ben, and his seamed, care-worn face broke into a toothless smile that, nevertheless, never touched his pale blue eyes.

"Strangers, are you?" he asked. "What'ya got? If ya got what I want, ya gets yer apples."   Again he smiled, but his cold eyes scanned Ben in an appraising look that said, *I can get a lot from this deal.*

Ben gave it some thought, and reached into his pack. He fumbled in the outside pocket for a moment, then placed an object on the table between himself and the vendor.

The man stared at the trade item laying in front of him, and to Ben's astonishment, began to salivate profusely. Hershey Bars were mostly gone, but obviously not forgotten by this man.

"How — how many apples ya want?" the vendor asked as he wiped drool from his flabby chin. "Is that the real thing? Shit, I ain't seen one of them in *years!*" He tentatively touched the candy with one long, filthy finger, and turned desperate eyes at Ben.

Ben saw the desire, the *hunger* in the man's eyes, and inwardly chuckled. *Where's the shrewd wheeler-dealer now?*

"One apple is all I want — that, and some information," Ben said. He saw the vendor's eyes shift warily to the wall behind them, and Ben hastened to reassure the man.

"Don't worry about them, my good man," he said as he pushed the chocolate bar slowly across the table. "What we want to know won't bother them, and doesn't concern them. Now," and Ben laid his hand over the candy, "do we have a deal, or not?"

"What do ya wanna know? I know just 'bout everything there is to know 'bout this town — lived here all my life. In fact," and the man swelled with pride, "I used to manage the produce section at the big Woodman's Supermarket down the road. 'Course, it ain't no supermarket no more. Word is that the government is gonna turn it into a barracks or somethin' — but I'll believe that when I see it."

Ben smiled faintly at the information that the man had just imparted. *A barracks?* "Is the college still open? And the library — can anyone get in?" Ben thought that the other man would answer readily enough, but he grew sullen and stubborn.

"Gotta see the Moderator for that, I guess," he muttered, and he eyed the chocolate with greedy longing.

Ben picked up the candy and tossed it to the vendor. "Where can we find this 'Moderator'?" he asked. With a nod toward the center of the floor, the man tore the wrapper from the candy. He didn't even notice when Ben reached over and picked an apple from one of his baskets.

With a nod to Jesse, Ben walked over to the Moderator's booth. As they drew near, they could see that the filth and decay had obviously not entered into the realm of the Moderator. The opulence of that ten by ten foot enclosure was astonishing even to the Walkers, and the health and wealth of the occupant was like that of a rose among weeds in this Hellish place.

Ben and Jesse stood just outside the booth waiting to be noticed, and both men watched in disgust as the Moderator slowly and methodically stuffed enormous amounts of fruit into his fleshy, pale-lipped mouth. Finally, his patience at an end, Ben rapped on the rail of the booth with his knuckles.

The Moderator turned a baleful stare on Ben, then resumed eating once more. Ben reached out to strike the railing again, but Jesse caught his arm.

"Hold it, Ben," he hissed. "We've got company."

Ben turned from the booth with slow deliberation to face four men, their carbines aimed at Jesse and himself.

A voice, deep and self-assured, boomed at them from behind their backs.

"You, I am afraid, have just made a grave error in judgment," the Moderator said.

CHAPTER FORTY

Ben paced up and down the length of the holding cell feeling like a caged animal. He berated himself for letting impatience get in the way of prudence yet again. It seemed to him that was the way it had always been for him—jump in with both feet, then let things work themselves out. Of late, however, this method had not been working out the way that he planned— the Damon Kane incident was a prime example.

Jesse, meanwhile, was seated on the floor in the far corner, his knees pulled up to his chin and his cloak wrapped around him. He appeared pale, and his breathing was shallow and rapid. The claustrophobia, which had been his bane since childhood, was rearing its ugly head, and he was trying to doze so that he would be unaware of the walls that threatened to close in around him.

The two men had been roughly escorted to this room several hours earlier, searched, disarmed, and locked in. They still retained their other possessions, which they had spent some time in repacking into their backpacks after they were emptied and searched. Jesse's cache of gold, which he had secreted in a hidden pocket of his cloak, remained safe, as did Ben's holographic imager and tape recorder. It was apparent that their captors were not as interested in what they had as in what they were after.

Jesse awoke from a light sleep when he heard Ben mumbling to himself. He looked up with bleary eyes and saw that Ben was in his classic thinking out loud pose—head cocked to one side and angry eyes staring into empty space. Seeing that Jesse was awake, Ben stepped across the tiny cell and squatted near his brother.

"Jesse," he exclaimed, "did you happen to pack any of your holographic projectors? Please say 'yes'!" Ben eyes were wide with the look of excitement he got when he had an idea.

"Sorry, Ben," Jesse said. "I didn't pack any projectors, but I did pack several discs. *You* have the projector." Jesse rose stiffly to his feet and went to his pack. He unzipped one of the side pockets and removed two small cases. Then, with a glance at his brother for permission, removed the 'Anna' projector from Ben's pack.

"Here you go, Ben," he said as he handed the holographic discs and projector to his brother. "They should be multiple image discs, but I'm not

348

sure; you see, I packed about a dozen of them in the plane, but I just grabbed a couple of them at random when we landed. If you look at them, there should be a small number near the spindle hole. Read them off, and I can tell you what they are." Jesse wiped beads of sweat from his forehead with a shaky hand, and waited for Ben to call off the codes.

Ben squinted as he attempted to make out the tiny numerals. "Oh, here they are—one, five, and nine on this one. The other one just has a zero on it." Ben handed the discs back to Jesse, who double-checked the numbers. "So, what are they?"

"Number one," Jesse explained, "is a birch tree. Five is a boulder, and nine is what I call the 'black hole'." At Ben's puzzled look, Jesse elaborated.

"The 'hole' is just that—a hole that can be projected onto the ground, walls, anywhere. It shows the illusion of depth, but of course, has no reality." Jesse grinned. "I haven't used it outside of the project room yet, but it definitely works.

"Now, let me see the other one. Oh yeah—zero. That's my 'empty space' disc—the one that we used for simulated invisibility." Jesse hesitated, then a thrill of excitement passed through him. "Invisibility! That's it! I have an idea, Ben. If I can split the beam into two channels, and get the projector to read both discs at the same time..."

Ben grinned and nodded as he and Jesse hunkered down and began to plan their escape.

The door to the cell banged open an hour later, and two burly guards strode into the room. On the far wall of the small room, a jagged hole gaped at them, and the two Provo soldiers stood dumfounded for several seconds before taking action.

"Shit!" exclaimed the sergeant as he ran for the hole closely followed by the other soldier. Bending over to pass through the hole, both men reached it simultaneously; they were knocked off their feet as their heads struck the wall behind the illusory hole with wet thuds.

Several feet to the rear of the two stunned men, the air shimmered as Jesse turned off the projector. Ben was already on his feet and running over to the guards, hatred and fury gleaming in his eyes. As he reached the sergeant, Ben kicked the man squarely in the face, then he grabbed the man's rifle and brought its butt crashing down on the other's head. Methodically, with a grimace of near-satisfaction on his face, Ben pulled a knife from the sergeant's belt and slit the throats of both soldiers.

Jesse watched this with a grim though not displeased expression, but made no move to interfere—it was not *his* wife who had been killed by the Provos. Ben stood, wiping the knife on the shirt of one of the dead men, then walked over to his brother.

"Ben," Jesse said calmly, "we've got to get going." He bent over to disarm the guards, handing an automatic pistol to Ben, who took it while staring in numb disbelief at the carnage he had created.

"Yeah," Ben said hoarsely, "we'd better go." He walked over to his pack, grabbed it, and with a look out the door, left the room.

"Wait, Ben!" Jesse picked up his pack and the projector, and raced after his brother. He shoved the discs into his pack, clipped the multiple imager to his belt, and caught up to Ben. "Stay close, and I'll turn on the zero projector." He did so, and the two men vanished except for a slight shimmer akin to heat waves. "The battery's only good for about another half-hour, so we'd best high-tail it out of town."

Ben stopped and whirled around, grabbing Jesse's cloak in his fist. "NO!" he roared. "I came here for a purpose, and I intend to accomplish it!" Ben realized that he was violently shaking Jesse when he saw the blank, icy look in his brother's eyes. He slowly released his hold, and Jesse smoothed out his cloak. "Sorry, Jess."

Jesse took a moment to respond, and when he did, it was through thinly pressed lips. "Don't *ever* do that again. I'm leaving here, with or without you," he continued in a deadly, implacable tone. "We can be to the planes in twenty-minutes, and on our way to Fond du Lac or Milwaukee in twenty-five. I have no intention of getting killed here—or anywhere, for that matter.

"If you want to, you can stay here, and I'll head for Pacifica. If not, we can always check out a library in some other town, some other time. Are the books worth dying for?"

Ben stood silently for a moment. *What was I thinking?* he asked himself. *Do I want to die that much?* "You're right—again," he said softly as he began to walk down the corridor. "Let's get the hell out of here!"

With that said, Ben began to jog down the hallway with Jesse following close on his heels.

I'm going to have to watch out for him, Jesse thought with a silent, bitter laugh.

The Moderator was in a very foul mood. His lunch had been disrupted, and the long walk down the hot corridors of the government building had covered his flabby body in an oily slick of perspiration. His light robes and baggy pants, which normally hid his bulk, now clung to his rotund, porcine torso like a second skin. To make matters worse, he had vomited up most of his lunch at the sight of the carnage and the hot smell of blood in the holding cell.

With the diplomacy of fear, the Moderator's Provo escort tactfully ignored the steaming pile of puke inside the door, and continued with his report.

"I still don't know how they did it, Sir. From the looks of it, there wasn't even much of a struggle, although both men have wounds on their heads consistent with the bloody smears on the far wall." The officer pointed out the spots, and the Moderator felt another wave of nausea run through him.

He fought down the impulse to regurgitate again, and stared at the soldier through heavy-lidded eyes. "Did these men have families, Captain?" The officer nodded but did not meet the baleful gaze of his superior.

"Cut their rations in half for one week, Captain," the Moderator continued imperiously, "as punishment for the poor performance of their duties. After that week, double their rations as compensation for the loss to their families." *Generosity,* he thought, *coupled with discipline. I have these people right where I want them!*

The Moderator smiled, his face pale but eyes steady. "Send out a search party to find those escaped prisoners. Alert the airbase to be on the lookout for any unauthorized traffic, just in case they weren't traveling on foot. Have them shoot down any UFO's.

"Send word up and down the line to our bases, with full descriptions of the prisoners—but be sure that they are captured alive. I have some questions for them."

The Moderator turned from the room and shuffled several steps down the hall, certain that his orders would be obeyed. Suddenly, he stopped and whirled around. "And Captain? Clean up this mess."

"Yessir," the officer responded crisply, hiding a feeling of disgust at the duty he had to perform.

Ben and Jesse reached the planes out of breath, but without incident. They rested for a brief moment against the brush camouflage of the ultralights, and Jesse lit a cigarette, "to get my lungs going again," he quipped. As he began to uncover his craft, a faint beeping sounded from the projector at his waist, and the circle of invisibility around him disappeared. Jesse took a minute to replace the battery and the disc, and tossed the device to his brother.

Ben shook his head as he snatched the projector from mid-air, momentarily startled by Jesse's abrupt appearance, and began to uncover his own plane. Soon, both craft were ready, and they rolled them onto the broken blacktop. They stowed their gear in the supply lockers, and climbed into the cramped cabins.

Jesse donned his FM headset, and waited patiently as Ben did likewise. They started their engines and taxied down the bumpy asphalt.

"*Ben, I'd like to make a suggestion,*" Jesse's voice carried clearly as he pulled back on the stick and was aloft.

"*Go ahead,*" Ben replied absently.

"*Since we're 'hot' right now, it's probably not a very good idea to stay in the area. I'd like to bypass Fond du Lac; more than likely, they have another Provo garrison there, and just as small a population. Chances are,*" Jesse speculated, "*that they've already sent out our descriptions to the other bases in the area – and we've had enough excitement for one day.*" Jesse did not need to elaborate; he was sure that Ben understood.

"*So what are you saying?*" Ben asked. "*Do you want to go straight into Milwaukee, or hole up somewhere until the heat is off?*" Ben tried to hid his contempt for the idea of hiding, but his voice carried the feeling too well.

Jesse chewed his lip for a second to bite back the acid comment that he wanted to make; then, his emotions under control, he stated *his* decision. "*Why don't we go directly to Chicago? It's the center of the Provo government, and*

St. John should be there. Besides, being in a different state, the heat may not be on us." He chuckled.

"Who's going to be looking for two escaped fugitives among the millions of 'Shytown'?"

Ben considered this, wondering why he had not thought of it. It seemed to be increasingly difficult for him to think clearly, as if a London fog had settled inside his skull.

Chicago *would* be the logical choice; it would definitely have libraries to access, and should prove to hold a wealth of information about the set-up of the Provisional U.S. Government.

"All right," Ben drawled, *"Chicago it is. But let's keep low speed and altitude on the way. Treetop level and under sixty knots. We can be sure that the Provos had low-level radar installations along the route south, since Chicago must still have a functioning airport."*

Jesse nodded, then threw a 'thumbs-up' signal to Ben through his cockpit window. Ben returned it, and the two planes skimmed the ground as they veered toward Chicago.

Excerpt from the Journal of Jesse Walker — July 13, 2022:

I am growing concerned about Ben's state of mind since our deposition from Paradise. He's been making grave errors in judgment ever since Anna was killed, but this is ridiculous!

While Ben has always been the stronger of the two of us, I fear that Anna's death may have triggered something deep within him. His concentration and decision-making skills are deteriorating, and I am forced to remind him of simple things on a regular basis. I fear for my —our —safety if he doesn't regain his grasp on reality.

We're en route for Chicago, hotbed of the Provos. Before we enter, however, I have to be sure that Ben has his head on straight — if he can't, or won't, I'll leave for Pacifica.

With him, or without him. His choice...

Ben's mind wandered as the plane flew through the night sky. He glanced over to where Jesse's plane should be, but the flat black fuselage blended into the shroud of night. Ben's thoughts were scrambled, and he was irritated with himself because he couldn't seem to keep his concentration centered on anything for more than a few seconds. Just flying the plane was a chore.

I'm just tired, he thought, but he knew that it was more than that. Pictures of Anna, memories of better days, kept crossing his mind. *And Paradise!* he thought bitterly. *Lost!*

Ben reached over to the dashboard and depressed the button on the holographic projector. At that precise moment, a pocket of turbulence caused the plane to jump, and his hand jerked the projector hard against the windshield. A cover fell from the back of the case, and Ben glanced incuriously at it.

In the dim light of the instrument panel, Ben saw a tiny button set just above the exposed batteries. With a sense of wonder that felt unusual after the past few weeks of numbness, Ben placed the case on the dash and pressed the tiny switch.

Like the image that 'R2D2' had projected of 'Princess Leia' in *Star Wars*, a tiny, fuzzy likeness of Anna hovered in the air just inches from Ben's eyes. The hologram was about ten inches tall and flickered faintly. It turned to face him, and Anna's tiny eyes seemed to look directly into his as she smiled.

Already in a state of shock, it came as no great surprise to Ben when the small simulacrum began to speak.

"*Dearest Ben,*" the voice of his dead wife said from the projector, "*if you see this, then I must be dead. Jesse arranged for this to be a type of 'living will' for me.*

"*While I cannot know the manner of my death, I can only hope that it was with honor.*

354

"I have left you this message in the hope that it will help you to overcome any grief you may feel at my passing. If I am gone, that's all there is to it. You," and the image pointed its finger at Ben for emphasis, *"are still alive, and must carry on for both of us."*

The image of Anna smiled and brushed away a stray lock of hair. *"Hard times may be ahead, my love, but you must not lose heart. You have a dream, and must continue to see it fulfilled. It is up to you to see that your dream does not die with me – it is no longer just your dream, for you have imparted its promise to many.*

"Carry on, Ben. Carry on for me, and for all of us who have shared in your vision.

"I love you, Benjamin Walker, and always shall." Anna smiled sadly from the hologram, and the image faded away.

The brothers flew over, but not into, Fond du Lac, and Jesse's guess had proven accurate. The city was well-garrisoned with Provo troops, leaving Ben even more dismayed than before. He remembered fondly the days when he was a college student at the University center, and how he had become, against his better judgment, an aspiring author.

So much had happened since those relatively carefree days. He had moved out of Fond du Lac in search of work, and he and Jesse had begun several collaborative writing efforts via the Internet and regular mail. Events had carried them across time, both of them barely surviving, until the day in 2011 when Ben had brought Jesse the news of his windfall.

That lottery win had been the basis of everything that had happened in their lives ever since. Good, bad, or indifferent, Ben was grateful for having had the chance to live a full life – a life of dreams fulfilled.

From that young dreamer of twenty-nine years old to the older and more capable leader he was at forty, Ben had grown and changed as circumstances dictated; however, the price for that growth had often been high.

Ben recalled with fondness the formative years; the building and recruiting of Paradise; the difficult times immediately following the Collapse, when Paradise was often faced with the decision of sharing its wealth, or keeping itself alive. That decision had rested solely with Paradises' leader –

Ben—and to this day, he wondered if he had made the wrong choices.

In 2017, the Plague Year, all Hell had broken loose. The Plague, a variant of Bubonic plague, was a virulent, extremely contagious, and deadly disease. The chills, vomiting, and fever struck suddenly, and without a full medical staff, all the Paradisans could do was treat the symptoms, keep the stricken isolated, and pray.

Ben was one of the lucky ones; the Plague was close enough to the strain he had been vaccinated against during his military service that he suffered nothing more serious than flu-like symptoms. So it was that he and a few hardy others who had served their fallen country were pressed into the service of tending for those too ill to care for themselves.

Ben watched helplessly as many of his friends and associates sickened, then died miserably—and he had keenly felt the suffering of each person. None had affected him more, though, than that of Eugenia 'Genie' MacAllister. Ben had held the six year old in his arms, trying to keep her warm when her body was growing steadily colder by the minute. He remembered it as if it was just yesterday.

Genie's parents had died a day earlier, but her symptoms had not appeared until early the next morning. Ben had made his rounds of the community, and had heard the little girl weakly crying out for a mother who was no longer alive. Ben, always with a soft spot for little girls and kittens, had picked her up, cradling her gently in his arms. In her delirium, she cried out, "Daddy?" and Ben had looked down at her emaciated, fever- reddened face with tears in his eyes. "Everything's going to be fine, Genie," he soothed her. "Daddy's right here."

In the infirmary, he had rocked the little girl back and forth until she was still. Ben reached down with his hand to sweep a stray lock of hair from her sweat-beaded forehead with a tender smile on his face. He stood up to take her back to her bed—and it was then that he noticed that she was no longer breathing.

A long time later, Ben had carried her small body out to be cremated with the others. He could not watch as the flames destroyed the bodies, for in the few moments that he had cared for the little girl, he had loved her as if she were his own daughter. He knew that he would never again be able to see a child in pain without seeing the pain- and fever-wracked face of little Genie.

Paradise had, in fact, survived the Plague better than many of the surrounding communities. They had lost over three dozen people, but stories that filtered in months later claimed that the death toll in some areas had been as high as eighty-five percent.

In the four years following the Plague, Paradise had seen a time of unrivaled peace and prosperity. Except for a few scattered raids by nomadic bandits, there was little to worry about. Even the weather had been cooperative, and Paradisan farmers consistently brought in bountiful harvests.

They had expanded their trade, and new building construction had followed: A new schoolhouse, with electricity and heat. A library and research center (*still not finished,* Ben recalled bitterly). A local radio broadcast. New generators for the hydroelectric dam.

The dream had become a reality! While it had not happened overnight, nor without hardship, it was Ben's idea of Utopia. The population had expanded as Ben and Jesse led excursions further and further from Paradise's borders. They had grown from a hamlet of forty or fifty people to a community of well over two hundred, and were approaching self-sufficiency when, without warning, the first harbingers of disaster were heard.

The 'Central Command'—Cencom—and its fanatical leader Dwight Cochran, had entered the picture, disrupting plans and making war—almost a forgotten subject—appear imminent. Ben had foreseen such an eventuality, however, and had taken steps to prepare.

The cost had been high. To keep the dream alive, it had taken the lives of nearly a quarter of the Paradisans—a heart-breaking total. Ben's only comfort was the computer analysis that told him that the battle had been fought at an optimum level with minimal casualties. *Minimal casualties!* Ben would never forgive himself for the deaths of his people, even if through their sacrifice they had bought the freedom of their friends and neighbors.

The months after the battle had been a flurry of activity. His courtship of long-time friend Anna Graycloud, his marriage, and the abrupt and devastating end of his honeymoon. Jesse's despondency over the vision of a dead Moira in the aftermath of the Cencom attack, and the subsequent changes in both his appearance and demeanor. The attempted take-over of Paradise from within by the traitorous Damon Kane, and his death at Ben's hands. The deposition of the Walkers, and their escape from Paradise.

A long trail of events leading to the present, and Ben had played a starring role in nearly all of them. By rights, he had led a full life and deserved to sit back and let someone else take the worry seat, but he knew that as long as he was alive, he would stand in the foreground and continue to take a hand in events.

Jesse, Ben knew, had never cared for his older brother's penchant for swift and violent action, but Ben had noticed that lately Jesse, too, seemed to be falling into that mold.

Ben wondered if he had been perhaps too cold and cruel during his life. Maybe more sensitivity would have won him more friends instead of allies. *Sure,* he sneered to himself. *And it would have opened me up to more attacks from potential enemies, too.*

He absently activated the hologram of Anna, staring at it vacantly while immersed in a morass of memories. He knew now that he had truly loved her. Anna had melted all his strength, and he was only now coming to terms with his loss. His eyes focused on the image floating before him, and he smiled.

"Thanks, Anna."

Ben wiped his moist eyes with the back of one hand and took a deep, trembling breath. He felt as if a vast and overpowering weight had just been lifted from his shoulders, and a surge of renewing energy pulsed through him.

Looking out of the plane's canopy, the night sky again seemed full of the limitless possibilities that it had once held for him.

Jesse adjusted his throttle and banked away from the position he had been holding near the *Phoenix*. He glanced over in time to see the tiny image of Anna Walker fade away, and a smile flickered across his sober features.

"Go to it, Anna," he whispered as he guided the plane through the night.

Moira Doyle wandered despondently around the cabin, her eyes sad as she pictured Jesse in each room. She had spent many an evening curled up in front of the fire with him, and while she was now living in his house, it seemed as if something vital was lacking without Jesse here, too.

She could not—*would not*—believe the allegations against Ben and Jesse. *Gentle Jesse, a murderer? Never!* she thought violently as, with a great, heaving sob, Moira collapsed in front of the heart crying long into the night.

Isaac Peters sat across the desk from his son-in-law, Jeff. Isaac's ebony skin was glistening with sweat, and his smooth brow held furrows that had not been there just a few short days before.

The two men sat silently, both lost deep within their own thoughts. An open bottle of whiskey sat upon the desk half empty, and each of them— the freshly appointed leader of Paradise and his new, young deputy—held a full glass in their hands.

"Okay, boys, let's open her up!" shouted Rob Tulliger to the group of a dozen men milling around the entrance to Ben Walker's home. They were itching to loot the place, not so much for what it held as for whom it represented.

At Tulliger's command, they rushed up to the locked doors and windows, prying, hammering, and breaking glass in an effort to gain entry. At last, the heavy oak door gave way, and the party of men ran inside.

A voice startled them into silence as they entered the main room. "SECURITY BREECH: SHUTDOWN ORDERS IN EFFECT. TEN SECOND COUNTDOWN BEGINNING. TEN...NINE...EIGHT...SEVEN..."

Tulliger looked around, wild eyed, and ran from the room, followed closely by his men.

But not soon enough.

Moira was awakened by a brilliant flash of light that cast sharp shadows across the great room in Jesse's cabin. A deep roar rattled the windows, and Moira sprang to her feet and rushed to the front door.

Flinging the door wide, she looked aghast across the compound. To the southwest, a fireball was slowly rolling into the night sky, casting a blood-red glow on the landscape.

Isaac rose unsteadily from his chair and staggered over to the window. He, too, saw the fireball, and made note of its position.

He smiled for the first time in days, and walked to where his glass sat on the desktop. Raising it high, he grinned at young Jeff Barker.

"Here's to Ben Walker — that son of a bitch," Isaac slurred. He tilted his head to drain the glass, and fell flat on his back with a crash.

Jeff, spluttering with drunken glee, drank his own glass dry and fell from his chair.

"To Paradishe," he saluted as he, too, fell into alcoholic oblivion.

Shortly before midnight, as the two brothers were considering landing for the night, the short-wave radios in both planes crackled into life.

"ATTENTION BEN AND JESSE WALKER. SECURITY PROGRAM FOUR-EIGHT-TWO-GEE-AITCH SHUTDOWN INITIATION IMMINENT. SECURITY BREECH IN PRIVATE HOME OF BEN WALKER UNDERWAY. TEN SECOND COUNTDOWN READY.

"DO YOU WISH TO HALT COUNTDOWN?"

Ben smiled grimly as he remembered the things in his house, the times with Anna, and all that it had meant to him.

"Commence countdown," he spoke calmly, simply into the microphone.

CHAPTER FORTY-ONE

Before landing for the night just south of Milwaukee, Ben had insisted on a slow over flight of the city to determine the extent of Provo control. To the dismay of both men, it was overrun by military might.

Not only were the old Summerfest grounds being used to house thousands of troops, but the marinas also held hundreds of small, heavily armed military craft. The shoreline had been turned from a place of fun to a place to *shun*---and Ben did not like that at all.

They landed, made camp, and got what rest they could.

"Phoenix to Nighthawk. Come in, Nighthawk."

"Nighthawk," Jesse's voice replied clearly from a few hundred feet away. *"What's up, Ben?"*

"I'm not sure. I just get the feeling that we may be flying into a situation that we can't handle. What do you think we'll find in Chicago?"

Jesse paused before replying, trying to remember all the scraps of conversation he had overheard during his travels. *"I think we'll find that Chicago is going to be like Appleton, only on a grander scale. Imagine millions of people living like those in Appleton, with a select few holding the masses in abject fear--and we have to remember that St. John is supposed to be based in Chicago, too."*

"That's right, Jess. We'll have to deal with him."

"Yes, Ben," Jesse said firmly, *" we will. Are you up to it?"*

Ben fumed momentarily before answering. Certainly his actions of the past few weeks had not enhanced Jesse's confidence in him, but a good night's sleep and some soul-searching had dramatically improved his outlook. *"Yeah, I'll be okay. I just won't be the guiding influence in our relationship any more – we're partners now, Jesse."*

In his cockpit, Jesse chuckled. *"It's about time that you realized we've been partners for over ten years, Ben! I'm tired of being your 'little brother', and I think, in your own way, you're just as tired of being the 'big brother'. Why can't we just be brothers, and leave it at that?"*

"Works for me-- Brother."

Jesse shook his head, but inwardly he felt released from a bond that had been becoming increasingly unpleasant for him of late. *"Back to the subject. Have you given any thought to how we should enter Chicago? How we can be integrated into its society without losing our freedom to move about and do our own 'thing'?"*

Ben answered immediately, his voice confident and sure for the first time in recent memory. *"I think we should land in the suburbs, conceal the planes, load up with minimal weapons and equipment, and walk right in. I have a feeling that the locals will be too busy trying to survive to worry about two more faces among many.*

"The only problem we have to worry about is staying away from Provo troops; however, from what I surmise of the conditions in Chicago, they probably don't spend any more time in the Lower areas than they have too."

"I agree," Jesse said. *"One suggestion, though; we should carry along as much food and medicines as we can without being too obvious. They'll be worth more to starving, sick people than all the gold I have with me--and it just might make us some friends."*

"Sound thinking, Jess. Where do you want to land? Up near Evanston, on the beach? Or should we try to penetrate the city more, and shoot for Lincoln Park?"

Jesse mulled over his choices for a minute. *"Well – I'd love to land right on Navy Pier, but for safety's sake, at least until we have the lay of the land, Humboldt Park would be the prudent choice. It's close enough to the Loop to give us a quick getaway if necessary, but far enough away to make a discreet entrance – and the lagoon area should be overgrown enough to hide the planes."*

"Humboldt Park it is," Ben decided. *"We'll have to play it by ear when we get there. In the meantime, let's maintain our low speed and altitude. Phoenix, out."*

The planes dipped another several meters until their landing gear was nearly skimming the wave tops. Ben glanced at his altimeter, which was reading twenty feet. *Awfully close to the water,* he thought. *It would be really easy to lose it flying this low.*

He grimaced, set the throttle at sixty knots, and settled back in his seat.

The altimeter read ten feet, fluctuating from as low as five to as much as twenty, and the proximity alarm beeped loud enough to startle Ben from his melancholy reverie. He grabbed at the controls of the craft and pulled it up to forty feet, and saw that Jesse and the *Nighthawk* were already at that height and veering slowly toward him.

"*Nighthawk to Phoenix,*" Jesse said calmly.

"*Phoenix, here.*"

"*Chicago is just a few miles away, and we're coming up on Humboldt Park. I've been checking carefully, and I haven't seen any activity at all – not a vehicle, not a person. Seems a little ominous, wouldn't you say?*"

Ben could see the grim, argent-framed face of his brother through the cockpit canopy of the *Nighthawk* just thirty feet away from his right wingtip. "*Let's hope that it means that no one is around to see us land, Jess; don't always be so suspicious!*"

Jesse flipped his middle finger at Ben, and then turned it into a thumbs-up as he flashed his brother a smile. "*Let's find a place to land, then. I'm sick of sitting!*"

"*Okay, little br – *" Ben cut himself off. "*Okay, Jesse. Let's go kick some ass!*"

EPILOG

New Beginnings

"Welcome to my parlor," said the Spider to the Fly.

September 2022:

John Walker struggled up the side of the steep hill, sweat streaming into his eyes and trickling down his back and sides. Grabbing at saplings and brush for handholds, he hastened to reach the top of the hill where his supplies awaited him.

About halfway up his ascent, John turned and looked through the dawn mist to where the town of Pacifica lay. The streets were deserted, and the buildings sat vacant with shuttered windows and drawn drapes. The distillery was closed, and for the first time in years no plume of white vapor rose from the twin stacks atop the sturdy brick edifice. The fields outside of town were blackened, and here and there yellow smoke billowed from still smoldering crops.

John sat down heavily, his lungs laboring to take in the sweet morning air, and opened his canteen. As he drank deeply, he reviewed the events of the last two months.

First, there had been the letter from St. John ordering the residents of Pacifica to vacate the premises. John had done his best to try and dissuade St. John from his course of action, but no amount of pleading, threats, or cajoling had changed his mind.

With increasing regularity, small squads of troops had begun to escort inspectors into Pacifica to ensure that preparations were being made to evacuate by the target date of September first. John had been less than courteous to these officers; while he *had* cooperated with them, he had also insisted that they find nightly accommodations elsewhere. He would not allow them to take up residence until the first of September, and then only under protest.

His own people had been resistant to the impending end of their community, but after John had made public the letters from St. John and explained the law to them, they had settled into a state of sullen resignation. Many had packed up and left immediately, though there had been nearly a thousand who, like John, had clung to their homes—until yesterday.

After St. John's ultimatum, John had decided that he was not going to relinquish Pacifica without a fight. His only problem then had been how to fend off ten thousand or more trained soldiers with a band of a thousand peace-loving citizens. A solution had eventually presented itself, but John had resisted this very final but effective method until he had exhausted all other avenues.

Most puzzling of all had been the strange reply given to him upon his last attempt to contact his nephews in Paradise. He had tried the open channels one last time, and had been given the runaround—for the *last* time.

When he tried the private emergency channel that Jesse had given him, he had gotten through at once—but not to Ben and Jesse.

John resumed his climb, and his brow furrowed as he remembered that last, odd conversation.

John entered the numbers 650.22 on the frequency keypad of his battered short-wave transceiver, and held the microphone close to his mouth. "Pacifica calling Paradise," he enunciated clearly. "Jesse, this is John Walker. Do you read?" He released the send switch with a sigh. He was losing any hope of reaching his nephew when, with a burst of static, a strange voice came on the air.

"*PARADISE HERE,*" the voice intoned. "*STAND BY FOR A RECORDED MESSAGE FOR JOHN WALKER OF PACIFICA.*" The voice went silent, and John listened to the hiss and hum of the empty airwaves with growing excitement.

"*Uncle John,*" the recorded voice of Jesse began suddenly, "*if you hear this, then Ben and I are no longer in Paradise.*

"*Things have been slowly going to Hell here, through no fault of ours. We opted to consolidate with one of the outlying communities—and that is how we made our mistake. Members of that group have begun to take over sections of Paradise, through means both legal and illegal.*

"*Ben and I are leaving for the capitol of the Provisional U.S. Government—Chicago. It is July 11, 2022, and we are preparing to depart within the hour.*

"*I don't know when, if ever, we shall return.*

"*I have keyed the computer to monitor all transmissions going through the* public channels in Paradise, with instructions to relay this recording to you on your first attempt to contact me via the emergency channel."

The recording paused, as if Jesse were collecting his thoughts. *"John, I know that things must be getting rough for you if you've broken our mutual radio silence. I wish that we could be there for you, but I seriously doubt that two more bodies would be of any help – and we have problems of our own.*

"If things get too bad, and you have nowhere else to go, we expect to be in Chicago by late July. If you elect to leave Pacifica for any reason, look us up. We'll be expecting you.

"I have to sign off – we're ready to go.

"Good luck to you, Uncle." The message ended, and the monotone voice of the computer came back on-line.

"JOHN WALKER. DO YOU WISH TO LEAVE A MESSAGE FOR JESSE WALKER OR BEN WALKER?"

John thought briefly, and replied. "Yes. Tell them that Uncle John is on his way."

"MESSAGE RECORDED. WILL THAT BE ALL?" Seconds of silence followed as John stared in amazement at the radio. "VERY WELL. THEN I, TOO, WISH YOU GOOD LUCK, JOHN WALKER. PARADISE, OUT."

The radio fell silent except for background noise, and John sat alone in the radio room, his decision made.

When John finally crested the hill, he flopped onto his back and closed his eyes while the hammering of his heart slowed down. He dozed, and was awakened by a deep, thunderous vibration transmitted through the hard-packed dirt beneath his head.

He struggled to his feet, muscles screaming in protest at the unusual strain that they had been subjected to during his climb. He made it to an upright position, feeling muscles that he had never known he had, and looked down into the valley below.

The early morning haze had dissipated, leaving the sky a clear and crystalline blue. Pacifica lay some two miles down slope from him, and the deathly calm that had covered it like a shroud was gone. In its place, a bustle of activity ran throughout the community.

John pulled a pair of binoculars from his knapsack and focused on the town. Even at that distance, he could make out the gray-green uniforms of the soldiers scurrying through Pacifica: Provos. A long convoy of vehicles was heading for Pacifica, and John estimated that all the trucks and cars would not be in the center of his abandoned home for at least another two or three hours.

John rummaged through his bag, smiling grimly as he located a small remote control device. He extended the whip antenna, leaned back against a tree trunk, and fell asleep.

The sun was on the downside of noon and the air was still and warm when John roused from his nap. He was disconcerted at first, until he remembered where he was — and why.

Clipping the radio device to his belt, John stretched and walked to the edge of the small plateau. He raised the binoculars to his eyes, and aimed them at Pacifica.

The convoy was gone, and the town looked alive again. Smoke was pouring from the distillery stacks, and many of the other buildings were showing signs of new habitation. Vehicles sat everywhere, more automobiles than John had seen in ten years. Men ran in cadence down side streets, and near the razed fields, large tractors were busily engaged in plowing under the ashes of the destroyed crops.

John swore silently, and scanned both roads that led into Pacifica. For at least five miles in each direction, the roads were devoid of traffic. He grinned as he turned and placed the glasses carefully back into his pack.

He took several minutes to lash his supplies to the back of his motorcycle, and then walked back to the edge of the hill. John slowly pulled the radio from his belt and held it lightly in his hand. He glanced from it to Pacifica, then back again.

Pulling a plastic cover from the single button on its face, John remembered something an old farmer had once told him.

"Son," the man had drawled, "it don't do your dog no kindness to let it suffer. You got to be able to put it out of its misery when the time comes. It'll thank you for it."

His thumb poised over the switch, John looked down at Pacifica with tears in his eyes. "Good-bye, old friend."

He pushed the button.

The distillery seemed to shimmer in the early afternoon sun, then burst with a great gout of blue and orange flame. John saw the holding tank explode from the heat, splashing five thousand gallons of flaming alcohol over the town. With relatively smaller explosions, the homes and other buildings began to disappear in clouds of flame and smoke as the other charges laid by John and his friends detonated. Through the smoke, John could see survivors running toward the borders of the town, only to see that route cut off by a wall of flame and debris as the border charges exploded.

Other and smaller explosions could be discerned as flames consumed the vehicles, full of fuel and ammunition. John turned from the conflagration as a wave of heat and sound blew up the hillside. He had seen enough.

Pacifica was dead.

He threw one lean leg over the seat of his classic '98 Harley-Davidson, and tossed the radio into the weeds as he started up the bike with a roar.

He drove carefully down the far side of the hill, tears obscuring his vision. When he reached the main road some three miles west of Pacifica, he headed south.

He did not look back.

Moira woke with a start, and for the third day in a row, it was a race to see if she could reach the bathroom before the vomiting began.

Today, she won the race — but the prize was no more pleasant for it. Finally, she stood looking in the mirror at her pale, freckled face outlined by straggles of her auburn hair. She rinsed her mouth, brushed the worst of the tangles from her hair, and shuffled into the kitchen. The thought of food make her stomach do flip-flops, and she decided on a glass of cold cider in lieu of breakfast.

With a growing sense of dismay, Moira lifted the taut nightgown over her belly and sat down. She ran her hand lightly across her once flat abdomen, and felt the growing curve refuse to go away no matter how hard she tried to suck it in.

She regarded her bulging belly and slightly distended navel in disgust for a moment, then put it from her mind. *I really must get more exercise,* she thought absently.

She drank the rest of her cider, decided that it was going to stay put for a while, and walked into the great room. She turned on the CD player, pressed the random play button, and fell back onto the couch, thoroughly exhausted.

Moira lay there for some time listening to the music as it cycled through Jesse's eclectic selections, and tried not to concentrate on how she had gained so much weight over the past few weeks. She had never before in her life had a problem with her figure, and had just convinced herself that it was old age—she *was* nearly twenty-three, after all—when *it* happened.

She felt an odd stirring just above her pubic hair, and sat bolt upright on the couch. She stared at her belly as if it would bite, and watched as the front of her nightgown trembled, ever so slightly, in unison with the vibration in her abdomen.

Moira's face broke into a wistful, sad smile even as her eyes filled with tears. She relaxed back on the couch, laid a hand on the curve of her belly, and anxiously waited for it to move again.

"Damn you, Jesse Walker," she whispered happily. "Damn you!"

She would check with Doc Riley later, but she was already certain.

Moira knew that she carried Jesse's baby.

Hundreds of miles away, Jesse whipped his hair from his eyes with a flick of his head, and aimed the shotgun at the leather-clad man before him. He had acquired the gun and a pocketful of shells from a dealer just off of Division Street. Ben held his pistol ready, but knew in his heart that Jesse could handle this situation.

"Move it, or lose it," Jesse hissed. The man moved on without a backward glance, and the two brothers went from the sunlight into the Shadows.

"Chicago—my kind of town," Jesse said through clenched teeth.

"Yeah," Ben agreed. He holstered his pistol, signaling Jesse to be on alert. A sudden thought occurred to him, but he hesitated a minute before voicing it.

"Do you ever miss Moira?" Ben asked finally.

Jesse whipped around and glared at Ben through steely eyes, then turned and resumed walking stiffly, his cloak flapping out behind his rigid frame.

Ben walked a step behind Jesse, and waited several minutes for an answer that was not forthcoming.

"I thought so," he muttered to himself.

The next few years would see the Walkers involved and embroiled in a war fought on many levels — battles on many fronts, with allies and enemies blended and confused by the fog of violence, and a flickering glimmer of hope.

But that is another story, for another time...

www.ingramcontent.com/pod-product-compliance
Lightning Source LLC
Chambersburg PA
CBHW030356030726
47497CB00002B/370